Forever Family

a novel

TJ BRAGG

Book Formatting by Derek Murphy @Creativindie
Book and Cover Design by Jerry Todd

FOREVER FAMILY

Copyright © 2024 by TJ Bragg.

All rights reserved. Printed in the United States of America. No part of this book may be used or reproduced in any manner whatsoever without written permission except in the case of brief quotations embodied in critical articles or reviews. This book is a work of fiction. Names, characters, businesses, organizations, places, events and incidents either are the product of the author's imagination or are used fictitiously. Any resemblance to actual persons, living or dead, events, or locales is entirely coincidental.

For information contact :
http://www.tjbragg.com

Book and Cover design by Jerry Todd
ISBN: 979-8-9890096-0-2

First Edition: April 2024

10 9 8 7 6 5 4 3 2 1

Forever Family

PROLOGUE

CLARA

"Daddy! Look at me!" Clara climbed over the weatherworn boulders to loom above her father. Determination distorted her face as she pulled herself to the highest platform. Giggles escaped as she looked down at him and balanced on the top stone.

"Catch me, Daddy."

With arms stretched like an eagle, Clara leaped from the ledge. *I can fly,* she thought as the wind licked her cheeks. Catching her effortlessly, her father twirled her around before guiding her into a graceful landing. Her silky dark blond curls embraced her neck before settling on her shoulders.

Northern Ohio's Nelson Ledges State Park hosted a family camping event on Labor Day weekend, complete with designated camping spots, fishing tournaments, and both guided and unguided hiking trails. Natural rock formations, strange tree structures, jagged cliffs, thrilling rock tunnels, and two stunning waterfalls made this park unique. Hazardous conditions generally prevented overnight camping; however, due to financial burdens, enthusiastic park rangers planned and supervised this event, ready to create a memorable family experience.

Tom Wilson, Clara's father, had scheduled this family trip as a way to relax after a demanding summer spent organizing the Great Lakes 200th anniversary celebration. As the lead director and historian at the Great Lakes Historical Society, he spent many hours with the fund-raising gala supporting local heritage. Clara, along with her three-year-old sister, Lucy, and their mother, Mary, provided their assistance to the best of their abilities in creating promotional advertisements. After the festivities had concluded, her father proposed a camping trip as a means of strengthening their familial connection.

The camping trip almost didn't happen. Clara overheard her mother's protests about spending the night in a freezing tent, but ultimately, she agreed to go for the benefit of the family. Even the beautiful weather recognized the importance of strengthening family bonds that holiday weekend.

Birch, maple, and beech trees decorated the sky, and various ferns and flowers embellished the ground. The foliage resembled something Lucy drew with a bright green crayon with speckles and bits of yellow, representing the kingdom of fairies with vibrant colors and magical formations.

Clara's fearlessly tackled every rock and tree stump in her path. Lucy, inspired by Clara's movements, mirrored her actions stationary form. She couldn't figure out what caught his curiosity.

"What's wrong, Daddy?" Clara stretched her neck around her father to look for the obstruction.

"I believe I've discovered an ancient artifact." The solid wall structure made it impossible for her father to bend his hips. "Could you reach around my leg and pick up the rock near my shoe?"

Clara's fingers wiggled through the dirt, and she grabbed a small, pointy object. The jagged edges were sharp against her skin as she turned it in her palms, yet the sides were as smooth as glass. "What is it?"

"I can't be too sure until we get more light. Hold on to it tightly. I can see the end of the cavern ahead."

As she clutched the mysterious stone, its sharp edges pressed into her delicate flesh, marking an impression. It didn't take long to squeeze through the other side. The trees filtered the sunlight, casting shadows on the object in her hand. The sun snuck through the canopy of trees reflecting sparkles of light off the surface. She admired the sharp edges with her fingertips.

"I wanna hold it!" Lucy wiggled her fingers at Clara. "Gimme!"

Giving in to Lucy's relentless persistence was easier than hearing her fits and whines. *Of course, she wants something I have.* Clara's eyes rolled with annoyance as she begrudgingly handed over the object. She turned to her father, waiting for answers.

A slight arch formed in his eyebrow as he instinctively adjusted his glasses. "It's called a projectile point or arrowhead." Her dad's voice mirrored years of academic experience. "Long ago, humans lived in this area and used these tools to survive and hunt food."

"That means they killed animals." Clara smiled teasingly as

she whispered to Lucy.

"Ew, gross." Lucy thrust the stone back into Clara's hands, then ran to her mother.

Clara's face beamed with pride as she rotated the object between her fingertips. Her curiosity grew, as she offered the object back to her father.

"Keep it. It will bring you luck."

Clara's smile grew to mimic her father's.

As he left to join the others, Clara admired her new treasure. Her ears perked up to Lucy demanding something in her mother's hand. *I need to hide this from Lucy.* Making sure no one was looking, she removed her backpack, opened the center compartment, and located her soft brown teddy bear. Her fingers probed for the tear underneath the teddy bear's crimson bow tie, pulling the seam apart and securing her treasure within the fluffy fibers. The pillowy filling tickled her skin as she forced the arrowhead farther into the fluff. *There.* She returned the bear to her bag and sprinted to catch up with her family.

An unfamiliar sound caused her steps to slow and her head to tilt. "What's that noise?" Deep humming resonated through the stone beneath her feet, filling the empty spaces between the trees and stone walls.

Clara's curiosity heightened her imagination as she envisioned lions and panthers leaping through the trees and pouncing on the boulders below. With caution, the girls approached the corner of the rock wall, stretching their necks to catch a glimpse of the other side.

Lucy clenched the hem of Clara's shirt, closing the gap between them for protection.

Ignoring her sister's pull, Clara leaned around the corner, and placed her hand on the chilly, damp surface. Her parents exchanged glances and smiled at the girl's peculiar behavior.

Clara's jaw dropped as she took in the incredible sight. "Wow!" *It looks like a giant faucet.* She ventured beyond the protection of the stone barrier and marveled at the magical display of water splashing upon the rocks.

Lucy pushed past Clara and jumped into a pool of water collecting at the base of a ginormous waterfall.

"Welcome to the Minnehaha Waterfall," her father announced, theatrically widening his arms to introduce the scene ahead.

Clara and Lucy hurried closer, laughing as the water freckled their faces.

"Be careful, girls. The rocks are slick. I don't want you to fall." As the girls stepped over the slippery stones, their mother anxiously interlaced her fingers.

Clara cast a quick glance over her shoulder, mindful of her mother's concern for potential dangers. She always worried. Ignoring the warnings, Clara climbed boulders closer to the waterfall as Lucy paused and covered her ears to drown out the growing thunder of water.

The sunlight reflected off the cascading water, leaving a kaleidoscope of colors trapped within the misty droplets. The leafy canopy accentuated the beams of light piercing through the gaps and added to the majestic scene. Clara lifted her arms and noticed how the beads of water on her skin captured some of the rainbow colors.

"Wait until tomorrow!" her father yelled above the noise.

"We will visit a larger waterfall that hides a cave."

Clara and Lucy shared an excited look.

"Can we go now?" Amidst the thunderous cascade, Clara's voice seemed muted.

"Not tonight, honey," her mother said. "We've got to set up camp before it gets dark. Tomorrow will bring plenty of new adventures."

"Please, Mommy?" the girls begged.

Their mother's hand rested on the small of the girls' backs as she guided them away from the falls. "Tomorrow. Let's get going. I bet Daddy can light up a campfire so we can enjoy some hot dogs and—"

"S'mores!" The girls' eyes sparked with renewed enthusiasm, mirroring the vibrant colors of bursting fireworks. Clara remembered shopping for the tasty ingredients yesterday. Her mouth watered when she imagined her first bite of the gooey treat.

As they ventured back onto the path, Clara's father took charge, guiding the family past an open field and beyond a rustic sign that warmly greeted the Wilson family. Caution tape wrapped around trees marked the safety zones to prevent nighttime exploration. Campers were advised to remain within the designated areas until sunrise due to the potentially hazardous environmental conditions.

"We're here!" Clara said, spinning in circles. She noticed Lucy running into an open field, prompting a game of tag.

"I'm going to get you!" Clara giggled behind her.

Lucy laughed and picked up speed. She quickly rounded a tree and slipped beneath the warning tape.

"Lucy, stop!" Clara accelerated when she saw Lucy

approaching danger.

Lucy turned her head, curious why Clara was yelling, but kept her pace.

"Stop!" Clara screamed.

Lucy stumbled over an exposed tree root and instinctively extended her arms for impact, but Clara rammed into Lucy's shoulder and knocked her on her side.

"Whatcha do that for? I'm telling," Lucy squealed while rubbing her hip, which had hit the ground.

Clara struggled to find her voice through her labored breathing. "You almost fell down that hole!"

Lucy and Clara crawled on their hands and knees to peer into the dark abyss. "Wow! Why's the earth cracked?" Lucy asked.

"Clara, Lucy!" Their exhausted parents trailed close behind, their voices sharp and breathless.

"I knew this was too dangerous." Clara's mother pulled the girls away from the ledge. "I knew this was a bad idea." A few tears cascaded down her cheeks as the girls returned the tight hug.

"You girls, okay?" their dad asked.

Clara nodded as she brushed the dirt from her knees.

"Jeez-a-wheezy, Clara, that was quick thinking. You protected your sister from getting really hurt." Her father positioned himself between the hole and his family and escorted them back within the safety of the yellow caution tape.

"Did the earth break?" Lucy asked.

The anxious tone in her father's voice was still evident when he laughed. "No. This park has big holes, tall cliffs, and broken rocks. Nighttime is dangerous. If we stay within the boundaries, the yellow tape will protect us tonight. Do you understand?"

"Yes, Daddy," the girls replied in unison. Clara lowered her head, sensing trouble even though she helped her sister.

"Let's pitch the tent and light the fire." Her dad clapped his hands and rubbed them together. "I know some tasty treats waiting to be roasted!"

The girls looked at each other and giggled as they ran to collect their abandoned gear near the welcome sign.

Clara watched her mom say something to her dad, then wiped her trembling hand over her teary eyes. She had never seen her mom display any signs of fear before. Her mom's face turned red, and she clenched her fists tightly. Her dad placed a gentle hand on her arm, but she angrily swatted his hands and turned her face away from him.

Her mother brushed off invisible dirt from her jeans as though brushing away her fear and walked to the campfire to prepare the site.

* * *

"One more, Daddy, please?" Clara begged.

The sun hid beneath the land, leaving the crackling fire to supply the only light around the campsite. Clara felt the warmth of the flames on her face and the sweet residue of marshmallow and chocolate on her lips.

"More s'mores, more s'mores!" Lucy chanted.

"It's getting late," her mother said.

"Come on, Mary. Live on the wild side!" Her father smirked. "Just one more."

The girls turned to their mother expectantly.

Despite her rolling eyes, she smiled at the girls and took out the ingredients she had just put away.

"Yeah!" The girls presented their roasting sticks to their father for a new marshmallow. He leaned back to avoid getting poked in the face. Their mother prepared the other components after unpacking the graham crackers and chocolate.

There was nothing that brought Clara more joy than seeing her family gathered around the campfire, even though she found the tree roots she sat upon a bit uncomfortable. The sinewy roots of the ancient tree slithered their way around the flickering campfire, provoking a mysterious image of a serpentine creature weaving through the rolling waves of earth.

Clara beamed with joy as she watched her mom and dad wrap in a loving embrace while Lucy happily licked her fingers to savor the delicious remnants. Clara couldn't remember a happier family moment.

"Daddy?" Clara interrupted the calmness. Her fingers traced the smooth, sinuous curves of the root seats. "Are these man-made or nature-made?" Visions of cutting and pasting various objects into the categories in school crossed her mind, but these roots didn't look anything like her other tree pictures.

"Nature-made." Her father cleared his throat to prepare his academic tone. He was always eager to spread his vast wisdom like a butter knife on toast. "The tree roots in this area love sunlight. Instead of staying underground, they come to the surface to soak up the sun and expand toward water. That's why they are often on top of rocks instead of below them."

Strange and unusual things often piqued Clara's interest. This definitely qualified.

She shifted until she found the perfect divot in the root to relax and roast her marshmallow. With her marshmallow barely toasted—as if it had spent a few seconds in the presence of the campfire and decided it had had enough—she was ready to create her s'more.

Lucy, on the other hand, set her marshmallow ablaze. Her dad helped her extinguish the flames that reduced her marshmallow to charcoal, just the way she liked it. The girls licked the melted, sticky residue off their fingers as they devoured their delicious handiwork.

"Okay, time for bed." Their mother stood from their father's embrace and pointed at the tent. When Clara and Lucy turned to their father for support, he dismissed them with a shrug and smile. With a hint of hesitation, the girls left behind their comfortable spot next to the crackling fire. Sensing the chill creeping closer, they quickly sought refuge within the tent.

Clara took her teddy bear out of her backpack and cuddled into the soft fur as Lucy unrolled her sleeping bag close to Clara. Her mother waited for them to settle before covering them with a thicker blanket and tucking them in for the night. Her father watched with a smile from the opening of the tent.

"Good night, my sweet girls." Her mother grinned with her soft eyes as she tucked the girls beneath the blankets.

"Good night, ladies," her father added from the entrance.

"Are you going to bed?" Clara asked.

"Your mother and I need to watch the fire until it's gone. Fire can never be left unattended, even a smoldering one."

"I'll watch with you."

Clara's mother placed a hand on her shoulder. "You've got to get some sleep. Tomorrow will be filled with more excitement and adventure."

"Okay. Good night. I love you, Mommy." Clara hugged her mother. "I love you, Daddy."

"Love you, Mommy. Love you, Daddy," Lucy chimed.

"We love you, too. Now get some rest." The night's gentle breeze rustled the fabric of the tent while their mother leaned over and planted a tender kiss on each of the girls' heads, bidding them sweet dreams. She lingered by Clara's side. "Look after your sister."

"I will."

Once the girls were alone, Clara shifted on her side, pulling the blankets under her chin. "Good night, Lucy."

"Clare Bear?"

Not again. "Not tonight, Lucy. Just go to sleep."

"Clare Bear, please?" Lucy begged.

Clara didn't have the patience to deal with loud, whiny Lucy. Before surrendering her teddy to Lucy, she gave him a big hug.

Lucy often demanded her teddy at night, especially when the darkness scared her. None of her other stuffies seemed to settle her fears. Clara sacrificed her bear for a good night's sleep.

"Sorry, Teddy," she whispered. *One day, I will never let you go.*

"Lu-Lu loves Clare Bear." Lucy smiled proudly as she cuddled the teddy bear in her arms.

"Clare Bear loves Lu-Lu. Now good night."

Her pillow felt like a cloud of marshmallows gently caressing her tired head, guiding her toward peaceful dreams.

* * *

A beautiful ray of sunshine found its way through the tent and delicately kissed Clara's eyelids. She responded with a hint of unease to the intrusion, attempting to turn away the light with her hand. With a gentle touch, she brushed away the remnants of sleepiness from her lashes and carefully surveyed the interior of the tent.

Where is everybody?

The bedding of her parents remained undisturbed, exactly as it had been the previous night, while Lucy's sleeping bag lay crumpled beside it.

"Mommy?" *They must be outside.*

Clara's arms reached overhead as she let out a long yawn, invigorating her muscles. She kicked the blankets from her legs, eager to start her day, then rummaged around for her sandals. Clara's lips curled into a smile as she recounted kicking her shoes off like they were performing for a high-flying acrobatic show with Lucy's laughter filling the night. Their father tapped the watch on his wrist, as if the girls could tell time, and silently urged them to be quiet.

With the grace of a clumsy flamingo, she wrestled her feet into those stubborn shoes. After getting her shoes on, she pulled the fabric to open the tent. An icy breeze forced her to retreat inside and hunt for her jacket.

Jeez-a-wheezy, it's cold.

Clara discovered her coat sleeve protruding from beneath the blankets, as if it were desperately trying to break free from quicksand. She pulled it free, put it on, and then fastened the zipper. Although the garment was thick, the elusive cold snuck between the seams, causing internal cascading chills. She rubbed her arms to smooth down the hidden goose bumps.

The gentle breeze carried wisps of smoke from the smoldering campfire, meandering through the forest canopy. In the early-morning, the air was filled with the melodious tunes of birds as they serenaded the world. Meanwhile, agile squirrels performed their acrobatic feats, effortlessly leaping and darting across the branches of the trees.

Clara cautiously distanced herself from the tent. The sound of the leaves beneath her feet crunched through the stillness, their crackling unexpectedly amplified.

"Mommy?" When no one responded, she raised her voice.

Where is everyone? Her heart trembled with fear. The woodland noises intensified. She strained her ears, desperately trying to catch any noise that would indicate her family's presence. Every sound reached her ears, except for the ones belonging to her family.

"Daddy? Lucy? Where are you guys? This isn't funny." Clara's fingers instinctively tightened around the fabric of her jacket.

Are they playing hide-and-seek? They wouldn't leave me alone.

Clara ventured a few more steps away from the safety of the tent, her heart pounding. She wrapped her arms tightly around herself, trying to steady her trembling body.

The smoking embers captured Clara's attention. Their faint glow beckoned her. As she drew near, her pulse quickened, and anticipation boiled with uneasiness. Against the circling tree roots, a pair of mysterious, shadowy figures emerged. A sigh of relief escaped her lips as she recognized her parents' hunter-green and maroon jackets.

Why are they sleeping outside?

"There you are! Why didn't you answer? I can't find Lucy." No response.

"Hello?" Clara climbed over the roots and tapped her mother's shoulder gently.

"Mommy, wake up. Lucy's gone."

Something's wrong. Ew! What's this sticky stuff on Mommy's coat?

Clara pulled her hand away with a mysterious substance sticking to her skin. Her expression tightened with a mixture of disgust and curiosity as she felt the gelatinous moisture between her fingers. She tried to remove the wetness by rubbing her hand against her pants, only to discover that it had spread farther.

"Mommy?" Clara's voice trembled with uncertainty as she rolled her mother over.

There was something unnerving about her vacant expression. Her mother's hazel eyes, once filled with warmth and familiarity, were now shrouded in a translucent gray haze. Clara's muscles tightened. Terror gripped her trembling lips as a solitary word slipped through: "Mommy?" That solitary word, once a source of comfort, now clawed at her lips with an unbearable torment.

Blood seeped from her mother's chest, pooling on the forest floor, staining the earth red.

Clara stumbled backward, her mind struggling to comprehend the horrifying sight. She turned to her father, yet it was not her father who lived within that lifeless expression. Her body staggered and twisted over the coarse roots, until she found herself landing amid the smoldering embers. Despite the searing pain in her right palm, she was completely unaware, consumed by the agony in her soul.

She spun on her knees, determined to find solid ground beneath her. With every breath, she could feel the adrenaline in her veins, urging her to move faster. She sprinted into the safety of her tent, her mind racing with horrible thoughts that couldn't be true. Huddled beneath the protection of her blankets, she longed for the nightmare's conclusion.

"Mommy! Daddy! Help me!" Clara's tears flowed uncontrollably as she rocked, her burned hand cradled gently against her chest.

Those aren't my parents. It can't be them. We're safe in the yellow tape. The yellow tape protects us.

Her parents radiated affection and warmth. *Those* people emitted fear and coldness. Beneath the covers, she nestled her knees closer to her chest, seeking peace in the darkness. Endless tears streamed down.

"Lucy, where are you?"

CHAPTER 1

CLARA

The piercing bell of Clara's alarm jolted her awake precisely at 7:30 a.m. *Oh, that blasted noise.* Exhaustion threatened to pull her back to bed, but she knew surrendering wasn't an option. She pushed the tangles from her face and willed her vision to focus on her old-fashioned alarm clock.

"Jeez-a-wheezy!" *I must have slept through my phone alarm!* Despite being unpleasant, the alarm clock served as a reliable backup to her phone, which she occasionally slept through. With a burst of energy, Clara forcefully struck the alarm clock, disentangled herself from the sheets, and leaped out of bed, seizing her necessary tools for the bathroom. Due to the distant location of the bathroom, meticulous preparation became imperative.

Living in a college dormitory offered both advantages and disadvantages. The bathroom posed a significant disadvantage. Sharing a bathroom with twenty-four girls, along with a few unexpected boyfriends, was less than ideal. Since her roommate stayed at her boyfriend's, her living situation was quite favorable compared to others. She used the entire room to create a cozy living place with blues, purples, and encouraging posters such as *"Hang in There"* and *"We Can Do It."* Her simple style helped her relax.

Clara secured her robe around her waist before retrieving the room key from her previously worn pants and proceeded toward the shared bathrooms. She showered, put on a little makeup, and left her dark blond hair in a short, wavy mess, styled without the use of a hair dryer. Morning beauty rituals were of little concern.

While crossing the corridor, she ensured a firm grip with her toes to prevent her flip-flops from sliding off her damp feet. She put on the skirt and blouse she'd picked out last night, then struggled to put on her black Mary Jane pumps. After grabbing her book bag, she stumbled out the door. Remembering her finished assignment, she lunged backward to stop the door from closing, and grabbed her pages from her desk.

She looked at her watch and walked faster. Clara hated being late. It rarely happened. Quickly, she descended three flights of stairs and discovered her friend waiting calmly at the bottom.

"Good morning, Sunshine!" His enthusiastic smile was not enough to jump-start her morning. The young man offered Clara a cup of coffee, which she graciously accepted.

"Bless you, Benji." Before progressing to her first class, she paused to savor the strong fragrance. As she took her first steps, her book bag slipped off her shoulder and collided with her arm, causing her hot beverage to spill. She hissed through her teeth as the drops splashed on her hand, reddening her pale skin.

"Here. Let me get that for you." Benji swung her book bag over his and together they walked to class.

Fourth grade was the catalyst that had brought Clara and Benji together in a lifelong friendship. As a new student, Clara had found herself socially awkward and friendless. Spider Attack was a game played by the kids at recess under a metal-bar dome. She decided to participate but was quickly caught by "the spider." Benji came to her rescue, and they became inseparable.

"Rough night?" Benji asked.

"Yeah. The nightmares are back." Clara cradled her coffee cup with both hands, looking absently at the coffee residue staining the lid.

Benji took a deep breath and let it out slowly. "Clara, I'm sorry. You should've called. I would've come over."

"I know. It caught me off guard."

Benji checked his phone, the iridescent sticker of a shark glittered in the sunlight. "Looks like we're power-walking today. You know Dr. Flickinger's temper when we're late for History."

Clara cautiously sipped her coffee as Benji quickened the pace. Her skirt rippled behind her in a silky stream. When they arrived, Benji gently opened the classroom door and gestured for Clara to pass through. The professor gestured animatedly at the front of the class as she spoke about the rise and fall of the mighty Roman Empire.

Benji closed the door behind him with the stealth and precision of a ninja. Meanwhile, when Clara sat at her desk, her chair scraped against the tile, echoing throughout the classroom. Ducking her head and gritting her teeth, she attempted to avoid drawing attention.

Benji shuffled through the door, only to be met with a disapproving look from Dr. Flickinger.

"Sorry," Clara inaudibly mouthed.

Benji sat down next to her, grabbed his notebook, and began taking notes. He didn't seem to care about getting caught. The professor's teaching was accompanied by a symphony of clicking keyboards and scratching pens, as if he were conducting an ensemble in the classroom.

* * *

"That was brutal." Benji let out a breath as he finished writing in his notebook, placing his pencil between the pages to mark his spot.

"My other courses aren't nearly this challenging." Clara stowed her materials in her backpack. She spotted Benji's dropped pen and returned it to him.

"Thanks." He let the pen fall into his pack. "Wanna meet for lunch later?"

Clara scratched the back of her neck and turned her necklace chain around to find the small silver pendant. "I'll probably grab a cup of coffee and head to the library."

"Clara, please don't. Meet me for lunch. I'll buy!" Benji tilted his head forward and batted his eyelashes, looking up at her with puppy dog eyes. "P-p-p-please."

Clara snickered. "We have a meal plan."

"You'll have more fun with me than at that dingy old library. That's the Benjamin guarantee!"

Clara held her book bag straps tightly. "There's just a few

articles I want to research."

Benji's shoulders fell. "You've read them all, hundreds of times. I know you. You'll be poring over those microdiscs, and I won't see you for days. When you finally surface, you'll look like you narrowly survived the Goblet of Fire. Just let it go."

"It's microfiche and you know I can't. The truth is out there. My sister's still out there. I promise I'm not going to barricade myself. I just want to double-check a few details."

Benji sighed. "You're at least meeting me at the pub?"

"Every Thursday night. I wouldn't miss it." She smiled.

Benji wrapped his arms around her and squeezed her tightly for a moment. "Don't go all cavewoman on me. I'll see you tonight." He waved as he jogged away, his chestnut hair barely moved from his styling products.

Clara valued her friendship with Benji, but he didn't understand her desire to find her sister. She imagined Lucy out in the world, alone and scared, not knowing where her family was or how to find them. She could never abandon her sister.

JENNA

"Order ready for Mr. ... Stroker. Mr. Willie Stroker?"

Snickers and crude comments emerged from the group of students standing around the college's central coffee shop.

"Oh, guys. Not again." Of course, the young barista was aware of the childish pranks, but she played along, pretending innocence to increase customer tips.

Jenna had begun her employment at Java Junction, shortly after her arrival on campus two months ago. Even though her supervisor had warned her multiple times not to engage unruly clients, she found pleasure in the attention and the gratuities. She scanned the crowd, searching for the coffee owner. Among the sea of students, she noticed one boy trying to conceal his laughter. His friends playfully nudged him forward.

Look at him, all shy and avoiding eye contact like he's about to ask his crush to prom. Will he have the courage to face the barista?

The young man's uncertain steps carried him closer—his youthful appearance hinting at his recent graduation from high school—as he reached a nervous hand out to claim his cup of coffee.

"Have a willie nice day, and don't stroke it too hard." The timid student blushed when Jenna winked at him. She leaned over the counter, her blouse slightly opened, revealing a glimpse of her smooth, rounded skin. With a playful gesture, she gently rattled the tip jar, silently conveying her expectation.

Her emerald-green eyes were highlighted by her long, wavy brown hair as she flirted with the customers. Except for the few rigid stick-up-the-dark-side-of-the-moon types, her daily income indicated that most of the clientele enjoyed the attention.

"Order ready for ... Clara." Jenna rechecked the ticket. "Just Clara?"

"Does that bother you?" the owner of the coffee asked.

Jenna handed the coffee to the girl at the counter. It took her a moment to realize she was referring to the boys' vulgar humor.

"Not at all." Jenna smiled at the girl who averted her eyes.

As the girl grabbed her coffee, she abruptly pulled back, bringing her finger to her lips. Her face contorted in discomfort, as though she experienced a searing burn.

"Careful, coffee's hot." Without another word, Jenna turned to help the next customer—a young man with a guilty expression on his face, as if he had just swiped a cookie from the cookie jar.

A tap on her shoulder startled Jenna. "Oh, Marcy. Sorry, I didn't hear the gate open. You're up!" She stopped abruptly in the middle of the young man's order, his face melting in disappointment.

Jenna caught sight of her watch. "You're a little late. Everything okay?"

"Yeah, just stuck at the library. That chick that flirts with the entire male population was working. I just pocketed my book. Everything working?"

"Rebel!" Jenna's hand connected with Marcy's arm in a playful slap. "So far, so good. Running low on coconut milk. I dispatched Gofer Boy for restock."

"Sounds great. See ya."

Untying her apron, Jenna draped her makeshift uniform over the counter before swinging through the side gate with her messenger bag. She spaced her courses to allow time for socializing and working, which she considered socializing with pay. Even as a first-year student, she adapted to college life as easily as Medusa to snakes. Before putting her phone in her lower cargo pocket, she checked it for the time and missed calls.

The passage of time did not influence Jenna as she persisted in walking at her usual pace. While she was rarely absent from class, she was frequently tardy. Criminology was one of her favorites, although she didn't much like the professor. Professor Lancer despised her, but she was performing well in the sophomore-level class.

"Hey, Jenna!"

She shuddered, her shoulders reaching her ears like a turtle hiding its head in its shell. The high-pitched voice evoked memories of nails scraping against a chalkboard. She sighed before planting a false grin and picking up her pace. *Puberty still eludes you, I see.* "Hi, Joshy. I missed you at Java." *Not really.*

"I picked these up for you." He presented a bouquet of wildflowers as he quickened his steps to keep up with her, but she never slowed or acknowledged the gift.

"You know I can't accept them, but they are beautiful." She felt bad about destroying the poor boy's heart. He did, after all, leave generous tips, but she was not interested. She willed her class to be closer.

"When will you give me a chance? I'd do anything!" There was a new pitch in his voice as he begged and turned his puzzle ring around on his middle finger. "Would you rather I was a woman? That can happen."

You already sound like a woman. "Joshy, I'm sorry. I simply don't date men or women. I'm here to focus on my studies." *Truth in parts is preferable to lies, right?* "I'll see you tomorrow—bye!" She quickened her step to a jog, leaving him behind as he dangled the flowers by their stems.

Upon arriving, she wished for the ability to transport herself to her classroom. *But alas, the elevator awaits.* Jenna despised feeling confined, especially with a can of stinky, perspiration-smeared humans pressed up against each other. Being late was a benefit to minimize such crowded inconveniences.

Behind her, another student reached past her and pressed the already lit button. *He must require assurance that, despite the choices of others, he remains in control.* Jenna rolled her eyes away from the man's actions.

The doors swung open, revealing an empty container. Jenna entered and selected the fourth floor, while the guy selected the fifth. She crossed her arms and leaned against the railing.

Her neck tingled, prompting her to turn and catch the guy quickly looking away. "Can I help you?" She straightened her back to address his obvious deception. She didn't recognize him as one of her regulars or classmates.

"Sorry, I didn't mean to stare. I just thought you looked familiar, but I ... I'm sorry."

Likely story. How many stalkers can one girl get in a day? "Just keep your eyes to yourself." Jenna longed for the elevator doors to open and put this awkwardness out of its misery.

"Okay, sorry. I'm Ben." He extended his hand.

"*I don't care.*" When the doors opened, Jenna slipped out to avoid any further interaction. There was an undeniable sensation of his eyes following her out into the hallway. *Creepy*.

Outside the classroom door, she checked her watch. *Only four minutes late. At least stalkers help me get to class on time.*

Opening the door, she entered and crossed the room to her seat. Professor Lancer ignored the interruption and proceeded with her lecture.

Jenna saw the jumbled mound of freshly stapled papers and slid her assignment into the middle of the stack before returning to her seat. Using the digital pen that came with her tablet, she began taking notes while she scribbled in the margins until the end of class.

* * *

An unpleasant, recognizable male voice shouted above the noise of the crowd, interrupting Jenna's stroll to the café.

Not again. When will this guy back off? She didn't bother with the fake smile. "Hey, Joshy. I'm on my way to somewhere else. Can't stop to chitchat."

"Do you want to have lunch with me?" Joshua asked as he side-galloped beside her to keep up with her pace.

Angry mutterings escaped her at the thought of having to change her plans. Her face scrunched up in a silent snarl, her frustration evident as she quickly developed new intentions. "No, Sugar Bear. I've got homework."

"How about dinner?" Joshua course-corrected.

"Meeting my dad. I'm not interested in going out, Joshy," Jenna said more sternly. "Keep it friendly. See you later." Jenna's mind shifted, and she found herself drawn to the library with its hallowed halls and whispered secrets, providing the sanctuary she needed to find solace and solitude.

"Jenna!"

What now? Jenna turned her head over her shoulder and spotted her friend Kyle and exhaled a sigh of relief.

With a genuine smile, Jenna said, "What's up, Kyle?"

"Are you going to the WaHo tonight?"

A few blocks from college, underage teenagers gathered in an abandoned warehouse to drink and socialize. Her eighteen years of age required others to bring the beverages.

"Yeah. I can't stay long, but I plan on making an appearance. I wouldn't want to disappoint my fans." Her heart had swelled with pride as the partygoers erupted in cheers, demanding an encore after her last karaoke performance.

Parties were never planned, but after a beer or two, Jenna would convince others to sing and dance with her. Her voice was pleasant and goofy, not professional, but others encouraged her for their own amusement.

"Great! See you then!"

CHAPTER 2

CLARA

Flipping through the newspaper archives, Clara couldn't find anything she hadn't seen before. The cold and dingy basement of the library provided her with a safe, comfortable environment away from other people. She preferred the isolation of hard research to search engines and streaming databases.

Clara eagerly searched through various periodicals and magazines from the Labor Day weekend fifteen years ago, feeling a sense of expectancy building as if she was on the verge of a discovery. In her search for the elusive piece of information, her concentration strained with each microfilm clip.

Clara abruptly pushed herself away from the table, causing her chair to emit a piercing screech against the unforgiving concrete floor. Her face scrunched up in a grimace as the noise assaulted her ears once again. She let out a sharp exhalation and reached for her phone. A message was waiting from Benji: *Don't forget about me.*

Benji's right. She flipped the switch to turn off the microfiche monitor. Hazy phantom images haunted her vision. Clara returned the films and collected her things. Climbing up the creaky stairs to the brighter first floor, she squinted like a spelunker coming out of a deep dive.

Clara's shoulders drooped and her head hung low as she caught sight of the person behind the circulation desk. *No point picking up my schedule. She'll ask me to cover one of her shifts, again.* Clara avoided the front, lowered her head, and bolted for the rotating doors.

* * *

Happy Hour at the Fyte Pub occurred every Monday through Thursday from 6:00 p.m. to 8:00 p.m., with the final call at 9:00 p.m. Most of the patrons walked from the dormitories to get cheap food, sodas, and beer. Marshall Campbell, the owner, dubbed the place Forget Your Troubles & Enjoy; the main attraction being the infamous Happy Hour card presented with each entrée and each beverage with five pull tabs—two of them revealed *Full Price*, two offered *Half Price*, and the final tab read *Free*. Talking and meeting new people helped most college students forget the rigors of academic obligations. Benji and Clara traditionally hung out on Thursday nights to relax among the crowd, although for Clara it was anything but relaxing.

Avoiding further lateness, she walked across campus without dropping her book bag at the dorms. *No twinkling lights. Either*

Marshall's late or I'm earlier than I thought. Multicolored twinkle lights announced Happy Hour. Precisely at eight o'clock, the lights were switched to the ordinary nontwinkling white lights.

Outside the dimly lit tavern, Clara's footsteps echoed softly as she ascended the weathered steps leading to the porch. Opening the squeaky door, she was utterly bewildered by the mayhem within. A group of individuals gathered around the jukebox, engaged in a spirited debate over the perfect song to set the mood for the evening. Meanwhile, shadows danced across the tables as patrons moved about, seeking connections and engaging in clandestine rendezvous. Glasses clinked and chairs scooted, making it hard for Clara to focus through the chaos to find her friend.

She found Benji at the bar before she shut the door. She clutched her bag tightly against her chest, her eyes darting anxiously from person to person as she hurried past. To a stranger, they may have thought she was guarding a treasure trove of priceless diamonds concealed within the guarded package.

"Nice of you to join me. Relax." Benji gave her a brief side hug as she sat down on the uncomfortable stool beside him. He was completely comfortable and calm. While Benji seemed to be able to blend in with his surroundings and make friends with anyone he met, Clara felt more like a social leper, constantly ready to hide in a corner.

"It's packed today." Clara's skin felt warm and clammy, her breaths shallow as she struggled to maintain composure.

"Focus on me, not them." Benji gently removed her book bag from her lap and placed it on the floor. "Cheyenne? Tall tap, please."

Clara remembered ordering root beer floats until she turned twenty-one over the summer. As she took a sip of beer, she wrinkled her nose in distaste. Yet she couldn't deny the soothing effect it had on her, allowing her to unwind and let go of her anxieties. During her conversation with Benji, she noticed a root beer float being delivered to the opposite end of the bar, indicating her preference.

Clara noticed Benji's Happy Hour card tabs were all pulled. "Tough luck."

He shrugged, completely unbothered about his results. "Who needs a free drink when you've become the grandmaster of indifference, like a Zen master of nonchalance?"

Clara smiled as Benji slid her card closer.

"Experience the thrill of pulling a tab. Will it be treasure, or will you be sad?"

A chuckle escaped Clara's lips. Benji possessed a certain knack for putting her at ease in situations that pushed the boundaries of her comfort.

She pulled the middle tab and frowned. *Full Price*.

"Treasure!" Benji bellowed with a pitiful pirate accent.

"What? It's *Full Price*." Clara turned the card over so that he could have a clearer view.

"Yes, but I'm buying for ye tonight. Cheyenne, drinks are on me tab. Thank ye." The bartender saluted and kept serving other customers.

"Benji, you don't have to do that." A subtle smile surfaced as she lightly grazed his arm.

They tapped their glasses together. "Cheers."

Clara's tense shoulders eased, her body finding a more

suitable position on the unforgiving wooden stool. Anxiety and fear teamed together like two mischievous sprites, constantly vying for her attention, but Benji possessed an unwavering ability to keep these troublesome companions at arm's length. Without him, she would be lost.

"How was the library?" Benji asked, yet Clara noticed his lack of genuine curiosity.

"You're right. Same things, nothing new." At the bottom of her glass, Clara could see effervescent bubbles escaping gravity, and the sight captivated her.

"Hey, I've got a wild and crazy idea." Benji swiveled his stool toward Clara. "Why don't we road-trip to Maine and eat lobster on the beach? Or visit Disney and play with Mickey?"

Clara considered, her body contorting with discomfort. His motive was evident. He knew the importance of the upcoming weekend.

"Anywhere you choose!" Benji's fingers intertwined with hers, his grip firm and unyielding. A wordless plea was written on his face as he stared into her eyes.

She developed an uncomfortable sensation from his hand on hers, as if his fingers were slimy seaweed from the deep sea. She wanted to let go but didn't want to upset him. This wasn't a sympathetic act. This was selfish. *He says, "It's time to move on," but I can't bring myself to forget.*

"You don't have to decide today. Please consider."

Clara thought about what to say next and swirled the beer in her glass. "This year feels different, somehow."

Benji's shoulders drooped as he sank into his seat, releasing her hand, clearly displaying his disheartenment. She peered into her swirling vortex. "Like something's about to change. I don't know." She sipped the bitter elixir. "Will you still go with me? I promise this will be the last year. Then, if you want, we can travel to Bermuda and go parasailing. But I need this year." Clara's fingers grazed his hand for a fleeting moment, but she quickly pulled away when their eyes met.

"I will always be there for you. If you need another year, we'll do it together."

Clara noticed that he was sincere, but his slouching posture betrayed his disappointment.

"Thanks, Benji." Clara gently touched his arm.

He looked at the gesture for a moment before talking about something else.

"Did you see that TikTok video of the little girl performing a cartwheel and the little boy attempts to show her up? It's hilarious!" Benji took out his phone from his back pocket while Clara shook her head.

Clara leaned in to watch Benji's comedic video. The young girl performed her semicartwheel, and then it was the little boy's turn. "Oh my goodness. He just puts his arms straight up and drops like a plank, flat on his face!"

"I know! He's the next face-plant superstar. Why is it so funny to watch kids fall? They're just tiny humans doing their thing, thinking everything's possible, and *bam* ... face plant! Did you see the other one with the toddler girl rolling all the way down a hill after she slipped?" Tears pooled at Benji's eyes, due to the uncontrollable fit of laughter that erupted.

Clara, against her better judgment, couldn't help but join in the amusement.

JENNA

The abandoned warehouse off campus was a well-known gathering place for rats, college students, and squatters. No one planned parties, but people seemed to always show up. Boards hung in front of broken windows, vines covered the deteriorating bricks, and the roof sagged into the front corner. It was in danger if the big bad wolf threatened to huff and puff.

The dilapidated appearance didn't stop Jenna from attending a few drinking sessions with her friends. Her newfound independence, since starting college, provided an escape from her father's rigorous, unrelenting expectations, as well as an opportunity to explore more than what society considered acceptable for a young lady.

Hidden behind an alley dumpster, a swinging wooden panel concealed the easiest entrance into the warehouse. Pushing the panel out of the way, Jenna crawled inside and found the spiral staircase leading to the second floor. What started as faint music intensified the higher she climbed each stair.

"Livin' on a Prayer." Must be '80s night. The floorboards pulsated with the beat of the music and groaned with the pressure of each step.

"Jenna!" the partygoers shouted as she entered the far room.

"Thanks, guys. I feel like frickin' Norm." She gladly received the salutations.

George and Kyle shifted on the sofa to make room for her while Lisa handed her a bottle of beer from the cooler.

"What's up?" Jenna said as she plopped down between her

friends.

Kyle reached for Jenna's bottle and opened it for her. "Not much." He handed the bottle back and gave her one kiss on the cheek, which she returned with two. He smiled devilishly at her as they shared a secret communication.

Her favorite lyrics began playing and Jenna bolted from her seat midconversation, blaring out "Life Is a Highway." She pulled Lisa from the arm of the couch to join her, and the two of them danced and sang into their beer bottle microphones. Song after song, drink after drink, Jenna enjoyed herself until an unfamiliar set of hands grabbed her hips and tried to dance with her. She slapped the hands away and continued to dance with her friends.

Every now and then, the new attendees couldn't resist testing the waters of her playful nature, but those who were acquainted with her were well aware of the limits she set. She has a reputation for knocking men to their knees when they become too friendly. She danced with a mischievous spirit yet possessed a fierce strength when boundaries were trespassed.

"Hey, listen up, guys!" someone yelled from across the room. "Mark's brother got his dad's gun, and we're going to blast out the windows at the old farmhouse. Who's coming?" Responses of varying enthusiasm filled the room.

Lisa cast an inquisitive glare at Jenna.

"Not I," Jenna said. "I've already started drinking and I only partake in one illegal activity at a time. Besides, I've got to get back home. You guys enjoy. Shoot one out for me!" She squinted closer at her watch, willing the hands to stop spinning.

"Jenna, I'll walk you home."

She felt her body transform into a live guitar string, vibrating with tension as the sharp voice pierced her ears. *Joshy?*

"I can manage on my own." Jenna started to chuckle, picturing what her father would do if a boy walked her home. He didn't take too kindly to *friendly* companions. On the other hand, maybe that was how she could get Joshy to stop stalking her. She shuddered with the thought.

Before leaving, Jenna double-checked that her phone and foldable pocketknife were securely in their proper places. Her father gave her the knife years ago, after teaching her effective defensive techniques. *Protect yourself no matter the cost.*

Jenna's foot slipped off the edge of a step, causing her to lose her balance. She stumbled down four steps before landing on the next platform of the spiral staircase. She felt a pair of hands grip her hips, steadying her. Instinctively, she recoiled and tightened her fists. She hated being touched. Her hips were a magnet for unwanted attention tonight.

Can't a girl stumble in peace without feeling like a human squeeze toy? Jenna grunted but tried to convince herself that the unknown grabber was just trying to help. Despite the contact, she continued her descent, determined to reach the bottom safely.

The last occupant left the wooden panel ajar, probably in a hurry to join the party or too inebriated when they left. *How rude!*

Jenna wriggled her way through the narrow opening and glanced up at the dark sky. As the moon rose, its gentle light spilled over the landscape, creating a soft, hazy glow that bathed the world in a subtle illumination. She couldn't help but feel a sense of disappointment. The city lights were so bright and overpowering that it was impossible to see the full expanse of the sky. She longed to see the stars and constellations that she knew were up there but remained hidden by the light. A few raindrops trickled down her cheeks, and she closed her eyes to embrace the cool night air, forgetting the open panel she'd left behind. The cold drops felt peaceful as they eased the warmth in her cheeks.

Her arms were being guided into a jacket, and she tried to remember if she'd even brought a jacket tonight. She allowed the unknown person to help her put it on. Her delicate fingers grazed the strange scarlet material enveloping her skin.

"This isn't mine," she said to the gift giver.

"I know. It looks like it's going to rain."

Joshy? "I am not your concern, Joshua. Leave me alone." Instead of ripping the jacket off, Jenna hugged the jacket closer to her body and stumped away from the alley.

With a determined focus, she placed one foot in front of the other, focusing on the ground beneath her. The sidewalk, though familiar, was far from even, and she knew that one misstep could send her tumbling to the ground. The flickering streetlamps, surrounded by buzzing insects, cast darker shadows along the cracks, making balance nearly impossible.

A few stray cats skulked in the shadows, but otherwise the streets were empty. The streetlamps' feeble attempt to illuminate the streets only increased the darkness with dancing elongated shadows. Walking home at night never felt so nerve racking. Autonomy felt empowering and therapeutic. But tonight, she'd consumed a tad beyond her usual limits.

The crisp night air felt refreshing on her warm skin. She caught a glimpse of her apartment's stairwell. *That was fast.* She glanced at the dark living room window on the second floor. If she could sneak to her room unnoticed, she might avoid a parental battle.

Even though she loved her father dearly, he was overbearing at times and way too nosy.

With a heavy sigh, she shook her head, clearing her thoughts so she could focus on being quick and stealthy. Her hand found its way to the smooth metal railing, cool to the touch. A familiar and unpleasant pressure against her hips caused her to startle.

"What the ...?" Jenna's body twisted, forcefully pushing the invader aside. As the intruder's ring contacted her arm, a sharp scratch etched its way along her delicate skin. "Joshy?" She glanced at the darkened window, her voice dropping to a whisper. "What the blazes are you doing here? Did you follow me?" As she went for her knife, her fingers struggled with the fabric of her pocket. Despite her efforts, she struggled to find the opening.

"I wanted to make sure you got home safely without any problems." Joshua beamed with self-satisfaction. He reached for her.

"Besides the one that followed me home." She swatted his hands away. "You shouldn't be here." Jenna nervously glanced up the stairwell again, then back at Joshua.

"Jenna, I really like you. I think I love you. I think you'd like me, too, if you let me try." He advanced for a kiss, causing her to stumble and fall against the metal steps.

A sharp impact struck her lower back, causing her to wince in pain. A dark shadow passed over her at the same time and shoved Joshua back with the force of a linebacker. He tripped over the sidewalk, landing hard on the unforgiving asphalt. He scrambled back as the tall, dark, menacing figure towered over him.

"I hope to encounter you near my daughter again so I may have the pleasure of slicing your throat and erasing your existence." The shadows casting across Jenna's father's features intensified the danger he depicted.

In a flash of uncertainty, Joshua sprang up from the ground, emitting a tiny squeal as he darted off. He resembled a startled creature straight out of a vintage cartoon, where perilous situations prompted a comical display of legs whirling like a whirlwind. Jenna covered her mouth and stifled a laugh at the sight of her father's serious face.

She closed her eyes, took a deep breath, and prepared for the impending wrath. But to her surprise, nothing happened. She slowly opened one of her eyes and saw her father's indecipherable face above her. "I'm sorry, Daddy. I drank a bit and didn't know he was following me."

"You're late."

"I'm really sorry."

"Where's your knife?"

"It's right here ... in my pocket." She nervously patted her pocket, feeling the weight of the weapon trapped inside. "He didn't mean any harm. He follows me around campus like a lost little puppy. He's got a crush."

"That's no excuse to force himself on you." Her father's hovering figure made her feel as small as Alice did after drinking the mysterious potion that shrank her to itty bitty size.

Jenna hesitated for a moment, her lips parting as if to speak. But then she quickly shut her mouth and hung her head low. A chill shuttered through her as she sensed the weight of the red jacket slipping off her shoulder.

Her father inhaled deeply, his warm brown eyes shimmering with a hint of vulnerability under the gentle glow of the security light. He draped the red fabric over her shoulder and offered his hand.

Jenna accepted, and he helped her up. Her body jolted slightly, a reflexive reaction to the touch of his hand on the sensitive area of her back that still throbbed from the recent impact. He frowned at the reaction and guided her into the apartment. As they stepped inside and locked the door, he released her with a gentle push toward her bedroom.

"Clean up and get to bed."

"Yes, Daddy." *No lecture?* She watched him cross the room and head to his workshop in the back bedroom. *Is he losing his touch or losing control?* She had witnessed numerous situations where he lost his temper, especially when he felt that she was in harm's way. She sensed it, lurking beneath his calm facade, a tempest waiting to be unleashed. Though he tried to conceal it, she could see a flicker of anger and the subtle tightening of his jaw.

She staggered to the restroom and unintentionally slammed the door behind her. With a gentle shushing, she coaxed the door into silence, her heart fluttering with the hope that the boisterous clamor wouldn't awaken any dormant eruptions. Stomping feet echoed down the hall. She hoped they were not meant for her. When the entry door opened and closed, she relaxed but became curious. *Where's he going?*

As she stepped into the shower, the warm water cascaded down her face, cleansing her of the day's poor judgments. A slight sting pricked under her arm and at the small of her back as the water trickled over her recent injuries. She closed her eyes and let the water transport her to a world of relaxation and rejuvenation. The calming steam beckoned her to stay, but school awaited her in the morning.

In front of the mirror, she braided her damp hair and told herself not to drink so much next time. Careful not to leave wet footprints, she wrapped herself in a towel and tiptoed to her bedroom. She dropped the towel and quickly changed into the tank top and shorts she had carelessly tossed aside earlier that morning.

She kissed her teddy bear good night and projected her voice down the hall, "Good night, Daddy!" No response. *Guess he went to bed.* As soon as she slipped under the warm covers and nestled her head into the soft pillow, she drifted off into a peaceful slumber.

CHAPTER 3

CLARA

The inky abyss distorted the unfathomable figures prowling within the depths of obscurity. Mysterious beings vanished into the ether, fleeing with every precious breath of life. This place was branded in Clara's memory along with the fear and terror that felt all too familiar. *Please wake up.*

Once again, she found herself deep in the heart of the woods, surrounded by the tranquillity of nature. Inside her tent, she sought refuge, wrapped in the comfort of her scratchy camping blankets. As she sat in silence, her neck tingled, and her arms prickled as the leaves rustled softly nearby. Despite her muscles refusing to move, she knew that the horror would persist unless she mustered the courage to cast aside the security of her blanket. With a trembling hand, she removed her shield and slowly parted the fabric of the tent. The smoke slithered like Medusa's unruly hair away from the smoldering campfire her father had started last night.

The crackling sound of toasted marshmallows and the laughter of family around the campfire had transformed into a haunting tale of wickedness. Tonight, darkness enveloped everything, leaving behind only the void where goodness once resided. The wilderness offered no sounds or evidence of nightlife. Not a single cricket chirped. Not a single lightning bug glowed. The darkness pressed Clara to the ground and manipulated reality. She approached the final family gathering with careful stride.

Why did Mommy and Daddy sleep near the fire instead of with me and Lucy?

Clara's footsteps echoed through the silent forest, the dried leaves crunching beneath her feet like a series of miniature explosions. Her parents' forms did not rise and fall with the rhythm of life. No snores came from her father.

No. They're not sleeping. Her spine shivered with an icy touch, causing her body to crumble under its weight, leaving her gasping for breath. Her stomach churned, a wave of nausea rising with each sway of her body. She squeezed her eyes shut, summoning darkness to shield her like a protective cloak from the truth she couldn't bear to witness.

"Please wake up, please wake up."

Breaking the silence, the roots of the trees pulsated and groaned as they crept over the jagged stones. Clara's nostrils were filled with the pungent scent of soil as the writhing tentacles slithered out from the rocks, leaving behind a trail of crumbled debris and porous bark.

"Clara, sweety, where are you? Help us." The voices of her parents drifted through the shadows of the trees, their presence felt but unseen. Nearby, their physical bodies remained still, blending into the darkness as they rested by the crackling fire.

"They're not here. They're not real." Clara's fingers clung desperately to her knees as she willed herself to awaken from the depths of her subconscious, urging her mind to break free from the chains of sleep.

The roots twisted and writhed, their gnarled fingers stretching hungrily toward the anguished cries near the campfire. "Clara!"

"They're not here. They're not real." Her ears popped as she slapped her palms over them.

Her parents' lifeless forms lay on the ground, their ankles entangled in the tentacles of fibrous roots. Their flesh was torn by the rough splinters that were pulling them down beneath the surface. Their arms sprang to life, their fingers transforming into sharp claws that scraped against the gritty soil. Clara's heart pounded in her chest as she witnessed her parents being dragged beneath the surface. Her mother's head slowly tilted to the side, revealing dark, empty eyes. Her father's mouth hung open, a black abyss swallowing all the light.

"Why won't you help us?" Accusations echoed through the air, the voice of her mother echoing, even though her lips remained still.

With a determined squeeze of her eyelids, she immersed herself in darkness, embracing the rhythmic motion of her rocking. Her head swayed in defiance, a gentle rebellion against the world around her. "I'm not here. It's not real."

The earth rumbled beneath, and Clara watched as a gaping chasm appeared, consuming her parents in an instant. A thick cloud of dust billowed into the air, gradually descending, and obscuring the scene. The overwhelming feeling of stillness followed. She clamped her hands over her ears, desperate to block out the overwhelming images that surrounded her.

Rocking gently, she curled into herself, finding a small measure of comfort in the protective embrace of her own body. She gnawed on her lip, coating her tongue with the metallic spice of blood. The roots expanded, wriggling, and probing the ground, their hunger driving them forward. The night skies were dimly lit, with dark clouds obscuring any remaining light. Her muscles ached, frozen in fear. She could taste the briny tang of her own perspiration. As she braced for the worst, the breeze whispered words of helplessness and despair in her ears.

"Clare Bear? Why did you leave me?" Lucy's soft voice rumbled with the distant thunder.

"I didn't leave you, Lucy. I can't find you." Blame consumed her mind, unleashing a torrent of tears.

"The trees are angry. I'm scared."

A flash of light momentarily brightened the land, revealing the slow approach of the tree roots. Screeching bats, whistling cicadas, and howling wolves intensified the pounding of Clara's heart.

Lucy stepped out from behind a tree. Her eyes, just like her mother's, were dark and intense. Her outstretched hand trembled as she longed for the comfort of her big sister's touch.

Clara remained motionless; her body frozen in place. She managed to loosen one of her arms, but the smoldering fire suddenly flickered back to life. The moment her hand came into contact with the scorching heat, she recoiled in pain, forced to retreat as her skin burned.

"I'm sorry, Lu-Lu. I'm sorry." Clara cradled her hand.

As Clara stepped forward, the darkness enveloped her, suffocating the light and developing into an impenetrable barrier, blocking her path to her sister. The burnt smell of leaves created thick and unbreathable air. The flames cast shadows on the trees, making the trunk appear to breathe. The towering tree sent roots around Lucy's neck. She clawed at the invaders as they tightened their hold like a boa constructor. The trunk of the tree cracked open, swallowing Clara's baby sister whole.

"Clare Bear!" In a haunting twist of fate, Lucy's anguished cries were abruptly hushed as the ancient tree swallowed her, its gnarled branches becoming her final sanctuary.

Clara's mouth opened wide, releasing a piercing shriek that echoed through the air. Her body jolted, breaking free from its frozen state. She rushed to the tree and clawed at the bark encapsulating her sister until her fingernails broke and her fingers bled. She felt tension in her ankles and had forgotten the roots. The pulsating heartbeat of the tentacles pressed against her skin and encircled her body. In surrender, she let her arms fall to her sides, her face tilting up to the verdant canopy of branches above. Like a gentle rain, tears cascaded over her cheeks, as if the very essence of her emotions was being released into the world.

"Lucy. I'm so sorry."

She felt the roots wrap around her, their grip tightening as they dragged her beneath the earth's surface.

* * *

"Clara." A phantom voice pulled Clara away from the darkness.

"Clara, wake up. It's just a dream."

Fingers tenderly combed through Clara's hair, releasing her from her mental prison. Her body convulsed as she frantically scanned the ground for the treacherous tree roots. The air was heavy with the lingering scent of burnt vegetation. She winced as a sharp pain shot through her hand, a vivid reminder of the burn she had endured. Gently, she held her injured hand against her chest, seeking comfort and protection. She took a deep breath, her eyes meeting Benji's with a sense of calm. He leaned in and hugged her closely and continued to run his fingers through her hair.

Clara's nightmares became more traumatizing as the anniversary of her family's death drew near. Benji had always been there for her. She sat up and looked about the room. The only light in the window came from the security lights illuminating the sidewalks. The only sound came from the hum of the air vents. She felt safer when Benji spent the night in her roommate's bed. Benji reached for a cup of water on her nightstand and offered it to her. After taking a sip, she handed it back. "Thanks, Benji."

"Do you want to talk about it?" Benji leaned over to set the cup down and patiently waited for Clara to answer.

"No. It's always the same." Clara raised her covers even though they could do nothing to warm the chill in her bones. "You don't have to spend the night, you know, if you don't want to."

"There's nowhere else I'd rather be."

Clara attempted a grin to Benji's soft smile. Her fingers slowly released their hold on the covers as she stretched out her legs, feeling the stiffness in her muscles. She settled back into her bed and flipped over her damp pillow.

Benji tucked the blankets around her before returning to the roommate's bed.

"Benji?" Clara's finger gently glided along the intricate seams of her bedcover.

"Yeah?" His hand froze in midair, hovering just inches away from the unfolded covers.

"Do you mind sleeping next to me?" She flushed with embarrassment when he didn't respond right away. "We could move the bed over," she offered.

"No. That's okay." He spun on his heels and made his way towards the adjacent bed.

Clara's face melted. She didn't want to make it weird, but she felt safer when he was close.

He took the pillow from the bed and joined Clara with a smile. "Move over."

She shifted to the side, a wave of relief washing over her. With a gentle gesture, she lifted the covers, inviting him to slide in. He wrapped his arms around her, and she snuggled into his chest and found peace.

* * *

Clara squinted as the sunbeams tickled her eyes. She stretched her arms out over her covers, knocking the extra pillow off the bed. The room looked empty, showing no evidence of any visitors. *Did Benji spend the night?*

A knock interrupted her confusion.

Wrapping herself in her fluffy robe, she hollered, "One moment!" She inspected herself in the desk mirror, tamed her wild hair with her fingers, and opened the door enough to see who was on the other side.

"Good morning." Benji's smile traveled from ear to ear while he presented a cup of fresh coffee and a paper sack.

Clara fully opened the door to allow Benji in.

"I grabbed us some breakfast. I expected you'd sleep in a bit."

Clara smiled and secured the door lock as Benji patiently waited for her to take the hot coffee cup. Her eyes softened as she inhaled the aroma of the bitter grounds. *Mental cleansing activated.* "Mmm. Thanks." She took a small sip to test the temperature. *Perfect.* She positioned her pillow against the wall on her bed and leaned against it.

Benji handed over a paper bag.

Clara peeked inside and saw a bagel with strawberry cream cheese. "Just one?"

"I ate mine in the cafeteria." Benji's lips thinned as he confessed. "I woke up kind of early and didn't want to wake you. You're so cute when you sleep." He swiveled a chair around and settled it at her bedside, winking. He lowered himself onto the chair, wrapping his arms around the backrest.

Clara's cheeks warmed, but she ignored the comment to focus on breakfast.

"Do you want to play dodgeball at one? A couple of the guys invited us to play at the rec center."

I doubt I was the one invited. "Nah. After class, I think I'll go to the library."

"Clara, you promised you wouldn't barricade yourself again. It only makes the nightmares worse." Benji leaned closer over the backrest.

"I can't help but think I overlooked something ... maybe a newspaper from another town. The printer doesn't work, so I've got to pull them up again." To be honest, Clara didn't want to bring articles into her dorm room. They should remain hidden in the depths of the library rather than exposed to the sunlight.

"Remember, your phone has a camera. If you change your mind, you know where to find me." Benji shuffled his foot on the floor and rubbed the back of his neck before taking a sip of his coffee. "Should I wait so we can walk to class together?" Benji stood up and replaced the chair at her desk.

"Sure, it won't take me long." Clara looked away from Benji as she collected her hygiene caddy and a fresh outfit for the communal bathroom.

CHAPTER 4

JENNA

Grinning from ear to ear, Jenna stretched out her arms resembling a superhero ready to conquer the world, taking in a deep breathy yawn. Her peaceful dreams were interrupted by a delightful aroma, a tantalizing blend of vanilla and cinnamon.

Daddy's making waffles! Pure joy spread across her face as she eagerly slipped on her soft, velvety slippers. Jenna shuffled into the kitchen, ready to satisfy her growling stomach. Sure enough, her father was finishing a fresh batch of homemade waffles, her favorite.

"Good morning, Daddy!" Jenna's eyes danced with delight as they trailed the steam rising like wisps of morning magic. She softly pushed his shoulder down so she could lean in and kiss his cheek.

"Good morning, Ju-Ju. Sleep well?" Her father placed an empty plate and a glass of orange juice in front of her while she rounded the table. While he might be strict, he was also quick to forgive and forget.

"The best!" She plopped herself into a seat. She clenched her teeth and forced a smile, determined to shield her father from the pain she felt. The ache in her back served as a constant reminder of the previous evening. "What's the special occasion?" Jenna surveyed the tempting sight before her: the golden waffles, glistening syrup, and the velvety butter slowly succumbing to its own warmth.

Her father filled his thermos with coffee and poured a small mug for Jenna. With a grin, he placed the final batch of gorgeous waffles on the table and gently squeezed her shoulder.

Her eyes narrowed suspiciously as she looked at him. She loved waffles. She loved his surprises, but they often came with bad news.

Is he prepping for a lecture about last night? The lectures, while bearable, were overshadowed by the impending dread of the announcements regarding their relocation. *I told him I'm done playing musical chairs across the states. I'm staying.*

"I'm working late today. The garden shed didn't meet Ms. Cassidy's approval. One of those home renovation shows changed her mind. She's paying extra for the modifications. Do you want to meet for a late dinner?"

"Sounds great! I want steak." Jenna fluffed out her bottom lip. "Please," she added.

"Steak it is," he agreed. "I'll stop at the butcher's on the way home."

She didn't need to be dramatic, but she enjoyed his affectionate smirk when she did. She was Daddy's little girl after all.

"We will discuss our next location at that time."

She slid her plate of waffles away in a silent protest. As the dish glided across the table, it lost its balance, crashing onto the floor and scattering porcelain fragments in every direction. Despite the unintended consequence, she chose to embrace her dramatic nature. "I'm not going anywhere. I have classes and friends."

"Like the friend last night." Her father's phone rang with a classic melody. He answered, unfazed by her words or actions. "Hello.... Yes, this is Nicholas Dean.... No, don't touch a thing. I'm on my way."

Jenna's lips touched the rim of her coffee cup, the warm liquid awakening her senses. Her eyes lifted, and a wave of defiance washed over her. He was accustomed to always getting what he wanted, but now she needed to assert herself and stand her ground.

"We will discuss this later."

"There is nothing to discuss. I'm not leaving."

After storing a waffle in his mouth and grabbing his coffee tumbler, her father gathered some loose tools on the counter and headed for the door. He mumbled something through the waffle and departed, letting the door close behind him without waiting for her response.

"See ya, Dad." Her lips curled back, revealing sharp teeth as she glared at the closed door. Her throat tightened, aching to release a shrilling scream, but she clenched her teeth, suppressing the urge, mindful of the new parents living just above their apartment.

Last night's events weighed heavily on her, a reminder of her previous mistakes. She took a quick look at the small, sensitive scratch beneath her arm. Every time a bad seed came her way, her dad packed them up and whisked them off to another state. His actions spoke volumes of his affection for her, but she had grown weary of his manipulative tactics. During her college years, she craved a taste of normalcy.

Jenna's father rarely said, "I love you," but he expressed his love in other ways. She loved the moments they spent working on projects together or the thoughtful things he would do for her, such as preparing her favorite breakfast. His intellectual efforts bridged the gap between actions and emotions, communicating his heart. She imagined emotions became challenging after her mother passed away. He never mentioned her and forbade Jenna to bring it up.

After serving herself a large waffle, Jenna slathered on the butter and savored her morning treat. The aroma of the magnificent breakfast filled the air. She refused to let her delusional father spoil the moment. It was still her favorite.

The scattered splashes of waffle batter strewn across the floor made her yearn for a furry companion to help clean up the chaos. Before class, she would need to clean it up. Precalculus didn't begin until 9:00 a.m., allowing her to take her time.

Jenna put her empty plate and cups in the sink and noticed a sack lunch resting on the counter. *He packed me lunch, too?* She opened the bag to check the contents and saw another favorite ... a peanut butter and banana sandwich. *My favorite breakfast, my favorite lunch, and my favorite dinner? Just because he was anxious last night doesn't mean he can be irrational today.*

It was a short walk to campus. Jenna's father had moved them closer to the university, so she wouldn't spend money on housing and transportation. She was accustomed to moving, having done so her entire life after losing her mother. Memories flashed of long, dark hair tickling her nose as the scent of green apple blanketed her with a kiss good night. It was hard to tell memory versus dream. Either way, she cherished the connection.

Jenna suspected her father couldn't sit still after losing her mother. He would pick up jobs in different states and move them faster than she could meet a friend. Temporary friend-making was difficult, but she adapted. They never stayed in one area for very long, and thus most of her schooling was online.

After graduation, Jenna told her father she was moving to Penn State for a normal college life. She refused his online degree demands. At eighteen, she could make her own choices. Later that day, he announced they were moving to Pennsylvania. She was so excited she nearly knocked him over when she jumped on him for a hug.

He wants to move? I'm two months into a four-year program. Not happening.

Java Junction was at the center of campus. She squinted her eyes to see who was working the counter. *Oh great. Karen.* The disappointment curdled her expression like sour milk. A twinge of anger tightened her chest. *No free coffee today.* Many of her coworkers were pleasant to work with, but Karen was a disgruntled militant.

"Good morning, Karen!" *You authoritative twit. What Sour Patch Kid did you suck on today?* "One venti black americano." Jenna leaned in with her phoniest smile.

"That's one *large* americano. Four dollars and sixty-five cents."

She's so rancid. "Just put it on my tab." Jenna waved a dismissive hand in the air.

"You have no tab. Four sixty-five."

Not a single smile. Can she take a joke?

"Oh, Karen. Lighten up, will you? Life is too short to be so glum." *You know your face may stay that way.*

Karen straightened her shoulders and flatly stated, "Four sixty-five." She held out her hand for payment while drumming the other on the counter.

Jenna pulled out a five-dollar bill from her pocket and handed it to Karen. "Keep the change." *You filthy animal.*

Smiling at her passive-aggressive quips, Jenna collected her coffee and begrudgingly continued her trek to class. A couple of playful squirrels dashed across her path and into a neighboring tree, causing her to stop abruptly. As she walked away, Jenna chuckled at the energized comradery. She soon spotted Kyle walking in the opposite direction.

"Hey, Kyle." She waved a friendly salute.

"Good morning, Jenna. Did you sleep well? You were a bit wobbly last night." Kyle snickered.

"Like a baby," Jenna retorted. "Hey, did you invite Josh Parker last night?"

"No. I don't think any of us really talk to the weirdo. He may have overheard us yesterday."

Jenna remembered his proximity and nodded to Kyle.

"How was window-shooting?" Jenna nudged Kyle's shoulder as she instigated the gossip.

"Turns out the kid lied," Kyle said.

"Are you serious?"

"Yeah, Mark's brother had a BB gun. He tried to pass it off as a real gun, but he's an idiot. He still shot out some windows. The rest of us just threw rocks until the farmer released the hounds. Then we turned tail and ran." Kyle waved his arms, acting out his tale. "You comin' tonight?"

Jenna contemplated for a moment. "Nah, not tonight. I've got a couple of classes and then dinner with my dad."

"Sounds boring. See ya tomorrow." Kyle turned and left.

Jenna continued her walk to her math class.

* * *

After class, Jenna headed to the library to check out a couple of books for her English research assignment. The library was relatively deserted, not unexpectantly since it was Friday. *Flirty Chick is working. Guess I'm swiping books today.*

The classical literature section was on the opposite side of the library. She knew exactly what she needed: a book on Greek mythology and *The Canterbury Tales*. Impressing her obstinate professor was now a priority. *Although I'm a first-year student, I'm an exceptional first-year student.* Even Professor Campbell would be impressed by her research and analysis skills.

Her finger dipped between each spine of the books, allowing her to scan each title. Chaucer was easy to find. She proceeded to the section on Greek and Roman mythology. *So many.* Jenna's hungry stomach beckoned for the sandwich, so she arbitrarily selected two titles. She put the three books in her bag. After throwing her satchel strap over her shoulder, she went outdoors in search of a pleasant place to eat her sandwich.

CLARA

The strobes from the microfiche generated blind spots in Clara's vision. She rubbed her eyes, then attempted to refocus on the articles. After spending two hours in the library's basement, she had learned nothing new. *Maybe Benji's right.* It had been nearly fifteen years, and she had yet to make any progress. *If the police can't figure it out, what makes me think I can?*

Remembering Benji's advice, she took out her phone and paused her thumb over the camera button. *There's no way I'm putting these images on my phone. Physical cues can intensify mental reminders.* She shook her head and put her phone down.

Feeling defeated, Clara shut off the machine, gathered her belongings, and trekked upstairs to the front desk. Susan was staffing the circulation desk, chatting with a few college boys while inappropriately leaning over the counter. They didn't appear to be having intellectual dialogue.

"Susan, can I get this week's schedule?" No response. "Please?"

"Excuse me." Clara's voice rose in volume for a moment before quickly quieting down. She glanced around, searching for any signs of offense, particularly the head librarian. "The schedule?" With a tight grip on her book bag, she rolled her eyes in frustration. Regrettably, this situation was all too familiar. She didn't know why today should be any different. Abandoning communications, Clara opened the swinging gate and located the printed schedule.

Four days? Susan's voice echoed in her head, urging her to work because she'd received an invitation to some big sorority event. Clara's eyes rolled again as she captured a quick snapshot before exiting the building.

The sun's harsh rays bore down on her, urging her to seek shelter. Despite the temptation, she resisted and raised her hand to shield herself against the sun. The vibrant green lawn seemed alive with the joyful sounds of students engaged in a spirited game of flag football. Her pale skin uncomfortably soaked up the sun. She scanned the area, searching for a tree with cool, inviting shade. Her mouth watered at the thought of enjoying a snack before her next class.

Off to the right, a tree provided a comfortable area thanks to its slanting trunk. Trees were an uncomfortable and disturbing place for her to relax due to her nightmares, but she had eventually come to use them as a form of therapy. *No one ought to be scared of trees.* At least this tree didn't have exposed roots.

Clara plopped her bag down, leaned against the tree, and rummaged in her pack for a snack. A bird landed next to her on a low-hanging limb. She gently smiled at her companion until it left a warm, white parting gift. She shifted away from the gift with a wrinkled expression. A loud crackling sound announced the discovery of her granola bar. Her face scrunched with disappointment at her flat, malformed food.

"Would you like the other half of my sandwich?" announced a voice from around the tree.

Clara straightened her neck to find the source.

"It's peanut butter and banana. It may sound weird, but it's the best sandwich on the planet."

On the other side of the same tree, a young lady whose long

wavy brown hair rippled in the breeze sat at a picnic table and held up half of a sandwich.

Clara dropped the tasteless treat into her bag and slung the pack over her shoulder. As she stood up, a sharp pain shot through her palm. She winced and examined her hand, spotting a tiny splinter embedded in her skin. With careful precision, she removed the splinter, wincing again as she felt a sting and saw a drop of blood emerge. She instinctively brought her finger to her mouth and tasted the metallic acidity. The girl welcomed her with a bright grin and motioned for her to take a seat anywhere with a dramatic sweep of her arm.

"Hi, I'm Jenna." The girl held out her hand as she partially rose from her bench.

Clara removed her finger from her mouth and presented her other hand to meet Jenna's. "It's nice to meet you. I'm Clara. You work at Java, don't you?"

"I do, 'Just Clara,'" the girl said with a wink.

Clara recognized the comment from yesterday and smiled.

Jenna placed her extra half sandwich on a folded napkin and slid it over to Clara.

"I haven't had a peanut butter and banana sandwich since I was a little girl. I used to love these things." Clara dropped her book bag on the grass next to her as she settled on the picnic bench and picked up the sandwich. One bite transported her back to when her family visited West Branch Beach. Her mother packed peanut butter and banana sandwiches for lunch. They called them PB&B sandwiches. The man-made lake was ideal for swimming and building sandcastles on its sandy shores. Lucy and Clara giggled as they splashed water back at their father when he chased them around the lake. After working up an appetite, they'd break to eat their favorite lunch.

"Are you okay?" The girl's voice interrupted her reminiscing.

Clara briefly blinked and finished swallowing her first bite before returning to reality. "What?"

"Looked like you were miles away. Did you have a good trip?" Jenna grinned.

"Oh, just remembering something." Clara shifted in her seat and looked at the sandwich before taking another bite. "What do you study here?"

Jenna placed a bag of chips between them. "Criminology. You?"

Clara involuntarily flinched as Jenna mentioned criminology, then quickly composed herself. "Literature."

A group of students started a game of frisbee on the lawn. Sometimes Clara wished she had the courage to join them. Her aim was precise when it came to stationary objects, but she lacked experience when it came to hitting moving targets. She imagined everyone wanting her on their team for her phenomenal gaming skills. All fantasy, of course. She had no gaming skills.

"Something wrong with criminal investigations?"

"No, nothing's wrong. I'm sorry. I didn't mean ... It just gives me the heebie-jeebies."

"Why?"

"Oh, it's not really a lunch conversation."

"Great, I'm not really having lunch. Go on." Jenna's curiosity drew her closer as she grabbed a chip and leaned closer.

Jeez, she's persistent. "Oh, okay." Clara moved her napkin from side to side and glanced over to the frisbee game. Reliving the emotions that came with telling her story was painful. When others discovered her history, they either treated her like an injured puppy or avoided her completely. *Just rip the bandage off,* Dad would say. "Well, my parents were killed fifteen years ago, and my little sister disappeared. I'm trying to figure out what happened." Clara bit her trembling lip as she awaited Jenna's response.

"A real-life unsolved mystery?" Jenna shifted with a grin spread across her face, as if she had just scratched a winning lottery ticket.

Clara shuffled uncomfortably. This was normally when people found a reason to leave or say they were sorry, like they had something to do with it.

"I want to hear the entire story," Jenna said, glancing at her watch, "but I've got class in a few minutes. Let's meet tomorrow at one." She jabbed the picnic table with her finger. "I'm great at researching historical stuff and solving puzzles." Jenna collected her things and stuffed them in her messenger bag.

"I don't know." Clara struggled with the social interaction and was at a loss for words as Jenna stood to leave and donned her crimson jacket. Clara chewed the inside of her cheek.

"It was great to meet you, Just Clara." Jenna didn't give Clara a chance to retract her self-invitation. "I'll see you tomorrow at one. Bye!" She waved good-bye over her shoulder as she left the open courtyard. Her red-hooded jacket billowed behind, as if she were late for Grandmother's house.

"What just happened?" Clara's lips moved silently as she expressed her thoughts, confusion etched across her face. *Have I just made a new friend? Is she genuinely interested in helping?*

Clara's thoughts were uncertain and indecisive. As she

lowered herself onto the bench, she suddenly noticed that she had been on her feet. The frisbee players cheered and high-fived each other. *I guess I'm meeting with her tomorrow.*

CHAPTER 5

JENNA

"Hey, Dad? You home?" Jenna entered her apartment and locked the door. Since her father's truck was parked outside, he was probably in his work studio.

"In the back," the deep voice replied from down the hall.

"Whatcha doin'? I thought you'd be home late." Jenna dropped her school bag on the couch as she jumped to smack the low ceiling entrance outlining the hallway.

"Working on a new garden box for Ms. Cassidy. How was school?" Jenna's father lowered his focus level with the plank he was measuring. His shop was scattered with projects in various stages of completion. The room smelled of sawdust, fresh paint, and sealant.

"Same old school." Jenna took a calming breath and asked the important question. "Are we staying?"

He briefly looked up, then returned to his work. "For the moment. But when I say it's time, we go."

Jenna's smile reached across her face as she ran over to hug her father and kiss him on the cheek. She then plopped on a spinning work stool and spun in circles. "I met a new friend today."

"Oh?" Midcalculation, her father arched his brow with a hint of suspicion. "Friend or *friend*?"

Typical parental intrusion. Her father, the great Nicholas Dean, was king of fifty questions. Most of the time, she didn't mind. She stopped spinning and smiled. "What would you say if it was *friend*?"

"I would say, are they brave enough to meet your father?"

Why do I try his patience, especially after last night? But Jenna knew why. She enjoyed the attention.

Her father's sturdy form stood and let go of the measuring tape. The tape retracted into its case with a sharp snap. He dropped the casing and shook his hand in pain, hissing through his teeth.

"Are you okay, Daddy?" Jenna popped off her stool to inspect his injured hand. Her fingers traced the outlines of a red mark, like a psychic palm reading.

Jenna found herself intrigued by her father's sudden change in behavior. His face was overtaken by a distant gaze, as though reliving a powerful moment. Worried that she had pushed him too far, her heart raced. In truth, she wasn't brave enough to bring someone home to meet her father. No one was good enough, and he trusted no one. Plus, he emitted a fragrance that screamed, "Stay away from my daughter!" A regular dating repellant. Her thoughts drifted back to the eighth-grade Sadie Hawkins dance.

Her father had volunteered to chaperone, as he usually did, and stood as a sentry protecting the queen. He stood with his arms crossed and eyed every breathing creature that attempted to have a conversation with her, including the stray dog that greeted her in the parking lot.

One brave soul stepped forward, offering his hand, silently asking for a dance. Aiden Barnes avoided making eye contact as he approached her intimidating father. She smiled warmly and took the boy's small hand. Being primarily educated online, she eagerly embraced the chance to mingle and have a good time with the other kids on the dance floor.

Her smile matched the swing of her dress as she twirled around the dance floor. She was thoroughly enjoying herself until she caught sight of her dance partner's ashen face, staring attentively over her shoulder. She followed Aiden's line of sight to her father, who sent her a forced grin before concentrating his attention on the boy. *Awkward.* Her dad's lack of people skills was evident.

Aiden appeared to agree and said he was tired of dancing. He abandoned her midsong, in the middle of the dance floor. Standing alone, Jenna could feel the weight of countless eyes. Her chest tightened and a flood of tears threatened to unleash.

Stumbling from the dance floor, she tried to hide her frailty from her new classmates. Aiden appeared among a group of boys across the way, their faces twisting into sinister smiles as they shared meaningful looks. Listening, she caught wind of their conversation about a challenge. A lump formed in her throat, as if it were ready to escape. With a fierce grip, she clung to her trembling frame, her heart propelling her towards her father, determined to conceal the tears that threatened to spill from her eyes.

"What's wrong, Ju-Ju?"

She couldn't bring herself to look directly at him, instead keeping her head down and staying close to his side. "I thought we were having fun, but they're laughing at me." Tears burst through like Old Faithful when she eyed the boys still smiling and pointing and poking fun at Aiden. Overwhelmed with emotion, she instinctively covered her face and cowered in the bathroom. The reflection in the mirror appeared blurred and indiscernible. She felt a sensation in her throat, as if a mountain lion were clawing its way out. She wanted to leave.

She emerged from the bathroom, her cheeks glistening with the remnants of her tears, a cold paper towel pressed gently against her skin. She felt the tickle of a runny nose and instinctively wiped it against her arm. She looked around for her dad, but he was nowhere in sight. *Of course, now he decides to leave.* No trace of the snickering boys, either.

Where are they? Most likely ruining someone else's hopes and dreams.

A strong hand took hold of her arm and pulled her back. She tried to pull away until she realized it was her father. He pulled her out of the building and lead her straight to their truck. She thought she was in trouble, but it was the only time his abruptness was welcomed.

***

The strike of a hammer jolted Jenna out of her trance. "No worries, Dad." The memories faded as her new story surfaced. She returned to her stool, spinning casually from side to side as she talked. "I met a girl outside the library. She was upset about something and looked at her granola bar like it called her a foul name."

"Like ... chicken?" He chuckled to himself.

"Ha-ha, Dad. Cool it with the dad jokes." She hid her grin to keep from encouraging him.

Relaxed, her father started remeasuring the boards, then sanded down the edges.

"Anyway ... I offered her half of my sandwich, and she told me an amazing story about her murdered family. She's going to tell me more details tomorrow. A real-life unsolved homicide. Isn't that fascinating?"

"Jenna, you know I have little interest in such things." His smile withered with the discarded grains of dust. "The past is painful. Rest in peace." The last words sounded monotonous and rehearsed as he crossed his fingers in front of his chest. Whenever he spoke about her mother, he would make that gesture, despite not being religious. Her father couldn't tolerate discussions of death or murder and often said those exact words to change the subject.

"I know, but I find it riveting." Jenna bit her lip, gauging her father's reactions. He continued his work, marking locations for nails and hinges, unfazed. She understood his hesitation in discussions of the past. Talking about it made him angry. Her mother's death and his past life were such painful topics that they inflicted permanent wounds. She hoped one day he would share.

"Is this a school project?" her father murmured through a chewed pencil.

Jenna relaxed and twirled in the stool until she felt a little unbalanced. "No. Not currently, but I know Professor Wolverton will require us to investigate an unsolved for midterm. I'll be getting a head start. Her family was killed, but the police never caught the guy. Her name's Clara something. Investigating should be a fun break from mundane schoolwork." As she sat beneath the whirring ceiling fan, a small dust ball descended onto her delicate hand. Without hesitation, she gently blew it away.

Her father positioned two boards together, eyed Jenna, and motioned with his head.

Recognizing the summons, Jenna jumped down from the stool and held the boards in place while he lined up the nail with his markings and struck the nail down with a single swing of the hammer.

No matter how many times he did that, Jenna was impressed. Construction work gave her father well-defined muscles that pulsed and glistened when he worked up a sweat.

She crafted a convincing puppy dog expression and peeked over the boards. "It'll help me improve my research techniques so I can write more effectively. Please, Daddy."

"No more late nights and your grades will not suffer. Understood?" Her father put his pencil behind his ear and held out his hand to settle the deal.

"Yes, sir." Jenna saluted and shook his hand.

He gave her a half smile and returned to his work. He was skilled at intruding and inserting himself in Jenna's social life. If he didn't approve of someone, he set earlier curfews and implemented ridiculous rules. She remembered packing up and moving states after the incident with the eighth-grade boy. He'd gotten more patient as she grew but was still protective.

Jenna believed her father feared losing her, especially after her mother's death. As a result, she tried to empathize with his protective behavior.

"I'll be done in twenty minutes and then I'm putting steaks on the grill. Go ahead and chop the salad." Her father assembled the wooden slats on the floor and positioned long beams to serve as legs for the raised garden box.

"Sure thing."

Jenna found it unusual but was grateful that her dad didn't mention anything about last night. *Guess he feels I've suffered enough. I didn't like being stalked and pawed at while I was out of sorts.* Jenna turned the television on in the living room while chopping ingredients in the kitchen. Her favorite comedy show had her laughing in tears as she prepared dinner.

CLARA

"How was dodgeball?" Clara set her tray across from Benji, who was occupying their usual table in the back corner of the café. She scanned the room, filled with noisy students that echoed across the enclosed space. The thick noise made her feel invisible and forgotten, yet also the center of unwanted attention.

"Oh, you should've seen it!" Benji's hand slapped the table as he told her a spectacular tale. "Don't eat the fruit salad, by the way. Bluh." Benji pointed to her dessert and stuck his tongue out. "Someone used salt instead of sugar. Yuck!" His body shuddered as his face crumpled like he bit into a lemon. "Instead of getting a scrumptious dessert, you get the Sahara Desert!"

"Thanks for the warning." The remaining items on her tray

suddenly didn't seem so appetizing, so she pushed the tray aside and grabbed her soda bottle. "So, what happened?"

"Yeah, right. Peter showed up with a girl he had a crush on. Kyle decided it would be amusing to divide them into different teams for a little friendly rivalry. He completely misjudged Pete's competitive nature. His team trailed by four points near the end. The ball went airborne. He caught it, getting Doug out, and immediately launched it at the girl. Ooh, it smacked her right in the face and broke her glasses on impact!" Benji threw his head back, laughing as tears developed.

Clara's brows peaked. "Is she all right?"

"Oh yeah, she's fine. But Pete's future with the girl is as shattered as her opticals!" Benji brushed away a tear as he tried to breathe away his giggles. "It was great!"

He paused to take a deep breath and sip his soda. "So, how was your day?"

"Not nearly as exciting, but I did meet a new friend ... maybe." Clara traced the edge of her soda bottle with her finger, waiting for his reaction.

Benji straightened his back, leaned in, and folded his hands on the table. "Really? Where? How? Details!" His interest was not surprising. Clara often stood on the sidelines, observing the crowd rather than diving into conversations and forging new friendships.

"At the library. Or rather outside the library. She shared her lunch with me. She's one of the baristas at Java Junction ... Jenna."

"I don't remember the name ... wait." Benji appeared puzzled as he attempted to recall where he recognized her from. "Is she the one that reads all those ridiculous names? With the vulgar humor?"

"That's her." Clara remembered a few of those names and

squirmed in her seat.

"Interesting." Benji sat back and put his fist up to his mouth in thought. "What did you talk about?" His face contorted with confusion.

His skepticism radiated like a beacon. Understandable. *What could a lively, flirtatious woman have in common with a timid, anxious girl?*

"Oh, mostly what we were studying. She's a criminal justice major. After I told her about my background, she seemed really interested and began asking me questions. We're meeting again tomorrow at one." Clara bit the inside of her cheek and pinched her thumb.

Benji paused a moment before responding. "Let me know how it goes."

"I was hoping you would come. It feels ... I feel ... I don't know. Will you come with me? Please?" Clara bit more firmly. Her tongue tingled with the taste of blood.

"Of course."

Clara exhaled in relief, freeing her poor tormented cheek.

"I'll let my dad know I'll be a little late. I was supposed to help him with lawn care tomorrow. So, you're doing me a favor!" Benji smirked.

"Thanks." Knowing her best friend would be with her, she relaxed.

CHAPTER 6

CLARA

Clara bit her lower lip as she checked the time on her watch. One sixteen. *Maybe this was a mistake. Maybe I misunderstood. Perhaps she got spooked.* Negative thoughts stacked up like a rickety house of sugar packets. Her nerves were jangled by nervousness and uncertainty. She rubbed her hands together, though she was not cold. The prospect of a new friend was exciting yet troubling—like a Popsicle. *Refreshing, but melts away.*

A dragonfly settled on a bolt that secured the wooden planks for the picnic table. *At least someone came to see me,* she thought as she watched her new winged friend take flight.

"Maybe she just got caught up with school stuff," Benji

offered from across the table.

Gray shadows outlined huge, billowing white clouds in the distance. The sun's rays grew stronger, brighter, and hotter. The air felt damp on Clara's skin and smelled of a fresh, earthy musk. The clouds mimicked the turmoil brewing inside. She lifted her chin, wishing for the rain to fall and hide the signs of her imminent tears.

Clara watched the clouds smother the sun, then a trail of ants crawling along the edge of the table caught her atttention. They are born with friends, adventure, and purpose.

"Sorry I'm late." Jenna smiled as she plopped her bag on the bench, sat next to Clara, and darted her eyes from Clara to Benji. "What did I miss?"

Clara shifted to the side to provide more space for Jenna and accidentally bumped her knee against the table leg. As a single tear trickled down her cheek, she swiftly brushed it away before the onlookers could catch a glimpse. She rubbed the pain away and felt her heartbeat against her chest, excited that Jenna showed up.

"You missed being on time," Benji said under his breath.

With a sharp look, Clara kicked him and then turned to Jenna.

"Ow!" Benji puffed out his lips as he rubbed the pain off his shin.

Jenna examined Benji for a moment. "Oh! I remember you. The gawking elevator boy!"

"What?" Clara asked.

"I wasn't gawking." His voice was low, stern, and crisp. "I thought I recognized you."

Jenna grunted and waved her hand dismissively.

Clara glanced between them, interrupting the awkward encounter. "Okay ... Jenna, Benji ... Benji, Jenna. I see you've sort of met."

"Oh yes, we enjoyed each other's company in a quaint little elevator ride," Jenna remarked cynically. "Anyway." Jenna rolled her eyes and faced Clara. "Let's hear all about your fascinating past." Jenna's lips stretched from ear to ear as she waited to get to the rest of the story.

Fascinating?

"Clara's been through a lot. She doesn't need someone playing it down like a crime show!" Benji fists hit the top of the table hard, shaking the attached benches.

The poor ants halted for a moment, then picked up their pace to retreat and scatter.

"It's fine, Benji." Clara placed a calm hand over his tight fist and silently pleaded with him to calm down.

"Take no offense. I've been captivated by unsolved crimes for as long as I can remember. I've never known anyone with a true story of their own. It's fascinating, intriguing, and worth solving. I mean no offense. Start at the beginning."

"Well, um." Jenna's energetic, carefree, and outspoken attitude was a personality trait Clara tended to avoid. Her teeth sank into her cheek, a small wince escaping her lips. Her hands clenched tightly in her lap, fingers intertwining as she struggled to find the right words.

"My family spent a weekend camping in Nelson Ledges State Park when I was six. It's close to Cleveland, Ohio."

"When was this?" Jenna shimmied in her seat and crossed her ankles underneath her.

"Labor Day weekend, fifteen years ago. It was me, my three-year-old sister, Lucy, my mom, Mary, and my dad, Tom. It was the first time we ever went camping. We intended to stay from Saturday to Monday." Clara interlaced her fingers and picked at her thumbnail.

"When I woke up Sunday morning, I found my parents next to the campfire and my baby sister was gone." Clara examined her hands, remembering the sticky darkness staining her palms. The burn scars whispered their story, their faint presence a gentle reminder of the past. Even now the emptiness of her mother's eyes haunted her thoughts.

Two birds flew overhead communicating in high-pitched tunes. They ignored her pain as they danced through the air seeking shelter from the incoming storm clouds.

"What did the police do?" Jenna asked.

"Many suspects were identified, but none were charged. The media blamed a local serial killer of murdering couples, although he never targeted children. He stole rings, bracelets, and necklaces from crime scenes. Dad's watch and Mom's bracelet were gone. Not all items were taken, so authorities didn't suspect robbery. The police had nothing. They suggested Lucy may have wandered off in the middle of the night and died in the woods. I don't believe it. Why would she wander off without me or our parents? If she was scared, she would have woken me up. I still think she's alive somewhere."

Clara peered off into the distance, expecting Lucy to materialize from around the building. Instead, a whisper of wind twisted through the rooftops, creating a ghostly howl.

Jenna smirked and rubbed her arms. "Ooh, I've got chills. What do you think happened to her?"

Clara put her hand over Benji's curling fingers. "I truly have no idea. Nothing really makes sense. If Lucy had wandered off, she would have been discovered, alive or not. A whole search party saw no trace of my sister outside the camping area. I think maybe the guy stole Lucy and sold her. She was only three, so maybe he sold her to a black-market adoption agency."

Benji spoke up. "They didn't find the family's footprints outside the camping zone. No wandering prints to suggest Lily left on foot. But there were two sets of unidentified footprints around the bodies that headed out into the woods in two different directions. One set matched prints found at another Woodland crime scene. The second set suggested an accomplice that night."

"Woodland? Is that the serial killer? How many people did he kill?"

"The media called him the Woodland Phantom. I hate how the media glorifies the criminals and minimizes the victims. The police accused him of eight murders, aways in pairs. My parents were the last, although other murders have similarities."

Jenna bit her lower lip and lowered her voice. "How did he kill them?"

Clara increased the depth of her cheek bite and dug her fingernail into her thumb.

Benji gently intertwined his fingers with Clara's, his touch offering comfort and reassurance. As he spoke, his eyes met hers, conveying his words with delicate tendencies. "The Woodland Phantom killed with the knife found at the Wilsons' crime scene. It also matched the wounds on the other victims."

"Wait a minute." Jenna gripped the table and straightened her back. "The killer left the murder weapon? What kind of murderer leaves the murder weapon at the scene of the crime?

FOREVER FAMILY

That's Killer 101 stuff!" Jenna pushed herself away from the table, straightening her back and crossing her arms. "Even with the murder weapon and bodies, the authorities still couldn't identify him? That's not saying much for the local authorities."

"The police think the attacker was interrupted and dropped the knife before making an escape. Perhaps Lucy or another camper interrupted, but no witnesses ever came forward." Benji squeezed Clara's hand and rubbed her foot with his own.

"Investigations are three parts—body, weapon, conviction." Jenna glanced between Clara and Benji. "Why did he stop with your parents? Do you think they knew him?"

"No," Benji replied. "At least we don't know any of the other victims."

Jenna turned to Clara. "Did you see anything?"

Clare Bear, whispered the faint echoes of her past. "No. My sister and I were sleeping. I had no idea Lucy left the tent."

"What did you do when you woke up?" Jenna asked.

"I … uh … I woke up. Realizing my parents were … gone, I hid in my sleeping bag until I was found later that morning. I was too scared to look for Lucy." Each word felt like pouring acid onto festering wounds. "Because of the family event, extra rangers frequently patrolled the grounds."

Clara took a deep breath and briefly closed her eyes. "The first ranger on-scene radioed for backup. I was hiding under the blankets, but I heard him open the tent flap and walk away. While investigating the scene, a detective found me."

"How horrible." Jenna's posture softened. "Did you hear them say anything?"

"Probably, but I don't remember. I just remember them

talking about my parents like they didn't exist anymore. Discovering me left them all bewildered. One officer took me to the police station and asked me questions, but I couldn't answer. I lived with my uncle Jonathon until he passed, just before I started college." Clara lowered her head and picked away at a chipped fingernail.

The three students sat in silence, digesting the information. Thick clouds illuminated from unseen lightning in the distance, making the shadows darker and more menacing.

Clara felt Benji nudge his foot against hers. Her brows lifted as she projected her thoughts. *I'm fine*.

"So ... have the police turned up anything over the last ... what ... fifteen years?" Jenna said.

"Different theories were published in magazines and newspaper articles." Clara looked up at the library where time takes a leisurely pace, and the burdens of everyday life melt away. "But people lost interest as time made them forget. I wasn't old enough to understand, but when I got older, I began researching."

The kids frantically gathered their stuff in the courtyard as dark clouds loomed overhead and the wind gained speed.

Jenna stood up and confidently announced, "Okay, I will help. I think we can make this work. You need someone with new ideas and strategies."

Clara glanced at Benji and then back at Jenna. "I've researched all the known media outlets through microfiche and all the social media blogs. I don't know what else to do," Clara admitted.

"Well, I don't know what micro-fish are, but for starters ..." Jenna adjusted her position on the bench and leaned against the table. "You said there were no witnesses for the actual crime, indicating other witnesses for other things, right?"

"Yeah, someone thought they saw a man in a green truck that night in the park, and later a man with a little girl driving in a truck. Police investigated, but …" Clara shrugged, indicating that they came up empty-handed.

"Well, we can reinvestigate. Talk to the witnesses." Jenna's eyes darted between Clara and Benji.

"Wait, wait, wait." Benji held up his hand. "You want to track down long-forgotten witnesses and bring up fifteen-year-old memories? First, I don't think people want us bombarding them with questions after nearly fifteen years. They already provided statements. And second, what lingering memories remain may be distorted with years of media, assumptions, and personal conclusions, assuming they're still alive! I don't think it's a good idea. Police have witness statements on file."

"Oh, stop being a pessimistic pile of poo."

Clara stifled a chuckle.

"You never know. They may remember something that didn't seem relevant at the time. It could be fun!"

"Fun!" Benji slammed his hand on the table and stood awkwardly from the bench.

Clara reached across the table to settle Benji's tense fingers. She understood the frustration he had but wanted him to understand her desire to know what happened.

"No, I'm sorry. I don't like it. Clara loses herself every year trying to find answers." Benji's soft eyes found Clara's. "Leave the pain in the past."

Jenna stood to match Benji's height. "Pain festers without

truth."

Clara processed their words. Both appeared correct, but this was new. *Why not try a different method?* She tightened her hold on his fist and felt his fingers relax as he sat back down with an exasperated sigh.

"Are you two, a thing?" Jenna said.

Clara let go of Benji and slid back on the bench. "No. Just friends. We've been best friends for a long time. He just worries."

"I see." Jenna examined Benji and Clara, clearly not believing her words.

A ping from Benji's phone pulled his attention. "Oh crap. My dad's help didn't show. He needs my help."

"Will he still have work if it's raining?" Clara said, gesturing to the dark clouds.

"You know my dad." He leaned closer to whisper, "You okay?"

"Yeah. Go ahead."

Benji caressed Clara's shoulder, delivered a warning glare to Jenna, and secured his bookbag on his back. "You better head inside," he said over his shoulder. "It's about to pour." He set off running towards the parking lot.

"I think we should start with one of these witnesses," Jenna said. "What do you think?" She looked directly at Clara as she settled her messenger strap over her head.

"I agree. I've collected their names in my notes." Clara motioned to her bag.

"Great!" Jenna scooped her phone from her bag. "We should exchange cells."

Clara extracted her phone from her skirt pocket.

"That's *Clara Wilson*, right?"

"Yeah, and you are …?"

"Jenna Dean."

A raindrop fell on Clara's cheek, and she looked up to the darkened skies with her palms held high. More droplets fell and Jenna began to laugh. They ran to the library just as the rain poured in a violent stream.

CHAPTER 7

CLARA

Meeting in the library was preferrable to chasing papers around the lawn as the afternoon storm rolled in. With fewer students around on weekends, it was simple to find an available table. Clara eagerly watched Jenna review the contents of her witness list from the yellowed pages stacked in a manilla folder.

The mountain of investigative materials that Clara brought with her were comprised of photographs, drawings, articles, notes, and clippings from various publications. Elongated shadows danced across the table as the dim light struggled to illuminate the room. She leaned closer to the desk lamp and folded her damp hair behind her ear. Clara bit the inside of her cheek, expecting Jenna to pick up on something immediately.

FOREVER FAMILY

"Is this it? Just the three?" Jenna shuffled through the pages, reviewing what Clara had collected.

Clara slumped. "Only three credible, unfortunately." Her expression melted like grilled cheese. "I got those by chance. The police officer knew my father from the Historical Society. The police got a lot of phone tips, but most of them didn't lead to anything ... money mongrels. My uncle offered fifty thousand dollars. These are the only ones the police considered worth investigating."

"Well, it's a start." Jenna straightened the documents and looked at the leading page. "So, where'd your boyfriend go?"

"We're just friends." Clara hoped the dim light hid the warmth she felt on her cheeks. "He goes home most weekends to do laundry and work his dad's lawn-care business."

"He doesn't like me much."

"He's a bit protective, like a big brother." Clara lowered her eyes, hoping Jenna wouldn't ask any more questions about Benji. She struggled with her feelings for him, but friendship was his only interest.

"Let's review the witnesses, shall we?" Stretching her shoulders overhead, Jenna relaxed. She slowly turned the pages, scanning the witness information. "Ms. Della Martin of Triadelphia, West Virginia."

Clara raised her head. "Yes. She reported seeing a man and a little girl eating breakfast at a truck stop in Wheeling, West Virginia, early Sunday morning."

"Mr. Jeremiah Reynolds of Newton Falls, Ohio?" Jenna continued.

"He was a park employee that Saturday night and witnessed a man driving a green truck. He didn't see anyone else in the vehicle, though."

"Interesting ... and ..." Jenna flipped to the next page. "Ms. Helen McGavin of Warrendale, Pennsylvania?"

"She witnessed a man and little girl checking into a hotel near Pittsburgh."

"Who should we start with?"

Clara shrugged but responded, "Why don't we start with the guy who saw the truck in the park? He's the first to witness something that night."

"Sounds logical." Jenna pulled the document about the park employee.

"Mr. Reynolds. Age fifty-six. Lived in Newton Falls. Employed as groundskeeper. He was asleep in his truck. The sound of an engine woke him, and he witnessed a green work truck driving off the property." Clara pointed halfway down the page to indicate the printed information.

"Why was he sleeping in his car?"

Clara handed Jenna a pencil sketch of the truck with an emblem on the side, and Jenna tilted her head for a better view. The sketch was a bit smudged and transferred some of the residue on the previous page.

"He told police he wanted to be available while the park was full of campers, but the police found out he frequently slept in his truck." Clara lowered her voice to a whisper. "Trouble at home." Regaining her normal volume, she continued. "Anyway, he heard a noise and noticed a green pickup truck leaving the lot with only its floodlights lit. He thought a man was driving but didn't have a clear view. The only light was a flickering streetlamp near the entrance of the parking lot. He mentioned a yellow work emblem—like a caution sign—on the passenger panel, but he couldn't read the words."

"A green pickup truck with a yellow caution sign? That shouldn't be too hard to locate." Jenna picked up the drawing and rotated it, examining it from various perspectives. "It wasn't. It led the investigators to a man by the name of Jack Drewitt, a local fix-it man in the Warren-Ravena area, but he was in jail and never became a person of interest. Detectives never interrogate Drewitt about his truck. After a few years, they tried to find him, but he had moved without a forwarding address." Clara thought a moment and continued. "Because Reynolds mentioned a man with a solid alibi, the lead investigator looked into him as a potential suspect, but no arrests were made."

"Interesting. So, either someone who knew Drewitt took his truck while he was away, or Reynolds tried to throw the police off his trail and frame the local handyman. Sounds like we need to put Jack Drewitt on our potential witness list. Why was he in jail?" Jenna scribbled notes in a notebook she took out of her book bag.

"The report didn't say. Drewitt couldn't have played a direct role because the investigating officer had arrested Drewitt earlier that day."

"Have you ever talked to these people?"

Clara shook her head and pushed away from the table. "Oh no. Police advised me to stay away. They said it could hinder their investigation, but they weren't making progress."

Jenna's grin reached ear to ear. "Interfering is what I do best!"

The fresh perspective and infectious energy helped alleviate Clara's distress. She was cautious, although her eyes betrayed a spark of hope.

"So, how do we find Reynold's phone number? It's been fifteen years."

Jenna retrieved her phone and typed. It took her a few minutes before she peered over her screen, smirked, and glanced back down. "Eight Jeremiah or J. Reynoldses listed in Newton Falls. Five of those have death certificates before the crime, and two were born in the last fifty years, which leaves one person. The stars have aligned to help us out."

"That's assuming he's still in the Newton Falls area," Clara said with her voice so low she might have been whispering to herself.

"Ms. Pessimistic. Mr. Benjamin must be rubbing off on you. If it's not him, we can call the park and say we're doing a research project on the park's history and ask about previous caretakers." Jenna clicked something on her phone and selected the speaker.

Clara heard the ring tone on Jenna's phone. "What! Now?" Clara's teeth sank into her quivering lip as her fingers wrestled with each other. She looked around the library to see what other students were doing, feeling they would be caught. Talking on the phone was prohibited.

"No time like the present!" Jenna announced, clearly not caring what anyone thought.

"Hello?" answered a raspy, baritone male voice.

"Good evening! Am I speaking with Mr. Jeremiah Reynolds?" Jenna's chipper voice intensified Clara's restlessness.

"Yes. Speaking."

"The same Jeremiah Reynolds that previously worked at Nelson Ledges State Park?"

"Who is this?" Suspicion resonated.

Jenna nodded, confirming he was the right person, and she

was prepared for her role. "I'm sorry. My name is Linda Lewis, and I am researching a cold case. I would like to ask a few questions."

"That was a long time ago. I told the police everything I knew." The man coughed and hacked into the line.

Jenna held the phone away as he finished. "Oh, I know. The case was never solved, and I hope a fresh look may help the investigation and help bring closure to the surviving family. Please, sir."

Silence followed. Not even static hissed from the speaker. Clara leaned in to ensure that the line was still connected.

"I don't know. I guess, but I don't have time now. Some other time," Mr. Reynolds said.

"That would be great. I'll call tomorrow at two? I won't take much of your time."

"I guess." The drawn-out response was coated with reluctance.

"Fantastic! We'll talk tomorrow. Bye!" Jenna hung up before Reynolds changed his mind. "And that's how it's done." Jenna wiped her hands of fictious dirt.

Clara imagined Reynolds looking at his phone thinking, *What the hell just happened?*

"How do you know he'll answer?" Clara asked.

"I don't," Jenna said, "but now we know that's our guy. We can reverse-phone-lookup and get his address."

"You mean, go to his house?" Clara never dreamed of talking to these people, let alone visiting them in person.

"Only if he doesn't answer. How else would we get the information? He agreed to talk. Now we make sure he doesn't back out." Jenna jotted a few notes into her notebook.

Clara gave this some thought but decided to follow Jenna's direction. She had never met Jenna before, yet she gave her hope because of her unwavering confidence, powerful determination, and unstoppable persistence.

"Who's next?" Jenna fingered through the pages. "How about Hotel Lady?"

"Helen McGavin was working at a motel near Pittsburgh. She said a tall, broad man with a full brown beard paid cash at two in the morning, registering under the name of Daniel Beau Cooper. The police suspected the crime occurred between 11:00 p.m. and 1:00 a.m., and the motel is about two hours away, so it fit the timeline."

Jenna slammed the papers down. "Seriously? D. B. Cooper? Obviously a false name. What did she see?"

Clara realized she had been completely unaware. *Jenna must not miss much with those scrutinizing eyes. Did the police recognize the name?* "Well, McGavin went to her car to find change for the vending machine. She noticed the man picking up a sleeping young girl from the passenger side of a green truck that had a yellow triangle on the door."

"When did she call the cops?" Jenna asked.

"Not until next week when she saw the news reports."

Jenna typed into her cell phone. After making a few facial grimaces and more typing, she reported, "Well, I've got some good news and some bad news."

"Well?" Clara waited.

"The good news, Helen McGavin is a unique name in Pittsburgh, and I found an article that matches your description." Jenna thinned her lips.

FOREVER FAMILY

"The bad news?" Clara bit her lip.

"She's dead."

Clara winced as the bluntness struck her, a sharp impact that seemed to radiate through her chest like a blow from a wooden bat.

"Died five years ago. According to her obituary, she worked in the hotel business for fifty years, died at seventy-two years old. There could be another with the same name who worked in the hotel business, but I doubt it."

Clara's hope dwindled. Uncertainty clouded her mind as she bit her lip.

"Nevertheless …" Jenna looked at the wall as she collected her thoughts.

Clara perked up. First, nobody used that word anymore. Second, that word meant Jenna had pieced together useful information. *What good can come from a dead end?*

"Assuming she saw our suspect … *One*, your sister was still alive after the crime. *Two*, the murderer took her, and *three*, they headed east out of Cleveland. East is far smaller than west."

Clara couldn't tell if this constant optimism was inspiring, exhausting, or dangerous. Jenna brought new perspectives—finding the flower among the thorns.

"But we could call next of kin and see if Mama left behind any stories. Then again, we wouldn't be hearing it from the source, and the information could be tainted."

Clara liked hearing Jenna express her inner conflicts. She put Clara's internal struggles into words.

"That leaves us … Ms. West Virginia." Jenna shuffled the papers until she located the paper with the next witness.

"Martin," Clara offered. "Della Martin was a seventeen-year-old waitress at a truck stop near Wheeling, West Virginia. She saw a man and a little girl eating breakfast in the café Sunday morning. The man ordered a large breakfast, but the little girl hardly touched any of it. They left in a green truck. She notified the police that Tuesday."

"So, they headed south after they spent the night in Pennsylvania." Jenna tapped her phone a few times, deep in thought, then started her digital investigation.

Clara examined the pages as Jenna flipped through her phone, but she knew what was on every sheet. She absentmindedly traced the grains on the table while tapping her foot to a rapid rhythm in her head.

"Bingo! Della Martin now lives in Atlanta, Georgia. She's the only 'Della' with a past address listed in West Virginia."

She's good. I doubt she's using a simple search engine.

Jenna selected the phone number listed, set the speaker, and waited.

Clara's heart sped up as the phone rang again.

"Hello?" a little girl's high, squeaky voice answered.

"Hello, sweetheart! Is your mommy home?"

A muffled static and an unknown rustling screeched across the phone as a child yelled, "Mommy! Mommy!"

"What is it, Chloe?" said a woman's voice in the distance.

"Someone's on the phone!"

"Oh, Chloe. I told you not to answer Mommy's phone." Crackling and buzzing filled the air, preceding the sound of a woman's voice. "Hello?"

"Hello. What a sweet child you have. Am I speaking with Ms.

Della Martin?" Jenna was natural with people.

"Yes. Well, Della Davenport now. How may I help you?"

"My name is Linda Logan, and I am doing a follow-up story on the unsolved Wilson murders. We are trying modern investigative techniques to try to bring closure to the surviving family. Do you mind if I ask a few questions?"

There was silence on the phone. "Ms. Davenport?"

"I'm sorry. I don't think I would be of any help. I told the police everything I knew."

"Often time helps bring new perspectives. Do you mind?" Jenna insisted.

"What do you want to know?"

Jenna mouthed, *Yes*, then straightened her shoulders and neck in a more professional manner. "The report indicates that you were a waitress at a truck stop in Wheeling. What did you see that day?"

"Um, a man and a little girl ate lunch, and then they left."

Clara's eyebrows rose and her lips curled at a slight angle as she glanced at Jenna.

"You mean breakfast?" Jenna corrected.

"Oh yeah. It's been a while. Like I said, I don't think I'll be much help." The woman was talking fast and seemed eager to get off the phone. "Chloe, put the cat down."

"What did they eat?" Jenna continued.

"Breakfast."

"Do you remember *what* they ate?" Jenna said.

"No. Probably some eggs, bacon, pancakes … stuff like that." The woman's tone was elevated to a higher pitch.

This isn't going well.

"Do you remember what kind of vehicle they left in?"

"A blue truck, I think." Ms. Davenport's voice became distant when she sternly said, "Chloe, I said put the cat down."

Clara and Jenna mouthed, *Blue?* at each other.

"Did it have any markings on the side, like a work logo?" Jenna continued.

"Oh yeah, it did. You know what it looked like, don't you?"

"Are you asking me if I know what you saw?" Jenna reached up and twirled a strand of hair behind her ears.

"Look, I told you it was a long time ago. Just look at what I said back then."

The lamp's light flickered, casting a dim glow across the table. The girls shared a curious glance. *Are we even talking to the right person?*

Jenna's shoulders slumped and she sat back in her chair. "You didn't see anything, did you?"

Clara never considered the possibility that any of these witnesses might be lying. Why would someone intentionally mislead the police?

The woman sighed. "No. I saw the news and called the police. I was young. I needed the money. I never got anything, though. Look, I've got a family now and don't want to be involved."

"You already got yourself involved when you told the police a lie. Thank you for your time." Jenna hung up.

The phone lay on the table. The words that came out of it were shocking.

Jenna broke the silence. "Well ... now we know no one witnessed them heading south out of Pittsburgh."

"We don't know which way they headed out of Pittsburgh,"

Clara said.

Jenna jotted a few things in her notebook. She clenched her pen between her teeth, pausing briefly before scrawling a few more words onto the paper.

"Tomorrow, we talk to the old man. He may be able to help." Glancing at her phone, Jenna started to collect her things. "I've got to go. But tomorrow's a new day. We talk to the old man and discuss suspects. Oh yeah, and we've got to look up Jack Drewitt."

"Thank you, Jenna." Clara spoke softly.

"For what?"

"For being here. I know we may not be able to find out what happened to my sister, but it helps to work this out with someone who believes in it as much as I do." Clara's eyes drifted downward while Jenna smiled.

"We do this together. Me and you. Let's have lunch at twelve before we call the old man. Sound good?"

Clara smiled and nodded.

Jenna picked up her messenger bag and waved over her shoulder as she headed out the door.

CHAPTER 8

JENNA

Jenna latched the bolt to the door and heard the familiar pounding of the hammer in the back room.

"Jenna?" her father called out.

"Yeah?" She paused to listen.

"Come here." Deciphering his straightforward reactions was quite challenging. She couldn't think of anything she did to upset him ... recently. *I'm not late.* Jenna glanced at her watch to be sure.

After tossing her bag to the wall and having it crash into the shoe rack, Jenna went to the third bedroom that was converted into her dad's work studio. It had been three months since they moved in, but each residence had similarities: the distinct aroma of freshly cut wood and intoxicating hints of paint lingering in the air.

FOREVER FAMILY

Despite her father's efforts to maintain clean air by using an air purifier and placing additional filters around the vents, the pleasant and comforting aroma of home remained unchanged.

Due to her father's construction business, they typically occupied an apartment for six months before finding a new home. Throughout her studies, she hoped to make this place her permanent residence, at least for the next four years.

Jenna passed by a collection of wood projects in different stages of completion on her way to the back room. She carefully opened the door, taking precautions to avoid causing any harm to the items inside. Seeing she was clear to enter, she swung the door open and settled herself onto the work stool. It seemed that her father was in the process of constructing either a bookshelf or a display cabinet.

"Mrs. Cassidy?" Jenna guessed.

"It's Ms. Cassidy, and no. Her neighbor. She saw the garden box and wanted shelves for her plants. Hold the frame."

Jenna helped her father hold the shelf's structure as he took the pencil from his mouth and sketched his intended cuts. He slipped on safety goggles, then cut through the planks, creating circles for potted plants. Focused on his lastest work of art, his face was expressionless and his muscles taut. Jenna enjoyed watching her father work.

Particles of sawdust started to fill the air in a dense fog. The furniture, rugs, and air ducts in the room were all covered in plastic, and a vacuum helped to clean the air. The remaining dust settled on the workbench, some tools, stacked wood, and some unfinished projects.

"That should do it." Her father stepped back to appraise his work. "How was your day?" He stuck his pencil between his teeth and swiped away loose particles with the back of his pinky.

"Exhilarating! I met Clara and we located the original witnesses. One was dead, one lied, and one wouldn't talk. We're trying again tomorrow." Her words practically slurred together as she recalled the details. Her heartbeat accelerated to match her enthusiasm.

"Jenna?"

"Yeah, Dad?" Jenna dusted off the workbench and hopped up to sit so she could feel higher.

She watched him push the powdered wood around on the plastic floor covering with his foot, as if the sawdust were covering his words. "I, uh ..."

"Out with it, Dad!" *"Uh" is not in his vocabulary. Something's wrong.*

He took his pencil out of his mouth and placed it behind his ear.

"I have ... a date." He avoided eye contact. "Tonight."

Jenna stared at her father. *What?* "With who?" She crossed her arms over her chest. *Don't say it. Don't say it.*

"Ms. Cassidy."

Ugh. Not her.

"She asked me to dinner."

"That's great!" *This is awful!* "Where you going?" *Is she using you for free services? What's that conniving woman after?*

"The Chinese restaurant on Third."

"Splendid!" *Instead of joining me for a movie tonight, he's decided to hang out with that tramp. I can't believe he would choose her over me!*

"You're okay with this?"

"Absolutely!" *Not at all.* "I hope you guys have a great time!" *I hope she chokes on a crouton and dies.*

"Good."

Jenna jumped off the worktable and dusted off the sawdust from her backside. "Is that all? I've got homework." *I need to go scream before my head explodes.*

"Yes." He turned the shelving unit around and began placing support structures at the legs.

Jenna left, swinging the door shut a bit harder than she meant to, and headed straight for her room. Calmly, she closed her door and leaned her back against it. Her chest hurt from the betrayal pounding against her ribs. She didn't like to share her dad with anyone. She eyed her pillow, peacefully lying on her unmade bed, unfazed by the recent news. She stumped to her mattress and box spring and threw her face into the pillow. The drill from the studio masked her screams.

He never goes out. I should be happy. But he's supposed to be here … with me! Despite her best efforts, punching the pillow increased her anger. The treacherous grip of deception and pain ensnared her chest, as if an angler had cast a line, hooked her heart, and betrayed her trust. She pictured Ms. Cassidy and struck harder, but the cushion remained unharmed.

Jenna dug her hand into her pocket. With a flourish of elegance, she unveiled her blade, setting it free from its hidden confines. The light sparkled off the edge of her blade. Her attention shifted to her pillow just beyond the blade, and she plunged the blade in. Her breath escaped with a mix of satisfaction and excitement as she embraced the violent action. She imagined Ms.

Cassidy's expression as the blade plummeted deeper into her vulnerable flesh. She thrust the knife three more times and took a deep breath. As her breath left her body, her heartbeat slowed, and the piercing pain dulled. She smiled as she turned and fell into her pillow as white downy feathers fluttered around her face.

CLARA

Very few students occupied the café. Clara often found herself spending weekends at Benji's dad's place. However, this time, she was grateful for the opportunity to have a conversation with Jenna. Jenna's presence filled her with a sense of boundless possibilities. She selected a turkey panini, slid her student ID through the reader, and headed for her usual spot in the back corner of the café.

With her focus on the floor, she didn't notice the student eating at her usual table until she approached. She looked up at the student surprised and unsure what to do.

"Can I help you?" the student snapped. The girl's lip curled up as her nose wrinkled and her eyebrows pulled down. Her face looked like she had a coat hanger stuck in her mouth.

"Sorry, I just ... sorry." Clara gripped her tray tighter and backed away. She found an unoccupied table and set her book bag on the neighboring chair. She retrieved her earbuds and inserted them. Peaceful silence. Clara didn't actively detest music, but she preferred acoustic tranquillity. Plus, the earbuds and her opened laptop provided the perfect *Don't talk to me* display.

Raindrops trickled down the large wall windows. Even though it was no longer raining, dark clouds still hovered over campus.

A vibration in her pack pulsed and hummed as it jingled her

room key. *Where's that blasted thing?* Rummaging through school supplies, she located the source of the offending noise and looked at the caller ... Benji.

"Hello?" she whispered as she removed an earbud.

"Hey, Clara. How's it going, and why are you whispering?"

"I'm in the café."

"You don't have to whisper in the café."

Clara heard a faint chuckle on the phone. "I know." *It feels awkward to talk to someone that is not physically here. Everyone would stare.* Clara looked around at the other students.

"Did Jenna stay to talk?"

"Yeah, hey, let me call you back in about fifteen minutes. Okay?"

"Sounds good. I'll be here." He chuckled once more before ending the call.

After finishing eating half of her sandwich, Clara wrapped the other half in a napkin and prepared to return to her room. She slid her chair beneath the table and looked around to make sure she hadn't forgotten anything.

The café wasn't far from the dorms. Clara knocked on her door before she inserted her key and pushed the door open. Setting her bag under her desk, she sat down on her bed and called Benji.

"Hey, there."

Clara pictured Benji's Cheshire grin as he answered the phone.

"So, what's new?"

"Well, Jenna and I called the witnesses." Clara traced the pattern on her comforter.

"Really? I thought you were just researching."

"Calling *is* part of researching," she said, repeating Jenna's words.

Benji took a deep breath and exhaled. "Was it worth it?"

"Yes. The West Virginia witness lied to the police. She never saw anything. Only wanted reward money. Tomorrow we're talking to the man that worked at the park."

"Wow. Really? Do you want me to come back early … to help?"

Clara knew Benji worried about her, but he was helping his dad. He needn't worry. Jenna had things under control.

"No. Jenna knows what she's doing. It's kind of nice hanging out with another girl." Clara picked at the geometric patterns on her comforter, waiting for Benji's response. She had no idea why she felt guilty.

"Okay." His voice sounded weak and thready.

Clara felt her heart sink into her stomach. "Wanna meet at the café for dinner tomorrow?"

"Sure. See you then." His tone was hollow and disappointed.

Clara stared at the screen flashing the word *Disconnected*.

That's one way to put it.

CHAPTER 9

CLARA

Tingling goose bumps ornamented Clara's arms, jolting her from a deep sleep. Muffled noises permeated through the floorboards. She peeked over the safety of her covers as she caressed her fluffy brown teddy bear. The darkness surrounded her, with only a faint glow projecting from a circling globe, which shimmered and twinkled, mirroring the glow-in-the-dark stars scattered across the ceiling.

As she sat in her childhood room, she strained her ears to catch the faint whispers rising from beneath the floor. *Is that Mommy and Daddy?* Clara scanned her bed, searching for any sign of the source of the noise emanating from beneath the floorboards.

Clara slowly untucked the sheets and climbed out of bed, dragging her teddy bear with her. She looked over at her sister, fast asleep, and tiptoed down the hall. At six years old, she had discovered the loose floorboards that betrayed her presence with a creak. Approaching the stairs, she rested her weight against the top post of the banister, her ears attuned to the sounds below.

That's Mommy and Daddy, but they sound strange. Her mother's tone changed octaves at a rapid speed. Her father's tone was stern yet calm. *Why are they so mad?*

Clara grabbed the spindles of the banister and descended a few more stairs until she could see the light spilling from the kitchen. As the voices became clearer, each stair felt more treacherous and steeper. Even with the dishwasher rumbling, she could hear what her parents were saying.

"I'm not imagining things, Tom. I know what I saw." Exasperation intensified her words.

"Calm yourself, Mary. Maybe—"

"Stop telling me to calm down. We need to call the police!"

The wooden spindles prevented Clara from going any farther, but that didn't stop her from pushing her ear between them despite the coldness.

"I don't think the police are necessary. He's harmless."

"Harmless?" her mom shouted. "He was staring at me through our bedroom window … while I was dressing! Stalker is one step from intruder and twice removed from attacker! I don't trust him near our family. This isn't his first offense. I knew he was a strange kid even when we were in school."

"I'll call him tomorrow. No need to involve the police. He's a single dad, struggling to raise his little boy. He's lonely and probably not thinking straight."

Her mom closed her eyes and took deep breaths … deep breath in, slow breath out. "Fine. Talk to him." She stood tall, shoulders squared, hands firmly on her hips. "But he's not going camping with us this weekend."

"What about his son?"

Clara saw her father gently touch her mother's arm, but she shook his touch away.

"We could just take the boy," he said.

Her mom shrugged his hand off again. "No. If Roger doesn't go, Benny won't, either. I don't want any contact with that man!" She put her arms across her chest and stood over her father until he bowed his head in submission.

"Fine, but I hate to disappoint the boy. He's already been through enough."

"*We* are not doing anything to the boy. His father is. He shouldn't be trespassing in the middle of the night, spying on me!"

"Fine. Like I said, I'll talk to him in the morning."

"Thank you. I'll check on the girls before I go to bed."

Clara saw her mom place a hand on her father's forearm before turning toward the stairs.

The clap of heels drew louder, forcing Clara to grab her teddy and run up the stairs on her toes to her room, where she climbed into bed and pulled the blankets up under her chin. Teddy tumbled off the bed, but she had no time to rescue him. Her eyes widened in panic, before she shut them tightly.

Did Mommy hear me on the stairs? Did she hear Teddy fall? Am I in trouble?

Her mother could easily tell if someone was pretending to be asleep by the tightness of their eyelids, so she relaxed her face. She got caught once for stealing a midnight cookie. As her mom stepped on the loose floorboards, she felt a wave of tension wash over her, but she tried to remain calm and relaxed. Her mom took softer steps. It appeared that she had removed her heels.

The scent of green apple warned Clara that her mother was close. She felt the mattress sink as her mother sat on the edge of her bed. She sensed the soft presence of her teddy bear snuggling up beside her, nestled under the covers. Her mother's dark, wavy hair tickled her nose as she leaned over and kissed her forehead, and she tried not to move.

"I love you, Clare Bear."

The gentle words wrapped Clara in a gentle embrace. She missed those words. She wished she could tell her mom that she loved her, too, and give her a hug, but she didn't want to get in trouble.

The mattress rose as Clara heard her mother's soft steps travel to Lucy's bed. Clara peeked through her narrow eyes. Her mother leaned over Lucy's bumper barrier, pulled up her covers, and kissed her forehead.

"I love you, Lu-Lu." Lucy shifted but remained asleep.

Clara's heart raced as her mother's figure slowly rotated, prompting Clara to squeeze her eyes shut. The wooden floor groaned with each footstep. The room fell into a hushed stillness as the sound of footsteps echoed down the staircase.

* * *

Clara bolted from bed, beads of sweat glistening from her brow. The chill didn't alleviate the intensity of the heat she felt radiating from within. She put her hand to her chest to ease her ragged breathing and heart palpitations. Phantom whiffs of green apple perfumed the air.

It was just a dream. She exhaled and allowed her muscles to ease. *Not a dream. A memory.* Her eyes flickered as she remembered the details. *Benji!* The alarm clock read 3:48 a.m. *Too early to call.* She threw her blankets against the wall, grabbed a sheet of paper, and sat down at her desk to write.

A flood of emotions and images splashed into Clara's mind like water spraying from a broken tap. Her memory pipe soon burst, unleashing a torrent of long-forgotten encounters. She wrote frantically before a single memory evaporated.

Her parents went to high school with Roger Lawrence but were unhappy when he bought the neighboring house the summer before kindergarten. That's when she met Benjamin Lawrence. They played together but only in her yard. Even though Benji had a trampoline, Clara and Lucy couldn't go over unless Mom or Dad was present.

After the murders, Mr. Lawrence watched over Clara until the police notified her uncle. When he wasn't asking numerous questions about the incident, he was pacing and mumbling noncoherent things. Eventually, he stopped asking Clara questions and watched through his kitchen window as the police searched through her house.

Uncle Jonathon arrived a few days later and brought Clara to live with him. She never talked about what happened even after he arranged counseling. She and Benji were reunited in fourth grade, although she was unaware that they had previously known each other.

Did he know?

Whispered secrets and unsettling doubts played a sinister game of Ping-Pong booming relentlessly within the depths of her mind, until a chilling realization materialized.

What if Benji's dad killed my parents?

CHAPTER 10

JENNA

Clara was not difficult to find in the back of the café. The only other people were huddled over a nest of books, laptops, and papers, clearly studying for an upcoming exam. Clara swirled her coffee absentmindedly, staring through the table.

"Hey, Clara! Whatcha daydreaming? If it involves me, I don't want to know ... or *do* I?" Jenna winked at Clara.

Clara turned her coffee around and took a sip. Her face soured in response.

"Sorry, I had a rough night." Clara sipped more of her coffee and spat it back into her cup. "Ugh, too cold. I'm going to get another. Do you need anything?"

Jenna held up her Java Junction tumbler and bag.

After retrieving her student identification from her bag, Clara returned to the dining hall and purchased a fresh coffee.

Jenna settled at the table, spreading cream cheese on her bagel.

Clara sat down and almost spilled her coffee when she set it down off balance. "Jeez-a-weezy!" She balanced her coffee and shook off the molten drips that splattered her hand. She placed her burning fingers against her moist lips.

Jenna smirked, "Okay, then. Never heard that one."

"Oh yeah. Only when I lose myself. My dad used to say it." Clara waved her hand to soothe the burns.

"What's made you so ... *graceful* this morning?" Jenna crunched down on her toasted bagel.

"I remembered something last night, but I need to talk to Benji first."

"Involving the case?" Jenna mumbled through a macerated bagel bite.

"I don't know yet." Clara peered into her coffee as if the answer had sunk into the dark liquid. Her stomach growled, interrupting her thoughts. She instinctively placed a hand on her stomach.

"Have you eaten this morning?"

"No. I didn't feel like food."

"Your stomach disagrees," Jenna said. She halved her bagel and slid it across the table on a napkin.

"Thank you." Clara examined her edible gift and took a bite. "My favorite ... strawberry cream cheese. I guess food does agree with me. Thanks."

Jenna and Clara tapped their coffee cups together and smiled.

FOREVER FAMILY

"So ... what questions do you have lined up for Mr. Park Man?" Jenna asked.

"His name is Reynolds, not Parkman."

"Ha, I only meant that he was the man from the park, but sure ... Mr. Reynolds?"

A loud noise of disappointment erupted from the students at the other end of the cafe. Jenna and Clara looked to see if they should be concerned, then returned to their own conversation.

"Well, first of all, I'm curious to know if he was under the influence. What kind of home troubles drives a man to sleep in his truck in the middle of the woods?" Clara said. "He could have lied about things to keep from losing his job."

"Unlikely. If he was drunk or stoned, he would've told police he didn't see anything. He knows something. But we'll have to tread carefully. He's the hang-up-on-you type if he decides the conversation's over."

"Do you think he'll answer?" Clara sipped her coffee after taking another bite of bagel.

"Even if he doesn't, he'll talk." Jenna spoke with authority and confidence. She knew if he didn't answer, she would drive to his house and get the information. Nothing stopped a Dean from accomplishing their goals.

Jenna watched Clara glance at the faded marks of an absent watch.

"Jeez. Today's starting out rough." Clara rubbed at her wrist as if the action would make her watch magically appear.

Knowing her pain, Jenna shook her head and tapped a button on her phone. "It's almost time. Want to call outside?"

"It's a bit windy. My dorm's close," Clara said.

"Sounds good." Jenna finished her bagel and threw away their trash.

Jenna followed Clara to her dorm. Since the wind carried a slight chill, Clara was relieved she had offered her room. The sidewalks were empty except for a few squirrels chasing one another up a lamppost.

"Weekends are usually quiet," Clara said. "What few students stay meet up in the apartments to party."

"Do you ever go home on weekends?" Jenna asked as they climbed the stairs.

"I ... uh ... don't really have anywhere to go. My uncle passed away before I left for college. He left me the house, but he had so much debt, the bank took it. I just live here for now."

"What about holidays and breaks?" Jenna watched the squirrels leap to a tree and was amazed at the distance.

"Benji's, usually." Clara paused and frowned before continuing up the stairs inside the dorm building.

Jenna noticed Clara's mood change. *Must be a sensitive subject.*

Upon their arrival on the third floor, a window unit turned off its humming with a machinic *clink*. Clara led Jenna to the last door on the left, knocked, and inserted her key.

"You have a roommate?" Jenna said as they entered the dorm room.

"Not really. My roommate moved in with her boyfriend the first week of school. Just habit to knock."

Clara put her belongings on the desk as Jenna sat on the spare bed.

"Ready to call Mr. *Park* Man?" Jenna chuckled and leaned

back against the wall, crossing her legs. "I've got a question."

"Sure." Clara scooted close to the wall next to Jenna.

"Did you and Benjamin have an argument?"

Clara looked away. "No. What makes you think that?" She shifted in the bed, as if the words were ants crawling on her skin.

Jenna shrugged. "You're acting strange."

"It's not that. It's ... I can't explain. I should talk to him first."

"Interesting. Okay. It's a nunya situation. Got it."

"A what?"

"Nunya. None of your business."

"I don't mean to be difficult. I just remembered something and want to confirm with him." Clara traced the patterns on her roommate's blanket.

"About your history?"

"Maybe. I think we were neighbors and ... I just remember some things that have me a little alarmed."

"Girl. If you're not honest, I can't help." Jenna searched Clara's eyes and crossed her arms expectantly.

Clara pinched the fabric beneath her fingers. Her worried expression intrigued Jenna.

"Well, last night, I dreamed about an argument between my parents. My mom was very upset. Benji and his dad moved next door my kindergarten year, and I think his dad liked my mom." Clara picked at her fingernails.

"I thought you guys met in fourth grade." Jenna's arm rested on her knee.

"We did. I guess we both changed a lot in four years. I didn't recognize him. In fact, I forgot all about the boy next door."

He had to know, Jenna thought skeptically. *I can understand a little girl blocking out her traumatic past ... but a boy with a crush?*

Clara continued. "My mom caught Benji's dad peeping through her bedroom window and told my dad to call the cops, but he talked her out of it. She banned Benji and his dad from camping with us that weekend."

"The weekend they were ..."

"Yeah." Clara shook her head.

"Wow. Benjamin's dad was a Peeping Tom? Potential motive. Do you think he was involved?" Jenna's voice accelerated with excitement as if this new information were critical in solving the whole case.

"Roger Lawrence didn't have anything to do with my parents' murder. He may be a strange guy, but he treats me like family. He is not a suspect." Clara's remarks were defensive and cutting.

For Jenna, it was the most spirited display of emotion Clara had yet presented. Jenna was impressed she had some backbone hidden in that personality. *Overkill? Does she believe herself, or is she trying to convince herself?*

"No offense. There's lots of unknowns. Do you know why he was stalking your house? You must admit, it's a bit odd, especially the weekend before they're killed. Why didn't she call the cops?"

Jenna found Clara watching a cardinal perched on the windowsill that pranced along the windowsill, then hopped away and took flight.

"My dad felt sorry for the guy ... raising a child alone."

"And that weekend, they're murdered. Coincidence? Does Benjamin know the tension between your parents?"

"I don't know. He never mentioned we were neighbors. After I lost my family, I went to Cleveland and lived with my uncle. My early memories are spotty at best. I didn't recognize Benji when we met again, and he didn't seem to recognize me, either."

The same scarlet bird flitted back to the glass and pranced along the ledge. A red-beaked visitor soon landed, and the birds called to each other before flying away.

"Did your mother or father have any friends who were aware of the family feud?" Jenna said.

Clara shuffled her feet at the end of the bed.

Jenna followed Clara's eyes to the windowsill, where a blue bird had settled down with some twine in its beak.

Clara glanced at Jenna. "Actually, yes. Ms. V. Mom's friend Marci Verecamp. Lucy called her Misty. I forgot about her. She'd bring me and Lucy gifts … candy, toys. Once she brought us a cornhole set and a bubble machine. Lucy and I played dodgeball with the beanbags." Her grin spread across her face at the memories.

Jenna watched Clara grin as the blue bird danced in the sun until the scarlet bird returned and chased it away.

Clara's smile soon crumpled like a discarded Post-it.

Jenna snapped her fingers at Clara. "Where did you go?"

"The last time I saw her was the day of my parents' funeral. I was hiding behind a plant to avoid everyone telling me they were sorry for my loss. When she arrived at the church, my uncle got upset. He told her she wasn't welcome and physically ushered her out. She refused to leave and insisted she had a right to be there. He threatened to call the police if she didn't leave. She wiped away her tears after staring into the cathedral and left."

"That sounds as sketchy as a kid with a match. I wonder what happened."

"I don't know. She and Uncle Jonathon clearly didn't get along."

Jenna got a notebook out of her bag and jotted some notes.

"What are you writing?" Clara leaned closer to look over Jenna's arm.

"Marci Verecamp is a witness. We need to question her. Rarely is a funeral visitation denied. She must have some insights or ideas about the family quarrels." Jenna thought out loud as she tapped her pen against her lips. She looked back at Clara with renewed interest. "Did she talk to anyone else before she left ... like Roger?"

"Not that I know of, but I stayed behind the plant." Clara bowed her head and appeared to be biting her lip.

Roger, Marci, Mary ... What did this all mean? Does it mean anything?

Jenna dreaded interrupting Clara's mental conundrum, but her phone alarmed. "Ready?"

Clara snapped out of her thoughts and nodded in agreement.

Though Marci's involvement remained a mystery, they shifted their focus to investigating Mr. Jeremiah Reynolds. Jenna dialed his number, pressed *speaker*, and set the phone down on the bedspread.

"Hello?" a woman's voice answered.

Daughter? "Hello! Is Mr. Reynolds available? He's expecting my call."

"And who shall I say is calling?"

"Linda Lanson," Jenna said

"One moment, please."

Clara hit Jenna's arm. "That's not the name you gave

yesterday!"

"I'm terrible at remembering which names I use, but so are they. It's fine." Jenna waved dismissively.

"Hello?" the familiar raspy voice answered.

"Mr. Reynolds. Great to speak with you again. I have a few questions, if now is a good time."

"I thought your name was Linda Lewis. My nurse said you introduced yourself as Linda Lanson."

Clara smacked Jenna's arm again.

Clever guy. "My apologies. I recently married and I'm getting used to my new name." Jenna thought she saw Clara exhale with relief.

"Congratulations." His voice lacked care or interest. "I have a few minutes, but that is all."

"Great! I will try to keep this brief." Jenna straightened her back and positioned her notebook for action. "You were parked at Nelson Ledges the night the Wilsons were killed. What were you doing there?"

"Sleeping. I volunteered to stay on property in case the campers had an overnight emergency."

"Clearly, you were a very dedicated employee." Silence on the other end. "How would anyone know you were available?"

"The park has one entrance and exit. I parked in the only lot. *Park Ranger* was stenciled on my truck. Each of the campers had the park's emergency number, which transferred to my mobile."

Jenna waited for Mr. Reynolds to finish coughing before continuing. "How long did you work for the park?"

"Sixty years off and on since I was a kid. When my health permits, I still put in a few hours of voluntary work on the weekends."

"What is your current health condition?"

"Personal."

Unfazed, Jenna continued. "What did you witness that night?"

"It was hard to sleep in my work truck, so I frequently got up and moved around. I saw a truck exiting the park. Before you ask ... no, I don't know what time. My dashboard clock was busted, and I wasn't wearing a watch. It was late."

"Do you remember details of the truck?"

"Yeah, it was an old rusted green Ford pickup with a yellow caution work sign on the passenger door. Looked like one of the local handyman trucks." He cleared his throat before continuing. "The lights were off, and he was slowly pulling out."

"You said 'he.' Did you see the driver?" Jenna asked as she scribbled on her pages.

"There was only one streetlamp, but the shadow was a man's ... big shoulders, short hair."

"Did you notice any *smaller* shadows?" Jenna asked.

"No. I saw a man, not the girl the media reported. I don't know if she was on the floor or lying down. I don't even know if the man was involved. He could've been another camper that got tired of staying outdoors that night. A few other vehicles left earlier."

"If the lighting was so poor, how do you know it was a green pickup truck?"

"The truck passed directly under the light. I know what I know, and I know what I don't know." His tone tightened. "I don't appreciate anyone questioning my words."

"No offense intended; I assure you. Is there anything else you can think of that might help us with our investigation?"

"No, it's the same thing I told the police fifteen years ago, and you can't squeeze me for more than that. So, if you don't mind, I don't want to be bothered again."

"Just one more question." Jenna waited, but the line remained silent. "Were you intoxicated in any way that night?" She clenched her teeth, knowing how the man would respond.

"How dare you!" The phone disconnected.

"Well, that went well." Jenna tossed her pen on top of her notebook.

"But we didn't learn anything," Clara said.

"Sure we did. He wasn't lying. I know a liar when I hear one. The truck appeared to have a single occupant. You said it yourself—this was a family camping weekend. Where was his family? The green Ford pickup is our primary suspect."

CHAPTER 11

CLARA

Clara tapped her beer bottle rhythmically with her fingers, pausing only to check the time. Her mind was a battleground, with questions, anxieties, and doubts firing at her like cannons against a fortress. *How will Benji react? How will he respond? Can we still be friends? Do I want to be friends?* She had texted him earlier to meet at the Fyte Pub instead of the café, hoping drinks would ease the discussion.

She drank a few sips. As the caramel liquid tickled her tastebuds, the sharp bitterness, which was usually tolerable, made her choke. The icy malt flushed her cheeks and warmed her head. Clara rarely drank, especially when Benji wasn't around, but she needed to relax.

She stared into her glass, waiting for the words to rise in her glass with each bubble. As Clara tried to decipher the coded bubbles, Benji patted her on the shoulder. Her arms flailed, searching for balance as the shock jolted through her body, threatening to send her tumbling from the stool.

"I gotcha." Benji placed a hand on her back and helped her settle on the stool. He kept a supportive hand on her shoulder as he sat down. "Everything okay? You're a wee bit jumpy." Playful sarcasm gently rolled off his tongue.

Clara knew he was joking, but she couldn't smile. "Yeah, I'm fine. Just been a long weekend." She glanced in his direction but avoided making eye contact. Instead, she absently tore the label off her bottle.

Benji signaled the bartender for a drink. Clara could feel his eyes study her as he waited for an explanation.

"Hey, Lex, could I get an order of chicken tenders?"

"Sure thing," replied the bartender.

"Do you want anything?" Benji asked Clara.

She shrugged. Food was the last thing on her mind.

"How many have you had?" Benji pointed at her bottle, but she just shrugged.

"All right, out with it." Benji placed a hand on Clara's thigh. "Did something happen? Did Jenna do something?"

Clara frowned at his hand. *How could he think Jenna did anything? She's been nothing but helpful and friendly.* "No, nothing like that. Jenna and I collected a lot of information this weekend, and it's hard to ... it's confusing ... I really don't know what to think." Clara ripped off the rest of the label and flattened it on the counter, working to rid the wet material of wrinkles.

Benji placed a hand on her shoulder, long enough for her to feel the heat from his palm. A thud vibrated deep in her belly like a quarter flicked into a fountain. She shrugged his hand away.

"Don't get mad, but you're not giving me anything to work with. Why don't you start at the beginning?" Benji suggested.

The beginning? When I found out you've been lying to me! Looking around the pub, Clara realized it was busier than expected. "Can we find a quieter spot?"

Benji scanned the room, but discontent soured his expression. He signaled the bartender. "Hey, Lex? Do you mind if we sit at the table out back?"

"No problem. I'll bring your tenders." Lex eyed Clara. "You want another?"

Lifting her bottle to the light, Clara saw that she had consumed almost the entire bottle. She gulped down the remains and passed it across the bar. "Yes, please."

Clara noticed Benji pass her a strange look as he helped her off the barstool. He placed a hand on the small of her back as he escorted her outside.

An unexpected shiver caused Clara to embrace herself as Benji opened the back door. Frigid nights were expected after such cool breezy days. Benji wrapped an arm around her and led her to the outside seating. Her muscles relaxed after he switched on the patio heater, rubbed her arms, and sat next to her. The contrast of heat and cold beer gave her a moment of serenity, but then she remembered she was upset with Benji and scooted away.

Benji laid a hand on the table and turned to Clara. "So, what's going on?"

Inhaling slowly, Clara forced out a heavier breath. "The other

FOREVER FAMILY

witness confirmed seeing a green work truck heading east toward Pittsburgh. The lying witness led police to Wheeling." The fermenting bubbles floated in Clara's glass. She struggled to find another focal point.

The crease between Benji's brow deepened. "Investigating the past is dangerous ... for your emotions, for your state of mind, and for the others wishing to forget. The police will notify you of new developments. Let it go. Your sister is ..." Benji stopped himself from speaking. "She'd want you to move on and be happy."

Clara sipped her drink. He had said all this before. She knew she should listen, but forgetting her family would not make her happy. *It's easy for him. It's not his family that was brutally murdered and ripped from existence.*

"Clara, what's wrong? You rarely have two beers, especially on a school night. Talk to me." He put a gentle hand on her arm.

His deceiving hands sparked anger. "This is my fourth." Clara displayed four fingers and dared herself to voice the challenging question tormenting her. "Were we childhood neighbors?"

Benji withdrew his hand in surprise. He lowered his head and gripped his drink tightly. "Yes."

Clara straightened her back and slid away. "Why didn't you tell me?"

"You didn't remember me. I was hurt. I told my dad, and he suggested not bringing it up. He said the past was too painful. Since then, it never came up."

"Never came up? How about when you introduce me to your friends, and you say we met in elementary school?"

"That's true. We were in kindergarten when we first met."

"Absence of truth is still a lie." Clara's words were sharp and brought tears to Benji's eyes.

"I'm sorry. I didn't want to hurt you."

"Congratulations on a job well done." Putting some distance between herself and Benji, Clara took another swallow from her beer. She knew her actions were over-the-top, yet she was powerless to rein herself in. She shouldn't put him through this. He'd been nothing but a loyal friend, but she was fuming with rage.

"We still have fond memories of how we ended up together." Benji smiled at her as he tried to lighten the mood. "You remember us meeting over that spider game? I remember playing hide-and-seek in your parents' bushes."

"The same bushes from where your father watched my mother undress?" Clara's words were like daggers laced with poison. None of this was Benji's fault, but her anger focused on a target and wouldn't let go.

Benji squirmed. The depth of her resentment caught her off guard.

She was hurt by Benji's deception, and she wanted him to feel the pain she felt. Clara's past was full of dishonesty, violence, and loss. Benji, whom she considered her safe haven, ultimately betrayed her. She felt strange, detached from herself.

The two sat in silence until the stillness was interrupted by the arrival of chicken tenders.

"Would you like some?" Benji slid his offering to Clara, but she shoved it back.

"No, thank you." The plate held generous amounts of chicken tenders, fries, and a biscuit, but her appetite was not there.

Lex examined them with obvious concern. "Can I get anything else for you guys?"

"No, we're fine." Benji kept his focus on Clara as he spoke.

The bartender positioned herself in front of Clara, forcing her to make eye contact. "Are you okay?"

Clara's eyes welled up with tears that teetered on the edge of spilling over. "I'm fine. Thank you." She turned away.

The bartender took a long look at Benji before walking back into the pub.

Benji picked up a small glass container on the table and showed Clara. "Did you know that molasses is the sloth of the liquid world?"

"This isn't funny, Benjamin." Clara slammed her hand on the table and attempted to stand. Her legs gave out and she fell back onto the bench. Defeated, she said, "Everything I know is wrong. Out of all the wrongness in the world, you were my safe zone. I want the truth." Much of her childhood was forgotten with that dreadful night and replaced with terrors and nightmares.

"I know. I'm sorry. Before the incident, we were neighbors, briefly. Me, you, and Lucy played together that summer before kindergarten. Our parents didn't get along, but I don't know why."

Benji took a sip of his beverage before continuing. "I overheard your dad telling my dad not to creep around at night. They argued because my dad denied it. We were supposed to go camping with your family that weekend, but my dad said your family was crazy and wouldn't let us go.

"Then, on Sunday, the police brought you to my house. I tried to talk and play with you, but you wouldn't talk to me. After you went with your uncle, I learned what had happened. I didn't see you again until my dad and I relocated, and you were at my new school."

Benji drank from his glass once again. "I'm sorry I didn't tell you, but every time you get caught up in the past, you enter social hibernation. I thought it would be best if you didn't remember me, so you didn't associate me with your past."

So many questions ricocheted in Clara's head, but she didn't trust the words to emerge without detonation.

Clara felt the ground beneath her feet shifting. A pain pulsed behind her eyes, and she felt nauseated. "I'm sorry, Benji. I've got to go."

"Clara, please. We need to talk."

Clara staggered away from the bench, feeling as if she had abandoned the bones of her legs. "I promise we'll talk, just not right now." She balanced herself on the table before reaching into her pocket for a few dollar bills. After abandoning her beer, she staggered aimlessly around the building. As she turned the corner, she caught a glimpse of Benji chasing the bills as the wind danced with them.

She walked with spaghetti legs down the path. She kept her palms parallel with the ground, willing the shaking to stop as she approached three steps leading to the parking lot. She descended the stairs carefully but missed the last one. She clung to the railing before she crashed to the ground.

"Clara!" Benji shouted behind her.

Closing her eyes, Clara waited for the light-headedness to dissipate before confronting the voice. "I told you I need a break," she said as she swatted his helping hands away.

Benji stepped aside and held out her bag. "You left your purse."

After she used the railing to lift herself up, she snatched the strap and secured it over her head. She intended to express her gratitude with a simple "thank you," but the words that escaped her lips sounded different, not quite right. She brushed the dirt from her backside and almost fell again.

"Please, let me walk you home. I promise I won't speak. I just want to make sure you are safe."

Always so chivalrous. "I'm fine. I'm not walking far."

"May I say something, Clara?" Benji's voice remained soft and steady.

Hearing that voice brought a sense of security and comfort to Clara. Then she remembered how that voice had sucker punched her. She looked at Benji, waiting for him to say anything that would make everything right again.

"You are my best friend. Nothing will change that. I thought I was protecting you. Please forgive me. I ... I care about you ... and how you feel." Tears collected at the corner of his eyes.

She could tell he was hurting, too. She didn't want to lose him. Heat tickled her cheeks and brought tears.

"Benji ... I ..." Clara cautiously closed the distance between them. Her mind was a tangled web of emotions, and Clara felt off-kilter because of all the confusion.

Benji supported Clara's arms.

This time, she didn't fight him away. Instead, she tucked her head under his chin and wrapped her arms around his waist. She felt his heart pound against his warm chest. The warm, steady rhythm calmed her.

Unfamiliar emotions surfaced, threatening to spoil the moment. She grimaced, clutching her chest as her heart raced uncontrollably. Her stomach churned violently. The dampness on her skin was noticeable even in the cool of the night.

Clara searched Benji's eyes to find evidence of similar reactions.

He stared back at her but loosened his hold.

Please don't let me go.

His hands gently rested on her shoulders, causing them to warm under his touch. As they drew nearer, he kissed her. The cold beer left his lips soft and cool. His stubble along his lip and chin scratched her delicate skin.

She hadn't imagined a romantic relationship in a long time, but this felt natural. She returned his kiss, tightening her grip on him.

Benji pushed her at arm's length. "Clara, I can't." He lowered his head and backed away.

Anger grew exponentially as the hurt deepened. When she realized he was speechless, she stormed off. She was thrilled that her dorm was within walking distance.

CHAPTER 12

CLARA

Clara rolled over when she heard a knock at her door. She squinted as the rays of sunlight streaming in through the window caught her off guard. Her head throbbed painfully, serving as a stark reminder of the reasons she avoided excessive alcohol.

"Wake up!" Jenna's voice rang out.

Clara wasn't expecting Jenna this morning. She fumbled out of bed, but in her grogginess, she stumbled over her scattered garments and collided with the doorframe, causing a painful bump on her head.

"Ow!" Clara massaged her head, opened the door, and returned to bed to cover her face with a pillow. "Why are you here so early?" she mumbled.

"Early? It's eleven! I thought we'd grab lunch."

Clara leaned over to check her phone: 11:08 a.m. "I can't believe I missed my classes."

"Hangovers are mightier than the willpower to attend class," Jenna stated in her best academic impersonation. "I'm just sorry you didn't invite me." Jenna pulled Clara's desk chair around and sat down.

"I met with Benji last night." Clara leaned over her bed and reached for her water glass.

"I gathered that. No explanations necessary. Nunmy." Jenna waved away the words. With a sly smile, she eyed Clara and continued. "Must have been some meeting. You're still in yesterday's clothes."

Clara looked at herself and frowned.

"I'm guessing your *meeting* didn't go well?"

"He confessed that he kept secrets from me. We *were* neighbors and our parents *did not* get along. I felt so angry. I overreacted a bit." Clara rubbed her head. "I tried to leave, but he wanted to apologize." She hesitated. Her face softened and she looked away from Jenna before concluding, "Then I came home."

"Lies by omission."

"What?" *How does she know?*

"I can read you like a picture book after a week together. You're withholding information." Jenna pulled her chair up to Clara's bed, kicked off her shoes, and crossed her legs up on the bed. "If you want our friendship to last, be honest. If it's none of my business, at least I'll know where I stand."

I am honest, Clara thought defensively.

"Not that it *is* any of your business, but we kissed. It was a mistake." Clara grabbed painkillers from her nightstand.

"I thought you liked him?"

"As a friend. Kissing your friend never ends well." Clara swallowed two capsules and set her water down.

"Did *he* think it was a mistake?"

"Undeniably." Clara rolled her eyes as she remembered the rejection.

"Hold on. I need details. What happened?" Jenna popped off the chair and sat at the end of the bed.

Clara straightened her back and sat up. "We met at the Fyte Pub. I was nervous about asking him questions, so I got there early and thought I could drink some bravery. It went straight to my head."

"Did you eat anything after that half bagel?"

Clara's head dropped, her eyes avoiding contact with anything in the room, including her mirror. "Um ... no."

"Bad choice but go on."

"Anyway, Benji shows up, and I asked him about being neighbors. He admitted he knew but didn't want to say anything. He confirmed everything I remembered. I got pretty upset and left."

"Did you ask him if his dad or Marci knew anything about your parents' murder?"

"No. I wanted to leave. He stopped me to apologize. I felt bad when I saw how much he was hurting, and we hugged. The hug turned into a kiss."

Jenna's expression sparkled with delight. "Who initiated?"

"I don't really know. My head was spinning. It felt right, until he pushed me away. No explanation, just said he couldn't. Mad and humiliated, I stomped back to my dorm. I don't remember getting back, but I woke up to you pounding on my door."

"He couldn't." Jenna repeated Benji's words. "Why do you think he couldn't?" She sat with her legs crossed, gently resting one hand on her knee. Her other hand hovered near her lips, her finger lightly touching them as she pondered.

"I don't know." *I don't want to know.*

"Maybe he didn't want to ruin your friendship ... or maybe he didn't want to take advantage of a drunkard ... or maybe he was too limp to pimp."

"Jenna! Don't be so crude. It was just a kiss. To be honest, it wasn't our first."

"*Do* go on!" Jenna smirked and plopped herself next to Clara on the bed and patted her thigh.

"Prom night. We went as friends. Benji took me for a walk outside. Twinkling lights and colorful flowers blanketed the garden pathways along with the gentle sounds of a waltz from the ballroom. As we sat in a clearing watching the fireflies dance in the night, he leaned over and kissed me. In the heat of the moment, I kissed him back but soon pushed him away. It's not that I didn't like it. I was scared. The idea of having romantic feelings for Benji was completely foreign to me. He apologized, saying he was distracted. He hoped it wouldn't harm our friendship. Once I accepted the fact that he wasn't looking for love, I stopped thinking about us that way."

"There's no doubt that he wants more. That's why the topic's resurfacing. You stopped things because you were terrified; he stopped things because the conditions weren't right. You two have got to get into sync!"

Why must men be so confusing? Clara glanced at her phone. Four missed calls, five texts, and a message.

"Benji's been calling." She showed Jenna her screen. She checked her texts and voice mail. "Hey, Clara, I missed you this morning for class. I waited downstairs, but I guess you're sleeping in. I'll make sure to take Clara-style notes today instead of doodling." Clara could hear his forced chuckle. "I'll call you later. I hope you're all right. Bye." The texts were identical.

"Yes, he likes you. Me, not so much, but you ... absolutely," Jenna said.

"Let's change the subject." *She doesn't know him like I do. He's my friend.* "Give me a few minutes, and I'll be ready for lunch." Clara grabbed her hygiene kit and a change of clothes and headed to the bathroom.

JENNA

Jenna guided Clara through the campus traffic. After observing Clara's poor attempt to shield her eyes from the sun, Jenna handed her a pair of sunglasses.

"Thanks," Clara said as she secured the glasses with both hands.

The café was filled with the soft hum of students, punctuated by bursts of laughter from the more vivacious personalities. Jenna sat down in the center of the café with her sandwich and chips.

Clara accompanied Jenna after finalizing her decisions, but paused and glanced around, appearing uncertain about her next move.

Jenna followed her eyes around the café but didn't know

what she was searching for. "Are you looking for someone?"

Clara slowly approached Jenna. "Want to sit over there? Maybe it's quieter." Clara indicated a vacant corner table.

Jenna glanced over her shoulder and turned back to her tray to eat her sandwich. "No. This is fine." *It won't be any quieter over there.* She didn't understand how people could be scared about nothing.

Clara looked around the room again before sitting down.

Jenna ignored the skittish-deer behavior and continued eating her sandwich.

Clara spoke up. "So, you heard about my exciting night? How was yours?"

"Uneventful."

"Come on. Nothing? Really?"

"No, really. I watched a few reruns on TV while I worked on a paper for my Crim-Ev class." *While hating my father's new girlfriend.*

"Alone?"

"Yeah, my dad was out on a date, and I was all by myself." The snarl in her voice was unexpected, and she hoped Clara wouldn't notice.

"You're not the only one who can sense when something's missing from the conversation." Clara's face lit up with a wide grin, her fingers sliding the sunglasses up to rest on her forehead. As she did so, her hair was gently pushed back, resembling a stylish headband.

"I don't like it," Jenna blurted as she pushed her tray away. "My dad dating. It's wrong."

"Have you talked to him?"

"No. I should be happy for him, but I'm not." Without taking a bite, Jenna pushed her sandwich aside and folded her arms. "He works for her as a handyman. It should be a conflict of interest or something."

"Has he dated before? Since ... since your ...?" Clara's words were soft and gentle, but she couldn't finish the question.

"No. Never.... At least, I never saw him date. It's just been him and me. We look out for each other. I don't like him with another woman." *Especially when they are gold-digging tramps.*

"Maybe it's hard for him, too. You should let him know how you feel."

No way. "Yeah, maybe." *Enough about me.* "Do you remember any more about that family friend? We need to ask Benji."

"You're right ... we should. I haven't texted him back yet." Clara pulled her phone out and sent a message to Benji. "I'll see if he responds."

Of course he'll respond. Jenna rolled her eyes. *The girl is clueless about her lovesick loyal puppy.*

Before Clara could put her phone down, it pinged with a response. Clara studied the message and asked Jenna, "Does three work?"

"Yep. Wait, no, five. I have a shift until four, and Janet is often late."

Clara typed. "I can meet you at Java and we can go to the library together? I might skip my other class today and rest."

"Sounds good. See you at five."

CHAPTER 13

JENNA

"Ima? Ima Joe King? Come on, guys, it's not funny. Ima *not* Joe King." Jenna crossed her arms over her chest in a dismissive, motherly manner, with a pronounced pouty lower lip.

Jenna appeared to enjoy the antics as the males laughed at the childish monikers.

Clara longed to possess such audacity.

"Ben? Ben Derhover?" Jenna pursed her lips as she pretended to drop something, bent to pick it up, and snapped back up. "Ohh!"

Jenna's fake outrage amused Clara. *I can only dream of having such confidence.*

"Ms. Tayla? Ms. Jenny Tayla? Has anyone seen Jenny Tayla?"

The hackling boys nearly fell over.

Jenna placed a hand on her hip and pointed the coffee at the group. "Now, I know none of *you guys* have ever seen Jenny Tayla."

Jenna's eyes brightened when she spotted Clara, and she motioned for her to wait.

A bench was perfectly positioned at the edge of the walkway for her to sit on. The rough texture of the wooden bench grazed against the back of her exposed thigh. She quickly rose to her feet and leaned in to inspect the injury, only to find that it was just out of her sight. She gently touched the area of pain, and a small amount of blood stained her fingers. Despite her aversion to blood, this situation didn't appear to be too distressing. *Must be superficial.* She adjusted her skirt and moved to a different spot on the bench to prevent any further injuries.

"Last order, guys, and Karen takes over. Mia? Mia Rack? Can anyone locate Mia Rack? Oh, my goodness. Real funny, guys! Are any of these names real?" Underneath her seemingly innocent words was a biting edge. "It pains me deeply to think about the wretched upbringings that you may have had to endure." Her phony pout suddenly blossomed into a radiant grin. "Don't forget to tip the lady!" Jenna flung her apron at the next worker.

I wonder if her name is really Karen. I thought it was Janet.

Jenna walked up to Clara. "Are you ready for our next adventure? Inside the mind of Benjamin Lawrence ... Oooh." Jenna grinned and wiggled her fingers to appear mysterious and ghostly.

Clara let out a deep sigh and rolled her eyes. She absentmindedly brushed away some dust from the wooden planks.

"The time for awkwardness has passed. Leave your assumptions at the door and let in the facts. Let's do this!"

Clara clenched her teeth and nodded as she got to her feet.

"You really don't mind the dirty names?"

Jenna cast a quick glance over her shoulder and the dwindling boys. "Nah. The raunchy humor brings tips and makes not dating easier. Who'd want to date from that gene pool?"

Clara realized that the male population of customers had significantly decreased with Karen or Janet at the counter.

Benji was waiting for the girls on the library steps as they strolled up. He scurried to his feet and cast an apprehensive glance at Clara. "How are you?"

Clara avoided eye contact while Jenna said, "I'm doing quite well, Benjamin. Thank you. And yourself?"

He looked at Jenna. "Fine." He turned back to Clara. "And you?"

"I'm fine," Clara said, tilting her head away.

"Now that everyone is fine, let's find a study room, shall we?" Jenna opened the library door for Clara and Benji.

Clara stopped at the front desk to sign out a room while Jenna and Benji proceeded into a study room.

"Susan ... Room 4, please." Susan perched on the counter, leaning in toward the male students with her legs crossed. For Susan, ignoring actual customers was business as usual. "Susan?"

"Excuse me, Ms. Librarian!" Jenna's authoritarian voice startled Clara.

"We need Room 4 now. The room has already been requested by my friend. To maintain your employment or any job on campus, it is imperative that you refrain from engaging in flirtatious behavior with the male population of students and prioritize the responsibilities assigned to you. Failure to comply with this directive may result in the notification of the head of Student

FOREVER FAMILY

Employment. Your behavior is absolutely unacceptable!" Jenna appeared to wave away the behavior with her hand and slapped her hand on the counter, causing Clara and Susan to flinch.

Susan sprang down from the counter, smoothed down her skirt, and scoured the overstuffed desk for the checkout clipboard. "Who are you to demand anything?" Susan snarled.

"My mother just happens to be the HSE of this university." With a dominating gesture, Jenna waved her hand.

Susan's complexion grew paler, and her hands shook as she passed the clipboard to Clara.

I've never seen Susan rattled before. Clara struggled to hide her smile as she witnessed Susan's embarrassment and shame. Those young men she was talking to bolted out of the building. Clara put her signature on the document and gave Susan a sly grin. When Clara turned, Jenna linked their arms together and they walked directly to Room 4.

As soon as the girls entered the study room, Clara spun around to face Jenna. "That was incredible! I wish I had that level of confidence. Do you even know the head of Student Employment?"

Sitting at the far end of the table, Benji angled his head ever so slightly, but Clara hardly noticed him.

"I don't think there is a head of Student Employment!" Jenna smiled wittingly. "Now, on to business." Jenna focused on Benji, her eyes sharp and focused, intent on unraveling the mysteries of his mind. She leaned forward in her chair, mirroring the posture of the investigator who often played the role of the intimidating bad cop. "Benji. What do you know about Marci Verecamp?"

Benji's forehead crinkled with a perplexed expression as he

reclined, contemplating. "Why does that name sound familiar?"

"Mom's friend, Ms. V. or Misty," Clara said. "They were inseparable. Did everything together."

"Oh yeah, she would bring candy and water guns. She seemed nice, but I really don't remember her that well."

"Any reason why my uncle wouldn't like her?"

"I don't know. We'd play in the backyard while she and your mom talked inside. She never stayed long."

Clara said, "That's right! She would leave before Dad got home. Marci and Mom were secret friends. We weren't supposed to mention her to dad."

"Strange. Hidden buddies bribing young children and making life difficult for the married couple?" Jenna scribbled notes in her journal. "Let's put that under *Things to Research*." Jenna aimed her pen at Benji with a dramatic swing. "Benji. Why did the Wilsons hate your dad?"

Benji turned his head sharply, staring accusingly at Clara. "Exactly how much did you tell her?"

"Everything. We're working together. Friendships require *honesty*, not assumptions and deception."

Benji leaned back in his chair, his shoulders slumped as he looked at the floor. His enthusiasm waned as quickly as a sun-dried grape.

Clara realized she stood tall above him, staring down like a teacher reprimanding a student.

Clara Anne Wilson! Clara heard the memories of her mother scolding her. *What is your problem? He said he was sorry. When did you turn into such a mean person?*

But Clara wasn't sorry. She was angry, and she hated herself for it.

"What my good friend is trying to say ..." Jenna gently patted Clara's shoulder as she took a seat. "Nothing is truly mysterious but the secrets stored in your mind. Please enlighten us with your memories?"

Benji folded his arms. A sharp huff escaped his lips. His appearance suggested he had just been roughed up for his lunch money. "What do you want to know?"

"Why your parents didn't get along," Jenna said.

"When I was four years old, my mom walked out on us. My dad raised me alone with no other family. I never saw her again and never found out why she left." Benji shifted in his chair, turning away from the girls. "I'm going to tell you something that defies all logic and reason, but it's all true.

"At bedtime, my dad would tell me magical stories about a mystery woman who would soon become my mom. From these stories, the brave and bold woman was captured by cruel pirates and had to fight for her freedom. He would save her just as a courageous knight would rescue a princess from a dragon. Several women were brought to the house to see if they fit his profile, but none of them matched until he met Mary with her two little girls at the shop. Even though he called her name, she kept going. He said with a big smile, 'Boy, there is your new mommy.' She fled the pirates to get back to us. Because her captors brainwashed her, she had no idea who she or we were. He believed everything."

Clara was about to speak, but Jenna prodded her arm to stop her.

"After two weeks, that summer before kindergarten, we moved into the house next door. 'No need to worry if Mommy doesn't recognize us,' Dad assured me. He had begun developing the antidote to release her memories. Even at the age of six, I found his tales peculiar. I was a freshman in high school before we found out what was wrong with him." Benji fumbled in the side pocket of his backpack and pulled out his water bottle.

"What was wrong?" Clara had thought she knew everything about Benji.

"Delusion disorder." Benji took a swig from his water bottle. "He takes meds and visits doctors for psychotherapy and counseling."

"I never heard of it," Jenna said.

"Previously called paranoid psychosis. He distorts the truth so that it conforms to his fantasies. He obviously had a thing for Mary back in high school. These feelings were sparked when he saw her in the supermarket, and he sincerely believed that she had miraculously appeared to be with him. He simply didn't understand how to make her view things his way."

"Why didn't you tell me?" Clara bit her lip.

"Since you didn't remember me, my dad told me not to tell you. You might also think less of my dad after hearing about what he was going through."

"That's exactly what I think," Jenna interrupted. "He has a delusional love interest in Mary and takes physical action to ensure that no one else can have her."

Benji's eyes burned with rage at Jenna's accusations. He clenched his fingers into a tight fist and struck the table. "My dad has never been violent to anyone!"

Clara pinched the bridge of her nose, blocking out Jenna and Benji's argument. "Did my parents know about Roger?"

When he turned to Clara, his venomous, angry tone subsided to a softer tone. "Whatever your parents knew, they made sure you girls didn't come near my place alone. They didn't trust my dad."

"Mr. Wilson knew your dad was crazy and banished him from that camping trip. He got deliriously furious, followed them, and resolved the situation," Jenna said. "Then he force-fed you false memories to hide his guilt!"

"Stop talking! My father was sad and hurt, not violent and murderous."

"Jenna ... we need facts, not assumptions. Your words. This is a sensitive topic, but we need answers. Benji ... please ... I'm not saying your dad did anything, but I need to know. After all that you've hidden from me, I ... The clues must be followed. Tell me what happened the night my dad went to talk to Roger."

Before continuing, Benji stopped to take a few deep, cleansing breaths and a drink of water. "We were building LEGOs in the living room when the doorbell rang. My father got up to answer, but before he did, he told me to stay and play. Even though your dad seemed calm, I knew right away that this wasn't going to be a friendly social call."

BENJI

Sitting on the berber rug in the living room, Benji laid out an assortment of building bricks on a flattened cardboard box to create a magnificent castle. His father leaned against the couch helping to pick out the gray colored bricks. A sudden, loud knock made them shift their attention to the front door. "Wait here, son." His father patted his shoulder as he stood, adjusted his flannel shirt, and walked to the door.

The living room wall obstructed his view, but Benji could hear the dad from next door.

The house was filled with tension as the two men stood in the doorway, their voices revealing a mix of emotions. As Benji worked on building his castle, he couldn't help but listen closer.

"Hey, Roger," Mr. Wilson said.

"Tom. Everything all right?" his dad replied.

"No, Roger. Mary caught you outside her window while she was dressing."

"I didn't know she was dressing." His dad's voice was almost a whisper.

"Why were you standing outside our window at all?"

Benji's curiosity got the best of him as he inched closer, hoping to catch a glimpse of what the adults were discussing. He cautiously glanced around the corner of the wall separating him from the front door, only to be caught by his father's watchful eye. With a subtle gesture, his father silently signaled for him to retreat to the living room. Benji hid behind the wall, but strategically positioned himself near the edge.

"I thought I heard something and wanted to make sure everything was okay."

"That's very kind of you, but you can't come on our property. Mary was going to call the police, but I convinced her not to. Stop sneaking around our place."

"I'm not sneaking. I want to make sure Mary is safe."

"Mary is not your responsibility." Mr. Wilson's voice grew louder. "I protect Mary and the girls. If you want to remain friends, you need to learn boundaries."

"I'm sorry, Tom. I'll apologize to Mary."

"I will tell Mary. She doesn't want you anywhere near her. You scare her."

"I didn't mean to scare her. I love her!" his dad almost shouted.

The air became heavy, almost suffocating, as the tones shifted. Benji leaned down on the floor and peeked around the corner again. Mr. Wilson's face turned red, his face scrunched, and he clenched his fists. Benji scampered back to his building bricks. He directed his attention on his castle tower, attempting to drown out the growing volume of conversation.

"No, you don't! Your high school crush is over, and so is this talk. I think you should start looking for a new place to live. We don't want you to live here anymore."

"It's hard for you to understand, but Mary and I are meant to be together."

"Enough! Roger, step back. Whatever is going on in your mind, you need to stop pretending and start living in the actual world. I'm done. This weekend, you're not going camping. Find something else for your boy to do. You've made it impossible, Roger."

Roger muttered under his breath as the door closed, "No, you have."

CLARA

Clara was so focused on what he was saying that she didn't notice how tightly she was biting her lip. A coppery coating formed on her tongue from a warm metallic drop. Her heart pounded heavily in her chest. At the back of her throat, she could feel the nauseating liquid rising.

"Excuse me." Clara bolted to the bathroom.

JENNA

"That went well." Jenna's tone dripped with sarcasm.

"Why did you come here?" Benji asked.

"I'm helping my friend solve her mystery."

"You are not friends with Clara. I am."

"It sounds like you're doing a great job of it, too. Please don't think of me as one of your friends." Jenna shifted her focus to her notebook, brimming with the valuable insights she had gathered.

"Everything was fine before you came along."

"Deception and dishonesty are essential to any successful relationship. Are you sure you didn't inherit your father's mental troubles? Maybe we should spike your water bottle with some of his meds." Unfazed by the verbal counterattacks, Jenna doodled in her notepad. *Yeah, it's a cheap shot, but he deserves it. I did nothing, and he's firing missiles like I'm target practice. Possessive much?*

Benji stifled a groan. He got out of his seat and started pacing the confines of the room, knocking over a chair in the process.

He's gesticulating and grunting like a caged gorilla. Ooh-ooh, Eee-eee! Jenna had a quiet laugh and kept writing in her notebook.

When Clara entered the study, Benji straightened his chair and turned to face her. Red and swollen eyes hinted at the overwhelming fog of uncertainty clouding her mind.

CHAPTER 14

CLARA

It was agreed to temporarily put Roger's narrative on hold, much to Benji's relief. As the girls proceeded to have a conversation about their upcoming topic, Benji excused himself and ventured off to procure a selection of snacks from the vending machine.

"Are you interested in discussing potential suspects or moving on to evidence?" Jenna flipped through her notebook.

Clara organized the papers, fitting them together like a puzzle. "Let's keep talking about the suspects. I promise I won't ignore evidence, but please, don't bring up Benji's dad. Not today."

"Agreed. I'm curious how the police would evaluate Roger."

"Not today. Please," Clara said.

Jenna's shrug was noncommittal and left room for

interpretation. Clara hoped Jenna would understand.

"Hey, here's some lip oil. You're working on biting a hole through your lip." Jenna slid a small tin across the table.

After carefully opening the lid, Clara dipped her ring finger into the oil and applied it to her lips. "Thanks." As Benji reappeared in the doorway, she returned the container.

"I stocked up on both sugary and savory snacks in addition to the standard soda, tea, and water."

"Thanks, Benji." The grin on Clara's face was quite wide for the modest offering, but she sincerely hoped that he could understand the true nature of her intentions. Despite feeling angry and confused, she valued their close friendship and didn't want to lose it. She felt safe with him even when she didn't feel safe on her own.

Even with a deep crater etched in his brow, Benji managed to conjure the hint of a smile.

"Hey, what do you call cows that won't give milk?" No one responded. He tossed a box to Clara. "Milk Duds!"

Clara accepted her favorite candy as a gesture of reconciliation and ate a piece.

Jenna cut off the unspoken remarks and brought the conversation back to the investigation. "So, the police considered two persons of interest ... Jack Drewitt and Ryan McFadden."

Jenna handed Clara the paper containing information about the suspects. Clara hadn't thoroughly examined these pages since last year.

"As the main suspect, Jack Drewitt, in his early twenties, had a tungsten-solid alibi. He took over his father's construction business and used the company work truck, a green Ford F-150 with a yellow triangle logo on the door. By day he was a friendly handyman, but at night he was a violent drunk, according to people in the area. By age twenty-one, his criminal record would be good enough for a true crime book. In fact, some of the prints on the murder weapon matched his."

Jenna looked back and forth between Benji and Clara. "Why wasn't this guy arrested? They convict people for much less."

Benji spoke up while Clara sipped her soda. "He was already in jail. Unrelated charges. His arresting officer was on the case and told investigators that he had taken the man into custody himself after a bar fight that Saturday night. Pretty good alibi. They assumed someone took his truck with the knife in it and used gloves."

"For each murder? That's impossible. Drewitt must have shared the truck with someone on a regular basis. What did he say about the evidence against him?"

Clara spoke. "There's no record of an interview with Drewitt. Years later, they tried to track him down, but no one knew where he had gone. No friends, no family, no forwarding addresses, no social media accounts, no credit card transactions.... Vanished."

"Sus." Jenna paused to turn a page and wrote in her notes. "Let me see what my sleuthing skills turn up. What about this other character?"

"Ryan McFadden," Clara said. "He was the prime suspect in the Woodland Phantom killings. Assault, assault with a deadly weapon, domestic violence against his parents, and illegal trespassing were just some of the crimes listed by the time he was nineteen years old."

"Is there a record of *his* interview?"

"Sort of. He lawyered up quick," Benji said. "Everyone said he did it, but there was no evidence. No fingerprints, no DNA, no witnesses."

"What about his alibi?"

"He wouldn't say. They questioned him for hours, but without proof, they had to let him go."

"Where is he now?"

"Dead. The next year, he was incarcerated after a bar incident and stabbed with a shiv." Benji grabbed a bag of chips off the table and opened the bottom of the bag.

"Doesn't sound like a popular guy. Hey, do you know your bag's upside down?" Jenna cocked her head, as if deciphering the brand from an unconventional angle.

"Every time! It drives my OCD bonkers!" Clara slapped his arm. Benji chomped on his chips with a carefree smirk, and she rolled her eyes.

"Was Ry Mac ever arrested?"

"Not for the murders," Benji said through crunching bites.

"So, he still could have done it?"

Clara turned to Benji. "Theoretically, but nothing ties him to the murders except suspicions."

"Let me get this straight. They had more than enough evidence for the guy locked up than for the guy actively attacking people? Now, that's messed-up." Jenna grabbed her phone and started typing.

Benji lounged in the chair, his feet casually resting on the table and his arms leisurely stretched behind his head. Clara craned her neck to catch a glimpse of the activity on Jenna's screen.

"I'm checking for Ry Mac's info. Several news articles. This one is interesting. McFadden robs a corner store with a knife. Could it be the murder knife?"

"No," Benji said. "The murder weapon was a black Gerber StrongArm. McFadden carried a silver pocketknife."

"Was the murderer a righty or a lefty?" Jenna pinched at her screen.

"Right-handed," Clara said.

"This guy appears to be a lefty." Jenna held her phone for Clara. "His arresting picture shows him with the knife in his left hand. There's another picture with him making a gesture with his left hand at the journalist. While definitely a troubled kid, he's not likely our suspect."

Benji agreed. "The police were seeking a scapegoat to appease the community's concerns. They protected themselves by pointing fingers at an easy target, finding a scapegoat instead of the true culprit."

Jenna scribbled notes in her notebook, then paused and lifted her eyes. "And you said there were no more killings after your parents?"

Clara pulled her knees up to her chest. "No. I mean yes, we said that. There are no additional homicides that are directly linked to the Woodland Phantom's methodology. Some believed it really was McFadden because no murders happened after he was caught and killed. Due to the tremendous media coverage surrounding my sister's disappearance, other news outlets assumed the serial killer remained dormant. Perhaps he was waiting for the media frenzy to die down."

"It was all over the national news, and people's imaginations ran wild with possibilities," Benji said. "Speculations that the killer was imprisoned for tax evasion or had a heart attack. Another account said he fled the country after killing the child. The media coverage would overwhelm the killer. Some say he felt so guilty he committed suicide. You let a story run open-ended and people fill in the blanks."

"But there's no proof she's dead," Clara quickly added. "It was all gossip and superficial speculation, but nothing substantial."

Benji fidgeted with the edge of the table while Jenna drummed her finger over her notes.

"What do we do now?" Clara said.

"We collect the facts, investigate, and locate little Lucy." Jenna glanced at her notes. "What do we know? We know the only person with damning evidence was already locked up at the time of the last killings ... Drewitt."

"We know the suspect was driving a vehicle that matched Drewitt's work truck," Benji added.

"We know a similar truck was reported traveling toward Pittsburgh and not West Virginia with a little girl matching my sister's description."

"What do we *not* know?" Jenna said.

"Who is Marci Verecamp?" Clara said.

"What is Roger Lawrence's involvement?" Jenna said.

Benji shot Jenna a narrow glare as she shot one back.

"What happened to Jack Drewitt?" Clara said, completely oblivious to the silent conflict between Jenna and Benji.

"What happened to Lucy?" Benji whispered.

"There are fifty more questions for every answer." Jenna jotted additional notes.

"What did you write in there?" Clara asked.

FOREVER FAMILY

"Every idea I think of, really. It's how I organize my thoughts."

Jenna checked her phone. "I've gotta go." She sprang from her seat and hastily began stuffing items into her bag. "I'll see what I can dig up on Marci and Jack. Benjamin, you may want to ask your dad a few follow-up questions."

Benji's face wrinkled as he crossed his arms.

"I'm just saying." Jenna shrugged. She put her notes in her messenger bag and opened the door, inhaling deeply.

The aroma of freshly brewed coffee filled the room, enticing Clara's senses.

"Ooh, that smells good. I'm going to grab a coffee before I leave campus. I'll see you guys tomorrow!" Jenna reached over the table, grabbed a bag of chips, and gave a quick wave as she left.

Benji and Clara realized they were alone.

Clara frowned as she filed papers into her folder.

"Clara? Do you want to walk around campus?" Benji asked as he shoved the extra snacks into his bag.

Do I? Not really. "Sure."

Before following Benji out of the study room, Clara carefully arranged the seats around the table. She couldn't help but flash Susan a smile as she walked by the front desk, despite Susan's scowl.

Except for a few students going to Monday night classes and the slender shadows escorting Clara and Benji, the sidewalk was empty. The wind rustled the leaves as it made its way through the buildings of the university. Clara inhaled deeply as the lovely scent of honeysuckle carried on the wind, helping her to release the tension built up in her shoulders.

The birds swooped and dipped through the branches, busy

making their last nesting preparations for the evening. The high-pitched chirp of crickets and the low-pitched croak of lake frogs convey an illusion of being immersed in nature.

Clara closed her eyes, embracing nature's a cappella performance and envisioning herself soaring beyond her problems.

"Are you okay?"

Clara blinked. *I forgot Benji was with me.* "Yeah, just enjoying the fresh air. What about you?"

"I'm good."

"You know, Jenna was insensitive, but your dad might know something that could help."

"Yeah, I'll talk to him. But he didn't hurt nobody."

"I know," Clara whispered. Roger would never knowingly cause harm to anyone. It was also difficult for her to accept the possibility that he was mentally unwell. Their conversation froze in the uncomfortable pause that followed.

"Clara, check it out." Benji pointed across the street. The owners stood beside the fence as their many canine companions ran after each other. "That little dog is chasing the big dog."

A chuckle escaped Clara's lips at the absurdity. "Look! There's a cat close behind." *We're just missing the mouse chasing the cat.*

"I can't stay mad at you." She gently punched his arm. "I guess I understand why you didn't tell me, but just remember that it hurts worse to learn you lied and kept secrets from me. I trust you. Don't make me question your words."

"Never again will I betray your trust. That's a Benjamin guarantee!" Benji traced a cross over his chest and saluted Clara.

Laughing, Clara connected her arm to Benji's, snuggling against his warm body as they strolled through campus.

CHAPTER 15

JENNA

The sheer quantity of data available online was astounding. With her keen eye for detail, Jenna felt she could solve any mystery. People's likes, dislikes, histories, plans, friends, adversaries, strengths, and weaknesses were all discoverable via social media. Combined with data from the White Pages, Jenna could create a comprehensive demographic of the person. Except ... Jack Drewitt.

Is this guy real?

It was unusual for Jenna to come up empty. *Everyone dabbles in social media at some point and forgets the information remains. Not this guy. He didn't even advertise his construction gig!*

"How did this guy stay in business without a website?"

Maybe he didn't. That's why he left town.

Jenna discovered an old *Tribune Chronicle* article about Jack Drewitt. *Just one?* "A terrible drowning involving a little child in a nearby lake." Jenna read to herself. "She was survived by her parents, Paul and Cora Drewitt and her eight-year-old brother, Jack Drewitt." *That would make Jack twenty-two years old during the Woodland Phantom killings. It's possible.*

"Let's try arrest records." Jenna readjusted her posture on the carpet and placed her laptop on her legs.

In her room, there were only two pieces of furniture: a bed and a dresser. Unfortunately, she did not have a cozy seating area. Jenna's father typically sought out fully furnished apartments or rental properties to avoid the hassle of moving. However, Jenna decided to choose this place due to its convenient location near the university.

"Great." Jenna's face twisted in annoyance. "The site appears to be taking a siesta for some much-needed updates." She closed her active search tabs and launched a brand-new one, this time targeting Marci Verecamp.

"Bingo! Okay, let's see ... if Clara's mother died when she was twenty-six, assuming Marci Verecamp was about the same age fifteen years ago, she would be forty-one-ish." Scrolling through images, Jenna noted a couple of potentials. "This lady's forty-three." She discovered a woman with an enormous profile after doing some cross-referencing with Mary Wilson.

Hundreds of photographs documented this woman's life since she'd signed up. *Wow! She's an OG member.* The woman appeared to love life and be having a great time. The collection of pictures showcased her encounters in various activities, such as exploring new encounters, attending thrilling parties, and meeting captivating individuals.

Jenna scrolled through the earlier stories. Marci frequently posted. She gave off the vibe of a lively, upbeat, and sociable lady. *Someone I'd hang out with. Let's browse back to Labor Day fifteen years ago.*

Let's see ... September two ...

"Today, I said good-bye to my closest companion. The one friend whose existence I valued more than my own. The man who took her away from me can never earn my forgiveness. Just how selfish can one person be? She was adored by many and despised by none. Mary, I beg you to visit my dreams and haunt my days. *Mi amigo, te extrao mucho!*"

This must be her!

Above the message was a photo of two attractive ladies in their mid-twenties sharing a side embrace while smiling, glowing from the light of their glow necklaces, and raising their fishbowl margaritas in a celebratory toast. A cartoon heart framed their faces. Based on previous images, Jenna recognized the woman on the right as Marci. The woman on the left ...

* * *

"Mommy, I want juice," Jenna said in a small girl's high-pitched voice. She sat at a table in a tall highchair, leaning forward, waving an empty sippy cup.

"May I please have some juice?" the mother corrected.

"You *may* have some if I *may* have some." The young girl perked up and giggled as she sat straighter at the table.

The mother smiled and filled a sippy cup with apple juice.

"Thank you, Mommy."

"You're welcome. Would you like a bagel with your juice?"

"Yes, please. With pink cream!" The girl took a swig from her sippy cup, and a fizzing, crackling noise escaped.

The mother spread strawberry cream cheese on a half bagel and cut fresh strawberries on the side.

As the woman placed the plate in front of Jenna, a delightful scent of green apple wafted around her. "Here you go, Lu-Lu."

* * *

Was that my mom? But she called me Lu-Lu. Maybe she said Ju-Ju. The crease between her brow deepened as she attempted to recall more, but the sound of the front door unlocking distracted her.

Dad's home.

"Jenna?" The hall reverberated with the baritone voice.

"Yeah, in my room!" Jenna minimized the window and opened a new search engine to find more on Marci Verecamp.

Jenna heard her dad's heavy footsteps approach her bedroom, then stop. "You can come in, Dad."

Her father opened the door and entered. "Working on homework?"

"No, I finished my paper last night. I'm researching for Clara. It's nice to hang out with her." *I don't want to ask, but I know he wants me to ask. Ugh.* "How was your date last night?"

"Fine."

"Are you guys going out again?" *Please say no. Please say no.*

"Yes. Thursday night. She wants to go dancing."

She's a bona fide spell-casting, broom-riding witch! "You don't dance."

"*She* wants to go dancing."

Of course she does. She exploits her enchantments to manipulate innocent souls into squandering their hard-earned money on her selfish wants. "You realize she will expect you to dance with her, don't you?" *The grown man's level of obtuseness is shocking.* "You can always cancel." *Cancel, cancel, cancel.*

"No."

Damn it.

"Your growing up made me realize ... at some point, you may move out. You may need a woman's guidance."

What? "It's a bit late for that. I don't need a woman telling me what to do. Is that why you're dating? Because you think I need a mother? That's ridiculous, Dad. We've been on our own my entire life and survived just fine without another woman. If I need advice, I'll just ask you. I like just me and you."

"Huh."

Jenna attempted to interpret his absent expression but failed. *Does he really think at eighteen, I need a mother? Maybe through puberty, but certainly not now.*

"If you want to date, date for you. Don't date for me. I'm eighteen years old, and we've done pretty good together. I think I'm old enough now to make my own choices." *You shouldn't want to date. Dating fills a void. I should be enough.*

"I don't know what I was thinking. Guess I wasn't. You are my life. I only want what's best for you. Sometimes I don't know what that is."

"Daddy, I know that I can always count on you to protect me." Jenna set her laptop to the side and stood to embrace her dad. "I love you."

"I love you, Ju-Ju."

Lu-Lu. Should I ask him about that memory?

Her father leaned forward, craning his neck over Jenna's

shoulder. "Who's Marci Verecamp?"

Jenna released his grip and turned her attention to her laptop. "She was a family friend of the Wilsons years ago before they were killed, and I'm trying to find her." Jenna flipped her laptop over and settled on the floor near the far wall. "There's chicken pot pie on the stove."

"What do you know about the Wilsons?" A coarse and aggressive nature resounded in his deep voice. His nostrils flared, and his body stiffened, resembling an enraged gargoyle.

What's going on? Jenna matched her father's sharp and focused gaze with equal determination. "Do you know about this case? Fifteen years ago, it was all over the news. The Wilsons were murdered while one of their girls slept in the tent and the other disappeared. Clara's the girl from the tent."

The silence swelled into a disturbing stillness. Jenna's father remained unmoving, as if he had turned to stone. A chill ran up Jenna's spine as she felt her father's gaze pass right through her. The air felt heavy and unsettled. She could almost see darkness around his form.

"Dad?" Jenna whispered.

Her father closed his eyes, took a strong breath, then relaxed his shoulders.

"Where did you go? Are you okay?" Jenna attempted a grin, but her lips twisted in an awkward way.

"You will not hang out with this Clara." The sound of her father's voice was unfamiliar.

"There's nothing wrong with Clara. We're just trying to figure out what happened to her."

"The media lies."

"Tell me what you know." She could see his temper rise, but she couldn't stop poking it with a stick to find answers.

"You are forbidden to investigate the Wilson case."

CHAPTER 16

CLARA

"Where's that blasted paper?" Clara dumped the contents of her desk and smeared the documents around the floor. With her current investigative goals taking precedent, she forgot her academic obligations, including an anthropology assignment on the four possible ways to define a family unit, due tomorrow.

Popping bubbles started projecting from her phone. *Not now!* The stacks of papers concealed the submerged sound. Clara pushed papers around until she found her phone.

"Hello?" She failed to hide her irritation.

"Hey, Clara. Hope I didn't catch you at a bad time."

Clara calmed as she heard Jenna's friendly voice. She gave up on her search for the time being, sat back, and inhaled deeply,

FOREVER FAMILY

prepared to hear Jenna out. "No. I just forgot about an assignment due tomorrow. What's up?"

"I need to talk," Jenna's voice faltered. "Do you mind if I come over?"

Clara had grown accustomed to her perpetual sunshine, leaving her somewhat disoriented in her response.

Clara inspected the pile of papers on the floor and bit her lip. "Sure."

An unexpected knock made Clara jump. When she opened the door, Jenna was already waiting in the corridor.

In mockery, Clara's eyes rolled as she exaggerated her words. "At least you gave me a heads-up." She moved to the side, allowing Jenna to enter. Clara's cheeks turned a rosy shade as she observed the disarray of items strewn across the floor, reminiscent of a tornado's aftermath.

Moving strategically, Jenna navigated around to the roommate's desk chair.

Clara swiveled her chair around to face Jenna. "Is everything okay? I didn't think your dad allowed you out this late."

"I told him my friend Gerdy needed help with our group project. He wants me home by eleven."

Clara noticed Jenna surveying the scattered mess on the floor and casually shrugged.

Jenna stepped over the papers, snatched the water bottle from the desk and took a sip. "My dad knows something but refuses to tell me."

Clara stooped down, trying to organize the chaos while continuing the conversation. "Something from his date? What? Why do you think he knows something?"

Jenna shook her head. "Don't you have anything stronger to drink here?" She gulped the water like a chaser. "Marci Verecamp is all over social media. My dad came in my room and freaked out when he saw the name on my screen."

"What did he say?"

The desk chair screeched under Jenna's weight. "Not much, really. Just that the media lies, and I'm forbidden to investigate."

"Forbidden?" Why would he forbid research into a cold case? Clara reached for her water bottle on her nightstand and sipped the refreshing liquid.

"This project took a surprising turn. Karma for mistreating Benjamin. Oh, how the poison shifts hands." Jenna propped her foot on her knee and took a swig from the bottle, clearly pretending it contained something other than water.

"The media lies? What did they lie about?"

"I don't know." She took another swig.

"Did you ever live in Ohio?"

"No. Not that I remember. Before my mom passed away, I lived in Illinois, but we traveled all throughout the Midwest: Illinois, Pennsylvania, Tennessee, Kentucky, Indiana, even Georgia once upon a time, but never Ohio. Maybe my parents knew your parents?" Jenna traced the patterns along her cargo pockets. "Feels like I've been smacked right in the middle of the twilight zone. I've never seen my dad so upset and angry."

Clara leaned closer. "Did he say anything else?"

Jenna pulled her knees up to her chest. "I couldn't push him. Not then. His aura cast a menacing shadow. He knows something. Something clearly shook him to the core, and I couldn't tell if it was anger or fear. He stormed out of my room and locked himself in his office. I heard him pacing until he tipped over a stack of boards, swearing under his breath, and began sawing. I knew the therapeutic sawing might cause trouble with the neighbors, but I had no intention of getting in the way. When things settled, I told him I had to go."

After a moment, Jenna blinked and looked at Clara again. "I'm all right. It's just seeing my dad like that. He's always intentional and in control, and he lost it." Her voice trailed. "I didn't know where else to go. I don't have close friends."

That can't be true. "But you're popular. Lots of people hang out with you."

"Oh, I have a lot of hangout friends, but no true friends. I compartmentalize my school, social, and personal life. Too many risks on the personal level when we move all the time."

"I feel the same way. Benji is the only person I've ever felt comfortable with. Perhaps that's why I overreacted to his deception."

"You have every right to feel the way you do. If Benji's a true friend, he'll understand, which I have a strong feeling he will. He really likes you." Jenna winked, causing Clara's cheeks to warm.

"We've been friends for a long time. Longer than I can remember, apparently." Clara tried to hide her amusement at her own irony.

"I don't mean that kind of like. Benji's smitten. Twitterpated! He's in *love*." She puckered her lips.

It was as if Clara's cheeks were on fire. "Oh, stop. He's like a brother. Let's change the subject." Clara moved to her mattress and sat against the wall.

Jenna giggled.

In the subsequent uncomfortable stillness, Jenna started tapping her fingers unconsciously on her thigh. "Clara, may I ask a delicate question?"

"Okay." Clara's voice stretched.

"Do you remember your mom?"

My mother?

"If it's too personal, forget I asked."

"No, it's okay. My mom was beautiful and funny, and creative. She loved to travel but not outdoors. She was always wearing a charm bracelet with all the places we traveled as a family." Clara smiled. "She loved taking me and Lucy to the beach but hated swimming and the sun. She'd find the best spot beneath a tree to spread out a picnic blanket and watch us play. There are details about her that I have forgotten, like what she read before bed or what nickname she called my dad. Oh, she always smelled of fresh green apples. When I lived with my uncle Jonathon, I had him buy the same shampoo and conditioner, so I wouldn't forget her smell."

Jenna's face was filled with sadness, a shadow cast upon her once vibrant spirit.

"Do you remember your mother?" Clara said.

"Not really. I was three when she passed. I believe I still have dreams about her. I remember sitting at the kitchen table waiting for her to fix me a snack. Her dark, shoulder-length hair was naturally wavy. Still, I can't swear by the authenticity of those recollections. My father avoids all discussions about her. Years ago, he said he loved my mother so deeply that her death has prevented him from talking about her."

"Don't you have any pictures or videos?"

"No. After Mom passed away, my father said there was a fire

and we lost everything. Only a stuffed animal from my childhood survived. I love the crazy thing. My dad said it was a gift before my mother died, but I don't remember."

"No digital pictures?" *Who doesn't have pictures?*

"No. Strange, huh? The earliest photos I have are from the year I started school. My father didn't take pictures." Jenna glanced at Clara. "Why do guys keep secrets? They think we are too weak to deal with the truths of life. I'm not a kid anymore. I am a woman. I can handle whatever he tells me."

"Now it's up to us to discover the truth for ourselves," Clara said. "We can do this together. We'll find out about Marci Verecamp, Roger Lawrence, and now Mr. Dean."

"Nicholas Dean," Jenna added.

CHAPTER 17

CLARA

"Clare Bear? Where are you?" The sound of Lucy's voice echoed softly through the forest, causing the leaves to rustle in the gentle breeze.

"I'm right here!" In the midst of the tempest, Clara found herself consumed by an overwhelming sense of apprehension, causing her body to tremble involuntarily. Her lips moved with urgency, yet the turbulent gusts devoured her words.

"The trees are angry. I'm scared!" the ghostly voice trailed in the wind.

"Please, Lucy. Where are you?"

"I'm scared, Clare Bear! Why won't you help me?"

Clara felt a cold, wet substance making its way down her

cheek. She felt moisture. The pale glow of the moon melted into a dark, translucent liquid shimmering with supernatural beauty. She discovered a vast emptiness engulfing the sparkling lights of the nocturnal tapestry. Clouds swirled overhead, unleashing a deluge of weighty droplets from the heavens.

Lucy's bloodcurdling scream pierced the darkness, its chilling echo reverberating through the desolate abyss. The relentless rain intensified, transforming into a torrential downpour, as if the heavens themselves were sobbing in sheer terror.

"I'm not here. It's not real."

Clara's focus was hijacked by the sound of splashing water and its forceful impact against her leg. As the puddle waters grew larger, she felt a surge of fear press behind her eyes, and she frantically tried to find a place that offered a semblance of safety. With the murky depths rising, she clawed to a taller boulder, her heart racing. With each step she took, it felt as though she was gradually sinking farther down.

Lucy's scream cut through the clouds, intensifying the rainstorm upon the rugged rocks.

"Please, Lucy," Clara cried.

She could feel the frigid touch of the unyielding stones beneath her feet. The stones, slick with moisture, seemed to shift with each step, adding to her instability. Below her, the dark waters crept closer. Struggling to rise, she felt the unforgiving stones puncture her flesh with a sharp precision. Disregarding the agony inflicted by the stone's assault, she allowed her adrenaline to seize command. She forced her trembling body to ascend, clawing her way up the treacherous terrain. With her heart pounding, every step was a struggle against fear and exhaustion. The air grew thick as if nature itself held its breath in anticipation. With every passing moment, the path became steeper, more treacherous, as if the very earth conspired against her. Finally, she pushed herself to the limit, reaching a point where her trembling limbs could no longer carry her any higher. The realization struck her like a bolt of icy terror: She was trapped.

Crouching down for balance, she searched the sky for a place of safety as the frigid waters continued to rise. A tree limb above was just beyond her grasp. She steadied herself on her feet. As she leaped, the granite beneath her feet slid and her body involuntarily tensed, bracing for an impending collision. Blood coated her hands, the source of which she didn't know. She hated blood. She rubbed her hands on her skirt, but the blood remained stained on her hands, refusing to disappear.

As Clara's mind wandered, she couldn't help but fixate on her father's basketball lessons, particularly the way to stabilize her feet for a jump. *Power, speed, and skill. Balance, elbows, eyes, and follow through.*

In a swift surge of energy, she launched herself toward the twisted limb.

I made it!

Clara's life rested with the limb's questionable strength. A grievous groan escaped the ancient tree. Her grip tightened, causing the tree to emit a disturbing creak. As she attempted to lift her trembling leg onto the branch, a silence fell upon the air, suffocating any trace of sound. The tall trees, with their gnarled limbs that extended like bony fingers, appeared to be holding their breath, as if they were aware of the terrible tragedy that was about to transpire.

FOREVER FAMILY

The branch snapped with a sickening crack, sending her hurtling down into the frigid abyss. She shattered upon the partially exposed stone, a surge of agony coursing through her vertebrae, leaving her gasping for air as her figure twisted and contorted in unnatural ways. As she struggled to free herself from the treacherous branch, a searing pain shot through her right hand. She cradled her hand and rolled onto her knees, her lungs on fire for each desperate breath.

She extracted a jagged shard of wood from her bleeding hand, leaving her feeling helpless as the dark waves crashed against her feet on the platform. Silent tears slipped away. Her focus concentrated on the intimidating cliffs that loomed above, casting a shadow over her. No path to safety presented itself, trapping her in a nightmarish predicament.

Clara's scream pierced through the storm. "Lucy, please stop. You're hurting me."

Silence.

No howls echoed through the stillness; no raindrops pattered against the earth; no trickling of water could be heard; no signs of life stirred. Silent as the depths of the underworld, not a single cricket dared to utter a sound. No sound except for the ceaseless pounding of Clara's heart coursing through her body.

A mysterious hum resonated from the depths of the unknown, casting a haunting presence within the stillness.

What is that? It sounds like purring.

Clara concentrated on the towering cliffs. Water dripped beyond the brink. She cupped her hands into the clear droplets, trying to cleanse the blood staining her palms. A single, warm drop slid down her pale cheek.

Her fingertips pulled away with the crimson substance she feared most. She couldn't help but look up, compelled by the disturbing scene above. Crimson droplets cascaded from the heavens, staining the world below in a disturbing hue. The thick matter ran down the jagged rocks and into the raging waterfall.

A high-pitched shriek, eerily similar to a banshee's cry, resounded in the shadows.

"Lucy!"

A violent surge from the crimson waterfall pulled Clara's feet out from beneath her, dragging her down into the dark waters.

"I'm not here. It's not real." Her breath caught in her throat as her head emerged from the murky depths.

Her appendages convulsed in an unnerving choreography. Despite her rigorous swim training, her body refused to obey her commands. As she reached for floating debris, it dissolved into the dark metallic liquid with a single touch. Struggling to breathe, she encountered the red wave flooding her lungs, producing an intense burning sensation.

A compulsion compelled her to persevere. With each strike of the opposing current, her right hand pulsed in pain. The sticky liquid clung to her like a malevolent force, dragging her down with each motion. Every attempt to break free was met with resistance, as if the red liquid was determined to claim her.

Without warning, her right ankle was seized by a presence, rough and unsettling.

Lucy! Please! As she was dragged into the abyss, her tears were stolen, leaving her unable to express her fear.

Dragging her deeper into the darkened waters, the trees, hidden from view, ensnared her. Her feeble attempts to resist were

FOREVER FAMILY

futile as her limbs turned to mush. Her body was pulled down by the overwhelming power of the roots. Her lungs were ablaze with each breath as the thick red fluid replaced her oxygen. As she writhed in agony, the gnarled roots coiled tighter around her ankles, refusing to let go.

The air abandoned Clara's body, leaving her gasping and struggling for breath. The roots dragged her farther into the shadowy depths. Her final breaths echoed in the crimson waters, punctuated by the sound of bubbles departing her lips.

"Lucy!"

* * *

Her breath escaped in short gasps, as Clara sprang up in bed and kicked her legs. Her eyes were darting in all directions.

My room. This is my room.

Her hand quivered, the subtle tremor betraying her distress as she grabbed the glass of water at her bedside. Meanwhile, her other hand pressed against her chest, anchoring her wildly beating heart. The sight of the trees was truly captivating. Bathed in the warm embrace of the morning sun, they appeared to be ablaze. The wind stirred a flurry of colors, transforming the reds and oranges into mesmerizing dancing flames.

Something on the nightstand started vibrating, catching her attention. She noticed moisture on her pillow as she leaned over to grab her phone.

"Hey, Benji." Clara's voice strained from her dry throat. She took another sip of water.

"Oh man! You sound rough. You all right?"

"Yeah, what's up?"

"I'm downstairs. Thought you'd want to get breakfast."

"What time is it?" Clara ran her hand through her unruly hair.

"Seven-thirty."

Clara glanced at her old-fashioned alarm clock. She must have forgotten to set it. "Okay, give me a few minutes. I'll be down shortly."

"Sounds good. And don't call me Shortly!"

Clara disconnected the call, her lips refusing to curve into a smile despite Benji's feeble attempt at humor. She put her phone on the nightstand, took a few therapeutic deep breaths, and got up to collect her toiletries and outfit. The first thing she did was jump in the shower and try to forget about the past few hours.

On her way out of the dorm, Clara saw Benji lounging on the steps.

Benji stood to greet Clara and walked with her down the steps. His arched tone betrayed his concerns. "The trees?" he asked.

Clara shrugged. "Yeah. They tried drowning me."

"Jeez-a-wheezy, Clara." Benji placed an arm around her shoulders.

Clara smiled at Benji's usage of her invented expression.

"Seriously, are you okay?" He gave her shoulder a slight squeeze.

"Yeah. Just need some coffee."

"Oh, I forgot!" After turning around, Benji ascended the stairs to take two coffee cups off the platform.

"You are my hero, good sir!" Clara lifted the gift and bowed theatrically. Smelling the delicious, bitter coffee grounds eased her shoulders. "Mmm. Thanks, Benji."

"You're welcome."

They rounded a corner and headed for the student union's eatery.

"Clara?"

"Yeah?" Clara sipped from her cup.

"I called my dad last night."

Clara came to a screeching halt as she nearly choked on her coffee. Her eyes widened as she pressed for more details. "About …?"

"About him and your parents. He wasn't shocked, but he was caught off guard. After lunch, he said you can come over and ask him whatever you want."

After lunch? What would I say? Hey, I know you stalked my mom. Do you have any idea who murdered her? I wouldn't dare. Clara chewed her lip as she thought.

"I'll be with you," Benji said, understanding Clara's internal conflict. "He wants to share his side."

"I don't think your dad did anything."

"Maybe, but I saw the doubt in your eyes when I mentioned him."

She looked away, regretting her own thoughts. "Okay, I'll ask if Jenna's free." Clara took her purse off her back and reached inside for her phone.

He placed his hand over hers. "If it's okay with you, Jenna is a bit … much. Just you and me. We can update her after," Benji said.

"I guess you're right. Your dad relaxes with familiar faces. Should we pick up lunch before we go?"

"Sure. Mack Shack's on the way. Tonight, the film department's hosting *Movie on the Lawn* outside the Old Main. Wanna go?"

"Sure. What's playing?"

"*And Then There Were None*. It's a black-and-white Agatha Christie murder mystery."

"How serendipitous. More mystery." Clara's exhaustion sabotaged her witty sarcasm, preventing her from being able to muster a genuine smile. "Yeah. I'll go. It should be fun."

* * *

"Are you sure your dad wants to talk to me?" Clara shouted over the air circulating in Benji's Jeep.

A gentle breeze caressed Clara's face. Her cheeks were tinged with the red hue of the car she was riding in. They drove the less-traveled routes, embracing the refreshing breeze that flowed through the open windows since the air-conditioning system failed to function. The fall weather always kept her guessing, with its unpredictable shifts from cold to hot and back again, sometimes even within the same day. After several attempts at tucking her hair behind her ears, she realized she was losing the battle against the wind, and she pulled her hair back into a ponytail.

"Are you kidding?" Benji shouted over the roar of the wind. "I think he likes you more than me. He knew you'd talk to him someday."

What does he think I'll say? What does he think I want to know? If he was involved, would he tell me?

Clara had never had the patience for puzzles. Now it was as if her whole life were composed of pieces that weren't guaranteed to fit together or even come from the same box. No corner pieces outlined the frame of her life.

Open farmland spread out from the suburbs. Clara's heart raced as they neared, and she jerked when a gentle hand touched her leg.

"Relax. Woo Sah! Have you seen *And Then There Were None*?"

Clara realized she was biting her lip. "No. I read the book years ago but don't remember much."

"Good! The movie and book are different but good. The acting is …." Benji brought his clenched fingers up to his mouth and kissed them sarcastically. "Mwah! Superb! Here we are!" After making it up the lengthy driveway, Benji parked his Jeep behind his father's black Tacoma.

Between her uncle's passing and the start of college, Clara had stayed at this house for six months. She felt welcomed and loved by Roger and Benji. Roger and Benji shared the master bathroom so that she could have her own in the hallway, and Benji put all of his stuff in the cold attic so that she could have a warmer room. They went to extraordinary lengths to welcome her as one of the family. The attic offered a peaceful environment for listening to music, while the living area was perfect for watching movies.

Upon arriving, she began to have serious doubts about the place, something she hadn't considered before. The aging two-story house, once pristine white, now bears the marks of time and weather exposure. One of the side windows was still boarded up after a tree fell during the last storm. The front shrubs looked as though they hadn't been pruned in decades. The two attic windows gave the impression of watchful eyes condemning anyone who entered.

Benji entered first, oblivious to the gloomy ambiance. Once more, Clara looked up at the unsettling windows before following Benji.

She was greeted by a delightful scent as she walked through the entryway. *Mmm, cookie dough.*

Benji inhaled deeply and glanced behind him. "Mmm-mmm. You really need to visit more often. Dad only bakes for you."

Clara's phone vibrated in her purse. *Jenna.* She typed out a short message and returned her phone. She followed Benji into the kitchen, where she was hit with the smell of freshly baked chocolate chip cookies.

"Oh, oh! That's hot!" The baking sheet wobbled on the cooling rack as Roger flung the hot tray out of his covered hands.

"Hey, Dad."

"Hi, Mr. Lawrance," Clara said, following Benji around the kitchen island.

"Hey, kids. One moment."

Clara sat on a stool while Benji poured three cups of cold milk. Clara's muscles loosened up the moment the milk cooled her throat, and she melted into her seat.

"Clara, sweetheart, I'm glad you're here. Though I hoped this day would never come." The latter came out as a whisper. "Please let me talk without questions. I may not have the courage to continue if interrupted."

Taking off his toasty mittens, Roger set a plate of cookies on the center island. The glistening chocolate specks caught Clara's attention, promising a delectable experience. However, an unsettling feeling in her stomach hinted at a different outcome. Benji passed Roger a glass of milk, and he sat down across from them.

Roger took a sip of the milk, cleared his throat, and began speaking. "I wasn't popular in school. Distancing myself from other people made me an easier target for bullying and teasing. Navigating the day being ridiculed and abused by jocks, populars, and even stoners was like walking through my own personal nightmare. I hated school and everyone in it, until I met your mother, Mary Martinelli." Roger grinned while speaking her name. "She was the new kid at school, but her charm and outgoingness quickly won the hearts of everyone she met.

"I was walking to class when a popular kid slammed me against the lockers and asked me why I was so weird. I remained silent despite my rage surpassing my fear. Engaging only worsened the situation, I had learned. He kept calling me names and saying nasty things about my family until Mary walked between us and bravely snatched me away from the kid by linking her arm through mine, saying she needed my help." Roger's smile stretched.

"After we turned the corner, Mary asked if I was okay. To be honest, I was completely at a loss for words. I couldn't remember how to speak. She introduced herself, and I managed to ask what she needed from me. She smiled and said she thought I could use a friend. We became friends. Not super close, but friends.

"After high school, I didn't see her again until she was married with two beautiful girls." He glanced at Clara, then looked back into his milk. "When my wife left me, Benny and I were in a bad way. She left without a word and drained my bank account. We were left with no way to pay the rent or groceries. I managed to get a small pay raise. Enough to feed us for a couple weeks. We moved into a homeless shelter for a few months to save money, until a coworker of mine found out and offered his shed out back. It at least had privacy and electricity and no transients. Every day brought new worries about how I was going to keep my boy safe and fed. I tried to keep him from my fears with stories of grandeur. Later, I learned that my mind developed delusions to cope with stress. Mary appeared as my rescuing angel as she strolled down the grocery aisle. Me and Benny's luck had finally changed.

"I followed Mary to her house. You guys lived along Braceville Park. I saw you and Lucy helping your mom carry groceries inside. A happy family. *And* you looked around Benny's age. It was perfect.

"After everyone went into the house, I drove around the property. The Fates smiled upon me. Right next door, there was a house for rent. I pulled up to the curb and retrieved a flyer. I was able to put down a deposit and move in within a month thanks to the money I had saved.

"Mary recognized me immediately and flashed her contagious sunshine-on-a-cloudy-day smile." A grin spread across Roger's face as he gulped down some milk. "She introduced me to Tom. He was a good man, but I felt bad for him. In my mind, I believed Mary was under some sort of spell that prevented her from recognizing her true love. I liked Tom. He was an innocent bystander who fell in love with the wrong girl. I didn't want to hurt him, but I was determined to end the curse and give Benny the chance to grow up with the mother he was meant to have.

"You and Benny became good friends, but your mom became less comfortable with me. The curse was getting stronger, and I didn't know how to break it. She stopped letting you girls come over and banned me from her house. I assumed I was getting close to breaking the spell. That's why Mary was confused. She knew her life was changing, and she wasn't sure what to do.

"That brings us to the camping weekend. The night before, I

thought I heard something rustling outside. I went to your house and looked through the windows to make sure everyone was okay. Your dad was with you girls in the kitchen, filling your water bottles for bed. Your mom was in her bedroom, getting out of her work clothes. I am ashamed to say that I lingered for far too long, and she noticed me. I ran home after hearing her scream. I didn't mean to frighten her. I was trying to protect her. Tom threatened me when I told him Mary was destined to be with me. He became angry and said that me and Benny couldn't go camping. That hurt my heart … and Benny's."

Clara stole a glimpse at Benji as he lowered his face and munched on a cookie. Her stared at her own untouched cookie as Roger continued.

"That morning, me and Benny looked out the window and saw your van pull out of the driveway. Mary looked sad. As they pulled out, she and I locked eyes. Her voice echoed in my mind, calling for my help just like she had in the past.

"We went to a kids' pizza playhouse for lunch. Benny met new friends, and they all had a great time eating pizza and making fun of the animatronics for hours. His ability to see the silver lining in every cloud made me very proud." For an instant, Roger looked away from his milk glass and into his son's face. He raised the cup to his lips before resuming his speech.

"We didn't get home until late, so Benji took a bath, and I tucked him into bed. While I was reading in the living room, my thoughts kept returning to Mary. Somehow, I knew she was in trouble. I checked on Benji and found him sound asleep in his bed. He giggled in his sleep, and I knew he was happy. Nelson Ledges was only fifteen minutes away, so I decided to go check on Mary."

CHAPTER 18

JENNA

Sitting in the Old Main courtyard, Jenna leaned back on her blanket to let the sun gently warm her skin. The sunlight provided a refreshing break from the gloomy classrooms. She intended to spend time with Clara after class, but her plans fell through when Clara didn't respond to her text messages.

Guess I'm not needed. Nothing more than a morbid fascination, anyway. I bet they're talking to Benjamin's dad.

Jenna wasn't able to stay still for very long. She glanced at her laptop but dreaded the thought of schoolwork. "If they can investigate alone, so can I." She adjusted her posture and screen angle to optimize visibility despite the courtyard's shadows and reflections.

If she knew more about the case, she might be able to figure out how her dad was involved. "What a wicked turn of events. How in the name of Mother Nature is my dad involved in this ancient murder mystery?"

Jenna reviewed the media feeds on Marci Verecamp. Shielding her laptop screen from the sun with one hand, she delved into researching her new person of interest. Marci was frequently photographed at parties, capturing her vibrant personality.

"Marci enjoys sharing every detail of her life with the public. Let's see...." Jenna clicked on the profile icon to read her bio. "Tsk-tsk, Marci. Identity theft is real. Currently living in Cleveland, Ohio. Originally from Warren, Ohio. Majored in theater. Work, family, dating situation, likes, hobbies, and *bingo*! How to get in touch."

Etched on the front of Jenna's notebook were the words *The Woodland Phantom Murders*. She collected information on the Wilson family, the findings of the investigation, her personal insights, and potential suspects. In her closet, she had a stack of notebooks that were all the same and were from different investigations. Each problem was successfully resolved, mostly through her unique solutions. When she discovered a new interest, she would diligently collect information in a notebook, make educated guesses, and conduct initial research until she either solved the mystery or moved on to the next challenge.

"Marci, Marci." Jenna tsked as if scolding a kid. "I appreciate your efforts to simplify my search, but phone number, address? Once you even advertised a *Having a great time away from home!* photo, giving thieves an open invitation to ransack your house."

Prior to dialing the number, Jenna took a moment to flip through her notebook, refreshing her memory with the notes from the past few days.

"Jenna!"

She turned around, protecting her eyes from the sun, and saw her friend Dustin approaching. Returning her focus to her screen, she acknowledged Dustin with a wave over her shoulder.

Dustin rested his hands on his hips, trying to recover his breath. "Hey, how's it going?" he wheezed.

"Same as always. Missed you at WaHo Friday night," Jenna said without looking up.

"Yeah, I was working on an anthropology project. Josh was supposed to be my partner, but he ditched me to hang out with you guys. You haven't seen him, have you?" Without invitation, Dustin settled himself on the grass next to Jenna.

Even though Jenna was annoyed by Dustin's intrusion, she didn't want to make him angry by dismissing him. He was a regular customer who always left generous tips. Placing her laptop next to her, she raised herself up on her elbows to chat with him.

"Not since Friday. The guy gives me the creeps."

Dustin chuckled. "He's got a crush on you."

"Obviously. It-puts-the-lotion-in-the-basket kind of crush," Jenna mumbled to herself.

"Well, we were supposed to finish this morning, but he didn't show. Didn't even bother coming to class. It's due Friday. Group projects are the worst. I'm always paired with the lazy." Dustin leaned over and picked up a few grass blades. He blew them out of his hand and went on to pluck more.

Few students were on the lawn, but Jenna knew the emptiness wouldn't last. Most settled on the lawn between one and two in the afternoon to take advantage of the outdoors between classes.

Jenna watched the blades of grass flutter to the ground. "I hate to state the obvious, but did you try to call?"

"Yeah. Straight to voice mail."

"Did you ask Kyle? Don't they have math on Mondays?"

"Kyle skipped Monday. Hungover."

"Sorry about your luck. You can destroy him in the peer review."

"Definitely. I'm headed home. You stickin' around campus?"

"Yeah, for a little bit. Doing some research." Jenna settled into a seated position and placed her computer on her lap.

"All righty, then. See ya!" Dustin blew the remaining grass blades over Jenna.

A forced chuckle escaped her lips as she dusted nature off her clothing. When her phone started buzzing in her hand, she checked the notification.

Clara responded.

Yep, Clara's at Benjamin's. I forgot Movie on the Lawn, tonight. I like Agatha, but this isn't the time to test my father's patience. Jenna talked as she texted back. She received a thumbs-up in response. "Tomorrow at one it is."

Jenna looked around the campus grounds and shifted into detective mode. Sitting upright, she scrolled through different sections on her phone, finding it easier to see than the laptop screen.

"Okay … just you and me, Marci." By clicking over to Marci's profile again, Jenna was able to select Marci's cell phone number.

Jenna didn't have to wait long before she got an answer.

"Marci here!"

Very chipper! "Yes, hello, my name is Linda Listerman. Am I speaking with Ms. Marci Verecamp?"

"Yes. How may I help you?"

"I'm hoping you can provide information about Mary Wilson."

Silence. Jenna checked her phone to make sure the connection hadn't been lost. *Nope, still connected. Evidently, people don't want to talk to me.* "Are you still there?"

"Yes, sorry. I can't remember the last time I heard that name out loud. Who did you say you were?"

Not so chipper now. "My apologies for bringing up old memories, but this case has never been solved, and I'm hopeful that new forensic techniques may finally provide some answers to the surviving family members."

"Yes, well, I don't know how I could be any help." The cheerful voice was replaced with hesitancy and grief.

"How well did you know the Wilson family?" Jenna continued.

"I didn't really know the family ... only Mary. She was married to Tom Wilson with two little girls."

"How did you meet Mary?"

"We were best friends in high school." Marci's speech was deliberate and measured.

She's being careful with her words. Perhaps I should ask tougher questions. "Were you not friends with Mr. Wilson?"

"Not really. We didn't hang out. Just me and Mary."

She's telling the truth but not the whole truth. What is she hiding? "When was the last time you saw Mary?"

Jenna could make out a long, deep breath on the other end of the line. She absentmindedly played with a loose string on her blanket.

"I saw her the night before the family went camping."

"Tell me what happened." *It's like asking a teenager how school was.*

"We didn't really talk. Just ... hung out."

"Hung out?"

Silence.

"Was the rest of the family home?" Jenna asked as she tugged at the string.

"No, her husband was at work, and the kids played in the backyard."

Okay.... "What were you two doing?"

"Do I have to answer?"

"It would be in your best interest to provide accurate and truthful information to help the investigation. Failure to do so may result in legal action." *Too much?*

Silence.

Patience. Patience. Allow the silence to work its magic. The thread on her blanket continued to unwind.

"Mary and I were intimate partners. Her husband was unaware of our ongoing relationship," she whispered.

Holy crap, on a biscuit! "Are you saying that you and Mary Wilson were lovers?"

"Yes." Marci let out a sign that appeared to contain decades' worth of suppressed emotion.

"Did her husband ever find out?" Jenna asked.

"I think he suspected, but I have no idea if he knew for sure. I don't want to be painted as a devious homewrecker. I first met Mary before Tom entered the picture, but our love was rejected because of its unconventional nature. We stayed hidden. Mary loved Tom for who he was, but we were soul mates."

"Don't worry. We will handle this information with delicacy. Is there anything that she said that struck you as being strange or out of character that night?"

"No. Her behavior was totally normal, and she even looked forward to the family vacation, even though she hated the outdoors. She loved Tom. I may have been jealous of her split affections, but I was happy for her and her family."

"Do you know Roger Lawrence?" A bumblebee buzzed near Jenna's head, and she shifted away.

"Roger? Roger the neighbor? I know *of* him. Mary didn't feel comfortable around the guy. She said he gave her the heebie-jeebies. You don't think he did it, do you?" Marci asked.

"Nothing is for certain. Could he have ever suspected you and Mary were more than friends?" Jenna said. She released the thread after realizing her blanket had an expanding hole.

"I don't think so. He never spoke to me or left his house while I was there, so I don't know what he knew."

Sitting up on her knees, Jenna consulted her notebook to find the next question. "What about Jonathon Wilson?"

"Tom's brother? I didn't know him, either."

"Do you know why he refused your visitation at the funeral?"

"If Tom suspected anything, he may have shared his concerns with him. Mary described him as a protective older brother, but I never met him until the funeral. He looked just like Tom. I was surprised by his anger, but I wasn't upset. Mary and I had a beautiful friendship, and I'll always cherish our memories."

Jenna allowed Marci a brief pause before posing the next question. "Can you think of anything else that may be relevant to the investigation?"

"I pray you find the person responsible for stealing her from the world. If at all possible, I prefer that the daughter remain unaware of our involvement. I'd hate for her to think badly of her mom."

"I will keep that in mind during the investigation. Thank you for your time. Oh, one more question," Jenna said.

"Yes?"

"Do you know Nicholas Dean?"

"Nicholas Dean? No. The name doesn't sound familiar. Who's that?" Marci asked.

"No one in particular. What about Jack Drewitt?"

"As in Drewitt Construction? I know he was the most delicious handyman in Warren. I never employed him, but my neighbor hired him to build a shed. Oh, that man glistened. I heard he was a mean drunk, though. I don't think Mary knew him."

"Again, thank you for your help."

Once the call ended, Jenna looked away in shock. *A secret lover? What if Tom did find out? What if Roger felt betrayed? How will Clara react? How does my dad fit into any of this?* As she considered each new question, the answers seemed to slip away.

CHAPTER 19

CLARA

The familiar metallic bitterness invaded Clara's tongue. She didn't realize she was biting her cheek so hard. A tingling sensation crept through her body, gradually surrendering to a numbing effect that mimicked the grip of a boa constrictor, constricting the flow of life within her. The relentless thump of her heart sounded like it was banging on her eardrums as it reverberated through her skull.

She forced herself to exhale when Benji patted her leg, but it was as if all the oxygen in the room had vanished. Benji sat there, bewilderment written all over his face. He had no idea his father had left the house that night and followed her parents into the woods, and he had no idea how to help her now.

Nausea threatened her stomach. She questioned whether she

should listen to the rest of the story. *He was there.* Roger had stood in the middle of those tall trees. Did his shaking hands and his sweaty forehead mean he was about to confess? As she got ready for what was going to be said, her heart was beating fast in her chest. Could she handle the truth?

Roger's head swung back and forth like a pendulum, reflecting his struggle to express his thoughts clearly. He continued despite Clara's wavering thoughts. "The previous week, Tom and I had discussed the trip at length and even driven to the park to scope out the area. They were encamped somewhere between Minnehaha Falls and the lake's northwest shore. I left my car on a service road along Route 282 and hiked into the woods. I could see their campsite wasn't too far away thanks to the fire's reflection off the trees. I slowed when I heard the fire crackling."

Roger spoke with hesitation, his words carefully chosen and delivered at a slower pace. Tears threatened to spill from the corner of his eyes.

"Quietly making my way through the underbrush, I spotted her." His untamed beard caught the first tear as it rolled down his cheek. "She was just lying there, next to the fire. Tom, next to her. At first, I thought they were sleeping, but they didn't look comfortable. I leaned around the trees for a closer view. She wasn't moving. In the chilly air, her breath was invisible. Her chest didn't rise or fall. I grabbed a rock next to my foot and threw it into the fire. Sparks flew everywhere as the charcoaled wood fell, but she didn't move."

Roger went on, rubbing the stubble on his chin. "I whispered her name. No response. I left my hiding place and moved closer. That's when I saw the blood. I felt sickness rising in my throat. It dawned on me that danger could still be nearby. I scanned the area but found nothing ... no animals, no enemies, no signs of life, except for the crickets that kept chirping as if nothing had changed. I walked closer and whispered her name again. The milkiness of her eyes seemed to glow in the darkness. Without tears, blind to the world, and devoid of the kindness she previously radiated. Mary was gone.... Her lifeless body lay in a black puddle, her leaking heart giving the impression that she had been dropped onto an abandoned oil spill."

The tears could no longer be controlled. "Mary was gone. Someone killed her! I was right to worry. I touched the dark puddle, and it was warm. The murderer had to be close. At the time, I was too scared to be angry. I realized the police may think I did it because I was not supposed to be there. In a daze, I found myself back at my car and drove home. I didn't even think to look for you two girls. My world had ended. I barely remember getting home. It took deliberate force to unglue my fingers from the wheel. I finally went inside to check on Benny. He was still sleeping soundly ... peaceful, naive, and unaware. I locked myself in my room and grieved for the mother he'd never know."

Acid rose to the base of Clara's throat, causing her stomach to twist. Her throat became raw and moist with excessive saliva. She raised the glass of milk to her lips, but the pure white liquid made her stomach churn.

After muttering an apology, she bolted through the back screen door. Clara heaved as she leaned over the deck railing, but nothing came. She dropped to her knees, leaning against the wooden slats, and let her tears flow freely as she buried her face in her arms. She remembered finding her mom in the same manner

FOREVER FAMILY

Roger had described. A sense of powerlessness seized her, as if cold fingers were squeezing her neck. Everything she had known in the world vanished into thin air, leaving her stranded in that desolate forest.

A chilly rag was draped around her neck. When she looked up, she saw Benji's painful expression as he offered her a tissue and a glass of water.

"I'm sorry, Clara. I had no idea. I don't know what to say."

Clara took a sip from Benji's water glass before setting it down. She fiddled with her fingers until the skin was a mosaic of red and white splotches.

Benji took a seat next to her. She leaned into his arms. His light gray shirt darkened with her tears.

"I'm sorry. The pain remains a constant reminder, piercing and intensifying with each passing moment." Clara paused briefly, deep in thought. "I wasn't the first to find them. Your dad must have been afraid. And not being able to talk to anyone?"

Clara leaned against Benji, finding solace in his presence, and took deep breaths to calm herself. She felt a range of feelings for Roger and Benji, wishing they had been more forthcoming about their struggles. Roger's occasional gullibility could elicit sympathy, but when he chose to hide the truth from her ... from the police ... She found herself entangled in a fierce struggle of emotions, uncertain of which would ultimately prevail. She still didn't understand what truly happened that night. *His presence explained one set of footprints, but who else was there? Who killed my parents? Who took Lucy?*

Clara reached for the water glass and took a sip after a few moments of silence.

"Are you okay? Do you want to return to campus?"

"Yeah, I'm fine. But there's one more thing I need to ask your dad."

Benji got to his feet and helped Clara up to hers.

Just before entering the house, she straightened her skirt and dusted off the particles of dust clinging to it. Roger sat at the kitchen island, drinking a beer, staring down the bottleneck.

"Mr. Lawrence, thank you for telling your story. I know that wasn't easy. Finding my mother and father is something that still haunts me. If you don't mind, I have one more question."

Roger lifted his head from his beer. His eyes had turned red as tears waited to fall from them. "Go ahead, darling. Ask me anything."

"Did you drive a green truck?"

"No. A gray Civic."

"Did you see anyone else that night or have any idea who killed them?"

"I didn't see anyone. I've been wondering every day who could do something so horrible. The guy they call the Woodland Phantom killed your parents the same way those other people were killed. If I could find out who it was, I'd kill him myself. Maybe someone did find him and kill him."

"Do you think he took Lucy?"

Roger shook his head. "I'm sorry, Clara, but he's never let anyone live."

* * *

Despite the heat, Clara was relieved that Benji's Jeep didn't have air-conditioning. The forceful gusts of wind provided a convenient excuse to avoid talking. As she glanced out the window, a blur of

FOREVER FAMILY

fields and farms rushed past, accompanied by the pungent scent of cow manure lingering after the heavy rain. However, she was soon drawn to the serene sight of trees in the distance, which appeared to move at a more leisurely pace. Life was going at an incredible rate, but she still mourned the death of her family.

Benji was the one to finally break the awkward silence. "Do you still want to see the movie tonight?"

With a start, Clara opened her eyes. She must have zoned out. The school parking lot was full of cars and pods of students talking. "Of course."

Benji narrowed his gaze, apparently doubting her response.

"Really, I'm fine. What time do you want to meet?"

"Let's eat first, then find a good spot on the lawn. I've got blankets and pillows in the back." Benji thumbed over his shoulder.

"Sounds good."

* * *

Outside the student union, a twenty-four-foot inflatable movie screen blocked the art department's educational graffiti. Clara never understood the abstract designs. Once the sun dipped below the horizon, the stars and moon came out to illuminate the night. Many of the other kids had already spread out their blankets on the grass. It was a perfect night for an old-fashioned murder mystery. A few stringy clouds were passing in front of a nearly full moon. The air was slightly cool, just enough to make one's spine tingle. Clara spread the blankets while Benji took care of arranging the pillows to create a more comfortable arrangment. As she nestled down on a pillow, she readjusted her skirt. She patted the top of the pillow to invite Benji to sit next to her.

"Yes, but first ..." Benji moved his backpack to his chest and unzipped the top. "Refreshments!" He smiled triumphantly as he threw each item onto the blanket. "We've got popcorn, Twizzlers, M&M's, Raisinets, and ... Milk Duds!" Tossing Clara the Milk Duds, he grinned like a dog wagging his tail for his excellent behavior.

"You think of everything, don't you?" Clara smiled.

"And ..." He plunged even farther into the depths of his bag. "Dr. Pepper for me, and a Diet Dr. Pepper for my lady." Benji bowed gracefully as he offered the can of soda, like a chivalrous gesture to royalty.

A slight flush bloomed on Clara's cheeks as she accepted the beverage. "Okay, Sir Packs-a-lot. Have a seat. The movie's going to start any minute." Clara defizzed her can with a tap on the top.

Benji took a seat next to Clara. "Just to be clear ... is this a serious movie or a talking movie?"

Clara loved watching movies, but she didn't appreciate it when other people talked during the films. On rare occasions, she found Benji's comedic commentary amusing.

"Well," Clara mused. "We *are* in an uncontrolled environment with no reminders to silence our cell phones; the audience is likely to be unpredictable. Plus, today's been far too serious."

Benji's grin grew wider. He rubbed his hands together as he appeared to plan out the various ways he could make Clara giggle. The film then began to show ten little Indian clay sculptures.

Clara couldn't wait to put the past few days out of her mind for an hour and a half to mentally recharge.

"Would you like me to pop the top to your pop?" Benji asked.

With a grin, Clara passed over her beverage as she ripped open the package of Milk Duds.

Music echoed over the grounds as she watched the black-

FOREVER FAMILY

and-white film. Clara tracked the strategically placed speakers in the grass.

Stories in black-and-white often had fresh perspectives that couldn't be found in color. The styles of the 1940s were bold, expressive, and extravagant. No matter if it was the traditional camera angles, the original acting, the corny jokes, or the situations that "would never happen in real life," the viewer was kept interested and entertained.

"The butler did it. The butler with the rope in the conservatory. It's always the butler," Benji whispered.

"Wrong movie," she smiled.

With the wind rippling under her cover, Clara snuggled closer to Benji. He wrapped an arm over her, and the two of them sat comfortably in the moonlight as the fireflies began to sparkle and dance through the trees.

CHAPTER 20

JENNA

The campus was draped in a thin layer of fog that wouldn't burn off until the sun arrived, early in the morning. The atmosphere at Java Junction was vibrant and lively, but not from Jenna's usual clientele. She didn't typically work the first shift, but she couldn't sleep thinking about all the juicy details she would soon reveal to Clara. She reasoned that if she was going to be awake, she might as well be compensated for it. When Jenna asked for the shift, her coworker Marcus gladly turned off his alarm and went back to sleep.

She found the direct and efficient nature of the order-and-serve customers to be a pleasant change from the use of offensive monikers, but the tips were not as generous. There were more

FOREVER FAMILY

online orders than her usual shift.

"Robin? Robin DePlace?" After hearing her own words, Jenna snorted in surprise. "Is anybody Robin DePlace?" She laughed.

"I thought you might find that amusing." Clara smiled.

"She jokes! Ladies and gentlemen, she jokes!" Jenna said to the few zombie-like students making their way to class.

As she grabbed her coffee, Clara did her best to conceal her embarrassment.

"We still meeting at one?" Clara asked.

"Let's get together at eleven. I'm interested to know more about your exchange with Roger Lawrence. And I have some news that you might find intriguing!"

"What news?" Clara leaned closer to Jenna over the counter. Her thick blond waves cascaded upon her steaming cup of coffee.

"Watch your coffee!" Jenna slid Clara's coffee to the side.

Clara turned to the side and hit her shoulder on the frame of the countertop. "Ow!"

"Careful, Ms. Accident Prone."

"I didn't use to be." Clara massaged her not-so-funny bone. "Anyway, what news?"

"I talked to Marci."

"Hey, I'm ready to order!" A young woman stood on her tiptoes and leaned over the counter to attract Jenna's attention.

"I'll be there in a minute," Jenna snapped. She ignored the customer's obvious disapproval.

She turned to Clara. "Anyway, I want to tell you everything, but you might not like it."

Clara glanced over at the displeased customer. It seemed Clara was not a fan of her customer communication style, yet Clara remained curious about Jenna's knowledge. After all, jenna had to deal with that customer repeatedly, and she was never satisfied with anything.

"Jeez, Jenna! Cut the suspense! Just tell me."

"You've got class. I've got to work. This is hardly the place." She rolled her eyes, annoyed with the girl drumming her fingers on the counter. "See you at eleven."

Jenna turned to the irate customer as Clara left. "How can I help you, O Impatient One?" She performed an elaborate curtsy to the girl, who had a rather unpleasant expression on her face.

As Jenna brewed coffee for a group of tired students, her attention was caught by Benjamin as he joined the line. *Maybe I should ask him what he thinks? He knows Clara and her potential reaction.* Jenna rapidly prepared the orders in front of him.

"Hey, Jenna. Could I get a black Americano?"

"Sure." She started his order. "Benjamin? Do you mind if I ask you something?"

"I'm running late."

"It's important." She marked a cup with his order.

Without waiting for a response, she tossed her apron on the counter and informed the remaining customers that she would be taking a five-minute break. Jenna could make out the muffled sounds of FOX43 News from the next customers watching their phones.

"Catch up on your news. I'll be back before the next commercial."

While waiting for her to return, the two individuals in line grumbled but didn't leave. Jenna then escorted Benjamin around the back of the Java Junction.

FOREVER FAMILY

"Okay. What do you want?" Benjamin snapped.

It was clear that he was either not a morning person or irritated at the thought of talking to her. "Why do you always act like someone's got you in a constant wedgie? We should consult a proctologist to surgically remove whatever splintered wood remains lodged in your rectum."

"Was that your question? Concerns for my health? I have better things to do." As Benji started to leave, Jenna put a firm hand on his shoulder.

"It's about Clara."

Benjamin stopped in his tracks and slowly pivoted.

I knew that would slow him down.

"What about Clara?" Concern replaced most of his annoyance.

"Yesterday, I spoke with Marci Verecamp, but I don't think Clara will be thrilled with the results. Help me tell her who Marci is."

"Who is she?" Benjamin straightened his shoulders and repositioned his backpack.

"Mary's lover."

"Her mother was cheating? I don't believe it." Benjamin lowered his arms and Jenna could tell he was giving it some thought.

"That's what she said. She was reluctant to tell me and didn't want Clara to know."

"This isn't good."

"She didn't believe anyone knew about their relationship, although your dad and Tom might have suspected based on his brother's reaction at the funeral."

"My dad?"

"He had an excellent vantage point. He may have witnessed her dropping by while Tom was at work, occupying the children with outdoor activities, and then leaving before Tom arrived home." Jenna cast a sidelong glance at Benji. "It was not uncommon for him to peek through the windows."

A subtle crease formed at the corner of Benjamin's mouth. "Maybe we shouldn't tell her."

"Seriously? You want to lie to her again? Your most recent betrayal was as painful as a mission-driven assault bee. All she wants is truth. I'll tell her gently."

"Gentle as a wrecking ball against a house of sticks," Benjamin mumbled.

"Speaking of sticks, I know a great colorectal surgeon."

Benjamin, unfazed by the quip, continued. "I guess I can tell her."

"I'll tell her. I talked to Marci. Besides, we're meeting at eleven."

"Clara didn't tell me." Benjamin's voice cracked with sadness. "Where? I'm coming." There was greater conviction in his words.

Jenna curtsied. "Honestly, I can't imagine it any other way."

In a display of determination, Benji strode away, inadvertently leaving behind his cup of coffee.

Meanwhile, Jenna entered the Java gate. Without skipping a beat, she donned her apron and resumed her duties, attending to customers. It was clear to her that informing Clara was the right course of action. Benji's advice proved to be of little value.

As Jenna was pressing coffee grounds into the portafilter, she heard a static voice report, "Breaking news from Nelson Ledges

FOREVER FAMILY

State Park. This morning, a startling discovery has left investigators with more questions than answers. Bones have been unearthed at the park, sending shock waves through the community. Stay tuned as we bring you the latest updates on this developing story."

"Turn that up," she demanded as she abandoned the espresso machine and hopped onto the counter. The student complied, and Jenna took his phone right out of his hands.

"Authorities are currently conducting a thorough investigation into the recent discovery of human bones found at the foot of one of the treacherous cliffs in the vicinity. Two hikers discovered the remains at the base of a twenty-two-foot cliff. The forensic task force is currently on-scene, collecting evidence. Despite the Nelson Police Department's refusal to comment, a witness has come forward acknowledging that the remains belonged to a young child. The circumstances surrounding the child's death, whether accidental or intentional, remain unknown. Rest assured, dear viewers, that as soon as we receive any additional updates, you will be the first to hear it, right here on FOX43."

Jenna froze. "Holy curse of the mummy's tomb."

"Um ... can I have my phone, please?" asked the timid student.

Jenna snapped out of her media news trance. "Sure." She handed back the student's phone and went back to absently brewing coffee.

How will Clara react? What does that mean for our investigation?

CLARA

Why is this class so long? Clara's anthropology class was often one of her favorites, but today it was a distraction from more important matters. *Maybe I should have skipped.* Her mind kept wandering back to what Jenna had discovered despite her best efforts to listen to the lecturer.

"Ms. Clara Wilson?" Dr. Thiel put an end to Clara's mental diversion.

"Yes?"

"I asked you a question. Do you care to respond?"

Clara panicked. "Could you repeat the question, please?" Her cheeks grew a patchy redness.

"Ms. Zeniyah Hendricks. Perhaps you could update Ms. Wilson on what we've been discussing thus far."

The girl to Clara's left sat up straight and wrinkled her nose in response. "Yes, Professor. The question was 'How do the structures and dynamics of a family unit affect an individual's life?'"

"What is your response, Ms. Wilson?"

Clara glanced at the show-off before shifting her focus to the professor. "The family has the greatest impact on an individual's conduct, social conventions, and societal expectations. The structure of the family may provide insight into an individual's views and values concerning primary decision-makers, family customs, economic participation, and personal morals and beliefs. While the concept of family is often associated with blood relations, it is important to acknowledge that familial relationships can extend beyond biological connections." Clara looked at Dr. Thiel hopefully.

"Nicely stated, Ms. Wilson. Does anyone have anything to

add?" Dr. Thiel took her focus off Clara and moved it to another helpless victim who appeared to be staring into nothing.

Clara pondered on Jenna's potential knowledge, curious about what insights she might possess.

* * *

Clara stuffed everything into her bag and was the first one out the door when class was finally over. She sprinted down three flights of stairs to the first floor, hoping she wouldn't fall and break her neck. On her way to the library, she had to weave around students going about their business as usual. Jenna texted from the study room. After a quick text to update Benji, Clara picked up her pace. The library seemed to be miles away from her current location.

After entering the library, Clara ignored Susan at the desk and rushed directly into the study room. Instead of just one person, she discovered two. Jenna and Benji's conversation came to an abrupt halt, leaving them exchanging uneasy glances.

"What's going on, guys?" Clara alternated her sight between them. "Benji, how'd you get here so fast? I just texted." Clara's chest rose and fell rhythmically as she restored her breathing to a steady pace.

What were they talking about?

"Jenna told me you were meeting. I updated her about Dad. She wanted to tell you about Marci Verecamp." Benji avoided making eye contact by looking at the floor.

"Okay ... you're scaring me." Clara, unable to obtain additional information from Benji, turned to Jenna in search of an explanation.

"Clara ... there was more than just platonic friendship between Marci and your mother. They were intimate. They had a secret relationship."

"You're sure?"

"No deceit detected. She was reluctant to share this information."

Clara's mind wandered back to the distant memories. The story gradually revealed the purpose behind the secret gatherings, the exclusion of young people, and the exchange of gifts to maintain secrecy. "Do you think their relationship might have something to do with the mur—"

"No. I don't. Absolutely without a shadow of a doubt, the Woodland Phantom killed your parents. All those couples were murdered by the same person with the same weapon, according to the evidence. Who that is remains unknown. There's no indication of a second killer since we know who the second footsteps belonged to. I doubt Marci could take out an adult man and his wife."

Jenna continued with her theory as she paced in the study. "Serial killers have a compulsion to kill the same way over and over again as they aim to perfect their practice. To the untrained eye, the killer's choices appear arbitrary, but they are always motivated by something deeper. Identifying their plan and their purpose is the challenge. Authorities didn't believe the victims knew their attacker, because the evidence didn't point to crimes of passion. The males were attacked from behind, and the woman was apparently slain while in a state of shock. No words exchanged."

"So, Marci and Roger had nothing to do with the crime," Clara said.

"Not necessarily," Jenna replied.

"What do you mean?" Clara and Benji spoke simultaneously.

FOREVER FAMILY

"Maybe Roger felt rejected when he discovered your mother was seeing someone else, and he became jealous. Maybe he became so angry that he was determined to eliminate the couple that ruined his future. He confessed to being out there that night."

Clara shrank in her seat as if she were being crushed by an invisible force.

Benji slammed a hand on the table. "Would you leave my father out of this? You just said that the victims didn't know their attacker and that there was no evidence to suggest that the acts were motivated by passion. Plus, the killer left his own footprints behind."

Clara decided to steer the discussion away from Benji. "Jenna. Benji's dad is innocent. Drop it."

In response, Jenna crossed her arms as she leaned back, rolled her eyes, and said nothing.

Benjamin's face lit up with a look of appreciation.

"Jenna. Is that all?" Clara asked.

"Now may not be a good time."

Clara witnessed Benji give Jenna a perplexed look.

"Right now is the right time. I'm prepared to hear anything you have to say." Even though Clara's friends were careful around her, she always felt stronger than they gave her credit for. She was given a bad hand, but she didn't give up.

"Did you catch the news this morning?"

Benji and Clara exchanged a puzzled look, shook their heads in unison, and waited for an explanation.

"How about I show you?" Jenna said, pulling out her phone.

"Jenna, stop procrastinating. You're not one to be evasive. Just tell us."

Jenna sighed heavily. "Early this morning, a group of hikers discovered a child's skeleton in Nelson Ledges. Identity unknown, but evidence is being collected. I'm sorry, Clara."

"I don't understand why you're sorry. It's not Lucy. If my sister was dead, I would know. I would know." Even though she knew she sounded crazy, she looked to Benji for help. "Wouldn't I?"

Benji sat in silence.

All at once, a wave of doubt burst into her mind like a flurry of popcorn. *It can't be Lucy. Lucy is still out there waiting for me to find her.*

"I'm not giving up on Lucy. We will continue our investigation and follow the clues." Clara's demeanor exuded confidence, leaving one to wonder if her refusal to acknowledge the truth was merely a mesmerizing facade.

"Yes!" Jenna yelled. "That's my girl."

Benji gave Jenna a condescending glance before putting his hand on Clara's shoulder.

Clara rejected his hand with a shrug. "It's not her! You are free to leave if you have given up. But I will find her."

Jenna gave Clara a nod of approval.

Benji, however, lacked the spark of inspiration.

"What is it, Benji?" Clara asked.

"I really hope Lucy's alive, Clara, but what if those bones are hers?"

"I'm not going to entertain the possibility. Lucy is missing. Not dead. Where do we go from here?" After turning away from Benji, Clara turned to face Jenna.

"The search for Jack Drewitt and his green pickup truck continues," Jenna said. "And my dad has a secret. The problem is, I have no idea what it is."

"Let's collect the fragmented pieces of this puzzle," Clara said. "We won't let the news stop us from finding the truth. Besides, the media lies."

CHAPTER 21

JENNA

The study table was a chaotic scene with office supplies scattered everywhere; notes, files, and pens moving around as if in a quidditch match. Paper fragments were scattered around, resembling confetti at a festive celebration. Amid the disorder, Jenna's eyes darted across her scribbled notes, while Clara clumsily sifted through stacks of paper.

"Where is that name?" Clara's teeth clenched tightly as a low exasperated growl escaped her lips.

Jenna halted momentarily to closely observe Clara. *If she doesn't simmer down, she may ignite internal combustion.* A fleeting glimpse of Benji and she sensed a shared understanding. He remained still in his seat, hesitant to disturb Clara's agitated condition.

"I need that officer's name so we can call the police department."

"Clara, chill-lax." Jenna put her hand on the tangled papers, making Clara stop her spastic search.

Clara's exasperation escaped her lips in a gentle sigh. Her shoulders, burdened by the weight of recent news, surrendered to gravity. "What?" she responded sharply, her voice tinged with frustration and hopelessness.

"You know every detail of this case, but you're swirling all these thoughts into a cauldron of chaos, concocting a thick pile of mental sludge. Relax, regroup, and refocus. Close your eyes, drink water, and breathe." Jenna demonstrated a deep breath. "Besides, we don't need the name to call. They could look it up."

Jenna met Benjamin's intense and resentful stare. *He blames me for his girlfriend's weird behavior. A convenient target for his wrath and insecurity. She turned this fifteen-year-old cold case into the upcoming episode of CSI. We only have forty-six minutes to find the perpetrator and solve the case, otherwise our mission will be a failure. That would make an entertaining project.*

Clara's eyes fluttered open, her chest rising as she inhaled a long, steady breath.

"Feel better?" Jenna asked.

"I'm not sure what got into me. I feel like I'm racing against the clock to prove the media wrong before they find something."

"No one in the media knows what was found. The only thing that is known is the discovery of a human skeleton. The media holds a remarkable talent for converting whispered rumors into concrete truths. Back to *our* investigation."

"No one would hold it against you if you decided to let the police handle the situation," Benji whispered to Clara.

Jenna and Clara exchanged perplexed glances, their expressions mirroring a shared confusion.

Jenna crossed her arms. *Why is he set on sabotaging this investigation? It's like he's not on the same planet.*

"That is, they have more information and evidence at their disposal," Benji added. "Clara, this is more than just a mystery; it's your life."

"Exactly. It's *my* life. And what have the police done? Nothing. Unlike the police, *we* learned about my mother's affair with Marci. *We* uncovered Roger's obsession with my mother and his fight with my father. *We* are discovering more about this mystery than the police ever did."

Way to go, Clara, Jenna praised. Reclining in her seat, she grinned.

Benji crumbled beneath the weight of Clara's verbal barrage. He opted for a somber expression rather than engaging in verbal conflict.

"I've learned more about my history in the past five days than I have in the previous decade. We are moving on. If it bothers you, you can leave."

Benji's body language spoke volumes as he slumped into his chair, a picture of defeat.

"Guys," Jenna intervened. "Let's focus on the now." Benji crumbled before her eyes like a fragile sandcastle as he dropped into his chair. *Clara's got some backbone. Who knew? Serves him right for meddling. Pitiful puppy got put in his place.*

Clara glanced at Benji before continuing. "Okay. Jack Drewitt.

FOREVER FAMILY

His truck was spotted in the park. His fingerprint was on the murder weapon. He has an extensive criminal record. He is the perfect suspect. Problem: The leading detective arrested him the night before. He was locked up behind steel bars and never got questioned. Drewitt was released without knowledge of the evidence against him, and subsequently vanished." Clara shifted a few papers. "I recall having a conversation with the detective. He had quite a few years under his belt. I have serious doubts about his current state of existence. His name was Officer ... Officer ... Bishop! Arlo Bishop!" Clara's grin spread across her entire face, her eyes widening in delight.

"See! Inside out," Jenna said.

Jenna searched for the Nelson Police Department's number online and eyed Clara with a Cheshire Cat–like expression as she dialed. The receiving party answered, and Jenna inquired about Jack Drewitt's arrest history.

"Let me see," said the nasal voice. "Drewitt ... Drewitt ... yes, I have a few entries."

"I am particularly interested in the Saturday arrest on September second."

"Hold while I transfer you to the arresting officer."

"He's still alive!" Jenna blurted.

Jenna got a whack on the arm from Clara, who couldn't help but giggle as the secretary burst into laughter.

"Oh, I'm sorry. I didn't mean to be rude."

"No worries. Oh, that old-timer just won't quit! People keep telling him to retire, but he's, like, 'Nah, I'm not ready for the rocking chair just yet!' Everyone thinks he's playing hide-and-seek with the Grim Reaper. Hold, please.... Arlo! Line two." The music on the line had a little extra crackle and pop as it was delivered through a static chamber.

"Jeez, Jenna! Put a filter in your mouth before he answers the phone!"

"Okay, okay. I wasn't expecting to converse with a historical figure," Jenna said with a chuckle.

The static stopped, and a gruff, raspy voice took its place. "Sergeant Bishop."

"Yes, hello, my name is Linda Lawson, and I'm investigating the Wilson family murder case. Would you mind answering a few questions?"

"The Woodland Phantom murders?" a strained voice emanated from the speaker, accompanied by a distinct cough.

"That's correct, but particularly the Wilson family."

"I will provide information that is publicly available, but please be aware that this is an ongoing investigation."

Here we go. Jenna straightened up in her chair as Clara leaned closer.

"Has a suspect ever been identified in the case?"

"No," replied the curt voice.

"Do you have any new information or new leads?"

"No."

"Do you have any suspects?"

"No."

"What about the owner of the green truck and the fingerprint found?" Jenna asked.

"Jack Drewitt is a person of interest. Not a suspect." Sergeant Bishop's responses possessed a monotonous hum, as if he practiced them in his sleep.

"Was he interrogated?" Jenna continued.

"During the period when the homicides occurred, the individual in question was not subjected to any questioning or inquiry by law enforcement personnel."

"Was he questioned at any time?"

"No."

"Why not? If there was an abundance of evidence against him, why was he not subjected to interrogation?"

"According to the available records, the individual in question was incarcerated during the Wilson homicides due to a public altercation. He was apprehended and placed in custody Saturday night." The officer's lack of enthusiasm was evident in his responses. "Because of the holiday weekend, his court appearance was scheduled for the upcoming Tuesday. He had relocated without leaving a forwarding address after the definitive identification of his vehicle and partial fingerprint."

"Did you place an arrest warrant?"

"We intended to engage in conversation with him, not arrest him. He failed to report the potential theft of his truck upon his release. Our objective was to ascertain the whereabouts of his vehicle or to identity the person entrusted with his vehicle during his incarceration."

"Is it odd that a local would leave town without warning during an active murder investigation?"

"Not that odd. The Woodland Phantom featured headlines everywhere. People get spooked. Some leave. Jack lived alone and only talked to other people for work. He didn't have local friends or family to our knowledge." Officer Arlo Bishop's voice faded until there was no more sound.

Jenna had no idea if he had finished his sentence, fallen asleep, gotten bored, or was just thinking. She shrugged at Clara. "Did he strike you as the type of person to get spooked?"

The man grunted before speaking up. "Spooked or not, he was a self-employed handyman. He'd find work easy enough wherever. If his high-paying clients were leaving, he may have followed the money. All speculation."

"What would you say happened to the Woodland Phantom?" Clara leaned closer to listen.

"Whoever it is, like most uncaught criminals, is probably hibernating, incarcerated, or dead." Bishop coughed again, this time directly on the speaker.

Jenna held the phone away until he was finished. "What do you mean, 'hibernating'?"

"Once the police investigation closes in on a suspect, said suspect manages to elude law enforcement by entering a state of concealment and remaining inactive for a span of several years. In this case, a juvenile was reported missing, thereby prompting heightened involvement from both the media and law enforcement agencies, nationwide."

"Is it possible that the bones found today are those of Lucy Wilson?"

"No comment."

Jenna observed Clara's body wriggle and her face go white. "What happened to Lucy?"

"No comment."

"Are there any surviving family?"

Clara gave Jenna a puzzled glance.

"I need to know what he knows." Removing the phone from

her lips, she muttered.

"There is a surviving daughter who was released to a relative, but I cannot comment on any further details."

Jenna leaned closer and whispered to Clara. "He has no idea what happened after the murders."

Clara whispered back, "Ask when Drewitt was released."

"When was Jack Drewitt released from jail?"

"Probably after his court appearance on Tuesday," he said dismissively.

"Do you mind providing an exact date?"

A frustrated sigh and a low growl resounded around the room. "Hold on. *Marjorie!*"

Clara bucked back as she reached for her ear to alleviate the discomfort. "Good Lord, he can yell."

They overheard Arlo and Margorie's mumbled chat. *Fortunately for us, Arlo doesn't know how to put a call on hold.* Jenna increased the volume to listen in while tapping her fingers against her knee.

Ruffled noises emitted from the phone before the officer spoke again. "You there?"

"Yes, sir."

"September second," the voice muttered.

"That can't be right. My family died that night," Clara said.

"Sergeant Bishop. Are you sure? That is the night the Wilson family was killed."

"Wait a minute. Hold on.... *Marjorie!*" A loud thud was heard as the phone was dropped.

Jenna and Clara could hear Arlo and Margorie talking in the background.

"Let me see that. That's not right," Arlo said.

"It says here, he was released at 11:00 p.m. Saturday. No charges filed." Marjorie's muffled voice echoed in the background.

"No charges? He stabbed a guy in the leg. He should have been rotting in that cell until Tuesday." Arlo's voice sounded raw and strained, filled with intense anger and frustration.

"He was picked up at 8:08 p.m. after his involvement in a bar fight and released at 11:00 p.m. No details. No signature of who let him go."

"That man was walking before I finished my report? Shit."

Jenna, Clara, and Benji exchanged glances as they heard pounding footsteps approaching the phone.

The phone emitted a series of unconventional sounds as Arlo said, "No more questions."

Unlike some people, Jenna never gave up. "So, Drewitt was *not* locked up during the Wilson killings? Did I hear that correctly?"

"No more questions," Arlo grumbled.

"You had the primary suspect in your custody, and you just let him slip through your fingers? He truly must be a phantom." Jenna knew her time.

"No more questions. This is an active investigation. Good day." The phone went dead.

As the phone returned to its home screen, a hush fell over the room. Jenna exchanged meaningful glances with both Clara and Benji. It slipped her mind that Benjamin had been present. As the weight of the new information settled, a stillness fell upon the room, leaving everyone frozen in place.

CHAPTER 22

JENNA

"Holy oversight, Batman!" Jenna hoped her sudden outburst would spark a flurry of conversation, delving into the depths of the Holy Grail of knowledge. In a stunning twist of fate, she found herself utterly flabbergasted by the mind-boggling oversight committed by the esteemed guardians of law and order. How could the very institution entrusted with upholding safety and dispensing justice have stumbled upon such a colossal blunder?

Jenna examined the sea of reactions, like a captain scouring the horizon for shore. Amid the stunned reactions, her eyes settled on Clara, lost in a world of her own, her focus drifting through the study table. And there, Benjamin staring at Clara, as if he was trying to decipher the mysteries that lay within her vacant gaze.

Benjamin's hand quivered in the air, just above Clara's shoulder, only to retreat at the last moment, never making contact.

"This means we have a real suspect!" Jenna's voice resonated with a blend of encouragement and excitement.

"This means the destiny of my sister hung perilously in the hands of a collective of inept individuals who displayed a brazen disregard for their professional obligations," she said with a intense anger. "Their assumptions could have cost Lucy her life!"

"'*There is nothing more deceptive than an obvious fact,*' wrote the great Arthur Conan Doyle. Officer Arlo placed his unwavering trust in his own faulty wisdom, abandoning the mundane task of fact-checking. You know what happens when you assume. It turns Arlo into an asshole." Jenna took a few of the scattered papers and shuffled them into a clump.

"Jeez-a-wheezy! They matched the man's truck. His fingerprints were on the freaking murder weapon. His shoeprints probably matched. And they were too damn lazy to ask him a single question? They held him for less than a day, then had the audacity to let him skip town without a single damn word!" Clara's eyes darkened with rage.

Jenna witnessed Clara's fear diminished into smoldering ashes, replaced with a relentless phoenix of anger, its intent filled with bloodlust. "Fifteen years!" Clara's chest heaved with the internal emotional whirlwind.

"If it waddles like a duck, quacks like a duck, and tastes like a duck ... it's probably a duck. But let's not dwell on their blunders. What's our next plan?" Jenna asked. "How do we locate Mr. Jack?"

Benjamin remained frozen in his chair. *Apparently, he's never seen his bestie this angry.*

"The green truck." Clara's breath escaped her lips in a slow, deliberate manner as she allowed her shoulders to loosen and find a state of calm. "It's the sole surviving trace that the authorities have yet to obliterate. Ownership probably belonged to Jack Drewitt. As far as we know, it left the park on September second and traveled east. He probably thought that the police would be looking for his car, so there is a good chance that he left the truck in the middle of Pittsburgh in the hopes that it would become intercity chop suey and snatched a different car on his way out of the city. The pressure of being a fugitive can really make a person do some crazy things."

"It could be smashed and destroyed in any number of dumps within the last fifteen years. Discarded auto corpses frequently find their final resting place in salvage graveyards, their remains harvested for parts. Fingers crossed it didn't pull a vanishing act in an urban chop shop," Jenna said.

"Until we check, we won't know." Clara shifted to Benjamin. "You okay?"

"I ... I don't feel so good."

Feeling helpless while your friend gains self-confidence must be a real challenge. Experiencing a twinge of isolation and unimportance?

Clara placed a hand on Benjamin's shoulder. "You look kind of clammy. Maybe you should go home and rest."

Forever. Jenna scowled and fumbled through the paperwork like an inept magician searching for the correct card in a jumbled deck. *Since these two lovebirds are having a chat, I might as well gather some intel on the elusive pickup.*

"Yeah, I think I will." Benjamin hastily assembled his

possessions, carelessly cramming some of the snacks he'd opened into his backpack, oblivious to the disarray he created in his pack. "I'll see you tonight?" he directed at Clara. "At the Fyte Pub?"

"Sure. Get some rest. I'll see you later." Clara watched as he walked out the door.

"What's wrong with him?" Jenna asked. *Emotional spill, aisle three. Cleanup, please.*

"I don't know. We usually don't go to the pub on Wednesdays." The empty doorway served as a haunting reminder of her friend's departure. "He's not usually so ... but maybe he's ... I don't know."

"Maybe he's just overwhelmed. Rest will be good for him." *There's a weight limit on emotional baggage—please return home and unload.* "Now, do you have the truck's serial number in your extensive collection of data?" Jenna said as she shifted through the documents.

Clara turned away from the door and surveyed the papers on the table. "Yes, it's in the vehicle report." She sifted through the papers until she could find what she needed.

Jenna detected a distinct absence of investigative mojo. Devastated and despairing, Clara resembled someone who had taken a marshmallow to a sword battle. "Let's set that aside and enjoy a delicious meal. Fresh eyes will bring us new perspectives and potentials. My friends are hanging out at a warehouse close to campus. They're planning either world domination or another epic dance party. Both are bound to bring some entertainment. We can kick back and enjoy a couple of magical elixirs that make your worries disappear faster than a magician's rabbit."

"But I'm meeting Benji at the Fyte Pub later. You can come."

FOREVER FAMILY

"I'm not twenty-one, and the bartender recognizes my fake ID. Funny story." Jenna chuckled. "Meet Benjamin after we've had a few. Allow him a moment to recover while you indulge in some well-deserved amusement. What do you say?"

Clara paused briefly before giving in, much like a sailor succumbing to the Siren's enchanting song. "Okay. But what do you mean, 'funny story'?" she said with a smirk.

Jenna chuckled to herself. "The first week of school I drank a few drinks in the apartments, and some older college students wanted to go to the pub. When we arrived, I ordered a Crown and Coke but gave the bartender my real photo ID. He informed me that I was not twenty-one. I apologized and offered him my fake ID. I said, 'Now I am!' He was unimpressed. He kept my phony ID and banned me from the pub until I legitimately turned twenty-one. I found friends at the WaHo soon after."

"Jeez, Jenna! What were you thinking?"

"I wasn't thinking! I was already plastered."

CLARA

Sneaking through a concealed passage behind a dumpster did not instill a profound sense of certainty in Clara. As Jenna guided her, a cacophony of bagpipes, accordions, banjos, guitars, and drums echoed through the musty interior. With a mix of trepidation and anticipation, she tightly gripped the cold metal rails that guided her ascent to the upper floor. She was mesmerized by the distinctive melodies of a familiar American-Irish punk rock band. A pleasant surprise flowed through her veins, as if a previously unknown connection had been unearthed from the depths of her psyche.

"Must be a Celtic night!" Jenna called over her shoulder. "Warning: The guys love their kilts and it's true what they don't wear underneath!"

Jenna's unwavering confidence in this enchanting ambience transformed Clara's mere anticipation into a bubbling cauldron of exhilarating adventure. Caught in a whirlwind of emotions and warring instincts, Clara found herself frozen on the top stair. She fidgeted with the silver charm on her necklace. The shimmering bracelet on Jenna out-stretched arm caught her attention. She felt calmer when Jenna took her hand.

As they drew nearer, the music swelled in volume, enveloping their senses with its harmonic hug. The air was filled with the joyful symphony of laughter and the melodic charm of slightly unconventional singing, echoing through the vast expanse of the cavernous walls. The vibrations traveled through the sturdy wooden floors, gently tickling Clara's toes as if they were playful whispers from deep below the floorboards.

Jenna flung the door wide-open, her voice ringing out as she proudly proclaimed their grand entrance. "Good morrow, noble lords and fair ladies. Well met! I bring fresh meat for thine enjoyment! I do present thee Lady Clara of Penn State!" Jenna dipped into a regal bow, her eyes sparkling with warmth and excitement.

Clara's fingers performed an awkward flutter in the air to greet the curious onlookers.

"Hail, Lady Clara!" The jubilant crowd resumed their vibrant actions to the infectious rhythm of the music.

"Jenna." Above the blare of the stereo, Clara whispered into Jenna's ear. "If tonight is Celtic night, why do you sound like the

Renaissance fair?"

"Oh, these silly folks wouldn't have a clue! Unfortunately, my tongue just isn't cut out for an Irish accent, so I went for what I know. I could have unleashed my inner Klingon and received a chorus of grunts in response. Embrace joy, abandon judgment!"

Jenna linked her arm with Clara's and led her deeper into the room. The wallpaper with its vibrant pink paisley pattern cascaded down the walls, revealing the weathered wood beneath that had acquired a charmingly distressed appearance. The faint sound of the wood floors creaking was almost drowned out by the lively music and joyful atmosphere. People were enjoying themselves on various pieces of tattered furniture, some lounging and others dancing or gathered around the drinking table. At the far end, there were coolers filled with a variety of alcoholic beverages, sodas, and waters. In a dimly lit section, a mysterious figure was experimenting with various mixtures, surrounded by broken glass and boarded-up windows.

"Hey, Jenna! Who's your friend?" someone shouted.

"Kyle, Clara. Clara, Kyle. Quite the turnout tonight," Jenna said as she scanned the room.

"I had no clue Irish punk rock had such a huge following. As word spread, more people arrived." Kyle's hands wrapped around Jenna's delicate frame, pulling her closer in a tight embrace. With a smile, he pressed his lips against her cheeks and kissed her three times.

Jenna smiled and bopped Kyle's nose before he left to socialize with others. Then she turned to Clara. "Usually, five to eight people come to our themed nights, but it looks like there's over thirty."

"It's a lot of people!" Clara yelled from behind Jenna's back.

"Don't worry. Once the music absorbs you, all the people will disappear."

"Was that your boyfriend?" Clara inquired, her hand gracefully accepting the beverage Jenna offered.

"Kyle? No. He's the closest I have to a best friend."

"Why did he kiss you?"

"That's our secret language. He's had three drinks ... three kisses. I've had nothing, so I didn't give him a kiss back. That's how we look out for each other at these things. Not that it's dangerous here, but sometimes someone loses control."

Smart, Clara thought.

A lively new song filled the room, and Jenna stole Clara's free hand and guided her to the center of the makeshift dance floor.

Jenna's dance moves were truly impressive as she gracefully danced to the sound of bagpipes, all while managing to keep her drink from spilling. Everyone was enjoying themselves, all engaged in their own activities amid the chaos. As Clara tasted the drink, she couldn't help but cough at the intense, bitter flavor sliding down her throat. Her face contorted and her body trembled.

"In retrospect, I should've warned you. Mikey is always trying new drink combinations. They're not all bad, but they're all strong. Sip slowly!"

Clara's taste buds embarked on a daring expedition, exploring uncharted territories of flavor. Surprisingly, this time, the experience was far more pleasant. Gradually, her body began to sway in rhythm with the music. As the spirited elixir coursed through her veins, it ignited a cozy fire within, dissolving the icy grip of social anxieties that had once held her captive. She initiated

FOREVER FAMILY

discussions with random people, without Jenna accompanying her. She couldn't recall the last time she had experienced such a liberating escape from her own thoughts.

Hours into the night, the crowd started to thin out, with some finding cozy spots on couches or the cold floor. Jenna and Clara sat side by side in a plush chair, both enjoying refreshing sips of water as their eyelids fluttered close.

"It's time to go, Clara." Jenna gently tapped Clara on the leg and began to rise.

"Yeah ... or we could sleep here." Clara nestled into the vacant cushions, her head gently resting against the inviting arm of the chair.

"You are welcome to sleep here if you wish, but I need to go home. My dad worries. I can walk you back."

Clara's mind knew Jenna was right, but her body hesitated to act as she contemplated the prospect of waking up to a group of strangers who were recovering from a night of heavy drinking. She raised her hand, and Jenna helped her up from the chair. After a few unsteady moments, she managed to regain her balance.

Maybe we left our coordination in the cushions.

The girls walked hand in hand, steadying themselves as they descended the stairs and exited through the side panel. Jenna's head shot upward suddenly, resulting in an unintended collision with the wooden frame. As she safely guided Clara through the opening, she gently rubbed the top of her head. Jenna scratched her head when the girls stood up, and the girls couldn't stop laughing.

The moonlight cast a gentle glow upon their path, as if nature itself was eavesdropping on their conversation. As they walked to the dormitories, their voices intertwined, weaving a tapestry of shared experiences and whispered secrets. The night had gifted them with tales to tell, and they reveled in the magic of the moment, cherishing the bond that grew stronger with each passing word.

Jenna's footsteps ceased abruptly as her eyes were captivated by the expansive sky.

"What's up?" Clara glanced up and attempted to stifle a burst of laughter when she realized her clever wordplay.

"I felt a raindrop," Jenna said.

Clara lifted her hands into the air. "I didn't feel anything."

Jenna's steps faltered, her equilibrium wavering, as she inadvertently pulled Clara with her to the ground, hitting the hard, uneven terrain. They fixed their hair and brushed dirt off their garments as more raindrops began to fall. A torrential rainstorm erupted from the sky, drenching everything in its path.

Clara rose to her feet, surrendering her hands to the air, and gracefully spun around. She savored the invigorating touch of the icy raindrops dripping upon her delicate skin. A wave of unburdened bliss washed over her, transporting her back to the whimsical days of her youth before the darkness had consumed her innocence. To her delight, Jenna decided to join her in the impromptu rain dance. The connection blossoming between Jenna and Clara was so tangible, one could practically reach out and touch it.

Jenna suggested heading back to the dorms as the rain slowed to a misty drizzle. With a quick glance at her watch, her expression betrayed a hidden urgency beneath her calm facade. They trudged along the puddle-filled sidewalk, their clothes clinging to their bodies like second skins, until they finally arrived at Clara's dormitory.

"You can crash here. My roommate's never around." Clara wiped the falling rain from her cheeks.

"Thanks, but when it comes to my dad, I'd rather be late than not there at all. I'll see you tomorrow."

"I had fun. Thank you." Clara grinned as she swiped her key card through the electronic reader and opened the door.

"I bid thee farewell, Lady Clara. Anon." Jenna smiled as Clara giggled and entered her dorm.

JENNA

Leaving the busy campus behind, Jenna frolicked through the puddles that dotted the walkway like liquid jewels. Anticipating her father's presence at home, she picked up her pace. She hurried with unwavering determination, her feet pounding against the pavement, until her rebellious stomach staged a revolt, courtesy of the alcohol coursing through her.

In the middle of her brief pause, breathless and hunched over, she captured the fleeting sight of a silhouette vanishing behind a line of garbage containers. Her hand fell to her concealed steel, as if the adrenaline triggered an invisible magnet. With a flick of her wrist, Jenna revealed the gleaming blade, poised to strike. With cautious movements, she approached the location where the shadow had been hiding. The rain pummeled her, and she tucked her drenched hair behind her ear. Silently, she closed in on the garbage cans. With a sudden burst, she leaped behind the bins, thrusting her blade into her pursuer. An oblivious feral cat let out a chilling screech as the sharp blade pierced its hind leg, causing it to hiss in agony before darting away around the corner.

Jenna's heart fluttered with a mischievous rhythm as she inhaled deeply to regulate her breathing. Her eyes locked on to the mesmerizing sight of scarlet droplets cascading from her glistening blade. The force of gravity gracefully tugged a droplet from the blade, causing it to disperse into a standing puddle, resembling a majestic paisley pattern. The beauty of this forbidden element was truly unexpected.

A distant noise distraction her from the crimson pattern. Swiftly, she cleansed her blade on a forgotten newspaper, concealing it once more within her pocket.

Jenna's body stiffened as the night sky unleashed another merciless onslaught of raindrops, just as she was mere moments away from the safety of her apartment. Taking shelter beneath the stairwell's canopy, she twirled her hair and wrung her garments, extracting every lingering droplet of moisture. She climbed the stairs, kicked off her shoes at the entrance, and unlocked the door before entering on tiptoe. The creaking door betrayed her attempts at stealth.

"Shh!" She gestured to the door.

When she turned around, her father stood in the darkened hallway, staring at her. She stumbled backward in alarm. Frozen in stillness, she braced herself for his thunderous reprimand, yet he remained motionless.

"Dad? I'm sorry I'm late." The floor creaked softly as she took a step closer with caution. Never before had she witnessed such odd behavior. "Dad? Are you okay?"

Disbelief and terror scarred his expression, as if he had just come face-to-face with a haunting apparition. His eyes held many secrets.

Jenna, soaked from head to toe, stood motionless in the foyer, her wet attire and damp hair leaving a trail of droplets on the polished floor panels. Waves of dark curly hair slithered over her shoulders. Her spine shivered as the icy breath of the air conditioner whispered through the room. She hesitated, uncertain whether to break his train of thought or attempt a stealthy maneuver around him. Yet an unsettling feeling gnawed at her, signaling that all was not as it seemed.

"Daddy?"

CHAPTER 23

NICK

A young girl lay motionless, facedown in the tub, like she was forever trapped in a deep slumber. The murky water stroked her hair, as if it had a life of its own, moving in a hypnotic dance. The filth and grime clinging to unwashed floor mingled with the liquid as it overflowed the porcelain rim and flooded the tiles. A chilling mist crept along the mirror and pooled at the base of the vanity. As warm water splashed over his toes, the young boy stared his little sister.

"This is my fault," the boy whispered.

No. It's not your fault. It's their fault, Nick told the boy.

A figure darted into the bathroom, letting out a bloodcurdling shriek, and forcefully pushed the boy aside. His body went limp as he collapsed onto the cold, wet bathroom floor, his head making a sickening thud against the porcelain toilet tank. His body swayed with uncertainty as he tried to stand, but in the end, he opted to stay seated against the wall between the porcelain structures.

As the water continued to flood around him, a single drop of blood splattered into the murkiness. Searching for the source of the red droplet, he slowly raised his hand to his head. He pulled his hand away, revealing red stains on his fingertips. The red sparkled in the fluorescent light and remained smooth as it painted red trails down his trembling arm. Shrill wails pierced the air, drawing his attention away from the mesmerizing sight. The boy's mother emerged from the dark waters, clutching the lifeless body of the three-year-old girl in her arms.

"What did you do?" the woman accused the boy with a terrifying intensity while she tightly held her daughter.

It wasn't his fault. It's yours.

"She just wanted a bath," the boy whispered.

He's eight! Did you expect him to raise your child?

"What's goin' on back there?" a masculine voice roared from the corridor.

The voice's deep, menacing tone sent shivers down Nick's spine, as if it were the dangerous rumbling of an impending storm. The boy pressed himself against the wall, hoping to blend into the shadows and avoid detection.

Not him. Don't let him know!

"Jayla! It's Jayla!" Her scream echoed through the house.

The threatening footsteps drew nearer, even the house quaked in fear. The boy's ears perked up at the sound of heavy work boots, a sound he knew all too well.

"What did you do now, you little ..." The tall, bulky man with a barrel stomach paused in the doorway. As the bathwater rose, he spotted his wife gently rocking their youngest child in her arms.

"Paul, Jayla's dead. She's dead!" The woman's body rocked rhythmically, as if she was trying to summon the dead back to life.

The young boy approached the woman to catch a glimpse of his sister. A sudden and forceful blow from the man's hand sent pain across his face. The force collided with the innocent child and his body jolted backward, causing his head to violently strike the opposite edge of the tub. A bloodred mark materialized on his face. He clutched his throbbing head, and tears streamed down his face, as if his very soul was being wrung out of him.

Don't cry. Don't cry. It will only make him mad. Don't cry. Nick could sense the unsettling strength emanating from the boy. No child should have to get used to such unforgiving brutality. This boy had learned early on how to stay alive.

"Why weren't you watching her, you little shit?" Paul raised another hand across his chest, ready to strike.

Why can't I help him? Nick's frustrated voice echoed on deaf ears.

The father was about to hit the boy for the second time when the mother's outcry interrupted him.

"What are we going to do, Paul? What are we going to do?" Her mournful cries grew louder and more desperate with each passing moment. "Call 911!"

Without warning, the man struck the woman. "We are not calling anyone, Cora! The cops ain't steppin' foot in my house!"

The piercing shrieks of his mother resonated through the house like the wails of a vengeful banshee.

"Shut up, woman!" The man struck the woman's head with the back of his hand. "Let me think!"

The woman's cries turned to whimpers as she cradled her dead, drenched daughter. Her silence fell short of the mark. The man delivered another forceful blow to the back of her head, causing her to drop the little girl, their bodies colliding in a sudden fall.

Leave her alone!

The young boy cowered in his hiding place, afraid to help his mother. The tainted water soaked through his clothes, leaving them slimy and repulsive, yet he remained still. When his mother righted herself and took up the lifeless form, the boy's fingers shook as he battled to quiet the acidic bile bubbling in his stomach.

Don't draw attention to yourself, warned Nick. *Stay still.*

"The lake!" Paul said.

No!

"What are you talking about?" With tears streaming down her face, Cora gently stroked the young girl's dark hair as she lay there, completely still, and devoid of any signs of life.

"We'll dump her in the lake. It was an accident. She went outside to play. When we found her, it was too late. She fell in and drowned. It was an accident." The coldhearted man's face twisted into a sinister smile.

"I can't. I can't. My baby girl! My baby!" Cora's rocking became more frantic as she clutched her baby tightly.

"You can, and you will. Now get up, woman!"

Cora's trance was abruptly shattered by her husband's savage grip. He seized her arm and hauled her upright. A sickening thud escaped as the small body hit the floor, resting in an unnatural pose.

The boy shuddered and struggled to suppress his nausea.

The woman stretched her hand to the girl, but the man violently pulled her back, leaving her trembling with fear.

"Leave it! You've got to cover the body first! Go get the trash bags!" Paul ordered.

Paul shoved Cora out of the bathroom. She stumbled across the threshold and fell against the adjacent wall in the dimly lit hallway.

The small child, crouched in the shadows, squeezed his eyelids shut.

The intimidating figure of the man cast a threatening shadow over his quivering son. "When we leave, clean this room with bleach."

Silence. The boy's eyes remained closed, as though he dreaded what he would see if he opened them, and this horrifying scene became a reality.

"Do you hear me, boy!"

The impact of the steel-toed boot colliding with his rib cage left the boy gasping for air.

"Y-y-yes, sir," the boy rasped out.

"Yes, sir!"

You've got to say it correctly or he won't leave! Nick said.

The boy's voice was more confident as he obediently responded, "Yes, sir," his eyes met his father's with an unwavering intensity.

Satisfied, the man left the room.

The boy's body shook as he collapsed backward, his hand instinctively reaching for his chest. As he heard his father's ramblings echoing through the corridor, he braced himself and cautiously emerged from his concealed nook. The disturbing sight of his sister splayed out in a twisted shape made the boy question if it was really his sister.

Don't look!

Her lifeless eyes had a way of seeing right through him. They were not the same eyes the boy remembered. They were there for each other when things got bad. And things always got bad.

"Ju-Ju. My sweet Ju-Ju." The back of his dripping hands brushed her cheek. The pallor of her skin resembled the slimy and moist texture of the moss enveloping the dark swamp.

"Maybe a kiss will wake her up," the boy said.

It won't. It'll just make him mad! Nick's warning came too late.

Bending over, he pressed a gentle kiss onto her lips. "Please, Ju-Ju. Wake up!"

"Get away from her, you sick pervert. She's dead! Get out of the way!"

Paul commanded Cora to use the trash bags to cover the body while he aggressively escorted the lad away.

The boy cast a longing glance at his sister before being pushed out of the room.

Don't sit on the couch! No kids on the furniture, Nick reminded the boy.

As the boy settled on the floor in the living room, the withered floorboards creaked and groaned in protest. With his knees tightly hugged to his chest, he rocked back and forth, desperately attempting to soothe his own nerves. He slowly rotated his head to a thumping noise echoing through the hallway.

The man hauled a dark trash bag across the floor and

unceremoniously hurled it toward the rear entrance of the kitchen. The woman trailed behind in complete silence, head bowed low.

The boy felt a shiver run down his spine as the man's footsteps grew louder and closer. He looked up to see the man standing tall above him.

"What did I say, boy?"

"Clean the bathroom." The bow cowered closer to the couch.

The man's hand curled into a menacing ball, and his nostrils flared with an unsettling intensity.

"With bleach!" the boy quickly added. "Clean the bathroom with bleach, sir!"

A faint breeze blew through the open back door after the adults left. Gradually, the boy rose and stabilized himself before trailing them. The night's events left his head in a dizzying haze.

A tiny yelp made him turn around.

Leave the dog. You don't want to take the dog.

"Come on, Buckeye, but be quiet. Shh!" He gestured for the terrier to hush.

Why won't anyone listen to me? Nick's inner turmoil boiled with an unsettling exertion.

Buckeye belonged to the boy and his sister. He had been discovered aimlessly wandering through the forest, hunting squirrels. Their mother reluctantly agreed to keep the puppy, but warned them that if it caused any trouble, it would disappear. Naturally, they waited until their mother was mentally impaired before asking. The young kids tended to the small pup with great care, ensuring that it was nourished, exercised, entertained, and even permitted to sleep beside them once their parents dozed off or passed out. The children bestowed upon the tiny terrier the moniker "Buckeye" due to his peculiar habit of chasing fallen buckeyes, which they found quite amusing.

The boy knew where his sister was being taken. The lake was near the tree house he'd built. From that concealed fortress, he had a commanding view of the valley and the waters beyond, making it the perfect lair for a notorious pirate. In that isolated palace, he would take aim at unsuspecting rabbits and other creatures with his paintball pistol, using them as mere targets for his twisted amusement. His sister didn't like it when he hit or killed the animals, but she found it hilarious when he missed. Though she disapproved of his actions, there was a playful glint in her eye as she watched him in his twisted games. The location was just three peaks beyond their house.

Despite the scarce moonlight, the fortress loomed ominously amid the dense forests. He had started construction when he was five, about the time Jayla was born. For the past month, Jayla had been helping him decorate, using paint he scavenged from dumpsters outside the hardware store. She carefully cleaned the wound on his hand, gently applying lake water and bandaging it, after he accidentally cut it on the sharp edge of a paint can.

The boy retrieved the stick he had stashed by a nearby tree to release a coiled makeshift ladder resting on the holding platform above. With a whack with the stick, he hit the release lever and the ladder descended.

"Shh," he whispered to Buckeye, as if the dog created the noise of the ladder unraveling to the ground.

As he cast away the stick, a sudden sharp sensation shot through his thumb. Before climbing the makeshift wooden ladder, he sucked on his thumb to relieve the pain and pulled the splinter out with his teeth.

Buckeye barked once, and the boy hushed him again.

Just leave the dog.

"Give me a minute." The young boy arrived at the platform, and with a rope he and Jayla had crafted last week, he lowered a basket to the ground below. The dog leaped into the basket with an awkward elegance, eagerly awaiting its ascent as it swung in the air. With a determined grip, the boy tugged and tugged until the final tug hoisted the basket over the precipice, granting Buckeye access to the platform.

The child's lungs filled with cold, damp air as he turned his head, searching for his parents. They soon materialized from the edge of the woods clutching the black sack that glistened like obsidian in the night. They stumbled through the hazy lakeshore, their thudding footsteps muffled against the rocky terrain.

Paul's frustration grew, while Cora's tears silently streamed down her face. He released his hold on the bag and dropped it at her feet, pointing toward the boulders in the distance.

Cora's trembling hands grasped the bag, its weight dragging her down as she stumbled over the jagged rocks. Paul yelled something and pointed again toward the taller rocks. She struggled to drag the bag higher and higher until she was finally standing on top of the highest rock.

Once the bags were stripped away, Jayla's body lay there, exposed and vulnerable. The limbs were contorted into unnatural angles, giving the impression of a kid's clay mold.

You don't have to dump her! It's not too late! Nick yelled out to the woman.

The silence of Cora's inactivity was shattered by Paul's sudden and jarring outburst.

After another bout of sobbing, Cora turned her head away and pushed Jayla over the brink. As the toddler tumbled, her body careened down the rocky terrain, colliding, tearing, and twisting until she lurched and plunged into the depths below, disappearing into the black waters.

Jayla doesn't like the lake.

The man's call echoed, and the woman stumbled down the rocky terrain. Her movements were awkward as she carefully navigated the uneven ground. Paul scanned the field, ensuring that he didn't overlook something before nudging Cora back into the woods.

Nick watched the boy, whose unblinking eyes were transfixed on the lifeless body of his sister, silently drifting in the abyss. The murky depths enveloped her, her raven locks splayed out like tendrils of shadow.

"It's my fault," the boy said.

You are not to blame. They did this to her. They were cruel. They beat her, tortured her, and dumped her like trash. They killed Ju-Ju. They must pay!

Nick felt the boy's anxiety morphing into an ominous fury.

The young boy peered into the darkness, as if searching for something that should not be seen. The beating of his heart grew louder, and his breaths became shallow and ragged. His fingers coiled into a tight knot and his body became a rigid statue. A faint, chilling howl reverberated from the shadows.

As the boy spun around, his expression glinted with an otherworldly glow. With a swift and calculated movement, he sent the creature hurtling off the platform and into the darkness below.

A sudden yelp pierced the air as the canine tumbled down from the tree house.

On hands and knees the child crept to the edge of the platform and peeked over. As he peered down, he caught sight of his faithful companion lying motionless on the jagged stones, red droplets trickling down the coarse edges. The lifelessness of the dog was unmistakable. In the moonlight, the rocks were surrounded by a pool of sparkling blood.

The boy tilted his head.

"It's beautiful."

The veil of darkness shrouded Nick's vision.

JENNA

"Daddy, are you okay?" Jenna whispered.

"Ju-Ju. My sweet Ju-Ju. Why do you torment me?" Her dad broke his haunting silence, and Jenna's eyes began to swell with tears.

"I'm sorry, Daddy. I'm sorry I'm late. I was helping a friend. It started raining, and it took me longer to get home. I'm sorry, Daddy." Jenna begged her father for forgiveness, but he appeared deep in his own thoughts. He had a tortured, distant appearance as though he had just awoken from a terrible nightmare.

Her father closed the distance and pulled her into a tight hug. "You're safe now, Ju-Ju. No one can hurt you while I'm here."

"Yes, Daddy."

Jenna leaned into his embrace. She felt protected and cherished but confused by his sudden fear and pain.

He gripped her so tightly, it seemed he'd never let go.

FOREVER FAMILY

Jenna wished he would hold on forever. Never had she witnessed him so vulnerable and scared. Now, more than ever, she felt a deep connection with him.

"Now." Her dad held her at arm's length and studied her face. "I need you to get cleaned up and go to bed." He tucked a lock of hair behind her ear and kissed her forehead.

"Yes, Daddy."

Before going to her room, Jenna gave her father a final embrace around the middle. She closed the door and braced herself against it as it latched. She dropped to the floor and let her thoughts and emotions calm for a moment. She was quite close to her dad but wondered what had brought on his physical display of affection.

What was that about?

CHAPTER 24

CLARA

The wind howled all around Clara, who remained motionless while her hair twirled around her face like ghostly fingers. As she slowly regained consciousness, she realized she was lying on a bed of cold, rough stones. Nature's debris clung to her face when she lifted her head. Her arm scraped against the jagged stones as she raised her hand from beneath her head.

The heavens unleashed a blinding burst of lightning, exposing tendrils of ominous clouds creeping closer to her. As the night grew darker, a mysterious hand of shadows loomed over the moon and stars, as if ready to snatch them away and plunge the world into darkness. The air was thick and heavy, carrying with it a musty scent of soil and decay.

Unnatural shadows were created among the tall weeds whipping in the wind near the deep woodland that lay ahead. As Clara breathed in and out, the tree trunks swayed in perfect unison to her rhythm, as if they were alive and breathing alongside her. The rustling of leaves echoed through the silence as they desperately tried to escape the increasing wind, entangled in the twisted maze of branches that lashed menacingly back and forth.

The deafening roar of thunder rumbled through the desolate terrain, as if the very earth trembled in fear. Clara clung to an exposed root, her nervous fingers clinging to her only lifeline amid the frenzied whirlwind of scattered fragments. A sound spread through the air as the roots writhed and twisted their way out of the shadowy earth, resembling the crunch of compacted snow. For years, the remains of a child had lain hidden beneath the earth, unnoticed and forgotten. But now, as the soil and roots transformed into a tombstone, a skeleton had emerged, a haunting reminder of a tragic past.

It's not Lucy.

"Why didn't you save me?" From the abandoned grave, Clara could hear Lucy's voice escape from the neglected remains.

"It's not you!" Clara said as her hand stretched toward the bones.

Her gentle touch caused the bones to crumble into fine dust. Touching the particles caused them to slip through her fingers, swirling and dancing as they fell to the ground, their movements growing more frenzied as the storm intensified. Clara cowered in fear as sharp bone shards whizzed past her, narrowly missing her face. She stumbled backward, the ominous dust swirled around her and grew larger by the second. The wind howled, carrying more and more grit and debris. A spiraling vortex of dark clouds descended from the sky, merging with the growing dust storm below.

"I'm not here. It's not real."

Amid the howling storm, Clara's desperate cries were swallowed by the merciless winds.

As the supporting structures gave way, the trees let out a moan of pain and lifted from the ground to join the swirling mass. The twisted branches reached out through the atmosphere, resembling spears from an ancient battlefield.

The trees crashed together, causing showers of splintered wood to rain down upon Clara. She fell to the earth and shielded her head with her hands. Every particle that touched her hands sent pain coursing through her body. Her arms were stained with blood as the sharp edges tore through her skin.

Make it stop! Please make it stop! Wake up!

As the storm intensified, the gusts of wind grew more forceful, pulling Clara's helpless body across the barren ground.

No, no, no. Clara pulled at roots and vegetation sprouting from the soil, trying to find a safe hold.

The darkness enveloped her as her eyes widened, revealing the black void of her pupils. Her nails clawed at the earth, desperate for something to cling to in the abyss. As she stumbled on the jagged rocks, a sudden gust of wind lifted her into the swirling vortex.

"Stop!" A fearful shriek escaped her lips, reverberating through the heart of the tempest. The strong gusts whisked her tears away before they could land on her cheeks.

The gusts abruptly stopped, leaving the air still.

FOREVER FAMILY

Clara collapsed to the ground. She couldn't help but notice the lifeless forms of other storm victims scattered around her. The fabric of her attire clung to her skin, slick with sweat and an unknown moisture. The air clung to her lungs, as if it didn't want to be released. Her windblown hair was stained with red streaks from her bleeding wounds. She scanned the darkness, anticipating the next wave of terror that was sure to come.

The atmosphere became too thick and suffocating for comfortable deep, calming breaths. No matter how hard Clara tried, she couldn't seem to find a steady rhythm.

In, out. In, out, she instructed herself.

Clara's breaths grew shallow as she realized the air she needed to survive was slowly disappearing.

As the newly sprouting trees took root, they hungrily consumed any available oxygen, replacing what had been destroyed. The dark shadows seized the oxygen and greedily consumed it, feeding the plant's roots with an insatiable hunger. The subterranean roots moved stealthily through the earth, like a serpent hunting its next victim.

As Clara struggled for breath, the roots of the trees seemed to hear and abruptly twisted in her direction. With each turn in her attempt to flee, the roots pursued her with alarming speed. Their thirst for oxygen was ravenous, even at the cost of depriving her of the very air she needed to survive. A tentacle slithered around her, eager to ensnare her in its grasp. She narrowly avoided its grasp, but the feeling of its rough touch lingered on her scratched leg.

She fled, but her lungs struggled to draw in air. Another root snatched her foot and yanked her down to the ground. Her mind raced with terror and her body was racked with excruciating pain.

The trees constricted their unbreakable hold around her body and stretched their roots around her throat. Her legs thrashed wildly, desperate to escape.

Her vision faded into darkness, leaving only a narrow gap for her to peer through. Muffled screams attempted to claw their way out of her throat but failed.

Each airless breath caused tears to swell. With every gasp of air, the roots constricted more deeply. Her body was consumed by an icy chill, devoid of any warmth to sustain her. As the freezing tendrils crept up her spine, her veins turned to ice, and her limbs grew weak and lifeless. The shadows in her vision deepened. Clara's final memory was the exact moment when she exhaled her last breath.

I'm sorry, Lucy.

* * *

Inhaling deeply, Clara jolted upright, her breaths coming in ragged gasps. She covered her eyes with her palm and pressed her thumb against her temple to ease the sting of remorse and pain. The deep breaths she hungrily craved gave sharp pains in her chest.

Clara reached across her nightstand for her water glass, but all she could grasp was empty space as her raw, grainy throat cried out for relief. Peering from under her hand, she searched for the cup, but it wasn't there. She leaned her head over the side of the bed and found an empty cup on the damp carpet. Feeling defeated, she buried her head in her pillow and tried to rest for a while longer.

The alarm sounded, forcing her awake with the realization that the world continued despite her restless nights. She slapped her alarm until it stopped and then dragged herself out of bed.

FOREVER FAMILY

Coldness spread through her body as her wet clothes clung to her torso and thighs. She gathered her toiletries and went to the bathrooms for a quick cleanse.

When Clara got back to her room, she immediately started looking for her phone. She rummaged through her bag and saw that she had three missed calls and six messages from Benji.

"Benji!" she remembered. She had completely forgotten about him last night. Her heart plummeted at the thought of what she must have put him through.

The overwhelming guilt made it easier to forget her terrifying dreams. She gathered her belongings, loosened her hair with her fingers, and ran out the door without making sure it was locked and completely ignoring her academic responsibilities. She swung open the staircase door and dashed downstairs.

If he's not in the café, he'll be on his way to class.

Clara, focusing on her feet so as not to fall, almost ran into someone sitting on the last set of stairs.

"Oh, I'm sorry." She worried about the unfortunate soul she'd kicked in her frenzy. "Benji?"

"Hey, when you didn't show up last night, I got worried." Benji's appearance was disheveled, with unkempt hair, rumpled clothes, and tired, weary eyes accentuated by dark circles.

"Oh, Benji. I'm so sorry. After the library, Jenna and I met with some of her friends, and I lost track of time. Once I started drinking, everything became a blur. Do you forgive me?" Clara leaned in, her puppy dog eyes begging.

Benji let out a long breath. "Of course. You don't even need to ask."

Despite his best efforts, Clara was not convinced. She

experienced yet another rush of remorse pelting her heart.

Benji presented her with a warm cup of coffee. *He's been here awhile.*

"Thank you so much. This is *just* what I need." Her shoulders relaxed as she took in the acrid aroma. She was still feeling a little queasy from last night, but she couldn't show Benji. The chilled beverage didn't quite suit her palate, yet she refrained from expressing her opinion.

"So, what did you do?" Benji asked, but Clara sensed that he wasn't interested in the answer.

"Oh, we hung out with her friends, listened to music, danced, and talked. They were quite entertaining." Clara's expression brightened briefly. "I think you'd like them."

Benji raised a brow. "You don't dance."

"I did last night. Not well. Whatever it was, I felt calm and comfortable. For one night, I was able to forget about things and have fun."

Benji frowned.

Since he'd wound up being a part of that forgetting, she realized she'd chosen her words poorly.

"You look kind of rough for such an amazing night."

"I'm fine. The discovery of those bones has me a bit on edge," Clara confessed. "But I know it's not Lucy. I'm meeting Jenna shortly to discuss a few things."

"What about class?"

"I'm not going to class today. I couldn't possibly concentrate. The truth feels so close."

Benji paused before speaking. "Are you sure skipping class is a good idea?"

"It's only one day. Besides, I have already submitted my work, and the other lecturer just reads from a PowerPoint. The PowerPoint will have to wait."

"Okay, Clara. I'm coming with you."

"Actually, Benji, you don't need to. You can join us after class. I wouldn't want to be a bad influence." Clara nudged his arm with her shoulder affectionately.

A forced grin crept across his face.

"What's wrong?" Clara asked.

"I just didn't sleep well myself. Guess it's your turn to wake me up this morning." Benji's grin appeared more sincere.

"Well, let's begin with breakfast at your favorite eatery … the Café de la Campus!" A cheerful Clara escorted Benji to the cafeteria.

CHAPTER 25

JENNA

Jenna pressed her ear against the bedroom door, straining to catch any sound that might reveal her father's presence and activities within the apartment. She had yet to figure out what had prompted his prior actions. Although she relished the attention in the aftermath, the source of the strange behavior was still a mystery.

The birds outside sang a grating morning melody, the dog next door barked at nothing, and the garbage truck emptied cans and recycling bins on the corner. The smell of her dad's famous waffles drifted down the hall while dishes clattered in the sink. A normal morning on an ordinary day, but with unusual emotions occupying her mind.

This morning, she had intended to meet up with Clara, but

FOREVER FAMILY

something was off with her dad, and she needed answers.

"Dad?" Jenna hollered from her door.

"Yeah?" her dad replied, accompanied by the bang of a frying pan hitting the metal sink.

"Don't leave. I'll be out in a minute!" Jenna hastily slipped on a pair of fluffy socks and wandered into the kitchen.

Her dad put the last plate on the drying rack and dried his hands with a towel.

Jenna found homemade waffles and fresh orange juice waiting for her on the kitchen table. Her father added mint to orange juice for a unique flavor, and it was the best orange juice she'd ever had.

"Thanks for breakfast!" Jenna hugged him closely, leaning against his back. When he turned around, she gave him a peck on the cheek.

"You're welcome. I have a full day ahead of me, but I hope to be home for dinner." He gathered a few tools, zipped them into his duffel bag, and reached for the keys to the pickup.

"Dad? Are you okay? Last night, you acted a bit ... odd. I'm sorry for upsetting you. Please forgive me."

"It's fine." He shrugged and readjusted the duffel bag slung over his shoulder.

"I mean ... you've been ... weird the last few days."

A grunt was all that escaped his mouth. Then he reached for the doorknob.

"Dad!" Jenna's tone hardened, as she stomped her foot. "I'm worried about you!"

After a long sigh, her dad finally said, "I'm fine."

"Can I ask you a question?"

"Yes." His grip tightened on the handle.

"Why did you say that the media was lying about the Wilson case?"

Her father's posture stiffened, and his muscles tensed, yet he maintained his grip on the handle. Even from behind, she could sense the subtle tightening of his jaw. Her pulse race and her head spin at the awkward pause.

What is he hiding?

"Jenna, there are some things that are best left alone. That case being one of them."

"Please, Dad. Does it involve Mom?"

"No."

"Because that all happened about the time Mom died?"

"I've told you before, the past is painful. Let it be." He dropped his hand to his side.

"Did you live in the area? Did you know them?" Jenna continued.

"Jenna! Enough!" He faced Jenna. "I don't know anything about them. They helped me get back something I'd lost." Her father tightened his grip on his tool bag and returned to the kitchen.

"What did you lose? Why did you zone out last night? You said I torment you. How do I torment you?"

"You reminded me of a pain I've tried to forget." Her father got his coffee tumbler from the counter.

"What pain?" Jenna asked softly.

"My sister died very young."

Jenna's breath caught in her chest. "What happened to her?"

"She drowned. Now leave it alone."

"What was her name?"

"Enough!" After pounding on the kitchen island, her dad stormed off to the back of the apartment.

Jenna realized she'd pushed him too far. She couldn't believe she'd managed to extract so much information from him.

I had an aunt? She didn't remember her father ever mentioning extended family. *Perhaps I have other relatives.*

Her father emerged from the workshop, carrying his tool belt and hard hat. He avoided making eye contact as he headed straight for the front door.

"Dad?"

His response was mixed with a shallow breath. "Yes?"

"I love you."

"I love you, Ju-Ju, forever." Without a backward glance, he opened the door and left.

Jenna approached the open door and gently shut it. Worried about her father's hidden truths, her thought raced with inquiries. His avoidance hinted at the painful memories: perhaps the loss of his dear sister and beloved wife.

She sat back down and resumed eating the rest of her breakfast, lacking any fresh insights. She intended to get more information before calling Clara, but realized she had left her phone in her bedroom. She retrieved it and returned to her breakfast plate.

"Okay, Mr. Google. Please, help us locate a green F-150 that was last seen in early September, fifteen years ago. We are looking between Nelson Ledges and Pittsburgh…. That's about a one-hundred-mile drive using the most direct route." Jenna skillfully manipulated her phone with one hand as she sipped orange juice with the other.

"Thanks to Ms. Helen's assistance, we can now work Warrendale into the story—116 miles via I-80 and I-79." Jenna ate her waffles and kept on babbling through macerated dough. "After he checked out of the motel, he probably abandoned the truck. That would put the area of interest at roughly twenty miles around Pittsburgh."

Jenna didn't stop her sleuthing until her phone buzzed and a text notification appeared. "Well, hello, Clara," she said to the text. "You're up earlier than expected." Jenna smiled broadly as she confirmed a rendezvous time.

CLARA

Thursdays at the school café were always a big hit among students. The cafeteria offered a diverse selection of food, ensuring that it was quickly consumed before students departed for the weekend, particularly on holidays. The widely recognized *342 Unlimited 4U* logo helped popularize the three-for-two promotion. There was a mix of students who stored their food and others who had feasts at home.

Clara walked into the café lobby with Benji. There was more of a grin on his face than there had been this morning, but she knew it was still forced. Clearly, something was troubling him, but he remained silent. She wondered how long he had stayed at the pub waiting for her. They went different ways in the café, picking out what looked the best, and then met at the cash register. After Clara presented her student card and paid, she searched for a table.

The room was packed with hungry college students. She

FOREVER FAMILY

found a table in the center of the dining room and set her tray down.

"Don't you want to sit back there?" Benji gestured with his shoulder to the corner table where they typically sat.

"This is fine. Jenna's going to meet us, and she'll be able to see us better." Clara set her tray down when she noticed Benji's attention on the back table. She laid down her fork and napkin and began searching the room for Jenna.

Benji hesitated at the table, seemingly anticipating Clara's change of heart before placing down his own tray.

"Ah," said Clara, eyeing Benji's lunch choices. "You chose wisely. You can't go wrong with the mac 'n' cheese, taco, wings combo."

Benji sat motionless, staring at the food on his plate.

"Maybe you would like some of my turkey wrap, BLT panini, and broccoli salad combo." She pushed her tray closer to him.

Benji's disinterest and lack of good humor disappointed Clara.

"What's with you, Benji? You're not your usual self."

"I could say the same of you," he mumbled, poking his mac 'n' cheese with his spork.

Perplexed, Clara leaned back in her chair and crossed her arms over her chest. "What's that supposed to mean?"

"I just feel like you—" Benji started, but he was cut off.

"Clara!" Jenna waved over a fellow student from the checkout line as she teetered her tray over the railing.

Clara plastered a smile on her face, sat up straighter, and waved back.

"Can we talk later?" Clara whispered to Benji before Jenna approached. She hoped he could at least be civil. There was obviously something bothering him, but Clara was preoccupied with other matters.

Benji grunted as he slouched back, poking at his cheesy noodles.

"You won't believe what I discovered!" Jenna's eyes gleamed with excitement. She placed her tray on the table and glanced between Clara and Benji. "Who died?" She spoke apathetically as she sat down.

Benji's personality, Clara reflected.

Unfazed, Jenna continued with her exciting news. "I found the truck!" She stifled a laugh despite her best efforts to contain her excitement. "At least, I think it's the truck."

"What truck?" Clara questioned.

"What truck?" Jenna slid into a chair, her eyes widening in surprise. "*The* truck! Mr. Jack's green Ford!"

Clara's eyebrows lifted as her confusion gave way to comprehension. "You can't be serious?"

"Actually, I was quite extraordinary. My inquisitive fingers worked their alchemy in pursuit of the truth. In a matter of minutes, I located a possible match in Pittsburgh." Jenna's fingertips danced with mischievous delight, as if they were conjuring spells upon the invisible keyboard.

"My investigation led me to a scrap yard north of Pittsburgh, where sits a green Ford F-150. I spoke with a worker this morning. Six years ago, another junkyard gave them the vehicle after going out of business. The only documentation he received stated that it had been acquired fifteen years ago, abandoned with ownership unknown."

"Jenna! You are Sherlock Holmes reincarnated. That's

incredible."

"What good will it do to find the truck?" Benji mumbled.

Clara and Jenna exchanged puzzled looks, momentarily forgetting Benji's presence.

"What is wrong with you?" While Clara's concerns for Benji grew, she was absorbed in her search for truth. *Why does he fight me every step of the way?*

"We won't know until we go." At this, Jenna completely ignored Benji in favor of Clara. "Let's go tonight."

"Tonight?" both Clara and Benji replied, but Clara's tone hinted at a heightened sense of thrill, contrasting with Benji's astounded contempt.

"What better time? But I don't think this is the place to bring it up. Prying ears and all. Let's go to our investigative headquarters!"

"What?" Benji asked.

Clara grinned as she explained, "The library."

CHAPTER 26

CLARA

The building windows shimmered with a dazzling reflection as the three students strolled down the path leading to the library. With a dismissive swagger, Benji trailed the girls with his hands in his pockets, scattering loose pebbles off the sidewalk. Since the warm breeze wasn't helping to cool the heated tension, Clara rolled up her sleeves. Jenna whispered to Clara that she would meet her at the library after retrieving her pay from Java Junction.

Clara's body tingled with a strange sensation as she and Benji walked to the library. Benji's foot connected with a pinecone on the pavement, sending it skittering ahead. He avoided making eye contact and remained silent, showing his reluctance to start a conversation. Her stomach twisted, a physical manifestation of the tension that weighed heavily on her. It constricted her heart, making it difficult to breathe.

"Seriously, Benji, what's up with you?" She smacked his arm and refused to move, demanding an answer.

"I'm worried," Benji said without raising his head.

Clara remained silent, her arms crossed, and her face scrunched up, leaning on her hip. She silently pleaded for Benji to break the silence.

"You're different." With a swift kick, the pinecone was sent soaring off the sidewalk and Benji's expression fell as if he had lost a friend.

Clara relaxed her posture and narrowed her brow. "I'm not different." A gentle breeze blew from behind. Clara tucked her tresses behind her ears in an effort to control the ensuing chaos.

"You are." Benji met Clara's eyes. "You're missing classes, getting drunk with strangers, and making decisions that aren't your own. Chasing the past never ends well, and I ... I ..." He paused. "I beg you to rethink this." He placed a soft hand on her arm.

"That's not fair." Clara's hands tightened around his. "Benji, this time is different. Look how far Jenna has gotten me."

"Far enough to fall from a towering height. Every year, you put all of yourself into something new and it leaves you broken and scarred, leaving behind a trail of shattered hope. Each passing moment, my heart fractures, and I'm compelled to mend the both of us."

"No one said you have to do anything. This"—she pointed between the library and herself with her thumb and pinky—"is going to happen. You need to choose if you will be there with me or go home."

Benji lowered his head in defeat, allowing his feet to unconsciously guide him toward the library.

"We might not find out what really happened, but we are definitely finding more clues." Clara matched Benji's pace, determined to persuade him that their actions were justified. "In the past few days, we've uncovered more than the police have in fifteen years. Including their own blunders! Don't you think that's worth pursuing? I know everyone, including you, believes Lucy is dead. But I can't accept that. I'm not asking you to believe in her. I'm asking you to believe in me."

Clara watched Benji wilt. His face drooped, his posture defeated, and his shoulders caving. The Benji she knew was silenced; his strength stolen. *That Benji longed for a world filled with happy ponies and mistletoe, but that's not my world.*

"I need you, Benjamin," Clara said. "Please." By gently touching his elbow, she swung him around to face her. Clara looked into his eyes for some sign of acceptance or reassurance.

Benji sighed heavily. "Of course, I'm with you, Clara. I will never leave you."

Clara smiled and embraced her friend. Benji returned Clara's hug, but she was doubtful of his sincerity.

* * *

When Clara and Benji entered the library doors, it was as though the lights had gone out. Clara struggled to adapt her vision from the harsh outside glare to the soft golden lights within. The air felt heavy with the smell of citrus disinfectant and musty aged books.

Perched on the counter, Susan was in her usual spot, engaged in conversation with a group of youthful male students. She arched her back, leaning low, devouring the attention.

FOREVER FAMILY

"Hey, Susan. I need Room 4, please," Clara said as she approached the counter.

Susan's cheerful smile transformed into a cynical scowl. "You totally ghosted work yesterday," she snapped angrily through clenched teeth. She hopped down off the counter. "I had to bail on my sorority pledge because I had to be here!" She slammed a fist against the counter.

"Bummer. Room 4?" Clara rolled her eyes in annoyance and without sympathy.

Susan's perplexed and vexed countenance was met with Benji's nonsupportive expression. "I lost my sorority because of you!" Her voice rose to a shriek of indignation.

"Because of your bullying, I've lost even more. Your audacity to hurl insults at others is truly remarkable, considering you possess the uncanny ability to represent the epitome of an inferior species. Now sign me into Room 4!" Clara casually pivoted and strolled away.

Benji, the ever-loyal companion, followed in her wake, casting a watchful eye over his shoulder to witness the aftermath. Slouched in her chair behind the desk, Susan looked like a wilted flower in the middle of a bunch of young men who were spewing words of encouragement.

After entering the room, Clara placed her knapsack on the table and retrieved her water bottle. Benji walked in and began to shut the door.

"Leave that open." Clara motioned to the door. "Jenna will be here soon."

Obediently, he opened the door and cautiously sat two chairs away from Clara's workspace while watching her arrange her things.

A short while later, Jenna arrived. "What's up with Little Miss Perfect? She's blubbering like she just lost Miss America."

Clara shrugged.

"Whatever, let's get down to business!" Closing the door behind her, Jenna slid her messenger bag across the table to where Clara was sitting. She unzipped the tablet's case and removed the device, and Clara leaned in to find herself staring at aerial views.

"This dump could be where our truck is located." Jenna pointed to the image on the screen. "It's a two-and-a-half-hour drive, and they shut down at 6:00 p.m. If we leave campus by six, it will be quite dark by the time we arrive."

Clara squinted her eyes, trying to make out the blurry green shape on the screen. Clara found herself perplexed by Jenna's unwavering conviction that the truck was indeed the one that had gone missing.

"Why not go when they're open?" Benji asked.

"Where's the fun in that? Plus, who would allow a group of college students to wander the grounds freely?" Jenna rolled her eyes.

"It's just a pile of abandoned trash. How could we make things worse? They might even have the answers to our questions."

"Oh, Benjamin. One person's junk is another's treasure. People protect what's theirs. Whether junk or gems. You obviously have never done this before," Jenna scolded him.

"And you have?" Benji retaliated.

Jenna's diabolical smile crept across her face. "We'll have more freedom to do our own independent research once we sneak in."

"What about security cameras ... motion detectors ... dogs?"

"They have seven employees and no nighttime security. Most junkyards only install cameras at the main gate and administrative structures, not at each individual junk pile. And dogs? You watch too many movies. Who keeps dogs alone in a junkyard overnight?"

"You don't watch enough. Security dogs are more cost-effective than video surveillance. Not to mention, breaking and entering is illegal." The pitch of Benji's voice rose an octave.

"Now, who's saying it's worth protecting? And it's only illegal if you get caught."

"*What*? It's illegal whether you get caught or not! And you know what happens when you assume ... it makes *you* look like an *ass* in front of *me*."

Jenna responded with a defiant gesture and a cheeky raspberry.

Clara slammed her fists on the table, causing the two squabblers to freeze in surprise. "Either you two call a cease fire, or you both can go home and wait for my return! I will not risk being caught because you two can't control your mouths. Tonight is the night, and I need a reliable team."

Jenna and Benji exchanged embarrassed glances. Their deep-seated hostility manifested itself in a captivating performance, where opposing forces clashed in a never-ending struggle.

"Truce?" Benji asked.

"Truce," Jenna agreed. "For now."

Clara faced her. "Great. Now, Jenna, what are your plans?"

Jenna expanded the screen as Clara leaned in and Benji sank back in his chair.

"This is the main gate, where cameras are likely to be

installed." Jenna shot Benji an angry glare and stuck her tongue out at him. Clara elbowed her in the ribs. "The picture quality isn't great, but it's possible that there are cameras mounted on these posts. Thick woods border the northern and western edges of the facility, providing excellent cover. This," Jenna pointed at the southern end tracing the road, "is the most convenient parking spot. There is a pull-off near the location of the truck, and the road makes a sharp curve that provides natural cover ... right about here."

Clara and Benji followed Jenna's finger, tracing the potential path.

"Luckily, there doesn't appear to be a light post around the truck, so we'll be in the dark. Bring a flashlight."

"Won't the people on the other side of the street notice us?" Benji pointed to the line of houses.

"Not unless we advertise our presence. The fence is completely overgrown with thick vegetation. On both sides of the barrier, there are bushes that will camouflage. Given the proximity of the salvage yard, that pull-off undoubtedly encounters a significant number of abandoned vehicles. We won't be staying any longer than an hour at the most, and we'll be exiting the same way we came in."

"What if the fence is barbed or electrified?" Benji asked.

"I have a leather jacket to lay over barbs, and I doubt it's electrified in a residential zone. The street view reveals a wooden front fence, so I don't expect the remainder to be electric or barbed."

"Do you really think we can pull it off?" Clara panned in closer and observed the outline of a blurry green vehicle.

FOREVER FAMILY

"Don't worry, Clare Bear!"

Lu-Lu loves Clare Bear, a familiar voice echoed from her past.

"We can sneak in, snap some photos, and check out the truck, then slip out again before anyone notices." Jenna exuded an undeniable air of self-assurance.

"What are you looking for, exactly?" Benji asked.

"Anything. It's possible the suspect left something in the truck that can be used as proof. We won't know 'til we go!"

"Okay, I'm in. Let's do it!" Clara turned to Benji, expectantly.

"I'm in," Benji said, reluctantly.

"Fantastic! The Three Musketeers!" Jenna said.

"More like the three blind mice," Benji muttered.

CHAPTER 27

JENNA

Jenna moseyed back to her apartment and found herself with ample time to contemplate the evening. She didn't have unrealistic expectations, yet Benjamin managed to deeply affect her. His negativity was toxic.

Determining the age of either the satellite or ground views proved to be a challenging task. She might have coerced Clara and Benji into this adventure, or at the very least Clara and her shadow, but circumstances could shift, trees could be eradicated, debris could be relocated, and the occurrences under the cover of night were unpredictable. It all sounded quite thrilling.

As she turned the corner, a menacing growl and sharp bark startled her, causing her to stumble and fall against the curb, landing harshly on the concrete. Pain radiated through her left side. As she began to draw her blade, she recognized the beast that swiftly pounced on her and started licking her face affectionately.

"I'm so sorry!" a young lady's frenzied cry came from the nearest ally.

Around the massive animal, Jenna's focus fell upon Molly, a local adolescent who was known for her dog-walking services. The girl trailed the Alaskan malamute, clinging to an empty leash that whipped back and forth as she ran.

"Jeez-a-wheezy, Pebbles! You scared the nincompoop out of me!" Jenna heard every syllable that came out of her mouth. Once she regained her balance, she proceeded to brush off the gravel and dirt from her hands and cargo pants. She noticed a bruise forming around an abrasion on her hip. *When did this path become so perilous?*

"I'm really sorry, Jenna!" Molly apologized. "Since I was running late, Pebbles wasn't in the mood for a slow walk."

"No worries, Molly. Mr. Pebbles needs to learn some manners." Jenna gently massaged the dog behind his ears and then assisted Molly in reconnecting the leash. She carefully inspected the incision, tracing its path along her left side, noticing a small amount of blood staining the edges.

Pebbles gently pressed her snout against Jenna's hand, hoping for additional pets. To show her forgiveness, Jenna patted him many times, earning a dangerously strong tail thrashing in response.

"I know you were just protecting," Molly said in a low, soothing tone as her lips pouted. "Who could be mad at such a cute face?"

Fueled by a surge of adrenaline, Jenna thrust herself off the ground and jogged home. The absence of her father's vehicle meant she had a chance to clean up before he got home. At the foot of her staircase, she examined the battle scar on her side. Her skin was embellished with crimson droplets, like nature's own abstract artwork.

That could make an intriguing tattoo design.

Despite the warmth of the day, the stair railing felt extremely cold. As she climbed the steps, a brilliant flash caught her eye from the bushes. Her neck arched, straining against the weight of curiosity, as she peered beyond the tangled web of overgrown vegetation. She maneuvered under the rail and pushed the branches apart, determined to reach the sparkling object.

Is that a key chain? Jenna pulled the metal object out of the foliage.

It was a key chain bearing the initials *JS* in calligraphy along with the Penn State seal. Keys and student IDs dangled from the ring. *Joshua Schultz.*

He must have dropped them when he came after me that night. She hadn't seen him since that evening. In any case, she was relieved that he was either a superb illusionist or an expert at ghosting. This wasn't the first time someone had vanished after harassing her. She reflected on the unexplained disappearance of people who meant her harm. Then she and her father would move to a new location. *Didn't Dad want to move after the incident with Joshua?*

What if dad threatened them and forced us to move? Jenna arched an eyebrow as she looked at the apartment, then shook her head. *No. He couldn't. How can I think the worst?* She pocketed the keys and climbed the stairs to her apartment.

Anticipating her father's arrival, she gathered the necessary ingredients for spaghetti and set a pot of water on the stove to boil. She ventured into her room to prepare for an epic evening adventure.

"Okay, what shall I pack?" With a delicate touch, she traced her fingers along the fabric of each item in her closet, surveying the contents. *A day pack is perfect for transporting essentials.* She opened the pack and continued searching. "Leather jacket." She pulled her jacket off the hanger and stuffed it into her bag. The rhythmic rocking of the wire hanger captivated her. "A hanger ..." *You never know.*

Jenna decided to switch to a black top while still keeping her dark cargo trousers. She knew they would be perfect for carrying supplies. After that, she searched through her dad's work studio.

"I'll definitely need a flashlight." She grabbed the flashlight and a pair of gloves, positioned conveniently beside it. "Gloves! Of course. Duh!" She grabbed two more pairs of the black worker gloves for Clara and Benjamin. As she scanned the room one last time, she caught a glimmer of something intriguing. With a swift and decisive movement, she snatched the box cutter from the counter, concealing it within the depths of her bag, but not before she leaned over the table and struck her injured side against the work stool, causing her to wince.

"Oh. I'd better bandage that."

A first aid kit was installed on the wall near the entryway. Upon opening the case, Jenna carefully chose a selection of bandages and sticky tape. With her supplies in hand, she prepared to clean the wound in the bathroom. Her heart ached as she bid farewell to the crimson artwork decorating her flesh, yet the perils of potential infection compelled her to make this difficult choice. The wound was cushioned with gauze, and her midsection was tightly wrapped with sports tape.

There's no reason for that to fall off and leave my DNA behind.

She inspected her work before returning the remaining materials to the workshop. She decided it was a good idea to gather a small assortment of first aid provisions. Jenna surveyed the array of tools and materials scattered about the workshop. Amid the organized chaos, a small bag set at the far edge of the counter.

"Perfect."

Jenna navigated her way over her father's ongoing building projects, but she didn't quite make the clearance when her foot grazed the edge. With an unexpected burst of momentum, her body surged forward, landing beneath the work counter. She narrowly evaded a head collision with the unyielding leg of the counter.

"Jeez. Did he deliberately concoct a hazardous labyrinth of doom?" Jenna, after taking a moment to evaluate herself, leaned to her right side to get up, but noticed an intriguing detail in the wooden leg's backside. Etched into the timber were three small diagonal tallies, intersected by a solitary line. The marks were similar to the edge of a flat-head screwdriver.

As her fingers delicately followed the intricate markings, she discovered a subtle indentation in the smooth surface of the wood. Intrigued, she pressed her finger into the dent, causing a hidden compartment to slide out from the side nearest the wall.

"What the …"

Jenna struggled to rise from the floor, cradling her side in pain while carefully maneuvering to avoid hitting her head on the counter. Her fingers followed the counter to the edge, and there, hidden within the compartment, lay a small metal object ... a key. The key, though smaller than a conventional house key, possessed a stockier appearance, with a noticeably thicker barrel that led to the intricate locking mechanism.

Jenna turned the metal object, and with a soft exhale, she easily blew away the tiny bits of sawdust that were stuck to the surface's intricate patterns.

"Why would he go through the trouble of hiding a key? And what does it go to?"

The sound of her dad's truck beeping outside snapped her out of her reverie. She planned to give this riddle more thought later. Before she could begin tonight's expedition, though, she had to finish packing.

After closing the compartment, she carefully placed the key in her pocket before making her way to the kitchen. Sensing the need for sustenance, she procured a selection of items from the snack cabinet.

She popped open the fridge and did a fast survey, pausing at the turkey lunch meat. Her mind drifted to Pebbles and the conversation with Benjamin. "Just in case." She sealed the sandwich bag and tucked it into her bag.

The door latch started to wobble, so she quickly zipped up her day pack, tossed it on a dining chair, and headed for the stove. She placed the pasta in a pot of boiling water and simultaneously began preparing the sauce in another pot.

"I didn't think you'd be home this early," her dad said as he locked the door behind him.

"I'm going exploring tonight with a friend, so I figured I'd prepare dinner for you before I leave."

"What friend, where to, and how long?" His gentle voice turned cold and stern.

Jenna's skin prickled, as if a thousand tiny feathers danced along the nape of her neck. She could feel her father's eyes on the back of her neck. She hoped he wouldn't inquire further, but he tended to dig for details.

A fight is inevitable. The truth will bring it now; a lie will bring it later.

Perhaps if she told him the truth in a certain way, he wouldn't see it as such a big deal. "Clara. We're going to Pittsburgh for a quick visit and then back home. I should be back by two at the latest."

Silence.

Her cheekbones were ablaze with a searing sensation, while an ever-mounting tension gripped her shoulders. She dared not to witness her father's reaction, instead choosing to fixate on the simmering spaghetti sauce, diligently stirring it despite its lack of heat. Her stomach churned with the anticipation of her father's wrath.

When nothing came, she cautiously turned her head. "Daddy?"

After taking a few deep breaths and laying down his work materials, her father sat down on the couch. Curious by his unusual reaction, Jenna tried to lower the intensity of the sauce's temperature, only to realize that she had neglected to activate it. She moved closer to her dad.

Like the previous evening, he settled on the sofa and gazed

aimlessly across the room. "Daddy?" Jenna repeated.

"Jenna, if you keep going in this direction, I'll lose you again." His tone reflected despair and grief. "I've worked so hard to get you back and keep you safe. Don't leave me alone again."

"What are you talking about? You won't lose me. When did you ever lose me?" Jenna sank down next to her father and clasped her hands in his.

Covering her hands, her father firmly proclaimed, "I forbid you to go!"

Jenna recoiled in shock at the abrupt shift in demeanor, yet a fiery anger burned within her, fueled by his commanding tone. "I am going! You can't stop me. Maybe if you told me the truth I wouldn't have to find it on my own. I can't stand having my every move tracked. I'm eighteen. An adult. I can make my own choices."

Jenna sprang from the couch, snatched her backpack from the nearby chair, and stomped to the front door. Struggling with the dead bolt, then hastily departed, not allowing her father a moment to reply.

CHAPTER 28

CLARA

The campus was completely empty, except for a few tardy students who were running to their six o'clock class. Students typically congregated on campus on Thursday evenings for informal networking and mingling, but this holiday weekend changed things a bit. The picnic tables were under the watchful surveillance of a vigilant duo of stray cats, diligently scouring the area for any signs of scurrying rodents or delectable morsels left behind. The campus was bathed in a mystical glow, courtesy of the nearly full moon.

On the cold stone steps of the library, Benji and Clara sat in anticipation, scanning the surroundings for any sign of Jenna's arrival. Benji's foot nudged the fallen acorns and small stones, creating a soft rustling. Clara watched the cats as they leaped and darted at the squirrels that taunted and scampered through the branches above.

"Hey, relax. It's not too late to change your mind." Benji's hand delicately caressed Clara's chin, stopping her from biting her lip.

Her teeth sank into her lower lip, a subtle pressure betraying her inner conflicts. It was a small action, almost imperceptible, but she couldn't ignore the unease that coursed through her. The anticipation bubbling inside her, a mix of excitement and nervous energy. Her cheek twitched as she clenched her teeth, a silent protest against his touch. Swiftly, she evaded his hand, tilting her head away from his grasp.

"I've spent my entire life waiting for the truth. I finally feel in control." Clara could see the reservations in Benji's eyes. He was making her feel uncomfortable, so she intentionally stepped down a few stairs and looked down the drive for Jenna. The turbulent journey of his emotions was causing her to experience a mental whiplash.

Benji's face grimaced as he snatched his backpack off the ground, then held out his hand for Clara's bag. He tossed them through the rear window. Leaning up against the driver's door, he crossed his hands and waited.

"She's coming!" Clara's body jolted upward with a burst of excitement.

Despite his true feelings, Benji managed to muster a smile in response. Confusion clouded her thoughts as she tried to grasp his reasons for holding a grudge against Jenna, but she couldn't afford to dwell on it at the moment. Clara smiled as Jenna approached.

"Hey, guys!" Jenna called out.

Clara descended the steps. "Why do you have on a long-sleeved black shirt? Tonight is going to be warm."

"Easier to hide in the shadows and avoid getting pricked by thorns. Unseen, unharmed, and unstoppable."

Clara inspected her bare arms, exposed by the short-sleeved purple shirt she wore. *Maybe Jenna has done this before.*

Ignoring the girls, Benji got into the driver's seat.

With her rucksack in tow, Jenna slid into the open window, and Clara settled into the front passenger seat.

* * *

Benji's Jeep approached the last corner, leading to the road pull-off indicated on the navigation app. He gently eased his foot off the gas pedal, then turned off the headlights, plunging the surroundings into darkness. Aside from the enchanting symphony of crickets and frogs, the vicinity lay abandoned, cloaked in a serene silence.

"You passed it!" Jenna's hand whacked Benji's shoulder, an abrupt and unexpected strike, as the Jeep glided past the gravel lot.

"I know. I'm circling back. Take it easy."

Clara's hands fumbled to unfasten her seat belt, making her movements deliberate and silent, as if the faint sound of the belt retracting could potentially betray their hidden motives. As she crouched in the shadows, heart pounding, she couldn't believe the rush of excitement coursing through her veins. Breaking into a business in the dead of night was something she never imagined she would find thrilling.

Benji parked his vehicle under a streetlamp, its light flickering sporadically. A thick layer of cobwebs covered the lampshade, while a pair of shoes dangled from its post, swaying in the warm breeze. The girls emerged from the vehicle as Benji stashed the keys inside a magnetic lockbox tucked beneath the driver's seat.

"In case we split up." He looked between Clara and Jenna and whispered, "For the record, we haven't done anything illegal yet. You still have time to change your mind."

"For the record, you don't have to go." Jenna's eyes rolled in annoyance as she snatched her bag from the Jeep and headed into the thick undergrowth.

Benji's shoulders slumped as he snatched his bag. He trailed behind Clara, his disappointment evident in every step.

No one was out walking their dogs or jogging on the quiet street. Clara failed to detect any blinds or drapes that were suspiciously drawn. The window coverings revealed no discernible slits, leaving no trace of lurking observers. No one suspected the students of breaking into the salvage yard across the street.

This is crazy! Clara felt the rumbling thrill coursing just beneath her skin. She turned and focused on Jenna, curious of her current activity, and followed her lead.

Jenna was crouched in the grass line, peering through the dense bushes, searching for the optimal point of entry. Thorny vines, bushes, and other aggressive plants guarded the fence that would be encasing the junkyard. Once they had overcome the initial obstacle of dense vegetation, they came across a chain-link fence that was topped with a menacing line of barbed wire.

Clara's regret for her clothing choice intensified as she trudged through the dense thicket. Her arms bore the subtle marks of a battle fought, etched with delicate scratches.

"Right, then." Jenna squared her shoulders and locked eyes with Clara and Benji. "We will need gloves and my leather jacket to get over the barbs. Once we're over, move through those bushes." She gestured to the right. "We'll come out directly in front of the truck."

A skeptical smile tugged at the corners of Benji's mouth.

Jenna retrieved the gloves and threw a pair to both Clara and Benji.

"Even the gloves are black? You thought of everything." The unsettling fact that Clara had failed to think of gloves heightened her anxiety.

"Turn off all electronic devices," Jenna said. "We wouldn't want any unexpected sounds proclaiming our presence. Ready?"

"Ready," Clara whispered. Her hands trembled as she fidgeted with the hem of her shirt

Jenna retrieved her leather jacket from her bag and tossed it over to Benjamin. "When I get up there, throw that to me."

"Maybe I should go." Benji's eyes followed the top of the fence line.

"Be my guest." Jenna stepped aside with arms widened in a welcoming gesture.

Benji passed her the jacket, but he kept his eyes on the barbed wire. He tugged at his gloves, making sure they were secure around his wrists, then began to scale the six-foot structure. The metal links bit into his skin despite the gloves, and he grimaced as he flexed his fingers a few times. He reached the top and gestured with his right hand. Jenna responded by tossing the jacket. The garment draped across the barbed wires. Exhaling a breath between puckered lips, Benji lifted his leg to climb over.

Clara's breath caught in her throat as she noticed a sudden descent from the fence, briefly thinking it might be Benji. His back

FOREVER FAMILY

pocket released an object that landed on the ground with a thump.

Jenna moved over to the item and used the hem of her jeans to wipe down Benji's phone. Her voice barely above a whisper, she reassured him, "It's all right." His phone remained intact.

Benji's lips parted, releasing a sigh of relief, as he continued to stretch himself over the fence.

Jenna assisted Clara in getting started on the ascent after she had stashed Benji's phone in one of her lower cargo pockets.

Benji crossed over the fence, jumped down, and landed heavily on the other side. He strained his ears to detect any other disruptions but seemingly found none.

Clara carefully examined the towering wall and positioned herself in line with the jacket above. She glanced at her skirt. *I did not think this through.* She savored a long, deep breath, preparing herself for the ascent. As she pulled against the wire mesh, the pain shot through her hands, the gloves offering little relief. Her delicate fingertips throbbed with pain as each grip tightened. She placed her foot on the first step, then the second, and continued climbing until her foot slipped. She heard Benji exhale through his teeth, but she quickly recovered. The pain in her hands intensified as the metal pinched into her skin and caused her entire body to stiffen.

"Careful," Benji whispered.

Clara's hand stretched around the jacket as she maneuvered her body over it. She braced herself as she lifted her leg over the razor-sharp wire barrier. Once she reached the other side, she carefully climbed down the chain-link fence instead of leaping down.

Hands tightened against her waist, and she took a jagged breath. When Clara realized Benji was assisting, she let herself be lowered. As she turned, gratitude filled her heart, but when she caught sight of his eyes, her expression froze. A spark ignited in her belly, causing her cheekbones to develop a radiant glow. She brushed off the sensation and turned to see Jenna climbing over her jacket without any difficulty.

With a graceful leap, she effortlessly propelled herself away from the fence, maintaining her equilibrium as she executed a flawless landing. Clara's eyes darted toward the abandoned jacket. She instinctively began rubbing her hands together, desperately seeking relief from the sting of the fence.

"Leave it," Jenna said. "We'll need it to cross back over, and it's a useful marker for the Jeep."

Hardwood trees wooded this side of the fence instead of prickly hedges. Their sturdy trunks reached high into the sky. Between them, the brambles weren't as overpowering. The dense woods enveloped the surroundings, casting profound shadows that offered an ideal sanctuary for concealment, but the stillness of the night made even the smallest of noises seem deafening. Every branch snap, leaf rustle, owl hoot, or woodpecker thud caused Clara's body to jolt.

Jenna darted from tree trunk to tree trunk, leading Clara and Benji closer to the open field.

Standing beneath the branches of a towering tree, Clara took in the expansive field before her. Her eyes adjusted, trying to capture any changes in the pattern of darkness. The scene that unfolded was quite different from the satellite image she had seen earlier, as the field was now arranged with heaps of crushed automobiles rather than parked intact vehicles. Darkness covered most of the field, yet it was evident that the truck was not in its expected location.

"I don't understand. It should be right here!" Jenna emerged from the cover of the trees and circled the first cluster of mangled vehicles, resembling a Jenga puzzle.

The freshly cut green trails between the heaps of crushed vehicles were dotted with dandelions and purple clovers. Clara looked around, feeling lost and uncertain. Wondering what their next move should be, she glanced at Benji. His lips curled into a contemptuous sneer.

Jenna examined the ground, as if a new plan would materialize within the soil. "We split up. If you see the truck, make an owl hoot, and then give the flashlight a little flicker on the ground, like this." She cycled her light on and off, illuminating the dirt, to demonstrate.

Benji shook his head. "Splitting up is a terrible idea."

"Again, you watch too many movies. This way, we'll find it faster."

"What if it's not here?" His voice brimmed with disdain.

"We'll set a time limit. Twenty minutes. If no one finds anything, we'll meet back here and leave. Sound good?"

"Okay," Clara whispered, unsure. Her heart raced with excitement at first, but soon a knot began to tighten in her stomach.

Clara's eyes met Benji's for a brief moment, silently communicating their unspoken agreement that they didn't want to go alone. Beyond the open field lay a vast labyrinth of twisted metal, a tangled web of abandoned cars, ancient appliances, and forgotten scraps of metal. Her vision became muddled as the shapes in the moonlight danced and transformed. Her body trembled involuntarily as her mind conjured up terrifying possibilities lurking within the darkness. She clenched her fists, desperately longing for someone to be by her side.

As a metallic clatter echoed through the night, Clara's body stiffened, locking her muscles in an instant. Crouching low to the ground, she swiftly moved to the right and took cover behind a pile of wrecked cars. She inched forward, her heart pounding, her breath shallow. The wreckage loomed before her, a chaotic jumble of distorted metal and debris. Her fingers vibrated with adrenaline as she carefully steadied herself against a small opening, allowing her to catch a glimpse of what lay on the other side. Her heart jumped as she spotted a person hiding in the shadows. The figure stumbled and tripped over scattered debris, exposing their location.

Clara's pulse pounded so hard she thought her chest might explode as the shadow got closer. The sound of her heart echoed in her ears, making her worry that the mysterious figure might be able to hear it, too. The dark figure loomed closer, causing her to contort her body against the ground, blending into the shadows in an attempt to evade detection. Clara's breath escaped her lips, a visible release of tension, as the faint beam of moonlight gently illuminated her best friend.

"Benji?" Clara's body straightened, her hands brushing the dirt from her knees. "Jeez-a-wheezy, Benji. You nearly gave me a heart attack." She placed her hands on her chest and inhaled deeply, attempting to calm her spastic heart.

"Sorry. This place is creepy as hell."

"Yeah."

"Why not go back and wait for Jenna at the Jeep? There's

FOREVER FAMILY

nothing here. Even if there was, we're not going to find it in the dark."

She pondered his comments until she heard the owl's call. "Jenna!" With a radiant smile, Clara grasped Benji's hand and pulled him through the chaotic stacks, determined to uncover the origin of the obscure call.

Her eyes narrowed as she scanned the ground, desperately looking for any trace of Jenna's flickering light. "Over there." A tower of scrap metal stood tall, casting flickering shadows as the light pulsated. Clara's heart raced as she quickened her pace, determined to find Jenna.

Panting and out of breath, Clara took a moment to calm her breathing before focusing on what Jenna's light revealed.

Clara's hand tightened around Benji's as they caught sight of the weathered green vehicle. Unconsciously, her jaw fell as she struggled to comprehend what she was witnessing. A green Ford F-150 pickup truck sat before her, its rusty exterior resembling a spreading cancer. On its door was a yellow caution logo, its inscription faded beyond recognition. Clara's body tensed and her face tightened. Right in front of her was the vehicle that eyewitnesses described.

"Are you all right?" Benji's hushed words slipped from his lips, reaching Clara's ears with a tender touch.

The truck emitted an eerie and foreboding presence into the heavy air. Goose bumps prickled up her arms like mischievous little sprites, the hair on the back of her neck standing upright. She approached the driver's-side door, scanning its surface. Her finger traced the outline of the faded logo, her touch gentle and tentative. Its worn exterior hinted at a lifetime of encounters, perhaps even holding the key to unraveling the mystery surrounding Lucy's disappearance.

Scattered scraps of metal and discarded vehicle parts obstructed the passenger side. Jenna's fingers struggled with the driver's door, its handle releasing an ear-piercing screech of rebellion. Given the presence of a concave roof, it seemed unlikely that the doors would have the ability to close, let alone lock. Yet it was locked.

Jenna placed her bag on the ground and began rummaging through its contents. She pulled out a wire hanger.

"Look who's been to too many movies now. You think *that* will open the lock?" Benji's face twisted into a scowl as he spoke.

By unraveling the metal's spiral, Jenna fashioned a long hook. She leaned against the glass, carefully maneuvering the hook through a small crack in the window and into the truck's interior. She tried moving the hanger up and down, but she couldn't find the correct angle to reach the handle.

"Okay, plan B." With a swift motion, she detached the hanger and discarded it over her shoulder.

The clanging sound of metal hitting the ground and bouncing off other metal items filled Clara's ears. Her body tensed as she searched for any signs that the noise attracted unwelcomed attention.

Jenna's hand dove into the depths of her bag, searching until it emerged, clutching a small container.

"Is that dental floss?" Clara squinted at the container.

"Trust me."

Jenna's confident smile reassured Clara, even though she had no idea what Jenna was planning.

FOREVER FAMILY

With a swift motion, Jenna seized a long strand of floss from the container and pulled it free with a sharp snap. After making a slipknot halfway along one edge, she moved the floss back and forth from the corner of the door's window until the string was visible inside. She skillfully guided the floss downward, inch by inch, gradually bringing the slipknot closer to the knobbed lock.

"No way." Benji edged closer to Jenna's right.

The slipknot moved back and forth, grazing the locking mechanism. Jenna skillfully fastened the knot around the knob by delicately manipulating the thread and swiftly pulling it tight.

Benji's hands mirrored her every movement.

Jenna reached above the window, bringing the ends of the floss together. She then twisted the strands around her hand and pulled upward. The three exchanged triumphant glances as they heard the satisfying thud of the door unlocking.

"Where did you learn to do that?" Clara leaned in, captivated by the sight before her. Dental floss, of all things.

"TikTok. Where else?"

Decades of abandonment and disregard had rendered the door's springs rigid, making the door challenging to open. Benji stepped up to help. He grabbed the door handle, his muscles straining as he applied pressure. The door resisted, its hinges creaking in protest before finally giving way with a grumble. The door crashed to the ground, leaving Benji standing there, still holding on to the handle.

Clara carefully climbed into the cab, swiveling her flashlight to illuminate the interior while making sure to avoid the protruding springs. The inside smelled of musty mold and mildew. A boulder-sized object seemed to have crashed onto the roof, causing the ceiling to dip low. Particles of fabric from the shredded ceiling cover were scattered throughout the entire cab, mixing in with a layer of dust. Clara's eyes stung as the tiny particles invaded. She wished she had brought a mask to filter the microdebris, as she coughed.

Jenna stepped up, ready to climb inside. "Why don't you check the back?" With a casual flick of her hand, she motioned for Benji to investigate the back of the truck.

His eyes rolled as he sharply turned and jumped into the cargo bed.

Clara watched him through the cracked and filthy back window, feeling a slight dip as he climbed into the bed of the truck. She shifted her focus back to the passenger side while Jenna scanned the driver's side. The beam of light crossed the worn floorboards, exploring the hidden corners of the glove compartment, and illuminated the space above the windshield visor. Yet it unveiled no secrets, no trace of the truck's previous occupant.

What was I expecting to discover after all these years? Trying to ignore the heavy doubts cluttering her mind, she carefully examined between the seats, feeling the texture of crumpled paper beneath her fingertips. It had the weight and size of a magazine or large paperback with a smooth, glossy cover and thick, crisp pages. Her fingers delicately slid beneath the literature, ensuring a gentle removal that wouldn't damage the pages. An Ohio road map. *You don't see these anymore.* As Clara flipped through the water-damaged pages, a document landed in her lap.

Curiosity sparked as Clara tossed the road map onto the floor. She carefully unraveled the trifold letter, eager to discover its contents. The faded handwritten letter revealed its age, its delicate

FOREVER FAMILY

ink slowly losing its vibrancy over time. Traces of water had gently erased some of the words, leaving behind faint imprints that hinted at a heartfelt message of gratitude. It seemed to be a letter expressing appreciation for outstanding work. Despite the ravaged parchment, two words stood out: *Jack Drewitt*.

"This is his truck!"

Jenna leaned closer, eager to catch a glimpse of what Clara held in her hands. She twisted her body to open the back window open. When the window wouldn't budge, she shouted, "This is Drewitt's truck! Examine everything!"

"The only evidence I'm finding is that birds enjoy leaving their filthy business all over the place," Benji grumbled from outside.

Clara flipped herself upside down in order to shine her light underneath the passenger seat. The gentle glow of the light revealed the dance of floating dust particles. Although captivating, their presence was irrelevant to the ongoing investigation.

Jenna stepped out of the vehicle and crouched down to examine what was underneath the driver's seat. There wasn't much that her light revealed, but she did notice a tear in the corner of the carpet liner. She pulled and tugged at the carpet, widening the hole with each forceful motion. The flashlight revealed a satin-like red material.

While pulling the red material out from the carpet, Jenna said, "I think I found a ribbon."

As Clara leaned over the seat, she briefly saw the red ribbon before a blinding light suddenly illuminated the area, obstructing her view of the object.

Security lights bathed the junkyard, exposing their position and leaving them vulnerable. The three novice detectives surveyed their surroundings, their heads held high, vigilant for any potential threats. The air filled with the echoing barks and haunting howls of distant dogs.

CHAPTER 29

CLARA

Clara's mind flashed back to her high school theater days, where the intensity of the lights had evoked panic and terror on center stage. The scrapyard came alive with a burst of light as each security light flickered and glowed, transforming the once-dark corners into vibrant displays of scrap heaps. Even from a safe distance, the growls and howls of canines sounded close.

Benji's eyes narrowed as he shot a sharp glance at Jenna, his frustration evident. Without a word, he leaped over the side of the truck bed, his actions speaking louder than any words could.

Clara delicately folded the paper, carefully concealing it within the depths of her bag. Meanwhile, Jenna thrust the ribbon into the confines of her pocket.

After stepping aside so Benji could help Clara out of the cab, Jenna explained the new plan. "The Jeep's too far. The river's closer. We can circle back through the woods."

Jenna's feet softly pounded against the ground as she sprinted north, presumably where the river was located. Clara's heart raced as she stole glances between Benji frozen in place and Jenna's retreating figure. "We should follow."

"The Jeep isn't too far." He pointed in the opposite direction.

"What about Jenna?"

Trusting her oldest friend, she didn't resist when Benji's fingers intertwined with hers, and they sprinted away together. The ground beneath crunched with the impact of stones and debris. Each step stirred up clouds of dust, swirling and curling in the air. All attempts at concealment were abandoned in favor of a faster getaway.

Above their heads, discarded metals and vessels loomed ominously, their precarious positions presenting a serious threat. Every distant shadowy figure transformed into more tangible obstacles.

Clara's footing faltered as she stared up at a metal obelisk blocking their path. As she stumbled, her ankle twisted unnaturally, wrenching her down to the ground as she slipped free from Benji's grip. Her fingers clenched, digging into her ankle. Her lip trembled as she clenched it between her teeth, a silent battle against the pain threatening to escape her.

"Get up!" Benji's voice cracked, exposing his fear.

"I twisted my ankle." Her teeth gritted, her body swaying rhythmically as she fought to suppress the welling tears.

"Can you stand?" Benji's attention was captured by the

FOREVER FAMILY

distant sound of muffled barks, diverting his focus from Clara.

After putting her entire weight on her injured foot, Clara grimaced in pain. Tears collected in her eyes as she looked up at Benji. He gently slid his arm beneath hers, providing support. Her brow furrowed and her lips tightened, creating a crinkled expression on her face. Attempting to outrun a pack of dogs was a futile endeavor. The sound of barking grew closer.

"Maybe we can hide." Benji's voice wavered. He scanned the surroundings, searching for a safe hiding spot.

With careful guidance, Benji assisted Clara in climbing into an overhead truck that had no doors. She used her arms to haul herself up and across the vehicle, feeling the frayed fabric like unruly stubble brushing against her legs. Their heads snapped in unison, drawn by the distant yelp that pierced the air.

Benji searched for any signs of danger. Satisfied that the coast was clear, he climbed in behind Clara.

Ducking their heads, Clara and Benji huddled deeper into the shadows. Her grip on Benji's hand tightened as the sound of male voices reached their ears.

"You see anything?" a deep and rough male voice said from beneath the front of the vehicle.

Benji pressed his finger against his lips.

"No! But Butch and Thunder are trackin' somethin'!" yelled a guy tethered to a couple of dogs a little way away.

"Over here. I think I heard something!"

Clara buried her head in Benji's chest.

The sound of heavy footsteps abruptly ceased beneath their hiding spot as dogs sniffed the air with a low, menacing growl.

"What'd you hear?" The dogs' barks drowned out the man's

attempt to speak softly.

"Shh!"

Clara's eyelids fluttered shut, her breath held in anticipation. Above her, a faint shuffling sound reached her ears. Her heart pounded in her chest as the dogs' growl intensified.

The sound of metal scraping traveled down the hood of the truck, eventually reaching a pile of debris nearby. The dogs' ferocious barks filled the air—as if in pursuit of the squeaky sound's source—echoing through the stacks, accompanied by a piercing high-pitched squeal.

"What happened?"

"Dogs spotted a racoon."

"Let's head back. I ain't seen nothing."

"Yeah, me, neither. Gotta get the dogs first. Butch! Thunder! Home!" the man hollered. "Besides, something got old Thunder. He's limpin'."

Clara and Benji exchanged glances, their tense shoulders relaxing as the sounds of human voices and barking dogs gradually faded into the distance. Clara's breath escaped her lips in a heavy sigh, her head spinning and her body growing feeble with nausea. As she tried to shift, Benji's palm abruptly halted her movement.

"Not yet," he whispered.

Security lights continued to shine brightly and illuminate everything even after the men's voices faded away.

"Shh ... wait here." Benji navigated around Clara, mindful not to disturb her injured leg. Before he descended, he twisted around and gave her a reassuring smile.

Clara strained her eyes, hoping to catch a glimpse of him, but he remained hidden from view once he hit the ground.

He pressed his feet firmly into the earth, anchoring himself, before stretching his arm upward to snatch the dangling mirror from a neighboring vehicle. Crouching low, he cautiously positioned the mirror to peer around the corner. He rose, apparently seeing nothing and abandoning the mirror on the ground.

"It's clear," he whispered, his voice barely audible as he motioned for Clara.

Her face contorted in pain as her left ankle throbbed, her body shifting ever so slightly to bring her closer to the edge of the vehicle.

"Set your foot here and fall into my arms. I'll catch you."

Clara followed the direction of Benji's extended arm, guiding her to the spot where she should place her foot. With a solid foothold beneath her, despite her wobbly legs, she looked back to find Benji poised to catch her. Leaning back, Clara placed her trust in Benji. Her heart raced as his strong arms enveloped her, guiding her down to the ground.

"Which way?" Clara's eyes shifted from one corner to another, taking in her surroundings.

"This way, I think." Benji glanced behind him, his thumb pointing in that direction.

"You think?" Clara's voice trembled.

"I got turned around!"

Perspiration dripped down Clara's face. Whether her anxiety was manifesting itself physically or the night was simply getting warmer, she had no way of knowing. The twisted maze of metal hindered any possibility of a straightforward getaway. Finding the perimeter fencing was their primary goal as it would lead them to the exit no matter where they were in the complex.

Clara clenched her teeth with perseverence despite the pain shooting up her spine. With each step she took, the sharp pain intensified, and her nausea increased, making it impossible for her to ignore the excruciating ache in her ankle. "I need a break."

"We can't. We'll stop on the other side of the fence."

Clara attempted to ignore her frantic friend, since her throbbing ankle demanded instant attention. She reduced her pace, letting Benji continue near a thick cluster of foliage. He ventured deep into its depths, searching relentlessly for the elusive edge.

"Over here!"

To Clara's left, she noticed some trembling plants. Her heart sank at the sight of the dense tangle of vines and branches. He approached her, his eyes filled with empathy. Without a word, he carefully lifted her onto his back, offering his strength to help her get to the fence.

A tall barrier emerged, its presence commanding attention. The sight was daunting, with the barbed wire snaking along the highest point, guarding it fiercely. Clara felt a tightening in her chest as doubt began to seep in, quietly suggesting that she may not possess the necessary strength and skill to overcome this daunting challenge, especially at this moment.

"We'll follow it and see if there's a hole or break or something," Benji said. He seemed to possess a sixth sense for discerning Clara's thoughts.

Not far from their location, the fence bent into a subtle curvature, providing them with a narrow passage to maneuver beneath its confines. With the greatest of care, Benji gently placed

FOREVER FAMILY

Clara on the ground, ensuring her safety. Displaying remarkable agility, he skillfully maneuvered through the narrow opening with a military-like precision, successfully avoiding any potential harm.

With a limping gait, Clara approached the sturdy chain-link fence. Despite the pain, she stooped to the small opening, granting Benji the opportunity to lend a helping hand. She found herself pressed against the unyielding earth, her body tense with anticipation. She extended her arms to find Benji, her fingers quivering in the dim light. Their fingers barely brushed against Benji's as he slowly pulled her through. As he helped her regain her balance, she adjusted her disheveled attire, ensuring that every speck of dirt and lifeless foliage was expelled from her itchy skin.

They clung to the winding trail of fencing, concealing themselves amid the lush undergrowth, until the prickly thorns and clinging burrs grew impenetrably thick. Emerging from the shroud of foliage, they pressed forward, only to stumble upon the well-known road that encircled the southern boundaries of the salvage yard. Their faces lit up with smiles as they discovered the road.

"Almost there!" Benji said. He crouched low, his back hunching forward, inviting Clara to climb onto his back once more.

Clara recognized the swerve in the road ahead and hope bubbled in her chest. She found a towering oak tree. She remembered it sheltered Benji's Jeep beneath, but the view of the gravel lot was obstructed by dense, oversize shrubs.

Benji's pace quickened, his arms instinctively encircling her legs while she clung tightly to his shoulders. They came to a stop at the opposite end of the shrubbery, scanning the vast expanse of gravel stretching out in front of them. The Jeep was gone.

"No, no, no, no, no!" Benji cried as he lowered Clara to the ground and sprinted into the vacant area ahead. He whipped his fingers through his disheveled hair, his eyes racing around the lot in a desperate search for his missing vehicle.

Clara hobbled forward, then paused when she noticed lights casting a vibrant glow in the distance. Flashing blues and reds reflected off the leaves of the trees.

The police cruiser slid to a sudden stop on the loose gravel, its tires kicking up dust and pebbles. A commanding voice yelled, "Hands in the air!"

CHAPTER 30

JENNA

Jenna's heart surged. Her pulse pounded in her ears, when the overhead security lights flickered on, revealing every nook and cranny, leaving no place to hide. Air entered her chest with a calculated deep breath, and a sense of calmness allowed her to strategize her next move. As her pulse quickened, she discovered an intensified thrill coursing through her veins. While Benji assisted Clara out of the truck, Jenna's mind conjured vivid images of aerial snapshots, disclosing the river as a more accessible escape route compared to the Jeep.

"Right. The Jeep's too far. The river's closer. We can circle back." The moment Clara's feet touched the ground, Jenna sprinted north, heading straight for the river.

Under the bright security lights, the ground sparkled with glass fragments and metal debris. Giant beams of light reflected across the windows and metallic surfaces, exposing Jenna's surroundings, leaving her feeling vulnerable and unprotected. She weaved through the maze of scrap metal and abandoned automobiles, her movements quick and agile. She scanned the surroundings, seeking out a path shrouded in shadows. Her heart skipped a beat when she glanced briefly behind her and saw that Clara and Benji weren't there.

Where did they go? Jenna's neck stretched as she peered around the final corner, hoping to catch a glimpse of her companions, but they were nowhere in sight. Ready to proceed with her plan, she presumed they got separated and would reunite at the Jeep.

The sound of dogs howling grew nearer and more intense. Jenna rummaged through her bag, searching for the one item she had convinced herself she would never need. With her knife, she sliced open the bag of lunch meat, allowing the enticing aroma to waft through the air and attract the canines. They were close. Real close.

Jenna heard the sound of paws thundering against the soil. She readied herself for the impending onslaught, clutching the lunch meat tightly in one hand and brandishing her knife in the other. Suddenly, a gigantic dog sprang in front of Jenna, its massive build trembling as it snarled at her. Frothy droplets dripped from its mouth, and dirt clung to the leash, hanging loosely from its collar.

With a mischievous glint in her eyes, Jenna unleashed her secret weapon: the bag of lunch meat. She flung the entire bag at the dog's paws, hoping the distraction would allow her time to escape.

The canine pawed cautiously at the mysterious opening of the sack, momentarily ceasing its growl in order to thoroughly investigate the tantalizing scent emanating from within. The plastic was no match for the dog's sharp teeth as it tore through, causing the lunch meat to burst out in a messy heap. Without hesitation, the dog devoured every morsel. Its nose twitched as it explored its surroundings, searching for any lingering treats. The growl intensified, as the dog bared his sharp fangs.

Ineffective beyond belief. Maybe I shouldn't have cut it open.

Jenna's body tensed as she assumed an offensive stance, her feet firmly planted on the ground and her grip on her knife tightening. She scanned the ground, searching for a rock or a piece of wood that could be used to coax the dog into action. With lightning speed, the dog lunged at her as she knelt down to snatch up a stone. The stone flew through the air, bouncing off the animal's side, but it had no effect on his speed. A surge of pain coursed through her arm as the tenacious dog sank its teeth into her delicate flesh. Undeterred, she summoned her inner fighter and countered, plunging her blade deep into the dog's front leg. The animal unleashed a thunderous cry and bolted away.

Jenna took a moment to catch her breath, feeling the adrenaline coursing through her. She rotated her sleeve to protect her wounds from grime and dirt as she ventured into the wooded area. After wiping her blade on her pants to clean it, she carefully put it back in her pocket and launched herself into a full-on sprint toward the northernmost edge. Deftly maneuvering around hazardous debris jutting out from the jumbled heaps, she finally arrived at the fence. She scanned the area, then focused on the barbed wire. Without a jacket to protect herself, she decided to trace the path of the barricade, searching for a safer route beneath or through the fence.

With frustration distorting her face and exhaustion weighing heavily on her shoulders, she trailed the fence. "Seriously? Nobody has flawless fencing."

Finally, a section of the fence offered an escape route. The barbed wire was crushed beneath the weight of a fallen tree. She spotted a low-hanging tree branch and leaped onto it, lifting her legs into the air. With nimble movements, she ascended the branch, her body rising higher. Pain radiated across her arm, causing her to wince. Once there, she stood tall, peering over the vast landscape stretched out beneath her. Clara and Benjamin were nowhere to be found.

Jenna felt the rough texture of the scaly interlocking branches beneath her knees and palms as she climbed higher and farther over the fence. Eventually, she reached the sturdy tree trunk. From her vantage point, she could see the entire place spread out below her. The salvage yard was a dazzling display of lights, with only a handful of defective lamps standing in darkness. Faint barks of dogs echoed from the southeast, yet there were no signs of police sirens.

With nimble grace, she climbed down the twisted trunk, then jumped down to the solid ground below. She wandered beside the fence, making her way in the southern direction where the Jeep awaited her. Thorny burrs and sharp twigs dug into her skin as she sought a simpler path through the dense foliage. A nearby streetlight revealed how close she was to the road. Despite the bramble being less dense near the street, she still didn't want to take any chance of being discovered.

Jenna navigated through the prickly weeds until she suddenly felt a sharp sting on the side of her neck. She squeezed her neck, her eyes burning with anger, until her hand snapped the offending limb in two. She glanced at her palm, noticing a small droplet of blood. The canine teeth had left unmistakable marks on her forearm. Several indentations marred her flesh, yet the crimson fluid had already formed a hardened crust.

Although her bag contained a first aid kit, her primary focus was on finding a way to escape this place. Cool and soothing, small droplets of sweat cascaded down her neck. The sensation of tingling on her neck was rather pleasant until dripping over the cut. Over and under more of nature's obstructions she went, until she heard the dogs barking with excitement.

Jenna strained her ears, hoping that the voices she heard weren't those of her friends. She crouched behind a dead tree stump, listening to two male voices amid the barrage of barking.

"What happened?" called a deep male voice.

"Dogs spotted a racoon," another man answered between labored breaths.

"Let's head back. I ain't seen nothing."

"Yeah, me, neither. Gotta get the dogs first. Butch! Thunder! Home!" the man hollered. "Besides, something got old Thunder. He's limpin'."

Jenna's lips stretched into a sly grin.

The voices gradually grew fainter. Jenna pressed on, her pace noticeably slower. The dogs were hot on the trail of a raccoon, causing her to tread more cautiously. She was unsure of the dogs' route and didn't want to draw their attention.

The leaves shimmered, revealing glimpses of the houselights on the other side of the street. Jenna increased her pace, scanning the area until she caught sight of Benjamin's Jeep parked beneath the oak tree. As she stepped out from the cover of the trees, her disheveled appearance revealed how the forest had taken its toll on her, leaving her feeling as though it had chewed her up and spat her out. Her heart sank as she scanned the empty lot, a sinking feeling settling in her stomach.

Having extracted the key from the metal case, she settled herself into the driver's seat. She inserted the key into the ignition but waited to start the engine. She drummed her fingers on the steering wheel. As she glanced behind her, she caught sight of flashing red and blue lights bouncing off the nearby windows.

"Sorry, guys." She flipped the key, and the Jeep rumbled to life. The road stretched out before her, winding through the darkness. With a steady hand on the wheel, she resisted the urge to switch on the headlights. Only when she had maneuvered past the sharp bend in the road did she finally allow the beams to light her path.

Jenna's mouth opened wide, releasing a piercing scream that echoed through the car. Her hands clenched into fists and collided with the steering column, the force reverberating through her body. She flicked the switch on the radio, filling the room with soothing melodies.

Even though it was risky, she had to find out if Clara and Benji escaped. She turned the vehicle around and drove back to the junkyard. Police cars littered the entrance with their blazing lights. In the backseat of the cruiser, Clara's and Benjamin's silhouettes were visible as the uniformed police appeared to be conversing with the owners.

"Jeez, Clara."

CHAPTER 31

CLARA

Hard liquor and musty body odor clung to the walls, transforming them into a fragrant gallery of questionable choices and questionable hygiene. Despite its valiant effort, the overpowering citrus disinfectant was no match for the unpleasant smells. The floors seemed to be clean, but the leftover marks from previous visitors created the illusion that the stains were slowly spreading up the baseboards. The light above the water dispenser was the only fluorescent bulb that flickered, rebelling against the overwhelming brightness in the police station.

Clara's and Benji's wrists strained against the cold metal cuffs, their freedom stolen as they were led down the luminated corridor. The sound of jangling keys rang behind them as they were ushered into a small, barren cell. Clara's head was bowed, but she couldn't help but notice the curious looks from the passing police officers. Their eyes silently conveyed judgment. Their frowns deepened, revealing disappointment. And the slight smirks on their faces betrayed their satisfaction as they successfully cleared the streets of delinquents. The unknown expectations terrified her. She'd never been in serious trouble before. Even the room was unexpected.

She envisioned a room filled with imprisoned humans, with most of them huddled together, trying to keep their distance from the unsanitary toilet while avoiding physical contact. The private rooms were uniquely designed, featuring doors with plexiglass windows and large acrylic walls. These transparent elements offered outsiders a clear view into the cells, replacing traditional bars commonly seen on television. The room was narrow and painted a pale cream color, with benches running the length of the room. There was a metal toilet and sink combination with a waist-high wall that provided minimal privacy. Clara frowned at the sight, determined to avoid using that feature for as long as possible.

The officer gestured for them to enter the room, and with a click, their handcuffs were removed. Benji led Clara to the bench, gently massaging his wrist as he surveyed the area. Clara winced as she favored her ankle, taking slow, painful steps. She lowered herself onto the sturdy, immovable seat, relief washing over her.

The officer, who had a tall and sturdy build, softly tapped his knuckles against the glass. "Miss, do you require medical assistance?"

"No, I believe it's just sprained," Clara said, wincing as she rotated her ankle. The rest of her body bore a multitude of gravelly grazes and raw pink scratches and rashes, evidence of nature's fierce assault.

"If you decide you need medical attention, let an officer know."

"Yes, sir. Thank you."

Clara's hand moved across the surface, brushing away imaginary specks of dirt near her seating area. She inhaled deeply, feeling her throat tighten in response to the intense aroma of citrus that filled the air. The space must have just been sprayed. The officers' voices murmured at a nearby desk, blending with the faint hum of a television tuned to the local news.

Benji positioned himself a few feet away from Clara, his head sinking into his hands. After a brief pause, he raked his fingers through his hair. He clenched his fingers tightly around the edge of the bench, as if he were anchoring himself to prevent drifting away.

Clara's brow creased as she watched him choose a seat across the room, confusion flickering across her face. He avoided eye contact with her, his face turning red, his brows knitting together, and his fists clenching. Except for getting caught, she would change nothing about tonight. No property was taken or damaged. As the police instructed her to empty her pockets, they remained oblivious to the fact that the document she handed over was not hers. She knew she shouldn't feel good about breaking the law, but she was excited. They'd found Jack Drewitt's truck, which the police had failed to find.

After a decade and a half of relentless pursuit, she felt a glimmer of hope that she was getting closer to discovering the elusive truth. She managed to make it through the night but remained perplexed about the events that had transpired and the reasons behind them. As a result, the memories from her past continued to torment her on a daily basis.

Just as she started pondering the implications of their discovery, the newscaster's voice broke her train of thought. "... child bones discovered at Nelson Ledges State Park."

Clara's head lifted. She hobbled to lean against the plexiglass partition. The pit of her stomach collapsed, mirroring the rush of the initial descent on a roller coaster.

"A forensic anthropologist in Cleveland examined the bones and established details to further aid in the investigation. According to the formal report, the remains belonged to a girl between the ages of two and four ..."

Clara's chest tightened with each beat, her pulse reverberating through her body. She leaned in, her ear grazing the tiny holes in the door window.

"... from the early 1800s."

Her body sank against the wall, her back finding support as she gradually descended to the cool tile floor. A sense of relief washed over her, evident in the gentle curve of her lips, which formed a smile. *I knew it wasn't her.* As she closed her eyes, the newscast replayed in her mind. Emotion amplified within her, and tears silently streamed down her face.

Clara noticed a police officer advancing, gesturing for her to join Benji at the back wall. She wiped away her tears and then propped herself up against the wall to stand. She stumbled over to Benji, who didn't offer any help.

"Do you need to make a call?" The officer's voice came through the small holes in the door.

"No. I'm a student at Penn State on my own," Clara said.

"I'm in the dorms, too. No one." Benji's voice lacked any hint of emotion.

Clara shot him a brief look.

"Trespassing charges are being discussed with the property owner. An officer will return with additional information."

When the police officer left, Clara's body sank against the bench as she crossed her arms and let out a long, heavy breath. She guessed Benji didn't want his dad to know he was sitting in a jail cell.

"Benji, did you hear the news? Those bones aren't Lucy. They're too old." A wide grin spread across her face as she leaned closer, her eyes sparkling with excitement.

The silence grew thick, suffocating any attempt to take a comforting breath. Clara's shoulders straightened as she subtly shifted her head to get a better look at her friend. "Benji?"

"Clara, I need to know if closure is so important that you're willing to jeopardize everything for it."

"I'm not ..."

Benji turned, softly grasping her hands, gazing directly into her eyes. "I love you, Clara. From the moment we first met, I knew I had fallen in love with you. I find your unique quirks quite fascinating. I find it charming the way you absentmindedly tap your pen against your lower lip, the sudden hiccups that arise after enjoying a few drinks, your nervous habit of chewing on your lip, and the delightful grin that appears on your face as you inhale a cup of freshly brewed coffee. You can't see the family right in front of you because you keep thinking about the ones you've lost. Not all families are united by blood. I need you to be a part of my life and my family.

FOREVER FAMILY

"Your past is destroying your future. Although I want to be there for you, it pains me to witness your continuous struggle and frustration as you try to unravel a mystery that beyond your reach. Every time you shed a tear, a piece of me slowly disappears." Benji's eyes turned a shade of crimson as he gazed at her with an intense yearning. "Choose me. Let me be your family."

She observed the intensity in his gaze, a silent plea for his feelings to be understood, yet she grappled with the challenge of articulating her own emotions. The thought of laying out her complicated feelings made her feel dizzy and sick. "Benji … I … You know I really care about you, but I can't give up on my family. I …" She reached for him, but he pulled away.

The door swung open with an officer who abruptly interrupted the painful conversation. Benji turned away from Clara as he shifted further along the bench, avoiding any direct contact. Clara silently begged for understanding before the officer spoke.

"There will be no criminal charges. You may leave at any time." The officer inspected both of them. "Do you need transportation back to the university?"

"No." Benji's shoulders drooped, revealing his dejected state. "I'll call a driver." Silently and without uttering a single word or casting even a fleeting glance, Benji rose and walked out of the enclosure.

Clara, feeling breathless from Benji's abrupt departure, leaned over the bench and against the chilly wall behind her to steady herself. An intense wave of discomfort rippled through her stomach, leaving her with the sensation of being struck with a powerful punch.

"Miss. Are you okay?"

"Um. Yes, of course." She stood up, perhaps too quickly. Her head throbbed as she struggled to regain her balance, her surroundings a dizzying blur. With a deep breath, she steadied herself and mustered the strength to move, trailing behind the officer. She exited the holding area with some degree of optimism, straightening the back of her shirt as she went. It felt right to be with Benji, but she could never leave Lucy. He had to understand. She'd explain it to him.

After the necessary paperwork was completed, her belongings were returned to her. The police officer on the opposite side of the counter began to slide a manila envelope with her name on it, but it accidentally slipped past her and fell onto the floor.

"I apologize, ma'am. I'm not aware of my own strength." The man's face lit up with a relaxed smile.

"No worries," Clara said, oblivious to his attempt at humor.

Clara retrieved the envelope and winced as she gingerly put weight on her ankle, feeling a throbbing sensation instead of the piercing jolt of pain. At a ledge nearby, she tipped the contents onto the surface. Pushing aside the watch, gum, and lip balm, she reached for the most important item she had with her. She carefully unfolded the letter from Jack Drewitt, taking her time to smooth out the wrinkles. Benji had to understand the significance. *Things happened so fast, maybe he didn't see it.*

With purpose, she pushed open the lobby door and quickly found the exit. The brisk night air hit her, causing her to stumble. She fought through the shock and strain, scanning the area for Benji. He was gone.

She walked back to the reception counter and inquired about her friend.

FOREVER FAMILY

"Oh, he left. He used the phone over there. Said a driver is about fifteen minutes out. You're welcome to wait in the lobby." The desk clerk adjusted her spectacles to prevent them from slipping off her nose.

Clara tightly clasped her hands together and nervously bit her lip as her pulse began to accelerate. She scanned the lobby and attempted to peer out the windows, but the interior lighting hindered her visibility. The realization hit all at once. She tried to breathe, but she could only let in small gulps of air. Her throat grew moist, a bead of sweat trickling down her neck. A wave of nausea washed over her as her stomach clenched tightly. "Where'd he go?"

"I don't know, dear. He left."

CHAPTER 32

JENNA

Jenna gripped the steering wheel tight enough that her knuckles turned white. The wind rushed through the open windows, stealing the cursewords escaping her mouth. She felt the cool wind around her hand as it glided in the night air, hoping it would help her find clarity.

What went wrong?

Jenna's mind became a chaotic whirlwind of thoughts, swirling with images of betrayal, abandonment, injury, disorientation, separation, and even the unsettling possibility of alien intervention. *Did they leave me alone on purpose?*

She flicked the lever on the steering column and looked over her shoulder as she guided the vehicle smoothly onto the shoulder.

Eleven o'clock provided a clear road, with only a few scattered vehicles passing by. She parked in the emergency lane, turned off the lights, and watched the stars through the open window. As she settled into her seat, the sounds of the night enveloped her. The melodic symphony of the night filled the air, the soft chirping of crickets and the gentle rustle of leaves blending peacefully with the gentle hum of passing vehicles.

As she relaxed her hand at her side, he noticed a gentle brush of silky texture against her wrist. A vibrant red ribbon peeked out from her pocket, catching her eye. With a gentle tug, the ribbon was released from its confines, allowing her to delicately lace the fabric through her fingers. The fabric's ends were frayed, and wrinkles were scattered throughout its twelve-inch length. It revealed tiny punctures at its core, hinting at past stitches. *Such a fragile object discovered within a battered, corroded truck.* Jenna twisted the ribbon in her fingers and fashioned a bow with the ends, imagining it wrapped through a little girl's hair, but something nagging inside told her that wasn't right.

Her pocket vibrated with a new message on her phone. She quickly scanned the screen, and read a message from Clara that read *Where are you?*

A surge of anger and hurt coursed through her veins. "Where were you?" she yelled at the phone. Jenna's face turned red as she clenched her fists. Her hand shoved the ribbon into her pocket, her posture straightening as she responded to Clara the exact location for pickup.

* * *

The police station was relatively quiet, except for one officer who was helping a vertically impaired person out of a patrol car. Every parking lot light remained in perfect working order, casting a dim glow across the vacant space amid the darkness that encapsulated it. Clara stood out, slouched on a weathered bench just beyond the main entrance.

Jenna parked the car, and the headlights illuminated Clara sitting nearby. Clara's posture briefly straightened, hinting at a momentary sense of relief before she slumped back onto the bench. Jenna turned off the engine. The headlights of the car slowly faded, casting a soft glow into the forest behind Clara. Clara stayed motionless as Jenna stepped out of the vehicle and made her way over.

"Hey, Jailbait? You okay?" Jenna's face lit up with a grin as she patted Clara on the back before taking a seat.

A rosy hue spread across Clara's cheeks while her face contorted with intense emotion. Swollen and stained with tears, her eyes narrowed and hardened. "You think this is funny? You left us!"

"Correction. You ditched *me*!" Jenna lashed back. "I had an escape route all planned. I turned around and you were gone."

Clara lowered her head. "Benji decided it was safer to go straight to the Jeep."

"Yeah, how'd that work out for him? Where is he?" Jenna scanned the lot, searching for the backstabber. She clenched her fists, her cheeks turning red with anger. Benji would never abandon his sweetheart alone in a strange city, especially with unknown dangers lurking in the shadows. He must have been around somewhere.

"I don't know." Clara's body curled into a tight ball, with her knees pressed against her chest. Fresh tears formed.

"What do you mean? He left you back there?" Jenna stood, adjusting the pitch of her voice to match. She spun around, gesturing with her thumb over her shoulder, pretending to know the exact location of the junkyard. In reality, she was completely clueless about its whereabouts.

"Not the junkyard. They let us go. No charges. Then he left." Clara brushed a tear against the knee of her pants and then lowered her head, concealing her face from view.

"He wouldn't leave you." Jenna's brows started to merge into one. "That boy is glued to you like a bee with a serious pollen addiction."

Jenna's patience was wearing thin as she sensed an underlying situation. She had noticed their constant dependence on one another, their inability to function on their own. There were other urgent matters that needed to be addressed. Curiosity tugged at her, urging her to uncover her dad's role in this story. What was he hiding? Their open and honest communication was the cornerstone of their relationship. She found herself compelled to return home to rectify their fractured state.

"It's none of my business. Let's go." Jenna reached out, and Clara accepted the gesture.

Clara stood up, winced in pain, and then fell back onto the bench, gently rubbing her ankle.

"What's wrong?"

"I twisted my ankle. I just need to rest it."

Jenna wrapped an arm around Clara, supporting her as they carefully descended the curb and settled into the Jeep. Despite the conflict coursing through both girls, Jenna helped Clara to the Jeep.

As they began their two-hour drive back, Jenna's frustration lingered. She couldn't help but feel abandoned when Clara chose to side with Benji in the junkyard, leaving her all alone. The girls sat in an unsettling silence while the wind ravaged them. Despite her frustration, Jenna was determined to delve deeper into their discovery, but Clara seemed to be avoiding any conversation, opting instead to stick her head out of the window.

Jenna gently pulled on the hem of Clara's shirt. "Will you tell me what's going on or are you going to just sit there and sulk?"

Clara sent a penetrating glare in Jenna's direction. She partially closed the window to muffle the noise. "After you drove off, leaving us behind, you're going to accuse me of sulking?" Clara's voice was barely audible over the deafening wind.

"You trusted the wrong person."

Clara raised her voice. "You drove off!"

"You're lucky I did. Thanks to me, this car is not being impounded right now."

"We got there, and the Jeep was gone."

"If you had followed me, you would have been in the Jeep with me." Jenna's breath escaped her lips in a deep sigh. "I had no choice. I had no idea where you were. Flashing lights appeared, and I was concerned the police would find Benjamin's Jeep. I decided to drive the block, but to my surprise, I spotted you sitting in the back of a cruiser."

The car's engine hummed softly, filling the silence with a gentle purr. Clara's head hung in defeat. She spoke with a trembling and gentle tone. "I think I lost my best friend."

Jenna cast a quick glance in Clara's direction, observing her appearance mirroring a withered blossom devoid of its former vibrancy.

FOREVER FAMILY

Clara cringed as her body throbbed with pain, but it was the emotional torment that truly consumed her as she hugged herself tightly.

"What happened?" Jenna asked.

"He said he loved me. The sincerity in his voice was undeniable. But he pleaded with me to abandon my search for Lucy so we could be together. He walked away when I couldn't. I see Lucy twirling into a room, her playful smile lighting up her face. How can I move on from the memories we shared, the laughter and the tears? Lucy's my sister. How can I give up on her? How can I let her go?"

"Do you like him?" Jenna noticed Clara discreetly picking at her nails. Her hands trembled as she clenched and unclenched them. Memories flooded her mind, replaying the moments when she had resorted to that familiar action.

"I do, but if he really understood me, he'd know how much Lucy means to me. She's the only family I have left."

"He'll come around. Perhaps he was too caught up in the adrenaline of the moment to think rationally. Give him time. You're stronger than him."

"Benji's the strong one." The words began in confidence, but as she reached the end, her voice wavered with doubt.

Jenna felt Clara staring at her. "You take charge; he takes cover."

Clara's hand shot forward, crashing into the dash with a force that jolted Jenna in her seat. Her back straightened, a fiery anger evident in her posture. "You've only known him a week! You have no right to judge."

"No offense intended. I believe he underestimates your

strength, and I believe you enjoy feeling protected." Jenna nonchalantly shrugged as Clara averted her gaze and fixed her eyes on the view outside the window.

Returning to school took longer than the journey to Pittsburgh. Jenna parked the Jeep in the parking area adjacent to Clara's resident hall. Apart from a boisterous cluster of students huddled in the distant corner of the parking lot, the campus conveyed an air of tranquillity, undisturbed by their nocturnal antics.

Jenna quickly opened the driver's door and rushed to Clara's side as soon as she saw her getting out of the car. "Let me help you."

"I'm fine." Clara's hand shot out, swatting away the intruder.

"I'm sure you are, but when help is offered, take it. Don't let anger cloud your judgment."

Clara rolled her eyes, but she still allowed Jenna to assist her in getting out of the car. Struggling to adjust her leg, she steadied herself on the door handle and Jenna's shoulder, as she carefully descended to the ground. Jenna helped her readjust so that she could close the passenger door.

"I can make it from here."

"No, I'll get you to your room. You still have stairs to climb. The last time I checked, your elevator wasn't working."

Clara scanned the steep slope that led to her dorms, but she remained silent, accepting the challenge ahead.

Before helping Clara climb, Jenna concealed the keys to the Jeep in the secret compartment. She found the walk to be less challenging than she had expected. Clara seemed to be doing better compared to her time at the police station.

FOREVER FAMILY

Clara unlocked the door to her room, and both girls promptly collapsed onto their respective beds. Neither of them moved for a few minutes, burdened by the weight of the night's events.

"Do you have a bandage for your ankle?" Jenna asked, looking around.

Clara motioned toward her closet. "There's a first aid kit is on the top shelf."

Jenna rocked her body, gathering momentum before lifting herself from the comfortable bed. In the closet, she found a red zip pouch with a white plus symbol tucked away beneath a forgotten sweatshirt. Standing on her tiptoes, she reached for it and then opened it on Clara's desk. She emptied the contents onto the desk and pushed items aside until she located the bandage wrap among the clutter.

Jenna knelt on the floor as Clara brought her leg over the edge. With a steady hand and a focused determination, Jenna skillfully wrapped the bandage around her injured ankle. She moved with care, ensuring that each loop was tight enough to provide support yet gentle enough to not cause any discomfort.

"Thanks," Clara said.

"Sure." Jenna scanned the room. She grabbed a pillow on the nearby bed. "Here, put this under your calf to reduce the swelling. Do you have any ice?"

"There's a frozen pizza pocket in the freezer."

Jenna retrieved the frozen pastry from the small freezer and placed it beneath her ankle.

"Where did you learn first aid?" Clara asked.

"My dad's in construction. Injuries happen. With sprains, you remember ICE. Ice, Compress, Elevate." With a playful grin, Jenna rose from her seat and faced the door.

"You can spend the night," Clara said.

"No. I don't want my dad to worry, but thanks."

"Okay. Good night."

After closing the door, Jenna experienced a sudden heaviness in her stomach. Glancing at her watch, she realized that it was later than she had anticipated. Acting quickly, she drifted down the stairs, stepped out of the dorm, and headed home. The towering streetlights stretched their long shadows across the pavement, while bats gracefully danced through the darkened sky. The streets remained empty, devoid of any other brave souls. Her body tensed as one of the bats swooped, its wings slicing through the air. The action felt oddly familiar.

As Jenna's mind wandered, an image materialized of a similar streetlamp standing tall on a warm, dark night. The lights flickered as bats darted in and out, their agile wings slicing through the air as they pursued their insect prey. As the bats performed their acrobatic dives, her laughter mingled with that of another young girl, slightly older than herself.

"Watch this." The older girl crumpled a long strip of aluminum foil into a compact ball as she swept her wavy golden hair aside. With unwavering resolve, she extended her tongue, retracted her arm, and launched the ball into the boundless expanse above. The ball left her hand, soaring through the air with all the strength she could muster, propelled by her petite stature.

Jenna found herself enchanted by the beauty of the metal ball, which appeared to reach the stars. The reflective glow from the moon captivated both Jenna and the whimsical bats as they swooped and darted through the dark, velvety night sky. Her laughter erupted with pure joy.

"You try!" The older girl grinned as she handed Jenna a fresh sheet of silvery material, allowing her to fashion her very own ball.

The girl's gift astounded her with its iridescent and light-reflecting properties. Crumpling the foil into a tight ball, she tucked her dark hair behind her ear and lifted her chin to the night sky.

"Go on, don't be scared." The girl's arm shot up, demonstrating the motion of a high throw.

The girl's face seemed to hold a sense of familiarity, as if belonging to a long-lost legend. Her eyes sparkled with a sense of wonder and curiosity, as if she held the key to a world of endless possibilities. With golden curls that bounced against her shoulder, she radiated a youthful intensity. Her flowy dress, adorned with vibrant hues that mirrored the colors of her mother's garden, danced in gentle ripples as she leaped up and down, fueled by an endless wellspring of energy.

Jenna's eyes shifted to the center of the swarm of bats. She marveled at the shiny ball, her fingers gently cradling it. Tilting her hand, she noticed the delicate curves of her petite hands. With a sudden burst of force, she sent the ball soaring into the air. Despite falling short of the other girl's throw, it seemed like it had the ability to reach the moon.

With lightning-fast poise, the bats' wings beat furiously upon the intruder who dared to encroach upon their sacred feeding grounds. They dove in the air, their muzzles reaching out to pick at the object. With each dive, their efforts grew more determined until the object slipped from their grasp and tumbled down to the ground.

Jenna's heart raced as she watched a bat hurtling toward

earth, daring the ground into a dangerous game of chicken. But just as disaster seemed imminent, the bat skillfully soared upward, narrowly avoiding catastrophe. Jenna erupted into giggles.

"Good job, Lu-Lu!"

Jenna's eyes snapped open, her body jolting with sudden awareness. The vividness of the memory appeared genuine.

"Who was with me? Why did she call me Lu-Lu? My mom called me Lu-Lu." Her mind became a storm of overwhelming thoughts, each question swirling and causing her expression to wrinkle.

Jenna's father's work truck was parked in front of their apartment. He'd handed her the keys to the dented old thing a couple of times, but she struggled to get the hang of the stick shift. The living room window above was shrouded in darkness. Quietly, she ascended the stairs, trying to avoid stepping on any creaky floorboards, and clumsily searched for her key.

As she slid the key into the lock, the doorknob turned effortlessly, surprising her. She turned the handle and felt it give way easily under her touch. Before going to bed, her father would always secure the door. She slowly opened the door and saw the empty room beyond. A surge of panic coursed through her veins, causing her skin to tingle with unease.

Jenna's hands trembled as she reached into her pocket, retrieving the cold, metallic handle of her knife. Dried blood stained the blade, a haunting reminder of the dog's attack. Upon realizing the absence of any other presence, she pivoted and discreetly secured the door with a soft click and tightened her hold on her weapon. Down the hall, only her father's door remained closed. With great stealth, she crossed the corridor toward her father's bedroom, carefully inspecting each open doorway along the way.

Her father's closed door was a regular occurrence, but tonight was different. He didn't wait up for her like he usually did, and the front door was left unlocked. Standing before her dad's closed door, she felt a wave of nausea wash over her. The house rule echoed in her mind, reminding her that she should never enter without his permission. However, an unexplained unease hung in the air, leaving her uncertain.

Summoning her courage, she gathered her nerve and pressed her body against the door, straining her ears for any signs of a slumbering presence. Nothing. With a deliberate slowness, she gingerly eased the door ajar, allowing herself a fleeting glimpse into her father's bedroom.

She couldn't help but feel a sense of relief wash over her as she listened to the soothing rhythm of her father's deep breaths, synchronized with the gentle movement of the blankets. In a hushed tone, she softly whispered, "I love you, Daddy," before silently closing the door.

After entering her room, she tossed her bag aside and collapsed onto her bed with exhaustion, yet she couldn't shake the feeling of unease that still lingered, refusing to be ignored. Maybe the events of the night left her on edge. As she prepared for bed, she started emptying her pockets and couldn't help but inspect the additional items that had found their way inside.

CHAPTER 33

JENNA

An unexpected sound jolted Jenna from her peaceful slumber. She shifted her weight, turning onto her stomach, and fumbled around the blankets in search of the racket-making phone. Last night, she'd struggled to put on a T-shirt and pajama pants before collapsing onto her mattress. The remnants of her earlier expedition clung to her hair, transforming her pillow into an unpleasant semblance of a bird's nest.

"Yeah?" Jenna said into the covers.

"Jenna? It's Clara."

"What time is it?" She rose and subdued her rebellious tresses with her careless touch. Nature's souvenirs from last night crackled as she extracted each from her hair.

"Nine."

"Ugh. What's up?" Jenna reached high above her head, her face expressing relief as she listened to the satisfying cracking sounds that ascended her spine. The tension in her neck, shoulders, and back gradually dissipated, leaving her feeling lighter and more relaxed.

"It's just ... I don't ... I need advice."

"What about?" Jenna's mouth stretched wide open, releasing a yawn. She displayed no interest in concealing it.

"Benji. But I'd rather not talk on the phone. May I come over?"

"Um ... wait a sec." Jenna unfurled her body from head to toe, as if she were a feline awakening from a deep slumber. She ventured into the living room, scanning the apartment for any traces of her father. A smile spread across her face as she glanced out the window, noticing his empty parking spot.

She shivered as the coldness of the phone pressed against her ear. "You can come over. How's your foot?"

"My ankle is much better. I'm keeping it wrapped up, but I'm walking just fine, no worries."

"Okay. I'm at Timber Heights, apartment 217, on Second."

"I know the place. See you in fifteen." Clara hung up.

After ending the call, Jenna tossed her phone to the couch and glanced around the room.

Jenna's hands darted across the apartment, snatching up objects scattered haphazardly. She arranged a jumble of magazines, her movements quick and frenzied. Her room was littered with abandoned garments, which she frantically stuffed into the closet before securing the double doors.

A satisfied smile played on her lips as she crossed her arms. Her fingers glided through her hair, exposing a small pine needle branch clasped between her fingertips. She took a deep breath; the scent of the forest and her own perspiration filled her nostrils, reminding her of her recent exertions.

Jenna rushed into the bathroom and turned on the shower with a flick of her wrist. She stepped under the warm water, feeling the droplets cascade over her skin. After a few minutes, she turned off the shower and grabbed a fluffy towel, drying herself off. Wrapping the towel tightly around her body, she walked to her closet to find the perfect outfit to entertain a houseguest. She stood in front of the mirror, admiring the way the V-neck top hugged her curves and accentuated her neckline. The jeans she picked out clung to her legs, highlighting her figure and giving her a confident, stylish look. She rummaged through her closet, searching for her wallet and other items tucked away in her old cargos. Suddenly, a faint tapping sound echoed from the door.

She bent down and used her foot to push the pile of discarded clothes back into the closet. Then she opened the door and greeted her friend.

CLARA

Clara stood before Jenna's front door, arms crossed anxiously over her stomach. A warm breeze blew through the corridor, causing the T-shirt on her back to slightly lift. Her body trembled, goose bumps forming on her skin as if a ghostly presence had brushed past her, despite the comforting midmorning breeze. The sound of movement on the other side of the door made her step back.

"Hey, Clara, come on in." Jenna widened her arm, inviting Clara to relax on the sofa.

"Thanks." Clara eyes lifted to the towel resting on Jenna's head.

Jenna followed Clara's gaze. "Oops. I'll be right back."

Clara skimmed the room, taking in the familiar layout of Jenna's apartment. The apartment greeted her with its pristine condition and minimalistic decor, leaving ample space for movement. It was difficult to believe that two people lived in this place. Clara, who lived alone, had a multitude of things scattered haphazardly around her dorm. It was a stark contrast to the other place she had visited with Benji just a few weeks prior. His friend was hosting a racing-theme video game night. He pushed the clutter into the corners, creating space for his guests to move around. Clara remembered the plush chair she'd sat on that sounded like the crunch of a bag of potato chips. In fact, there could have been a bag underneath. She took a seat on the sofa, nestling into its plush cushions.

Jenna emerged from the bathroom, her brown, wavy hair glistening with droplets of water, and settled herself on the other end of the couch.

"Hey," Clara began. "Sorry 'bout yesterday, for yelling. It wasn't your fault. We each knew the risks."

"Release the what-ifs and should'ves that bind us to the past and embrace the path that leads us toward the future. I think I read that in a fortune cookie or something. Friends?" Jenna extended a hand.

Clara's lips curled upward as she met Jenna's grip with a firm and steady handshake.

"Great! So, we discovered Jack Drewitt's truck. How freakin' awesome is that?" Jenna sank into the plush sofa, her legs crossed beneath her.

"Pretty amazing." Clara's thin lips compressed as she nodded, recalling the truck, but her mind was on Benji.

"Our primary suspect drove to Pittsburgh and abandoned his truck fifteen years ago. If he wasn't guilty of something, he wouldn't have run. Most likely, he stole another car because it would be too risky to use his ID to legally get one. But where did he disappear to? And did he have Lucy?" Jenna's finger grazed her lips, her face deep in thought.

"Oh!" Jenna's eyes widened with excitement as she pulled out a strip of vibrant red fabric from her pocket. Spots of faded color and stains from dirt, yet the redness prevailed. If only the frayed little thing could share its story. "Right before the lights sent us scattering like cockroaches, I found this ribbon."

Clara folded one leg on the sofa, her muscles tensing as she tried to find relaxation. Her newfound friend held a piece of evidence that could unlock the secrets of her past. The fabric looked familiar yet different. A subtle wave of disorientation washed over her, making her a bit light-headed. She questioned everything she thought she knew. During these encounters, Benji would often crack jokes or make lighthearted comments to ease the tension.

Jenna's fingers loosened their grip on the ribbon, setting it free to dance and spin its way into Clara's lap.

"It was under the driver's seat?" Clara's eyes inspected the fragile fabric, her fingers tracing its intricate patterns. On one side, a velvety smoothness caressed the fingertips, while on the other, a rough and coarse texture challenged her touch.

"Yeah. Tucked beneath the carpet."

The fabric whispered secrets of familiarity, teasing her mind with elusive resemblances that taunted her just out of reach. She curled the smooth side of the ribbon outward, forming a beautiful bow. As she admired her handiwork, a glimmer of recognition flickered in her soft eyes.

Jenna leaned closer as Clara tucked her legs beneath her and extended the bow, handling it with great care.

"What is it?" Jenna blurted while Clara's open mouth remained silent.

Clara's fingers tightened around the fabric cloth, pressing it against her chest. Memories flooded her mind, each one vivid and powerful. "When I was little, my mom gave me a teddy bear with a red bow tie. I'd take it with me wherever I went. Lucy was given a plush bunny, but she wanted to sleep with my teddy bear instead. At first, I didn't want to share him. I once yanked him away from her so hard that I tore the seam where his bow was stitched. I used the hole as a secret place to hide treasures so Lucy would never find them. I finally gave in and let her sleep with him to stop her whining. She was asleep with my teddy bear the night she vanished." Clara's hands gently lifted the fabric, revealing the bow as it unraveled into a straight line.

"And you think this could be the same bow tie?"

"I remember it longer, but it's possible." *Just not probable.*

The young ladies remained captivated by the swaying fabric, as if under a spell, until an unexpected vibration startled them both, causing their hearts to skip a beat. The fabric slipped from Clara's fingers, fluttering to the floor. With a sudden burst of excitement, she snatched her phone from her purse, eager to uncover the source of the vibration.

Jenna leaned forward and grabbed the material, her fingers spinning it in her hand. Her eyes flashed to her room and back to the material.

As Clara read the message, the hope quickly faded into disappointment.

"Not who you were expecting?" Jenna's expression spoke volumes, conveying her amusement and understanding of Clara's disappointment. She giggled as she twirled the ribbon in her hands.

Clara eyed Jenna, as if she were deciphering a cryptic riddle, before mustering a response. "No. I'm sure Benji's angry with me. He hasn't answered his phone. I'm not sure if I should give him space or break down his door." Clara's lip trembled as she bit down and anxiously tugged at the loose strings hanging from the couch coverlet.

"Honestly, I think space is a good idea. The man needs a cooler after yesterday's nighttime shenanigans."

"You're probably right. But that also presents another problem ... for me." Clara shifted uncomfortably on the soft cushions.

Jenna's face was filled with anticipation as she impatiently tapped her fingers on her crossed arms, awaiting an explanation.

"Every Labor Day weekend, I hike and gather flowers in Nelson Ledges to create a memorial for my parents. My mom had a passion for gathering wildflowers and admiring the beauty of various weeds. She loved dandelions and honeysuckle. My dad enjoyed pointing out the wonders of nature." Clara clenched her teeth, feeling the pinch against her cheek. "Benji normally takes me, but I haven't heard back from him. I didn't see his Jeep this morning, so he must have gone to his dad's. If he's too upset … I … I don't know if I can go alone." Emotions surged within her as tears welled up, a touching remembrance of the bittersweet mix of longing for Benji's presence and the daunting prospect of spending the weekend alone.

Jenna tucked the ribbon into her pocket. "I could go," she whispered, her voice barely audible.

Clara's voice filled with disbelief. "You'd do that?"

"I know we just met, but I'd love to see the scene of the crime."

Clara's body suddenly jolted, her eyes tightly closed.

"Perhaps that was insensitive." Jenna's words slipped out under her breath. "Still, I'd like to go."

"Thank you." Clara's heart raced as she noticed a slight unease, but she instinctively moved closer to Jenna and wrapped her arms around her. Jenna sniffed her hair, tickling her ear. Clara's eyebrows wrinkled as she pulled away.

"Do you use green apple?" Jenna asked.

"Yeah, why?"

"Oh, it's nothing really. This scent brings back memories of a perfume my mother used to wear. But I find it difficult to determine memories verses fabricated thoughts."

"My mom used to switch her shampoo and conditioner often, but her favorite was the green apple scent. I chose to use the same kind so I wouldn't forget her." As a little girl, Clara would eagerly await her mother's good-night kisses, cherishing the lingering scent of green apple that filled the room. Her eyes brimmed with longing. "Do you remember your mother?"

Unease and internal conflict washed over Clara as silence seized the room. "You don't have to answer," she added and picked at the seam in the cushion.

"I was just three when she passed away, but I remember snippets, like baking cookies with her."

"Oh, my mom baked the most amazing chocolate chip cookies! The smell of freshly baked cookies traveled throughout the whole house, enticing everyone with its warm, gooey deliciousness. That was me and Lucy's favorite." Clara closed her eyes as the comforting aroma caused her mouth to moisten.

"Those are my favorite. I think that's what Mom would bake ... coco cookies." Jenna's lips curled into a warm smile as she took a deep breath, savoring the phantom scent.

Clara's eyes fluttered open. *Coco cookies? Only one person I know has called them coco cookies. Jenna's smile is similar to hers.* "Did you ever have a sibling?" Clara asked.

"No. I'm an only child. But it's funny you mention it. Last night, I had a weird memory about playing with bats with another little girl. She may have been a neighbor, but I don't remember." Jenna reached for the glass of water sitting on the coffee table and took a sip.

Clara had not noticed it previously. "My sister and I would throw aluminum foil balls up to watch the bats swoop and chase after them."

"That's what we were doing." Jenna tucked her legs back underneath her. "Must have been a popular game as kids."

"Yeah." Clara nodded in agreement, although her voice carried a hint of uncertainty rather than confirmation. *It's not possible. There's no way.* She tilted her head, envisioning Jenna in her younger years.

Jenna narrowed her eyes to Clara's peculiar expression. "What? Is something wrong?"

"The other day, you called me Clare Bear. Why did you call me that?"

"It rhymes. Plus, I've got a plushie in my room that I call Clare Bear."

"Is it a teddy bear?" Clara's face turned pale as the blood drained away. *It's impossible to be a mere coincidence.*

"Of course. Hence the name Clare *Bear*!" Jenna said. "It's cute. It rhymes. Are you all right? You look like you've seen a ghost."

Clara felt the blood drain from her face. "I may have." She studied Jenna, prompting Jenna to shift uncomfortably.

Jenna's brow furrowed and her lips tightened, mirroring her confusion as she tried to follow Clara's rapid stream of ideas. Her face transformed, the lines of worry smoothing out as her comprehension deepened. "Whoa, you're crazy if you think I'm your long-lost sister. The implications are completely ridiculous and impossible. I have a family. Benji's right—you might need a break from this." Jenna's voice trembled with concern rather than anger.

"I'm sorry." Clara dismissed the thoughts from her mind. "Maybe I'm just tired, but can I see Clare Bear?"

Clara noticed Jenna's fingers tighten against the edge of the cushion beneath her.

The door latch jingled, and the two young women froze, their bodies tense and still.

"Just let me do the talking. I'm not supposed to have visitors." Jenna's body jolted upright as she sprang out of her seat, concentrating on the door.

Clara felt nausea brewing in her stomach. How could she have known she wasn't allowed over?

Nicholas Dean's hand froze on the door handle as he entered the apartment and saw the two young women in the living room. "Hello," Nick greeted, his lips pressed into a thin line, lacking any warmth. After scanning Clara, his eyes locked on to Jenna, silently demanding an explanation.

Thick mud clung to his black boots and tan work pants. His muscles strained against the fabric of the shirt, revealing their chiseled contours. A man who towered over others, his broad shoulders and muscular physique spoke volumes about his physical fitness. Clara couldn't help but be drawn to his deep brown eyes and black hair. His brow furrowed, his fists clenched, and his gaze sent a chilling warning that angering him would be a grave mistake.

"Hey, Dad. Are you okay?"

"Yeah." An awkward smile spread across his face, as if he could hear Clara's thoughts. "Some guys were tampering with a water main and busted the pipe. I tried to help." He bent down and used his foot to forcefully kick his shoes off, sending them flying outside the door. With a firm grip, he pulled the door, ensuring that it was properly closed.

Mr. Dean exuded a seemingly pleasant demeanor, yet Clara couldn't shake off a subtle sense of unease.

"Sounds exciting. This is my friend Clara. She came over to say hi. Isn't that nice?"

He scanned Clara from head to toe, taking in every detail. Clara's face paled, and she shifted her view downward feeling her stomach start to revolt. "I apologize. My manners must be stuck in

FOREVER FAMILY

the mud. We don't get visitors often. I'm Jenna's father, Nicholas Dean. I apologize, but I'm just buried in muck." With a sweeping motion, he motioned to his disheveled clothing. "Make it quick. I'm going to clean up." Mr. Dean ambled down the hall, his sleeves creeping up his arms with each step.

As Clara turned her head, she saw a tattoo peeking out from beneath Nick's rolled-up sleeve—a tribal tattoo featuring an eye at its core, gazing with intensity and mystery. She chewed on her thumbnail, trying to recall where she'd seen that design.

"Sorry about that," Jenna said. "He's nice, but he has limited people skills."

Clara's mouth hung open, her eyes widening in shock as she remembered the exact spot where she had last seen that tattoo.

"Are you okay?" Jenna cautiously moved forward, her eyes fixed on her father's fading figure. "He's really not that scary."

"Uh, no. Yes. I'm okay. I just remembered that I need something from the library." Clara's body jolted upright from the couch, scanning the area behind her in a frantic search for her purse. It was lying on the floor. It must have dropped after she retrieved her phone. As she reached down to grab her purse, her jagged thumbnail snagged on the rough fibers of the carpet. "I'm sorry to run, but I'll call you later today. Yeah?"

"Yes, of course. When are you leaving for Ohio?" Jenna's footsteps echoed behind Clara as they walked to the door.

"Um, tomorrow morning. I'll call you with details." As she turned away, her lips trembled, holding back the words that threatened to escape. The weight of her unspoken thoughts hung heavy in the air, a silent storm brewing within her. Her head swiveled like an owl surveying the forest.

"What are you looking for?" Jenna asked.

"My purse."

"You already picked it up." Jenna deliberately nudged Clara's purse, causing it to sway from her shoulder.

Clara patted her bag. "Silly me." A nervous giggle escaped her lips. "I'll call you later."

Jenna went to the door and opened it for her friend, whose purse strap dropped off her shoulder.

"Hey, I'll call after lunch?" Clara adjusted the strap before she turned away from the apartment and waved good-bye over her shoulder.

"Yeah, sounds good."

Clara caught the sound of Jenna's words, yet she refrained from pivoting in Jenna's direction. She was afraid Jenna would ask her why she was acting strange before she was prepared to provide an answer.

After walking a short distance through the parking lot, she retrieved her phone and dialed Benji's number. "Come on, Benji. Pick up!" Clara cast a cautious glance behind her, only to discover Jenna's peering from the second-story window. With an awkward wave, she propelled herself forward, increasing her speed.

"Come on! Put your ego aside and pick up the damn phone!" Clara's ears perked up as the line picked up. "Benji?"

"The mailbox is full...." Filled with discouragement, Clara shoved her phone in her purse and sprinted to the library.

CHAPTER 34

JENNA

Jenna leaned against the door as she locked it and peered out the living room window. She couldn't help but be intrigued by Clara's abrupt shift in behavior. Clara and her dad appeared shocked by the unexpected visit, but her recognition of him was evident. Her father's behavior had always been peculiar, but it wasn't enough to justify her sudden departure. Jenna wondered if there was some secret connection between them. *Impossible*.

Jenna watched Clara's rushed movements and tight grip on her phone, suggesting her urgent attempt to contact Benji. *What would Clara say if she could get a hold of him?* A faint rhythmic vibration flowed from her room, reaching her ears.

Clara's face stretched with a forced smile as she raised her hand in a friendly wave. Jenna mirrored her gesture before closing the living room curtains. Her breathing slowed as she closed her eyes, allowing the tension to melt away. The lingering scent of Clara's green apple shampoo eased her mind.

Jenna thought about the words she would say when her dad came out of his room. Was he angry? Annoyed? Her throat tightened, a dryness settling in. She decided to fetch a glass of water from the kitchen.

The door down the hall slammed shut with a loud thud. Her dad appeared from the dimly lit hallway, his new work shirt stretched tightly across his chest as he adjusted its length. His scanned the vacant living room before entering the kitchen.

"Jenna, we've talked about visitors. I don't like strangers and I don't trust her."

"I know, Dad. I'm sorry. But what's wrong with Clara? She's nice. She just needed a friend after breaking up with her boyfriend."

"Your *nice* friend nearly got you arrested last night." He cast a knowing look her way while his fingers emerged from the refridgerator with a pair of chilled water bottles.

Jenna squared her shoulders with her hands on her hips. "How did you know?"

Her focus remained on him, his figure gliding past her with an air of suspicion. With purpose in his stride, he stomped to the front door and picked up a fresh pair of work boots. A lightning bolt of realization shattered her worldview, and her eyes widened in response. "You called them?"

"I told you not to go." His voice resonated with authority and severity.

FOREVER FAMILY

Jenna stomped in front of him, blocking his path to the couch. "I can't believe you! How did you know where we were?"

"Don't get in my way." His eyes stared down on her.

Jenna confronted his obstinance head-on with her hands still on her hips, her eyes brimming with the same unwavering defiance. A multitude of questions and profanities ricocheted within her mind until, at last, one burst forth from her lips. "Did I have a sister?" *If he kept my aunt a secret, what else is he hiding?*

A deep, throaty sound escaped, allowing the tension that consumed him to reverberate through his entire being. Jenna studied the rhythmic vein on his forehead, deciphering its intense pulsations as if it held a secret message. The tension was palpable as his neck muscles tensed up like a stretched guitar string.

"Why won't you talk about the Wilson case?" Jenna insisted.

Taking his boots with him, her father silently turned and slammed the door as he left the apartment.

Jenna flinched with the loud sound. *What's wrong with him?*

Realizing the door held no answers, Jenna curled her fingers into fists. Frustration welled up inside her, and she let out a low growl, venting her exasperation. Her father was keeping secrets from her. If only she possessed a key to unlock his innermost thoughts. *A key. The key!* Her body stiffened, her eyes widening with anticipation. A mischievous grin slowly spread across her face, revealing the daring idea that had taken hold of her mind. As her father's absence stretched on, she found herself with ample opportunity to delve into the mysteries he had left behind.

Her hand tightened around the cold metal of the front door handle, and she used her other hand to lock the dead bolt. She gave it a firm tug, ensuring that the door was tightly shut. She tiptoed through the living room, her heart pounding with anticipation. Peering through the glass, she watched the tailgate of her father's truck disappearing around the corner.

She turned her head down the hall, and a malicious smile crept across her face. They were both respectful of each other's personal space, but she was furious. He had absolutely no right to betray her to the authorities in the salvage yard, so she took great pleasure in trespassing into his sacred territory. Her steps took her directly to his bedroom. Her fingers quivered over the cool, metallic doorknob. Yet an insatiable curiosity compelled her courage to turn the handle.

Jenna expected a locked door, but the door swung open effortlessly, as if inviting her inside. Despite knowing that her father was gone, she still scanned the apartment. She waited a moment for a siren or flashing lights to scare her away, but nothing happened.

She widened the door, scanning the ceiling for any concealed cameras. Despite her certainty that there were no cameras and no one else present, an eerie sensation crept over her, as if someone watched her every move. Silently, she slipped into the room, shutting the door behind her. With her back pressed firmly against it, she became a living barrier, blocking any entry. The room was enveloped in darkness, the blinds drawn, the lights turned off.

When she flicked on the overhead light, it did little to dispel the gloom. Like her room, there was a mattress on the floor and a wardrobe full of clothes. A flashlight sat next to a book near the mattress. *That will be useful.*

She snatched the flashlight and switched it on, leaving the book neglected and undisturbed. Her footsteps echoed off the walls as she moved restlessly, focusing on the illuminated spots. She stepped around the room, scanning every corner for any hidden details.

She pulled on both handles simultaneously, anticipating the door hinges to protest from excessive use, yet they remained eerily quiet. As she opened her father's closet, she noticed the neat arrangement of clothes and accessories, a stark contrast to the disarray of her own. His dirty clothes, including the muddy ones he had just changed out of, spilled out of the corner basket, creating a messy pile. Meanwhile, neatly hung articles of clothing decked the remaining space, showcasing his meticulous organization. On the highest shelf, storage boxes were neatly stacked next to piles of folded sweaters and jackets. Very little was kept on the floor except a small rug lining the closet floor.

The floorboards creaked underneath her toes as she stretched for the highest shelf and swept her hand under the stack of clothes. *Nothing.* She proceeded to do the same thing on the opposite side of the closet. *Nothing.* Uncertainty clouded her thoughts, but a nagging intuition told her that he was concealing a tangible secret. *Why else would he hide a key?*

She attempted to shine the light between the storage boxes, but her height hindered her effectiveness. As she searched for a solution, she noticed a stack of books beside her father's bed. *He always said to be a problem solver, not a problem creator.*

She carefully maneuvered them into the closet, sliding them across the floor with a soft shuffling sound. With precision, she placed one stack on top of the other, creating a tower of knowledge within the confined space. Her fingers traced the smooth edges of the sturdy hardcover books, feeling their durability and strength.

All the better to step upon, my dear, she thought, chuckling.

Balancing on the books, she carefully flashed the light under, between, and behind the storage containers. *Nothing*. She glanced at the boxes, contemplating whether to bring them down and inspect their contents. Uncertain about the amount of time available, she hesitated.

Content with her examination of the closet, Jenna carefully descended from the stacks of books and shifted focus to the mattress. She visualized the arrangement of the pillows and sheets in her mind before lifting the bed. She balanced the mattress on her back and used the flashlight to shine underneath. *Nothing*. She released her grip on the mattress, allowing it to settle back into its original position. She smoothed out the sheets, ensuring that they were perfectly aligned.

Jenna's flashlight swept across the room, illuminating the corners as she searched for potential hiding spots. Her keen eyes landed on two vents, their metal grates beckoning her curiosity. She held her flashlight up, peering inside each one. *Nothing*.

"Maybe he's not hiding anything." As she moved away from the vent, the floor groaned. After a moment of hesitation, she shifted her body so that she could better hear the hardwood floor's squeaks. She squinted, focusing on the floor of the closet. *Why does he have a rug in there?*

Jenna followed the light to the creaky location in the closet. The closet rug expanded seamlessly to the very edges, neatly tucked beneath the baseboards. She got down on her knees and slowly pulled at the edges. *Nothing*. She pulled at the borders until, at long last, the edge gave way. With the flashlight clenched between her teeth, her heart pounded in her chest as she inched deeper into the closet, tugging on the fabric.

As she inadvertently allowed the edge to flip back to the floor, a whirlwind of dust danced into the air. A sudden sneeze escaped her, causing tears to well up. Once the tickle in her nose calmed, she became aware of the wood floor below. She curled up the rug's edge and tucked it beneath her knee. With no concealed secrets lurking beneath the rug's surface, she used her fingers to explore each floorboard. No panel shifted.

Jenna rested her weight on her legs and put down the flashlight. It was possible that she had picked up some of Clara's psychosis. As she proceeded to mend the rug, she noticed a small hole in the baseboard in the closet's corner. She took up her flashlight and illuminated the hole. It was tiny, as though manufactured with a small drill bit.

Jenna's eyes widened as she noticed a slight shift in the baseboard. Curiosity pushed her forward, her fingers trembling with eager anticipation. With a delicate touch, she prodded at the movable panel, wondering what secrets it held beyond its unassuming surface. She maneuvered her free hand, her fingers wiggling against the rough grain of the baseboard as she felt the satisfying give. And then, she triumphantly yanked it off entirely, revealing a hidden space.

She carefully placed the baseboard to the side, allowing the beam of light to illuminate the dark cavern. She squinted as the beam of light reflected off an object within. Lowering the flashlight, she aimed its beam at the opening. She stretched her hesitant arm into the darkness, grabbing hold of a frigid metal box. She inspected the exterior of the container while holding it gingerly between her thighs.

"Maybe this belonged to the previous tenant?" Jenna said skeptically.

The battered black metal container, the size of a shoe box, bore the marks of time, its surface decked with weathered dents and a coarse, gritty texture. Certain sections of the black paint had faded, revealing an aged charm, while narrow silver scratches decorated the surface.

With a steady hand, she traced the outline of the keyhole, her finger gliding along its edges. A sudden rush of emotions overwhelmed her as her stomach plunged and her heart rose sharply upon the realization that she might possess the key. She slipped her hand into her pocket, exploring the fabric's texture as her fingers traced its every curve. Eventually, her touch led her to the key nestled within. Ever since she had found that key, she kept it with her.

Anticipation and anxiety overwhelmed her as she carefully examined the small key. Jenna's mind was filled with a whirlwind of emotions and hypothetical scenarios. *What's in this? Why hide the key?* Despite the potential implications, her insatiable curiosity compelled her to act. With her fingers held steady, she inserted the key into the slot. It fit.

Jenna twisted the key, but it remained stubbornly immobile. Her body stiffened, a visible tremor running through her as she made another attempt. She was disappointed and relieved at the same time. *What did I think would happen? I just magically found the right key?* she told herself. *I knew Clara's insanity was contagious.*

A new thought emerged, causing Jenna's frown to thin into a line. *Lefty-loosey, righty-tighty.* As she turned the key to the left, a distinct sound resonated through the air as the mechanism disengaged, causing the latch to spring open.

CHAPTER 35

CLARA

Fridays on campus were characterized by a remarkable emptiness, as if the very essence of life had momentarily withdrawn. The library, once a bustling hub of intellectual activity, now stood as a desolate ghost town, its corridors echoing with a haunting silence. On long weekends, college students lugged bags of dirty laundry back to their childhood homes. In between loads, they gathered in the living room, sharing stories and laughter with their families, cherishing the precious moments of togetherness.

Clara's dorm room was her sanctuary, a place where solitude enveloped her. The stillness brought her a sense of tranquillity, allowing her to focus and accomplish tasks. However, in this moment, memories of her stolen family resurfaced, nudging her

FOREVER FAMILY

heart with a bittersweet ache. Today, her steps were determined and focused.

Clara burst through the library doors, focusing on the stairway leading to the basement. Startled by the voice of an elderly lady, she experienced a sudden jolt, her heart nearly escaping the confines of her throat.

The soft voice, laced with concern, called out, "Clara?"

As Clara's ears caught the sound, a wave of regret washed over her. She couldn't help but think of all the hours of work that had slipped through her fingers. She turned around, her face flushed with regret, clutching an apology tightly in her hand. She braced herself for the inevitable consequences, anticipating the possibility of losing her job.

"Oh, Clara!" The lady's cane tapped hurriedly against the ground as she moved as quickly as her hobbled gait allowed. A smile played on her lips, radiating relief instead of fury.

"Mrs. Sullivan?" Clara's face twisted with confusion, shifting into awkward angles. "I'm sorry. I ..." Clara's words fell on deaf ears as the head librarian embraced her in a warm, tight hug.

"Where have you been? I've been beside myself with worry!" Mrs. Sullivan placed her hands on Clara's shoulders, carefully examining her as if searching for any imperfections or injuries.

A comforting embrace, like that of a mother's loving care, enveloped Clara. "I'm sorry, but I've been really busy." The sight of the librarian's tears caught her off guard. "Are you okay?" Clara couldn't remember Mrs. Sullivan displaying such emotion when Susan failed to show up for her shift.

"Oh, Clara. A student has gone missing. No one has seen or heard from him since last Friday. Then you don't show up for your shifts. Susan mentioned that you have been behaving strangely. I thought you went missing, too!" Mrs. Sullivan scanned Clara again, taking in every detail. She then pulled Clara into a tight hug, holding her with an even stronger grip.

"I'm really sorry I scared you. I promise I won't miss any more work." Clara patiently allowed Mrs. Sullivan to compose herself, wiping away her remaining tears and smoothing out her wrinkled skirt before posing her question. "Who's missing?"

"Joshua Schultz, a freshman. He was last seen at a party in a warehouse off campus. On Wednesday, he was reported missing." The elderly lady's head shuddered with worry. "The police have opened a case. They even came here asking about his social life and academic routine. But I don't recall him."

"That's awful." Clara's heart ached for the student. Her understanding surpassed that of most.

"Do you know him?"

"No. His name doesn't sound familiar."

"Well." Mrs. Sullivan's back straightened, and she tightened her grip on her cane. "I apologize for making a ninny of myself. I'm just glad you're okay. Please, be gentle with this fragile heart." Gently, she cradled her hand over her heart, allowing her breath to escape in a tranquil, unhurried sigh.

Clara grinned as she put her hand over her chest.

"Now, where are you off to?" Mrs. Sullivan revealed the stern features that Clara knew so well.

"Microfiche."

"Oh, Clara. You are such a nice girl. I want to see you live, not waste away in the basement. Chasing the past is like trying to catch smoke; it'll just leave you feeling ghosted and alone."

FOREVER FAMILY

"One last time, I promise. I think I found something, but I want to double-check." Clara had never understood the extent that Mrs. Sullivan observed and genuinely cared for her.

Mrs. Sullivan gently squeezed Clara's shoulders. "Please take care of yourself. Your family would want you to have a full and happy life. Remember that." She wrapped her arms tightly around Clara, holding her close for one last moment before returning to the circulation desk.

Clara was astounded by the librarian's warm smile and kind demeanor. Her life was often overlooked by most adults. Her heart sank as the weight of guilt settled heavily in her stomach, knowing she had let down Mrs. Sullivan. Her heart fluttered, and a fire ignited within her, urging her to prove herself.

Remembering her initial objective, Clara spun on her toes and descended the stairwell, into the library's dimly lit basement. Scanning the rows of dusty shelves, her heart was set on locating a specific news article. She stepped into the small room filled with rows of microfiche film, feeling calmness wash over her. The place offered a peaceful sanctuary, where one could escape the demands of the outside world and enjoy solitude. The scent of musty books and forgotten parchments wafted through the air, enveloping the surroundings in a comforting hold.

The microfiche slides she required remained nestled within the return bin, untouched since the previous week. The modern world deemed microfilm obsolete for research purposes and student rarely ventured down to the reader. Every time she left the room, the scattered items remained where she left them, unnoticed by everyone.

She pressed the button to activate the viewfinder and

illuminated the room with a soft glow with particles of dust sparkling in the air. With a shuffle, she began searching through the slides, searching for the *Tribune Chronicle*. With a practiced motion, she smoothly inserted the film and effortlessly fastened it with a satisfying click of the clips. As she scrolled, the film moved seamlessly, leading her to the article about the second series of murders. Her skin felt clammy as she leaned in her chair, unsure if it was her anticipation or the machine's warmth causing it.

"Here it is. The second couple found near Hickory Lake."

Clara scrolled through the article, carefully navigating a few pages until she found what she was searching for: an advertisement showcasing a family-run dairy farm in Braceville, Ohio. The ad proudly highlighted their recently constructed barn. Despite the monochromatic nature of the picture, the advertisement claimed that the wooden beams were painted in a vibrant fire-engine red. The local dairy farmers advertised a variety of cheeses and other dairy products available for purchase. The final words of the piece were a heartfelt "Thank you!" to one Jack Drewitt.

In the picture, the man leaned casually against his truck, one hand on his hip and the other resting on the bed to the right of the family. He stood slightly off to the side, not quite fitting into the frame. Adorning the inner surface of his left forearm was a captivating tribal motif, with an eye gazing intently from its core. Despite the pixelated and grainy quality of the shot, the man bore an uncanny resemblance to Jenna's father, Nicholas Dean.

The man's penetrating eyes caused her heart to pound in her chest, torn between beating or breaking free. He had no idea that the truth of his identity was exposed, all because of a simple act of goodwill. *No good deed goes unpunished.*

She pressed the call button for Benji's number once more, hoping for a different outcome. However, instead of hearing Benji's voice, she was greeted by the automated voice-mail system. "Damn it, Benji!" Clara's hand collided with the table, jolting the film free from the clips. She adjusted the orientation of the image, making sure it was upright. Then she zoomed in on the picture of the man, making it larger for better visibility.

Clara's mind meandered, drifting from one thought to another, preventing her from concentrating on anything specific. As she shifted in her seat, the sound of screeching filled the air. She leaned forward, a man met her eyes through the viewfinder.

Bold letters displayed the name Jack Drewitt, but she had somehow missed it every time she read the article. The significance seemed to have eluded her, perhaps because he had never been regarded as a possible suspect.

Clara peered deeply into Jack's pixelated eyes and inched herself closer.

"Did you kill my family?" Her cheeks flushed with boiling rage. "Did you take my sister?"

Her eyes widened as the data now formed a new thought. "Do you *have* my sister?"

CHAPTER 36

JENNA

As the metal key turned, the latch obediently raised its arm in a salute. Jenna stood still, her mind racing with uncertainty. What secrets could her dad be keeping? Should she open Pandora's Box or choose ignorance? She found herself caught in a dilemma, grappling with the potential repercussions that lay ahead for each option. She was aware that returning the box and attempting to dismiss it would only serve to provoke and torment her. She remembered the chilling depths of "The Tell-Tale Heart." Her skin crept over her bones.

She traced her fingers along the seam where the cover met the base. She took a deep breath, her chest expanding as she slowly lifted the lid of the container. The hinges protested with a low groan, their resistance evident as they fought against being opened. Confusion washed over her face as she furrowed her brow, examining the contents. She quickly grabbed the rolling flashlight and aimed its light into the container, illuminating all the dark corners.

The light revealed an assortment of jewelry, none of which appeared to have any significant value. Jenna carefully lifted each item, turning them over and placing them back in their original positions. *There must be at least fifty items here.* The display showcased a variety of jewelry, including wristwatches, chain bracelets, and gold and silver rings with intricate engravings.

Jenna thought one of the rings looked familiar. *This looks like Joshy's puzzle ring.* Her fingers traced the smooth surface of the ring, flipping it over to reveal the hidden inscription on the inside. As she scanned the letters, confusion formed on her lips. JCS. *Joshua Chance Schultz.* The puzzle ring slipped from her fingers, tumbling into the box. As it landed, the ring fragmented into three distinct pieces.

Another object among the trinkets immediately caught her eye. Jenna's hand shook as a silver charm bracelet landed softly on the back of her hand. Every charm shimmered and glistened in the flashlight, yet there was one in particular that transported her to a distant memory, one that had been buried deep within the recesses of her mind.

* * *

Jenna and another little blond-haired girl were greeted by a man who knelt in front of them, his smile radiating warmth and friendliness. A burnt orange sweater hugged his torso, complemented by a neatly tucked brown tie. His short brown hair, styled into a messy do with gel, added a touch of casual charm to his appearance. "Are you ready to surprise Mommy?"

"Yeah!" A wide smile spread across Jenna's face. She couldn't contain her excitement and began jumping up and down, her hands clapping. She turned to the other girl and they both shared in the thrill, their laughter filling the air.

"Shh." The man's lips curled into a mischievous grin as he gently pressed a finger against them. "We don't want to ruin the surprise."

The girls watched the man and couldn't help but imitate him, placing their fingers on their lips to quiet each other, their laughter barely contained.

"Daddy, can we see it?" the slightly older girl asked.

"You've already seen it." He chuckled. "You guys picked it out."

"Please, Daddy! Pretty please! With a cherry on top!" Jenna's lower lip swelled slightly, forming a subtle pout.

"Oh, all right. Who could say no to that adorable face?" His fingers grazed her cheek, leaving a tender touch in their wake. He glanced around the room, his eyes darting from one corner to another before he retrieved a small gift box from his pocket.

The girls' giggled with excitement as they admired the light blue box. He scanned his surroundings, making sure there were no prying eyes, then gently raised the lid. Excitement filled the girls' as he lifted the lid of the smaller box, unveiling its hidden contents.

"Oh, Daddy! It's the most beautiful charm! Mommy's going to love it!" A girl standing next to Jenna touched the charm, then swiftly withdrew her hands, giggling to herself as though it were on fire.

FOREVER FAMILY

"Can I hold it?" Jenna flattened her palm, and the man placed the charm in the center. Mesmerized by the gleaming silver, she carefully studied every attribute. "Jeez-a-wheezy." With delicate precision, her fingers traced the contours of a charming s'more pendant. Content, she gently returned it to its designated spot within the box.

"Are you girls ready?" The man's back and shoulders straightened as he smoothly slipped the box back into his pocket.

"Yeah!"

"Shh! Remember, it's a surprise." The man couldn't help but let out a hearty chuckle as he observed the playful antics of the two young girls.

"Follow me, young ladies … quietly," the man whispered, his grin never fading.

Jenna and the other girl exchanged mischievous glances, their eyes sparkling with suppressed laughter. They tiptoed silently behind the man, careful not to make a sound. The stairs creaked beneath their weight as they ascended, their laughter echoing through the house. They exchanged playful shushes, their excitement growing with each step, until they finally arrived in the bedroom. The doorknob turned under the man's hand, causing the bedroom door to swing open. He entered the room, lifting each leg with exaggeration as he approached the sleeping woman. The girls tried to imitate the dramatic performance, playfully covering each other's mouths to muffle their laughter.

"Mary?" The man's face drew closer, his lips brushing against the lady's ear as he whispered in a hushed tone.

The woman lay still while a sound slipped out from beneath the blankets. "Hmm?"

"Mary?"

The woman's words came out in a mumble as she struggled to shake off her grogginess. "What, Tom?"

The man's expectant stare caused the girls to erupt into fits of giggles.

"Surprise, Mommy!"

The woman's tousled hair fell across her face, and she brushed it away with her fingers. "Oh goodness!" The corners of the woman's lips curled upward as she greeted her early-morning guests. She sat up, her movements gentle as she arranged the sheets around her waist. With a warm smile, she patted the bed, silently inviting the girls to join her.

"To what do I owe this pleasure?" The woman's eyes fluttered open, heavy with sleepiness, as the girls crawled onto the bed.

"Happy Camping Day!" With unbridled enthusiasm, Jenna and her blonde companion reveled in their exuberance, their laughter echoing through the room as they playfully leaped on the bed.

The man extended his hand, presenting a soft blue box to the woman.

The girls nestled against the woman, inhaling the scent of a sweet green apple, their bodies occupying every inch of her arm space. She wrapped her arms around them, crouching down to retrieve the present that had slipped onto her lap.

"For me?" Her lips formed a tight line that transformed into a soft smile.

"Yes, Mommy. Open it!"

As she retrieved the velvety interior box, the woman placed the empty box on her lap. She smiled broadly at both of her daughters. The lid slowly lifted, revealing a sight that left her breathless. "Oh, girls. I love it. It's perfect."

"It's s'mores, Mommy! For Camping Day!" Jenna shouted. The early sun streamed through the window, casting a radiant glow on the small silver charm.

The woman stretched out her arm, offering the box to the man. "Do you mind?"

He steadied the charm between his fingers, used his teeth to open the link, and fastened it to its new spot on her bracelet. The woman's collection of dangling charms sparkled in the sunlight drifting in through the window. She rotated her wrist, proudly showcasing its magnificence for all to admire.

"It's beautiful! Thank you, Clare Bear. Thank you, Lu-Lu." She opened her arms wide and pulled the young ladies into a warm embrace. Gently, she leaned down and pressed a tender kiss on the top of each of their heads.

The young girls' faces lit up with joy as they pulled off their surprise flawlessly. The older girl's eyes glistened as she said, "This is going to be the best Camping Day ever!"

* * *

Jenna's hand quivered and she let go of the charm bracelet. She couldn't tear her eyes away as it dropped into the metal box, making a faint clinking sound. Gasping for air, she struggled to breathe as the walls and ceiling pressed closer, her vision blurring and head spinning. Her mind and body were in constant turmoil, torn between the relentless forces of confusion, disorder, and uncertainty.

Jenna's heart raced as she dashed to pry open the window with her fumbling hands. With a determined effort, she pushed aside the heavy curtains, revealing the outside world. Jenna leaned out the window, inhaling the cool air into her exhausted lungs. The gentle breeze brushed against her skin, calming the inner turmoil that had been battling for dominance.

Her nose twitched as the scent of smoke from the burning leaves filled the air, enveloping her senses. As she looked across the street, a mesmerizing flame flickered and swayed with the gentle breeze. Instantly, memories flooded her mind, transporting her to a different time and place.

* * *

As the crackling flames leaped and flickered, the faces of those gathered around the campfire were bathed in a warm, radiant glow. The dancing shadows played mischievously among the towering trees, adding an enchanting touch to the night. Jenna and the curly-blond-haired girl sat side by side on the tree roots encircling the crackling campfire. As they licked the sweet, gooey treat from their fingers, they were captivated by the sight of the woman's marshmallow bursting into flames.

"The marshmallow will soon disappear." The man's laughter echoed through the air as he sat on the exposed root beside the young girls.

"I like mine burnt." The woman's tongue lightly grazed her smiling lips. Her attention was fixated on the blazing marshmallow.

"Not only is it burnt, but it could easily audition for a role in a charcoal commercial! If you hit it hard enough, you've got yourself a diamond!" The man laughed, his face puckered with amusement.

"One can only hope." She winked.

The girls' mouths were filled with gooey marshmallows and melted chocolate as they laughed at the adults' witty banter. "One more s'more, Daddy, please?" the older girl pleaded, her eyes glassy with desperation.

"More s'mores! More s'mores!" The air filled with the sound of the girls' voices as they began to chant.

* * *

"Stop!" Jenna's hands shot up to her head as she desperately tried to silence the overwhelming flood of memories racing through her mind. She took a deep breath, her chest rising and falling rapidly. With a trembling body, she sank down to the floor, tears streaming down her face. She winced, clutching her head, as the internal struggle intensified. "I've got to get out of here."

Jenna's body shuddered as she slowly rose from the cold, hard floor. She used her sleeve to dab at the tears streaming down her face. She took a deep breath and began to head out the door. Her shaking hand drew near the doorknob, and she hesitated. She spun, absorbing every detail of her surroundings. Traces of her presence in her father's bedroom were scattered, betraying her recent visit. *Leave no trace.*

Jenna walked over to the window and closed it. She tugged on the drapes, adjusting them the way she remembered, then inspected the wardrobe. She delicately scrutinizing the contents of Pandora's Box, before sealing the lid on its crypt of curiosities. With a soft click, she secured the lock, ensuring that its contents remained hidden. Slowly, she slid the box back into its secret compartment. Her fingerprints left a trail in the dust, and she quickly wiped them away with her sleeve, hoping her father wouldn't notice until a fresh layer of dust concealed it. As she pressed down the rug and carefully adjusted the baseboard, she discreetly slipped the key into her pocket, then scanned the room, searching for any signs of something unusual. Without wasting a second, she dashed out of her father's bedroom.

She navigated through the workshop, carefully maneuvering under the desk to uncover the concealed compartment. After returning the key into the compartment, she quickly fled her father's space, darting into the sanctuary of her own bedroom. Leaning against the door, she took a deep breath and let herself unwind. As she stood there, she allowed a deep breath to let her mind focus on her beloved teddy bear.

She pushed herself away from the door. With deliberate strides, she approached her stuffed animal and bent to pick it up. The worn fabric, faded colors, and frayed edges revealed years of being loved and embraced. Without a word, she instinctively reached into her pocket, retrieving a vibrant red ribbon. She gently placed the ribbon around the teddy bear's neck, carefully adjusting it to create a perfect bow. "Clare Bear."

The bear slipped from Jenna's grasp, tumbling to the floor, as something moved outside of her window. She grabbed the edge of the windowsill as her father's work truck maneuvered in reverse, backing into a parking spot.

CHAPTER 37

CLARA

Clara's mind bounced with thoughts, like a bowl of popcorn on a trampoline. As she scrolled through the microfiche, her heart sank at the sight of the man's face. The haunting image sent shivers through her skin, as she couldn't help but remember the tragic fate that befell her parents. Her mother stared at her through the veil of milky white eyes. Her father's remained motionless, submerged in a pool of scarlet.

Jack Drewitt's wide smile dominated the frame while his cold eyes caused her to feel humiliated and sick. It was the same fake grin she had seen earlier today at Jenna's. He remained free after her parents had suffered by his hands, and he still had Lucy.

Clara tapped the camera on her phone screen, capturing a

photo of the newsprint displayed on the monitor. The printer remained in a state of disrepair, its once bustling hum now replaced by an unsettling silence.

Who can I tell? Who would listen? Should I go to the police? And tell them what, I solved a fifteen-year murder with microfiche? Benji. Answer your damn phone. Her tongue tingled with the unmistakable taste of metal. Her focus was so intense that she failed to notice the pain of her own bite.

Clara recovered her handbag and abandoned her workstation. The microfiche film remained untouched, and the machine continued to hum, leaving her discovery undisturbed. As she exited the library, she purposefully tried to steer clear of Mrs. Sullivan. She found it difficult to trust the words that would escape her lips. Her mind was enveloped in a shroud of fog, causing her thoughts to become incoherent and her expressions unpredictable.

Clara attempted to remain inconspicuous as she made her way towards the library doors, yet her footsteps reverberated through the hushed hallway despite her best attempts at stealth.

Mrs. Sullivan's voice drifted over her from the distance, bidding her farewell. She waved over her shoulder and pushed her way through the doors. She squinted against the harsh rays of the sun. Her uncertainty about her destination lingered.

The warmth of the sun enveloped her, bringing a sense of relief that washed over her. As she took a deep breath, the tension from the library basement began to dissipate. Gradually, her mind cleared, and she was able to think more clearly. Clara's wavy hair danced in the gentle breeze as she walked down a few steps. The serene environment provided her with ample room for introspection and deep thought.

The branches of a towering tree outside the library expanded out like open arms. A few leaves from the nearby trees had taken up residence on the picnic table. It was here, under its leafy canopy, that Clara's and Jenna's paths had first crossed. Her mind replayed last week's events, each detail etched with vivid clarity. Jenna had offered Clara her favorite sandwich, unleashing waves of childhood memories.

Clara's stomach let out a loud grumble, reminding her that she hadn't eaten since yesterday. No matter what course of action she ultimately chose, her first priority was to satisfy her hunger.

* * *

A distant rhythmic thumping broke the stillness in the third-floor dormitory corridor. There was no doubt the noise carried from Clara's dorm room. She pressed her back against the cool, rough surface of the wall as she inched forward, her steps slow and cautious. She clutched her key card with such intensity that her fingertips paled to a ghostly white. Holding her breath, she pressed her ear against the door as she slowly slid the key into the lock. The sound of a woman's angry sobs echoed from the other side.

Her knuckles throbbed as she rapped on the door, but the relentless pounding and banging overwhelmed the sound of her knocks. The door creaked open as she turned the knob, revealing her roommate, Becca, in a frenzy, flinging items onto her bed. Clara scanned the hallway, desperately seeking any indication of activity, hoping for someone to come to her aid. Feeling a sense of solitude, she cautiously entered, and shut the door.

"Becca?"

Becca furiously rummaged through her belongings, tossing items aside without so much as a glance in Clara's direction.

"Are you okay?" Clara remained close to the door as she scanned the room, taking in every detail, her mind working quickly to evaluate the situation.

"What kind of question is that?" Becca's lips curled into a snarl as she whipped her mascara-stained face toward Clara. "Of course I'm not bloody okay. Do I look *okay*?"

Black tears streamed down Becca's face, causing a shiver to creep up Clara's spine. It felt as though she was trapped in a horror film.

As Becca's eyes darted around the room, she reached for objects to throw. Meanwhile, her bed transformed into a chaotic mountain of stuff. Clothes, toiletries, and books were scattered haphazardly, resembling the aftermath of a miniature volcanic eruption.

"Where the hell is my ibuprofen?" Becca growled.

Clara's attention was drawn to the nightstand, where she grasped the bottle of pain relievers. She extended the bottle toward Becca, who snatched it and struggled with the child safety mechanism, her expression twisted with a mix of annoyance and rage.

Clara's outstretched hand froze midair as Becca's arm shot up, refusing any help. Clara lifted her hands in surrender as she instinctively retreated a step. Becca twisted the lid off and poured a cluster of capsules into her palm. Without hesitation, she tossed them into her mouth and washed them down with a gulp from her water bottle.

As Clara inhaled, she detected a scent that was not reminiscent of water. "I don't think you should—" Clara's words were barely out of her mouth when Becca cut her off.

"He dumped me! The bastard dumped me! Who does he think he is?"

Clara's heart raced as she lowered herself onto her bed, bracing herself for what she knew would be a lengthy outburst. Becca's words grew more muffled, and her pronunciation shifted, reflecting her mounting anger in her increasingly pronounced British accent.

"You want to know what happened? I'll tell you what happened! He cheated with some chem lab floosy. He denied it, of course, but a woman always knows. I know!" In a fit of frustration, she grabbed a dresser drawer and tossed the entire thing onto the growing pile of personal belongings, scattering the remaining items in the process.

"He told me to pop off if I couldn't control myself. He's an arse, and *I* have to leave? Of course, my dad's timing was impeccable. I hushed Damion and answered the phone. Do you know what that jerk did while my dad was on the other line?"

Clara's shoulders lifted and dropped in a nonchalant gesture.

"He comes up behind me and yells into the phone, 'She's having great sex with her live-in boyfriend!' While I try to convince my dad that the idiot is lying, he explodes in anger. Damion is laughing behind me as my dad says he's pulling me out of school. He was not going to let me become a tramp and squander his money. My own father, calling me a tramp!"

At this time, Clara understood that silence was her greatest ally. She nestled her body against the cool wall, running her fingers along the delicate seams of her quilt. She kept her head down, avoiding eye contact and hoped to blend into her bed.

"After I hung up with my dad, Damion said we were finished.

'No shit, Sherlock.' I launched my shoe at his head. Now my father is on his way here to pull me out of the dorms. He said I can commute from home. It's an hour's drive!" Becca scanned the room, searching for something, anything, to hurl. But there was nothing left. She paused to look at the pile she had assembled, and her body collapsed into its center. "It's not fair." Her shoulders slumped and her head drooped while her voice trembled with defeat.

The lingering silence created an atmosphere that felt more awkward than an avalanche of words. Clara hesitated, unsure whether her words would help or add fuel to the fire. "He's family. It sounds like he's worried about you."

"He's my *step*dad. The guy's not even real family."

"Family is forever, regardless of blood." Clara's mind raced to Benji. She made eye contact with Becca and a sinking feeling settling in her gut. It became painfully clear that she had made a grave mistake, aligning herself with the wrong side.

"Who asked you?" Trash bags overflowed with a jumble of miscellaneous items as Becca unceremoniously shoved items inside.

"Is there anything I can help you with?"

Becca reached for a discarded shirt and wiped it against her black tear-stained cheeks. "No." She stuffed the pile of items into a couple of suitcases that she retrieved from under her bed.

Despite not knowing her roommate well, Clara empathized with her. A wave of sickness washed over her as she considered the profound impact that a single truth could have on someone's life, causing her stomach to churn. Her mind wandered to the image captured on her phone. Emotions swirled within her, a mix of shock, betrayal, and disbelief. Her mind raced, trying to process the implications of what she had discovered. Clara's world shifted in an instant as the truth she had longed to uncover finally came to light. How would Jenna respond?

"Do you want me to leave you alone?"

"Do what you want," Becca said, defeated.

Even though Clara wanted to leave, she couldn't leave Becca alone after seeing her make a potentially lethal mixture. Becca's words hinted that her dad would arrive in about an hour. Clara chose to remain, blending into the background.

The book glided off the nightstand as she gently moved it, and she propped her pillow against the wall, creating a comfortable support. After reading the first paragraph six times, she became increasingly frustrated as she realized that she was having difficulty understanding the words on the page. Instead, her hands snatched a nearby notebook. She opened it, ready to capture the intricate web of details she'd discovered about Jenna and Nicholas Dean.

CHAPTER 38

JENNA

The stillness was shattered, as the doorknob rattled, and the sound of keys jingled through the hallway. As the dead bolt clicked open, Jenna's heart echoed the sound with a heavy thud. The apartment door closed with a resounding bang, sending vibrations through the walls. The floorboards trembled under the weight of thundering footsteps. Several heavy thuds suggested her father dropped his work bag onto the kitchen table.

"Jenna?" he called out. "Are you home?"

"Yeah." Her voice cracked, reaching a higher octave. A raspy sound escaped her throat as she cleared it, attempting to bring back the strength in her voice. "Yeah, in my room."

"Come here."

FOREVER FAMILY

"One sec." Jenna peered around her bedroom for something, anything that could help her, but the only thing she needed to hide were the mental ideas distorting her perception of reality. She hauled herself from the wall and straightened the creases in her outfit before seeing her dad.

Her father settled onto the plush couch, his hands holding a glass of ice water that shimmered in the soft glow of the sunlight streaming through the window.

Jenna poured herself a glass of water and said, "You weren't gone very long."

"The Clemonses are sick and had to rescheduled."

"That good news ... for you, not the Clemonses." A chuckle escaped Jenna's lips, though forced. She took a small sip of water, placing the glass back on the table. Her arms wrapped around her waist, her fingers fidgeting with the fabric of her shirt. She seemed uncertain, searching for something to occupy her restless hands.

"Jenna, come here." Her dad placed his glass on the coffee table, its weight causing a soft clink against the glass surface. He then tapped the cushion beside him, inviting her to join him.

She picked up her drink, looked around the room, and slowly approached her father. *Does he know?* She set her glass next to his.

"Haven't I given us a decent life?"

"Sure, Daddy. The best." Jenna lowered herself onto the seat beside her dad.

"I shielded you from harm and kept you safe."

"Yes, of course." Jenna's confusion grew as the conversation continued without a clear direction.

"Are you happy?"

Her eyes narrowed on her father, silently probing for answers.

"Yes, Daddy. I'm happy. My life is perfect in every way imaginable. What's this all about?" Jenna's fingers tightened around her dad's hand as she leaned in closer.

"You trust my words." A grin cracked along his face as he glanced at her from the corner of his eye. "Most of the time." His words slipped out quietly, barely audible. Her lips curled into a sly grin, a silent acknowledgment passing between them.

"Listen now." He dropped Jenna's hand and stood tall, his shoulders squared, and focused on her.

Her heart raced as she watched him, anticipation building with each passing second. The look in his eyes hinted at something important, something he was about to reveal. She held her breath, her mind racing with possibilities. Her palms sweat and her stomach churned with uncertainty. All she knew was that whatever he was about to say would change everything.

"Stay away from that girl. She'll make you believe lies." Her father's brow creased, displaying a troubling blend of concern and anger.

Jenna's anger from the previous night bubbled to the surface. "Tell me what happened fifteen years ago." Her voice trembled, revealing her desperate need for the truth.

He shook his head without a word.

Jenna jerked her hand back and straightened her shoulders and sat at the end of the couch. "I am eighteen years old. An adult. Tell me! Without knowing the truth, I can't let it go."

A composed expression never left her father's face. Her tantrum didn't appear to faze him. He lifted his water glass to his lips, taking a long sip before setting it down. Jenna's arms crossed tightly against her chest. The silence hung heavy in the air, but she remained patient, refusing to break the stillness.

"When you were three ..."

Holy crap! He's talking. Jenna leaned back into the cushions, her feet disappeared as she folded her legs beneath her. Emotions surged and her muscles tensed, threatening to consume her as she anxiously waited for him to unveil his well-guarded secret.

Her dad's eyes traced the path of each droplet of condensation as it trickled down his glass. His hand remained still as he his fingers curling around it. He brushed away the residue, his touch lingering on the surface. She noticed how he paused before speaking, searching for the right words.

"... you were taken away. One day, you were gone. I hated my parents for their neglect and wanted them to pay. I would have gone to the ends of the earth and wrestled Hades himself just to have you back. Suddenly, you appeared. My hard work brought you back. I spent every waking moment ensuring your safety and protection." Her father leaned in close, his hand draping over her lap.

Jenna's emotions swirled with fear, confusion, and unease. "I still don't understand. Where did I go? How did I return? What is the connection to the Wilsons and Clara?"

A heavy sigh escaped his lips as he slumped back in his seat. "I'm not sure where you went or how you returned. That family paid a price and brought you back, but the world will never understand. I didn't even know their name at the time."

Jenna's eyes lowered to the floor; her forehead creased as she absorbed the words. His words danced around in cryptic patterns, leaving her puzzled and searching for meaning as they weaved a narrative that revolved around a central theme. Her brows twitched in confusion as she attempted to make sense of the scattered puzzle pieces. "You were there?" Her words slipped out of her mouth, barely audible, as if carried by a gentle breeze. "I was there?"

"I found you that night and I returned you home."

"What about Mom? What happened to her? Did she know the Wilsons?"

Her father shook his head, his expression revealing nothing. "Your mother passed away before the Wilsons."

Jenna's knowledge about her mom was limited. Her father's lips remained sealed whenever her name was mentioned. No matter how many questions she asked, he would just answer with a few words. "What about Clara? What does she believe?"

"Because of what she has been told, she thinks you are her sister, but I know who you are. You belong to me."

Several of her memories suddenly came back to her. She had lived with a different family. Clara *was* the young girl from her memories. It was understandable why Clara believed them to be sisters. "What if we make her understand?"

A deep grunt escaped from him, resonating through the room. Restless, he rose from his seat and began to walk back and forth. He clenched his fingers, gripping his hair and pulling at it with a desperate intensity, fighting for new words. "Strange things happen in this world without explanation. You'll start doubting me as she fills your mind with poison. I lost you once. I will not allow it to happen again."

Straightening up, Jenna turned to face her dad. His emotions swung wildly, making it hard to keep pace. "Why do you think so little of me? No one can take me away."

"I was forgiven the moment you returned." His lips curved upward, only slightly, hinting at a cherished memory. "I promised to protect you at all costs. I love you, Ju-Ju."

"I love you, too, Daddy. I'm sorry I scared you. But trust me. Clara won't separate us."

A steely look replaced the warmth in his expression. Their hands intertwined, his grip growing stronger. "Since you met her, you've been coming home late at night, sneaking into businesses, snooping into people's lives, and taking her side over mine."

She brushed his calloused hands away, feeling the roughness against her skin. "You're being too hard on her. I was the one who got her to do those things." Jenna clenched her fists, her face growing red with frustration, standing to meet his intensity.

Her father's face contorted with a scowl, his fists clenching tightly. He spoke with a heightened strength and directness, his lips slightly curling over his teeth. He stood tall, his cheeks flushed a deep shade of red. "I forbid you to speak to that girl!"

Imitating his brutishness and commanding presence, Jenna clenched her fist by her side. A wave of nerves coursed beneath her skin, causing a rippling sensation. "That will prove to be quite the challenge, since I will be spending the weekend with her."

Two individuals stood face-to-face. Their faces reddened with intense anger. Their voices rose in a crescendo of heated words, each refusing to yield. Jenna's eyes narrowed as she tightened her grip on the edge of the table. She refused to let her illogical father gain the upper hand. He might appear intimidating, but she possessed an equal capacity for fear-inducing tactics.

A dangerous and sharp glare came from her father, but then his face flickered, unraveling a subtle change. His expression softened; his lips thinned to a soft line. She felt a pinch in her chest with his unexpected shift. A sudden wave of guilt washed over her, though its source remained unknown.

Her father sank into the couch, his hand finding its way to his chest. His stared into the barren depths of the fireplace, against the corner wall. Jenna glanced at the fireplace, but it was evident that his mind was elsewhere. His lips pressed tightly together, not a single word escaping.

Jenna's frustration boiled over as she emitted a low snarl. She pivoted and stormed off into her room. The door vibrated with a loud slam as she shut it behind her. "He is so infuriating. I just want answers." Jenna looked around her room, muffling her frustrations and throwing items on her bed to pack for the weekend, including her travel bag, a few changes of clothes, and of course, Clare Bear. She pulled the ribbon off the bear and stuffed it under her mattress with her foot. Her past might have been changing, but Clare Bear's would not be. Clare Bear was her sanctuary. The one thing she could rely on at this moment.

She walked into the bathroom and grabbed her incidentals from the counter. Jenna slung her bag over her shoulder, hardly noticing its weight as she walked down the hall, hoping to provoke a response from her father. He kept staring into the hearth as she rounded the corner, his hand still resting on his chest. He didn't look at her, just kept taking slow, steady breaths.

"I'm leaving now," she announced, her voice carrying the weight of her decision. "I'm coming back on Sunday. Call if you need anything." Her dad sat completely still, not even a muscle twitching. Her heart pulled her in two different directions, one urging her to stay and the other tempting her to leave. His actions had ignited a fiery anger within her, yet this behavior was uncharacteristic.

The door clicked shut as she left the apartment, sealing her decision. Her fingers trembled as they clutched the straps of her backpack, the tension in her knuckles betraying her inner turmoil. She scanned her surroundings, observing each direction as she weighed her options.

Clara expected Jenna to leave with her tomorrow, so she might welcome having a roommate for the night. Perhaps she could convince her of the truth and put her father's mind at ease.

CHAPTER 39

CLARA

Becca's stepfather angrily pulled her away from campus, while Clara sat on her bed, isolating herself as if she were invisible. The towering presence of Becca's father prevented Clara from escaping the family argument. Rather than causing a scene, she chose to sit back and observe as the father figure imparted a dose of tough love to his unappreciative daughter. Clara believed that one day, Becca would value her family's involvement, especially when she struggled to make responsible decisions.

Benji's phone remained silent, leaving questions as to whether he deliberately powered it down or allowed the battery to drain. After Becca left, Clara felt an unwavering resolve to pay a visit to the Fyte Pub, in search of any clues about Benji. Friday

FOREVER FAMILY

nights were always bustling with people, but despite that, she couldn't resist the urge to search for her friend. As she walked out of the dormitories, Clara noticed the empty parking lot below.

Clara pulled out her phone and selected Mr. Lawrence's number. He was one of the rare American citizens who did not possess a mobile phone. After a dozen or so rings, Clara hung up. Her heart ached with a deep sense of emptiness. Without allowing the thought to derail her, she continued on her path.

Despite the presence of city lights, the stars managed to shine through the evening sky, although their numbers were limited. She pulled her light jacket tighter around her body, attempting to shield herself from the biting chill that seeped through every tiny opening. She quickened her steps, feeling the adrenaline surge through her veins. Before she knew it, she stood on the front steps of the pub.

A wave of disappointment washed over her when she noticed the absence of any cars in the vicinity. Despite this, she couldn't resist the impulse to look inside. After gathering her courage, Clara finally entered the bar. As the air pressure shifted, her hair danced in wild, unpredictable patterns, eventually settling messily on her shoulders. Empty tables and chairs stretched out before her. The bartender put his phone down and greeted her with a warm smile.

"Good evening. What can I get for you?"

She looked around once more, but no one was there. It dawned on her that it was a holiday weekend. Naturally, customers would be scarce. She walked up to the counter and sank onto the unforgiving barstool. "Um ... Yuengling, please."

"Coming right up." The bartender tilted the glass and watched as the dark liquid tumbled into it, forming a frothy head.

A noise echoed through the room, and Clara's head snapped

toward the door. As she looked around the empty room, her heart sank, and she lowered her head over her crossed arms.

"Are you waiting for someone?" the bartender asked.

"Yes ... no ... no, I don't think so. I was hoping someone was already here, but I was wrong." Clara slumped in the chair, her shoulders drooping as despair washed over her. The pub seemed to absorb her desolation, amplifying it in the air.

"Not too many come around on holiday weekends." The bartender cast a questioning glance at Clara as he placed the drink in front of her.

She gently wrapped her fingers around the glass, relishing the refreshing sensation that spread across her palm. She observed as the bubbles rose from the depths, playfully popping as they reached the surface. Perhaps one of the bubbles could give her some guidance.

"I'm a great listener if you need to talk. Naturally, I may need to take a break to attend to other clients." He motioned to the empty barstools.

Clara managed to smile. "I wouldn't know where to start."

"I find the best place to start is at the end. What brought you here?"

"My friend and I had a fight. It was more of a disagreement than an actual fight, but it left him hurt and me confused. Now he's not answering his phone."

"People need time to find their own thoughts from time to time."

"That's the problem. I have important news. He's always been there. I don't know what to do." Clara's eyes silently pleading for answers to unspoken questions.

"Is the news important to *him*?"

She hadn't considered. Clara squirmed in her seat, unable to find a comfortable position. *Of course, it's important to him. It's the biggest news of my life.* Clara slumped and frowned. *Of my* life.

"Do you care for this guy?"

"Of course. He's my best friend, but he wants more. He wants me to give up everything for him. It's impossible." Clara's voice took on a gentle tone as she attentively absorbed the words being spoken.

Clara's throat burned as she gulped down the beer, but her confusion remained unresolved. *He deserves everything.* "I could see us together … someday. But there's something I need to do for myself first."

"It sounds like you know what you want."

"I guess I do." Clara's purse emitted a ringing sound. "I'm sorry, excuse me. Maybe it's him."

The bartender nodded and stepped away to create the illusion of privacy.

As Clara glanced at the caller ID, her shoulders slumped under the weight of anticipation. Her throat tightened, a lump forming and making it difficult to swallow. "Hey, Jenna." Her voice cracked. "What's up?" Clara's voice remained steady, yet a hint of uneasiness seeped through her tone. "Sleepover? Of course." Her face paled. "The Fyte Pub, but I'll be there in about ten minutes. Okay? Bye."

The bartender approached Clara as she rummaged through her purse. "Don't worry. It's on the house. Plus, you barely touched it."

Clara glanced at her nearly full glass. "Thank you."

"I hope things work out for you."

"Thank you—me, too. Bye." Clara shivered as she stepped outside, pulling her jacket snugly around her.

JENNA

Jenna rubbed her arms as she settled on Clara's dorm steps, her breath visible in the chilly air. The cool breeze caressed her face, providing relief from the lingering warmth on her flushed cheeks. The lampposts cast a yellowish glow, causing the pavement to ripple with darkness. Insects fluttered and swarmed around the artificial light source, drawn to the comforting warmth it radiated. Her eyes searched the sky. Anticipating the sight of bats, she found nothing but empty air.

In Jenna's mind, Clara wasn't much of a "social butterfly," and thus she probably wouldn't be found far from her dorm. It came as a shock to her when she realized she was in a pub. As Clara appeared over the bend, she jumped up. Clara's features were bathed in a golden light, the beams casting ghostly shadows as she passed through them. Her brow furrowed, her eyelids drooped, and her lips turned downward, giving her face a slumped appearance.

"Hey, girl. You doin' okay?" Jenna asked.

"Yeah, I guess. I still can't get a hold of Benji. I guess he needs space," Clara said.

"Yeah. About that ..." Jenna's feet dragged along the ground. "I have his phone." Clara's eyes narrowed in confusion. "It's dead. I didn't have a chance to give it back after the yard." Jenna's shoulders slumped, displaying her indifference. "He's probably still upset over getting arrested. He'll get over it."

Jenna's footsteps echoed behind Clara as they ascended the stairs to the dormitory. Clara's steps became heavier as she walked up the stairwell and down the corridor to her room. She slipped into her room, after her key card silently granting her access.

Jenna paused. The room looked ransacked and empty. She vividly recalled a lot more stuff across the room. "Redecorating?"

"No." Clara chuckled. "My roommate moved out. Her father discovered she'd been more focused on boys than her studies. It wasn't pretty."

"Ooh." Jenna's face contorted, her lips parting slightly as she emitted a low hiss, mirroring the roommate's agony.

Clara handed Jenna a stack of extra bed sheets she'd found in her closet. "Here, I'll help you." They worked together to make the bed and tuck in the sheets.

"Hey." As Clara smoothed out the bedding and looked up at Jenna with a subtle hint of curiosity. "I'm sorry for the assault of questions earlier."

Jenna fluffed her pillow and tossed it onto the head of the bed. She was unsure about how to introduce the information she had discovered. Although her father doubted Clara's ability to listen, Jenna was determined to make her see the truth. But how to start? "No worries. Thanks for letting me crash here. Things got heated with my dad."

Clara's eyes shifted from her phone's dark display up to meet Jenna's. "Your dad? Oh, right, ah … you're welcome."

Jenna tilted her head. "Are you worried about Benjamin? He likes you. He'll be back."

"It's not that." Clara's voice was so soft, it seemed like a gentle whisper meant only for the phone pressed against her chest.

"Care to share?" Jenna jumped onto the freshly made bed, waiting for Clara to speak.

Clara unlocked her phone and navigated to an image before handing it to Jenna. She took a step back and sat silently on her bed, waiting for Jenna's reaction. Jenna tilted her head, aligning it with the screen she held in her hand. In the screen shot, there was a pixelated farmer and his wife standing in front of a barn. She increased the size of the image. Clara seemed to be waiting impatiently for her reaction as she read.

"Jack Drewitt?" she read. "We know he was a fix-it guy."

"Look at the picture," Clara said.

Jenna scanned the top screen, focusing on the image once again. "That man on the side ... he sort of resembles my dad, doesn't he? Hmm?" Jenna rose from her seat and handed the phone over.

Clara's pupils dilated, her eyes growing larger. "Did you see the tattoo?" She pointed at the phone.

"Yeah, but it's grainy." Jenna shifted away from the conversation, reaching into her backpack for her notebook.

"Jenna! Your dad's got the same tattoo on his left arm!"

"Maybe," Jenna said, unconvinced. "The image is extremely pixelated. It's difficult to know for certain."

"Jenna? Hypothetically ... what if you were Lucy?"

Jenna set her notebook aside and rose from the bed. With a determined step, she moved closer to Clara and settled down beside her. This was the moment that could change everything. She had to find a way to make Clara see the truth.

"My father said something to me, and I need you to have an

FOREVER FAMILY

open mind." Jenna's breaths were deep and deliberate, as she pondered over every word with utmost care. She didn't have all the answers, but she had to convince Clara of the truth.

Clara scanned the image on her screen before setting her phone aside and shifting her attention to Jenna.

"The words my father spoke painted a different picture than the one you remember."

"He was there? He's Jack Drewitt?" Clara's voice escalated.

"I'm not claiming he is or was Drewitt. My grandparents stole me from my father when I was three years old. I ended up living with your family. We were sisters for a while until he discovered me and brought me home."

"So, you are Lucy?" Clara's eyes softened with tears.

Jenna noticed Clara's longing for a hug, but Jenna preferred not to receive physical affection unless Clara truly understood. She watched as Clara furrowed her brow, deep in thought.

"But that doesn't make sense." Clara searched Jenna's eyes. "You didn't just live with my family—you *are* family. I watched you grow up. I helped plan your birthday parties."

"My father said that you might not trust him because you knew me as your sister. Those people fed you lies about me and where I came from."

"Those people are *our* parents. You *are* my sister. Have you considered that he might be lying to you?"

Jenna's body stiffened as she towered over Clara, glaring intently at her. Her face turned red, and her fists clenched tightly. "My father is not lying to me. Ever since my mother's passing, he has been working relentlessly as a single parent to ensure my happiness and safety. I would know if he wasn't my real father."

"Not necessarily. A three-year-old child is susceptible to manipulation and brainwashing, particularly over a span of fifteen years. What if Nicholas Dean is Jack Drewitt?"

"Now, wait. Are you implying that my father is a serial killer and kidnapper?" Jenna stomped loudly against the floor as she paced in a tight circle. "Yes, he can be dramatic at times, but a killer? My dad said he found me, not murdered your parents and kidnapped me. He didn't know your family. It seems you're proposing the idea of a serial killer abducting a child and raising her as his own." She ceased her pacing and focused on Clara. "Perhaps your parents took me and attempted to raise me as their own. Someone discovered the truth and took it upon themselves to reunite me with my rightful family."

As Clara got up from her bed, her phone slipped from the sheets and landed on the floor. "You're taking this too far." Her brow furrowed and her lips tightened, a silent resistance to the truth evident in her body language. It was as if the words being spoken were hitting an invisible barrier, a different frequency altogether, unable to penetrate her thoughts.

"My dad was right. Maybe this was a bad idea." Jenna spun around, stuffing her notebook into her bag.

"No, Jenna. Please. I'm sorry. I don't want you to leave." Jenna watched as Clara's face transformed, shifting from confrontational to one of desperation. "I'm confused. The important thing is we found each other." Clara gritted her teeth and clenched her hands, but her grin was forced. "Please."

Jenna reached for the strap of her shoulder bag, lifted it off, and placed it down beside the bed. After a few moments of rummaging, her fingers closed around the familiar fabric of her pajamas and the comforting weight of her toiletries. "Can we agree that we don't have all the facts yet? This is a lot of information to process. We might both benefit from some sleep. In the morning, we'll be able to think more rationally."

"Yes. I agree, though I don't think I'll be able to sleep." Clara briefly made eye contact with Jenna before she turned to grab her hygiene caddy. "Would you like to see a picture of them?"

Jenna's head bobbed in a gentle nod as Clara obtained a picture frame from her desk. Clara slipped out the door after handing Jenna the old photograph. The faded image depicted a woman who bore a striking resemblance to her, standing next to a man she didn't quite remember. Jenna's mind raced with questions, but she couldn't bring herself to believe what her instincts were telling her. Clara's truth about her past seemed too unbelievable, too fantastical to be real. Memories of her childhood flashed through her mind, but they didn't align with the truth that she knew.

How could this be possible? Doubt crept into her thoughts, clouding her judgment, refusing the undeniable evidence of her past.

Jenna sank into the softness of the bed, questioning whether her dad's words held some truth. *What if Clara can't be convinced?*

CHAPTER 40

CLARA

As darkness fell, shadows crept along the ground with a predatory grace. The trees whipped in the wind, their branches almost touching the soil, but Clara could feel nothing. Miniature cyclones of dirt whirled around her, but her hair didn't move. Nature's tumult had no physical effect on her.

I know this place, but it feels strange. Clara studied the familiar forest setting, but nothing reached her senses. She couldn't feel the wind's strength. She couldn't hear the storm's thunder. Despite the dust in the air, she tasted and smelled nothing. She felt isolated in the midst of the pandemonium around her.

From the silence, a young girl's voice cried, "Clara."

"Lucy?" Clara peered through the ominous silent tempest, desperately seeking the elusive voice. She found nothing in the chaos.

Suddenly, she felt everything. Her skin tingled and her senses heightened.

The scene's intense display overpowered her senses. She covered her ears and crouched low to the ground as the storm was given life.

Forceful winds carried scents of pine, dirt, and humidity. To prevent toppling over, she lowered her head and dug her fingers into the grass. The frosty air burned her skin. Her hands went over her head, and she screamed as her body crumpled to the ground.

Sharp as needles, the dirt, debris, and pebbles pelted Clara's vulnerable body. She crushed her face against the soil, inhaling in the rubble with each cry. The icy air assaulted her spine like a barrage of darts. Her lips faded from pink to a bluish-gray tint, and her cheeks lost all their rosiness.

"Why didn't you help me, Clara?" the chilling voice reverberated. "It's all your fault."

A banshee's wail replaced the last syllable. Clara cowered, shrinking her body to its smallest form, while her hand pressed firmly against her ears. The wind howled through the trees, bending them to its will. Thunder rumbled in the distance, a warning of its controlling destruction. The mighty trees clashed with one another, their branches entangled in a fierce battle. The ground shook as stones were upended, their once-stable positions now overturned. Amid the chaos, haunting cries echoed through the air, their origin unknown, yet their impact was undeniable.

"I'm not here. It's not real."

Silence. Stillness.

Clara opened her eyes and slowly removed her hands, scanning for incoming dangers. Fear prevented her from caring that her shivering arms were covered with burns, cuts, and blood. Breathing became difficult, knowing this nightmare was far from finished. With each step, she could hear the creaking of the branches and the rustling of the leaves, as if the trees themselves were whispering a warning.

A warm gust caused her to turn around. As she stood there, a solitary red ribbon gently descended from the sky. It fluttered down, its worn edges and frayed strands revealing its age. Finally, it softly touched the ground, coming to rest right in front of Clara. As she reached down to grab the ribbon, flames engulfed it in an instant, burning her hand.

A band of rain slowly approached Clara, painting the landscape with its watery brushstrokes. She watched the rainfall as it descended from the skies and cast a dark shadow over the land. Yet, to her surprise, not a single drop of water soaked the ground. The rain crashed into the earth, leaving scorched remains. A single droplet of liquid fire burned its way through the solid stone.

Clara rushed in a fit of panic, but she stumbled and landed her knee on a rock. She tried to alleviate the pain with a massage, though with minimal impact. Flaming splashes of fire set its first tree ablaze. The liquid inferno poured down and swept through the woods, cutting off most escape routes.

Clara's pupils dilated as she resumed running once more through brambles and branches, ignoring the cuts and bruises she accumulated with each collision. A huge tree came crashing down, making her heart skip a beat and her feet stop dead in their tracks.

FOREVER FAMILY

With no time to assess safety, she ascended the brittle bark, breaking off branches as she went. When she spotted a clear area of grass on the other side, she leaped.

Clara dared to cast a fleeting glance behind her, only to witness the very tree she had once climbed now reduced to a pile of smoldering ash, as the relentless downpour of sparks continued to engulf the entire trunk. She quickened her pace, pushing through the tangled web of low-hanging branches and thorns that clawed at her clothes and flesh.

Clara let out a bloodcurdling scream as a searing agony shot through her arm. A single raindrop had seared a dime-size burn into her forearm. Her legs trembled with exhaustion, threatening to give out beneath her at any moment.

She ventured onward, seeking refuge from the scorching flames that raged around her. With no boulders in sight, she set her sights on a towering tree in the distance, hoping it would offer shelter from the inferno. As she drew closer to the base, the outline of a face slowly emerged from the shadows, sending tremors down her spine. Lucy's face, young and terrified, stared up at her, trapped within the deep ridges and furrows.

"Oh, Lucy." One hand covered her mouth as the other contacted Lucy's face. But as her fingers brushed against her coarse cheek, the features twisted and contorted, revealing the haunting image of Jenna, trapped within the crevices. "I knew it was you." Tears streamed down Clara's face.

Clara recoiled in horror, her heart pounding in her chest as she realized the true nature of the deception. Taking a step back, she tripped over an insidious root and fell, bracing for the inevitable impact that never came. As she plummeted into the abyss, the ground she stood upon drifted farther away. The darkness threatened to swallow her whole.

Despite her efforts, the sharp and steep stone walls created impossible holds for her to get a solid grasp. She descended further and further. The roots from the trees slithered down the gorge like vengeful serpents after her.

She hit the ground with a jarring thud, struggling to breathe as her body writhed in agony. Her surroundings whirled in a dizzying blur as she fought to regain her composure, her breath coming in desperate gasps, her chest rising and falling with each uneven intake of air. The impact had been brutal, knocking the wind from her lungs and leaving her helpless and vulnerable on the cold, hard ground.

Sizzling sounds made her tense in fear. In the depths of the narrow crevice, a cascade of fiery raindrops descended, leaving her trapped and devoid of any means of escape. The flames closed in, with no refuge in sight. No caves to seek shelter in, no tunnels to escape through. The inferno was coming, and there was nowhere to hide.

Seeking shelter, Clara pressed her back against the rough bark and dug her fingers into the gnarled roots. The winds howled, whipping up a frenzy that sent sparks flying in every direction. In a sudden, horrifying moment, the tree and its roots became consumed in a raging inferno. The scorching tendrils inched closer, devouring everything in their path.

The tree roots coiled around her torso, refusing to release their hold, as if determined to claim her for their own. She battled fiercely, but her efforts were in vain. She could feel their cold, gnarled fingers grabbing her ankles, pulling her deeper into their web.

"No, no, no, no! Let me go!" Clara cried. Her heart pounded with fear as she struggled against the suffocating walls of her prison, the flames evaporating every bit of moisture. "I'm not here. It's not real!"

Her forehead shimmered with tiny droplets of perspiration, each one a reflection of the intense heat surrounding her. The burden of defeat descended upon her shoulders as she was left with no alternative. In preparation for what lay ahead, she shut her eyes.

"Wake up!" Her voice cracked, willing herself out of this nightmare. Her tears ran down her cheeks but evaporated before they could reach her chin.

"Wake up! Dreams can't hurt you."

A burst of fire erupted from her hair, scorching her scalp and sending waves of searing pain through her body. The flesh on her bones started to bubble and melt, flowing down the twisting roots like wax dripping from a candle.

With the last of her breath, she begged, "Benji, help me!"

* * *

Clara jolted upright in her bed, her arms flailing out to her sides as if warding off an unseen force. She dared not even graze her own skin, drenched in a sheen of perspiration and gasping for air. She frantically scanned the room as she struggled to shake off the grip of the nightmare that had held her captive.

Clara closed her eyes. *It was just a dream. I am safe in my room. There is no tree. No fire. Dreams cannot hurt me.*

As the words escaped her lips, Clara realized she had been muttering them aloud. Jenna lay on the other bed, obviously concerned.

Clara's hand stretched for the bottle of water resting on her nightstand. She lifted it to her lips, allowing the cool liquid to quench her thirst and soothe her dry throat.

"Are you okay?" Jenna asked. "I know you're not, but will you be ... okay?"

"I'm sorry. Bad dream." Clara's hand moved up to her lips, gently wiping away any residue.

"Bad dream?" Jenna said. "I believe the professionals refer to them as night terrors."

"Yeah, well, I'm sorry I woke you up." Reaching over, Clara grabbed a face cloth next to her bed. She splashed a little water on it and started to wipe her face.

"I wasn't sure whether to wake you or let you sleep through it, but you've been screaming for quite some time. I'm surprised the rez didn't call the police."

"Everyone's home for the weekend, including her." Clara placed the damp cloth next to her glass of water.

"Do you want to talk about it?" Jenna asked.

Clara idly picked at the sides of the textured water glass, her mind wandering elsewhere. "If it's okay with you, I'd rather sleep than talk."

"Okay, but if you change your mind, I'm here." Jenna climbed back beneath the blankets and buried her head in the pillow.

Clara didn't look at anything in particular as she drank a few more sips and then laid the glass back down. Her heart pounded against her chest, a wild rhythm that matched the thundering thoughts in her mind. How could she convince Jenna that the man who raised her was an imposter? He wasn't her family. Her thoughts were whirling with uncertainty, but she knew one thing for sure: Her life would never be the same.

CHAPTER 41

CLARA

A shrill and piercing melody interrupted the last few moments of Clara's restless sleep. The chirping echoed through the room mocking her with its cheerful tune. With a deep, guttural groan, she arched her back and slowly turned to confront the rest of the room. Her breath seized in her chest as she noticed the trees outside ablaze in fire.

She jolted upright and rubbed her eyes in disbelief. The trees were not on fire. The morning sunlight casts a fiery illusion, turning the leaves into a vibrant palette of reds, oranges, and yellows.

"It was just a dream, Clara," she said aloud to herself.

She noticed the empty bed. The sheets lay crumpled and abandoned, as if they had been left in a hurry.

FOREVER FAMILY

The lock on the door clicked, and it swung open.

Jenna entered the room with a towel wrapped around her head and body. "Hey, I hope you don't mind. I borrowed some shower stuff."

"No ... yeah ... of course. Help yourself." Clara pushed the covers aside and stretched, perched at the foot of the bed.

"Are you feeling better?" Jenna said as she removed the towel from her hair and started combing the knots apart with her fingers. Her drenched hair looked almost black.

"Oh yeah, I'm fine. Nothing a coffee can't fix." Clara smiled. "Did you sleep all right?"

"Yeah," Jenna said. "So, what's the plan today?"

Clara leaned against her nightstand to check the time on her phone. "Jeez! It's already ten. I was hoping to leave earlier so we didn't get trapped out there in the dark. The drive is three and a half hours, depending on traffic. We can grab lunch and head out. After we visit the park, we can either book a room or return to campus. That is, if you still want to go."

"Sounds like a plan," Jenna agreed. "Could I ask you a personal question?"

"Sure."

"Don't you have any other family? You know. To go with you."

A somber expression emerged. "After Uncle Jonathon passed away, it was just me. Our family never communicated with my mom's side. I don't even know their names. Roger and Benji became my family."

"Oh." Jenna peered down at her feet, lightly gliding them across the soft carpet.

Clara's brow wrinkled as she watched Jenna, uncertainty

flickering in her eyes. Silence hung in the air as they exchanged glances, their body language betraying a hint of discomfort. "What about you? Is there anyone besides your dad?" Clara's voice trembled, barely managing to escape her lips as she whispered, "Dad." She felt her throat tighten, overwhelmed by a surge of emotion.

"No. My father doesn't talk about other family. We traveled so much, just me and Dad. I'm not sure what I'd do without him."

Clara paused, her mind racing as she considered Jenna's words. Convincing her of a different reality would be challenging. "Do you need anything before I take a shower?"

Jenna set the shower caddy down and walked over to her bag. "No, I'm good."

After selecting an outfit, Clara collected her shower essentials, which were still damp. Her favorite outfit was a violet skirt with blue and pink flowers paired with her supple green button-up shirt. In case she needed it, she tossed her black denim jacket on the bed.

"Hey, you'll need this." Jenna tossed her the room key.

"Oh yeah, thanks."

JENNA

Jenna's hands moved swiftly, tugging at the edges of the sheets until they were perfectly taut and free of wrinkles. Then she tossed the pillow onto the bed, letting it land perfectly on top. As she reached into her bag to retrieve her day clothes, she found her grinning companion.

"Hey, Clare Bear." She returned a friendly smile. "I'm sorry I left you in there, but Clara would definitely freak out."

Her fingers grazed the teddy bear's head, a small grin forming on her lips. With a tender touch, she turned the bear around, embracing it tightly. As she held it close, she caught sight of a loose red thread hanging from the back of its neck. Her thoughts wandered to the red ribbon shoved beneath her mattress.

"What am I going to do, Clare Bear?" Jenna believed her dad. It was clear Clara was not going to listen.

After learning Clara's identity, Jenna's father wanted to leave town, but that wouldn't stop her from pursuing her truth. Clara really wanted a family and seemed ready to say or do anything to make it happen. Jenna set Clare Bear in her bag and grabbed her pants. As she slipped her legs into her brown cargo pants, remnants from the previous evening escaped from their confines, thudding to the wooden floor.

"Jeez! I guess it's time to empty my pockets."

Jenna's pockets seemed to be a magical treasure trove of stuff. One could never predict what emerged from them. It felt like an endless illusion, where unexpected objects like a pack of gum or a tiny stapler appeared out of nowhere. Each time she changed clothes, she had to sort which items she really needed. One item particularly made her pause.

She flipped the phone over in her palms, admiring the shimmering sticker on the back, and slipped it into her pocket. She tucked her phone and wallet into a different pocket, while the side pocket of her book bag became a catch-all for miscellaneous items like documents, candies, and trinkets.

After donning a fresh T-shirt, socks, and shoes, Jenna found herself in solitude, lost in her own reflections. The image Clara had shared stirred a whirlwind of emotions she couldn't explain and threatened to overflow. The weight of her unspoken words pressed heavily upon her, a secret she could never share with Clara. *What does it all mean?* Maybe her dad's original name was Jack Drewitt, but there was no evidence to suggest that he was a serial killer. *If he hurt someone, it would be to keep me safe.*

Jenna positioned herself on the bed, crossing her legs. Her hand lifted as she envisioned the charm bracelet she was holding, picturing the delightful sound of the tinkling charms as they chimed in harmony. Furrowing her brow, she pondered the mysterious presence of her dad's possession.

With a click, the door unlocked and swung open. "I feel so much better," Clara said while towel-drying her hair.

Jenna shook her hand and buried it behind her back, as if Clara could see into her imagination. What would Clara do if she found out her mother's bracelet was hidden in a box in her apartment?

"We've got a small problem. I should've thought about it sooner." Clara's teeth clenched as she inhaled sharply.

"What's the problem?"

"Benji usually drives. I don't have a car." Clara chewed her thumbnail, dreading Jenna's response.

"We'll rent one. It's not big a deal." Jenna's lips curled upward, revealing a warm and genuine smile.

"You have to be twenty-four or they charge premium."

"Not with U-Haul. You only need to be eighteen." Jenna's smiled mischievously.

"Life hacks to the rescue," Clara said. "Hopefully, they have one available."

***

FOREVER FAMILY

Traffic on the road was so disorganized it resembled a massive Tetris puzzle gone wrong. The chaotic mix of cars, trucks, semis, and motorcyclists jostled for position like an obnoxious group of siblings squabbling for the last remaining pizza slice.

Jenna sensed Clara's frustration through her tight grip on the steering wheel of the rental truck, her knuckles almost turning white as she held on as if it were her only anchor through a turbulent sea. "Do you want me to drive?"

"No, it's okay. I know where we're going." Her eyes bulged and her grip tightened as an eighteen-wheeler swerved in front of the rental.

Jenna's body jerked forward with the sudden panic brake. "You can navigate," Jenna insisted.

"Okay, I'll pull off the next exit." Clara's eyes darted to her rearview mirror.

Jenna thumbed out her window. "Use the shoulder."

Clara flicked the blinker switch, her teeth grazing her lower lip. With an intense grip, she steered the pickup truck away from the bustling traffic lanes. Jenna released her seat belt and raised her feet, positioning herself to stand on the seat. She poised herself, ready to spring into action the moment the truck came to a halt.

Clara's hands trembled as she carefully shifted the truck into park. She exhaled deeply, her tense shoulders relaxing. She glanced at Jenna, filled with curiosity.

"Move that way." Jenna's finger glided across the air, tracing a line from the driver's seat to the passengers. She climbed over Clara, her rear end pressing against the windshield. With adrenaline fueling their moves, the girls flawlessly synchronized the maneuver, displaying their skill and agility without sustaining any injuries. As they accepted their new roles, they couldn't help but burst into laughter at their comical antics.

Jenna secured her seat belt across her chest. She merged back onto the bustling highway, blending into the flow of traffic. Resting one arm on the edge of her door, she maneuvered the steering wheel with the other, a calmer expression settled on her face.

"I can't believe we got this for less than the price of a standard rental."

"Yeah. U-Haul was always the way for me and my dad. It costs less and has more space."

The road stretched out before them, a never-ending ribbon of asphalt that they conquered with each passing mile. With Jenna behind the wheel, the lengthy journey felt shorter. As they passed the time with trivial banter about their academic pursuits and future aspirations, Jenna caught sight of a vehicle that seemed to be exhibiting rather suspicious behavior.

"Hey, look at the car!"

Clara followed Jenna's pointing finger.

The tiny two-door sedan staggered recklessly over the center line, swerving and jerking as if possessed by some unseen force. Its driver fought desperately to regain control, but the car continued to weave and wobble, threatening to careen off the road at any moment.

Jenna merged into the passing lane.

"Be careful," Clara warned.

"Yeah. Hold on." Jenna completed her switch to the other lane and accelerated. As they zoomed past the vehicle, Jenna caught a glimpse of the driver and Clara examined for signs of distress.

"Did you see that?" As they passed, Clara turned to look back over her shoulder. "That driver was drinking out of a sippy cup."

"I doubt that's apple juice." Jenna laughed.

CHAPTER 42

CLARA

Clara emerged from the car, eyes drawn to the ethereal white clouds strewn across the sky. The scene before her was like a work of art, with the clouds resembling brushstrokes on a canvas. The birds soared elegantly through the boundless sky, their melodic songs echoing through the air as they playfully pursued one another. The gravel crunched beneath Clara's feet as she walked. She scanned the empty parking lot, finally fixing on the dilapidated diner with its boarded-up windows and a closed sign hanging on the door.

Clara hiked up to the front door while Jenna got out of the truck, and she proceeded to read the notice. "Closed for renovations. Great."

"Plan B?" Jenna's foot accidentally hit a loose rock, causing it to roll down the dirt path. A cloud of dust billowed from the ground in its wake. As the particles descended, they created a soothing sound reminiscent of a gentle rain.

Clara looked at the screen of her phone. "I was thinking Elsie's Mocha & Munchies in Braceville or Severino's Pizza Parlor in Newton Falls, but that car crash cost us a lot of daylight. If we don't want to get lost in the woods at night, we should consume some of the food we packed."

"It's probably not the smartest idea to go on a trek fueled solely on M&M's and Dr. Pepper, unless we want to attract a trail of hungry squirrels and soda-loving birds. I say we break for pizza. Getting there won't take long."

A couple of hawks soared through the sky, their silhouettes gliding across the backdrop of the descending sun. Although there was still plenty of daylight remaining, Jenna was right. Surviving solely on sugar and caffeine would be difficult, especially considering the consumption of donuts and coffee earlier.

* * *

Jenna gripped the wheel tightly as the girls headed into town. Suddenly, a gust of wind whipped through the open windows. The air was filled with the enticing scent of freshly harvested sweet corn, blending with the earthy aroma of cattle grazing in the stretch of rolling hills. The combined smells created a powerful mixture that instantly awakened the senses. They navigated through a labyrinth of winding roads. Few people occupied the streets, suggesting this place was not a popular tourist destination.

Clara was looking out the window when she felt the U-Haul slow.

"Well, you don't see that every day," Jenna said.

As Jenna signaled her turn, Clara couldn't help but feel a sense of excitement as they carefully maneuvered around the old, rickety buggy. The sound of hooves hitting the pavement only added to the thrill of the moment. The man holding the reins was dressed in a rustic straw hat, suspenders, and a crisp white shirt. Beside him sat a woman in a boxy blue dress, her hair tucked neatly under a white bonnet. The two boys sat quietly in the backseat, mimicking their father's posture and movements with precision.

"Do you think they have simpler lives?" Clara's mind drifted away as she spoke, her voice taking on a dreamy quality as she envisioned the differences.

"I doubt it. They're forced to contribute to the greater good rather than personal gain. Just knowing that all those technological advancements exist would be enough to drive me crazy. I'd smuggle in a microwave." Jenna monitored the family in the sideview mirror.

As Clara glanced at the side mirror, she couldn't help but observe the family sitting together, seemingly at peace. However, their expressions betrayed a lack of joy or happiness.

"Sounds like the next reality show. I'd be the one sneaking in Netflix and exchanging my chores for viewing privileges." Clara and Jenna both giggled at the idea.

Clara presented her cup of coffee. "I'd probably get my Starbucks confiscated."

"Oh no, not your precious Starbucks! The horror! What's next, taking away your avocado toast? The world is truly a cruel place." Jenna placed the back of her hand on her forehead, playfully imitating a swoon, all while keeping her focus on the road.

"Can you picture cruising through the drive-through in a horse-drawn buggy? How do you stop a horse from sticking his head in the window and stealing the pastries?" More laughter erupted.

As the girls relished the serene twenty-minute journey to the town, the horse-drawn carriage appeared as a mere speck in the distance.

* * *

Amid the hive of activity at Severino's Pizza Parlor, an ensemble of seemingly organized chaos unfolded as delivery drivers transitioned in and out of the doors, workers bellowed out instructions, and customers retrieved their savory pies. The air crackled with excitement as the chaos unleashed an erratic whirlwind of thunderous sound that even rivalled the roar of a packed baseball stadium. The irresistible aroma of freshly baked dough, mingling with the tantalizing flavors of mouthwatering toppings, beckoned Clara and Jenna to embark on an exciting culinary adventure.

Clara scanned the faces of the people around her, but none of them sparked a flicker of recognition. It had been a few years since she was last here, and the passage of time had erased any familiarity she once had with the locals. In the absence of Benji, she tended to steer clear of densely populated areas, but Jenna's presence gave her some courage.

Clara leaned over to ask Jenna, "What do you like on your pizza?"

"I mean, I'm not picky, but plain cheese is the best of the best of pizza toppings. It's flawless and needs no introduction. But hey, if you want to throw some pineapple or anchovies on there, I won't judge ... much."

"As it so happens, cheese is my favorite. I guess we never outgrew the simplicity of a good old-fashioned cheese pizza." Clara ordered a medium cheese pizza, large fries, a couple of Pepsis, and two bottles of water. In exchange for Clara's credit card, the young cashier gave her a numbered alarm disc. She accepted the receipt and pulled Jenna's hand, leading them through the sea of people.

The weather outside was absolutely delightful. The sun's gentle rays offered a pleasant warmth, perfectly balanced by the presence of the clouds to prevent any excessive heat. Ideal for a pleasant al fresco meal. Clara led Jenna into an alleyway nestled between two stores, and soon found themselves in a cozy sitting area crafted by a wooden berm barricading the properties. Jenna found a soft patch of grass on a gentle slope and crossed her legs before leaning back. She closed her eyes and relaxed in the warmth of the sun.

"That was a zoo. Not the adorable type with pandas and monkeys, but the chaotic kind with people frantically fighting for items on Black Friday." Clara couldn't help but share the uproarious joke that Benji had shared with her. Her face subtly contorted with a hint of displeasure at the thought of her friend.

"I guess we found the local hot spot."

As Clara placed the alarm on the edge of the berm, the lights rhythmically blinked around the circle.

JENNA

When Jenna's phone made that familiar pinging sound, her mind was as wired as a squirrel on coffee. At her side, the alarm blazed

FOREVER FAMILY

with a fiery intensity, its red lights flashing with a sense of urgency.

Clara picked up the device as she chuckled to herself. "I'll get the food while you figure out who just jump-scared you." She laughed again before jumping from the berm and walking around the corner.

She unlocked her phone and saw a new voice message waiting for her from an unknown caller. *Apparently, we've traveled through the twilight zone of cell reception. No bars, no service, no hope.* After entering her code, she listened to the recording.

"Ms. Jenna Dean? This is the medical center located on Mount Nittany. Nicholas Dean has presented with symptoms consistent with a myocardial infarction. The patient's condition is stable, and he is currently resting. Our plan is to admit him for overnight observations, and he is expected to be medically stable for discharge tomorrow morning. Kindly respond to our call if you will be able to provide transportation for him at discharge. Thank you."

Daddy? She remembered him putting his hand on his chest, but she'd thought he was being dramatic. *Why didn't he say anything? Why didn't I protect him?* Jenna held her phone in her palms and stared at the screen as if she were holding a ticking time bomb.

* * *

Her vision was cloaked by the darkness of her mind's journey. Enveloped in layers of warmth, she found herself inside a tent. As she lay beneath the warm covers, she couldn't help but notice the soft walls were glowing. The delicate crackling and occasional popping sounds outside added to the mysterious atmosphere. The room was filled with rhythmic sounds, creating a feeling that was both soothing and comforting.

A tiny hole in the wall, emitting a fluttering coppery light, was the only source of illumination in the otherwise black space. Jenna was spellbound by the mystical forces that attracted her toward the radiant glow. She wriggled out from under the covers and stretched her hand to the warm light. She shoved the heavy fabric aside and gasped in awe as the flickering flames of the campfire danced.

The firelight glistened off the leaves of the trees, covering the landscape like mighty guardians. The campfire was working its magic, filling the air with the scent of toasted marshmallows and melted chocolate. She snuggled close to her teddy bear, seeking comfort from the gentle touch of the cool night air.

As Jenna stood outside the tent, a mysterious figure was hunched over the slumbering couple by the crackling flames. The shadows concealed the figures, but she couldn't shake the feeling that they were staring right at her. The figures seemed recognizable yet unfamiliar.

Something's not right. Jenna's heart pounded with fear as the world spun uncontrollably around her, so she clung to her teddy bear for protection. Shadows loomed ominously around the trees as glowing yellow eyes trailed her every step from the darkness above. She buried her face in her teddy bear and closed her eyes, trying to ignore the dangers hidden in the dark.

"Jayla?"

Her eyes slowly opened, drawn to the soothing voice.

"Ju-Ju. You've come back."

Everything will be all right now. Daddy's here to take me home.

CHAPTER 43

JENNA

Jenna's mind was lost in a sea of thoughts when Clara's voice shattered her trance.

"Hey, food's here." While settling on the berm, Clara gave Jenna the containers and drinks, casting a subtle glance at Jenna. "You look like you've seen a ghost. Are you feeling all right?"

Jenna attempted to push aside the peculiar recollection for the time being. "That was Mount Nittany. My dad had a heart attack." The phone's screen dimmed and faded into darkness.

"Is he okay?"

Jenna's eyes narrowed on Clara, her cheeks flushing red. Anger replaced her worry. With Clara's allegations against her father as a kidnapper and murderer, she questioned the sincerity of her concern. She inhaled deeply, striving to maintain composure. "They said he was, but they're keeping him overnight. I should give him a call."

"Do you need some privacy?" Clara carefully placed her beverage on the ledge as she rose from her seat.

"No," Jenna said. "I'll call him and be back." She pushed herself up over the concrete wall and began dialing her father as she moved down the alley behind the building.

"Hello?" a voice heavy with exhaustion and weariness answered on the other end line.

"Dad! What happened? Are you all right?" Jenna's nerves settled as she listened to his soothing voice. There was obvious concern in her voice, as if she couldn't help but worry.

Her father cleared his throat. "I'm fine. Where are you?"

Typical Dad, no nonsense and straight to the point. "Don't be mad. I'm in Ohio with Clara." Jenna's heart raced as she strained to hear her father's incoherent grumbling. "It's okay. Really. I remember."

Abrupt silence. Jenna scanned the screen, checking if the connection was still active.

The authoritative tone of her father asked, "What do you remember?"

CLARA

Clara watched Jenna as she raised her phone to her ear and vanished behind the building. She didn't trust Jenna's alleged father. He took her that night after killing their parents. He was weaving a web of deception, distorting her memories. She was absolutely certain. *How can you persuade someone that their father is not who he claims to be? Or that their entire history is a murderer's fabrication? Jenna is without a doubt my biological sister.*

Memories flooded back, vibrant and full of life. A collection of framed photos decorated the living room wall, capturing precious moments like Lucy's first birthday and Clara's joyous cake-smashing. As a family, they explored museums, marveled at aquariums, and splashed around in water parks. Lucy was always present for every single activity. She entered the family through birth, not abduction.

Jenna developed an explanation that paralleled Nick Dean's narrative. Her parents were unlikely to engage in unlawful activities such as abduction or secretly adopting a child, let alone successfully dodge detection or punishment. She remembered her dad's daring ice cream heist in the dead of night. Mom caught him red-handed, attempting to sneak an extra scoop on her cone. The memory was forever etched in her mind. How would he be able to hide an entire human child? *And my mother thought she was so clever when she slipped me a dollar's worth of quarters under my pillow for my baby teeth.*

Even though Clara was young when her sister disappeared, she believed she would know the difference if her parents had brought home someone who wasn't Lucy. She and Lucy were inseparable, best friends who were always by each other's side.

JENNA

Unaware of her intense hunger, Jenna eagerly opened the pizza box, relishing the enticing aroma that floated from the cheesy surface, and retrieved a slice. She raised it, observing the gooey mozzarella cheese as it stretched out and eventually separated. She lowered the end of the tail of cheese into her mouth, like a fisherman casting his line out to sea, and snatched her first nibble.

Jenna felt relieved that Clara didn't ask about her father. The girls sat back, their paper plates empty, satisfied smiles on their faces. Clara's hands moved fast, gathering the scattered garbage into a towering pile.

"That was delicious! What do I owe you for my half?" Jenna felt her pockets, unsure which held her wallet.

"My treat. You're my guest."

Jenna returned Clara's smile without arguing. Her fingers closed around the crumpled papers and discarded wrappers, their weight pressing against her palm. As her foot snagged on the uneven pavement, her balance wavered, but she managed to stay on her feet. She struggled to maintain her grip on the stack of items as she approached a nearby trash can. She crammed the trash into the narrow slot, smearing her hands on her pants before joining Clara by the rental truck.

Jenna couldn't help but observe Clara approaching the driver's side. She didn't mind if Clara drove, since they were no longer on the highway.

Clara spoke up while Jenna reached for the door handle. "Do you mind if I get some flowers? The shop's right there." A charming flower shop stood proudly on the corner of a bustling street, its colorful blooms spilling out from the shop's entrance, enchanting those walking by. "I usually pick flowers, but it's getting late."

"I'll wait here," Jenna said. Instead of remaining in the truck,

FOREVER FAMILY

she decided to relocate to the bed. She lowered the tailgate and effortlessly hopped up onto it. The truck dipped as she settled in, patiently waiting for Clara to return.

Jenna's mind was filled with thoughts, swirling, and consuming her, as she pondered over how to navigate this risky situation. *Will Clara listen?*

Convincing Clara to believe an entirely new version of the past would be challenging. Her entire life was spent looking for a family she didn't even have. Jenna could sympathize because she also refused to accept Clara's alternate reality. One in which Jenna's biological parents were brutally murdered and she was abducted and cared for by the Woodland Phantom serial killer.

Does she hear herself when she says stuff like that? We were great sisters, but it was just a dream. If she would just listen, we could be friends again.

Clara cradled a stunning bouquet of wildflowers as she emerged from the flower shop. The arrangement was bursting with vibrant colors and adorned with delicate sprigs of purple lavender and baby's breath.

Jenna hopped down from the truck bed and settled in the passenger seat. Clara presented the bouquet to her as she secured her seat belt with a satisfying click. The elegant aroma of flowery perfumes spread through the air, covering the musty odor of the rental.

"Ready?" Clara said.

"Yep."

Clara backed up slowly after checking the rearview mirror for oncoming traffic, pedestrians, and joyriders.

"Stop!" Jenna said.

The vehicle screeched to a halt, filling the air with the acrid scent of burnt rubber. Inches separated it from a speeding bicycle that had darted behind. Jenna spun around, only to catch a fleeting glimpse of the rider disappearing down the hill, his hand raised in a defiant gesture of disrespect.

"Where did he come from?" Clara said, her breath catching in her throat.

"Who knows?" Jenna glared at the reckless young man as he carelessly zoomed off. "Poor choices can get you killed."

"Well, let's hope the rest of the night is uneventful," Clara said as she began to reverse again after a few calming breaths.

One can only hope.

CHAPTER 44

CLARA

Nelson Ledges State Park was only a few minutes from the pizzeria. A delightful blend of cool and warm air enveloped the girls as they stepped down from the rented vehicle. In the midst of the soft whispers of the treetops, the sun played hide-and-seek with the horizon.

Fluffy white clouds floated like cotton candy in the sky. A soothing breeze brushed against Clara's skin. The temperature was perfect, setting the stage for a delightful hiking experience. The wildlife came alive with exciting sounds and sights. Squirrels bounded with confidence, navigating from one branch to another. Birds soared through the sky, their wings outstretched as they conquered the air currents, transporting last-minute materials for nesting before the bats swooped in to dominate the nighttime airspace. Meanwhile, bunnies hopped around the field, their noses twitching, scouring the grounds with their keen senses focused on the scattered purple clovers. Insects kept the air alive with their hum, chirp, and screech.

The lamppost at the entrance of the lot drew Jenna's attention right away. She reached for her bag and walked behind Clara. "That's where the groundskeeper saw the green truck, isn't it?"

"Yeah, he was parked just over there."

Jenna followed Clara's gesture toward the back corner of the property, confirming the location. Four vehicles currently occupied the gravel lot.

"That's pretty close. Is that the trailhead?"

Clara followed Jenna's eyes to a worn-out sign that hung on the opposite side of the road. "Yeah. There are four different trails ranging in difficulty."

"Which one are we taking?"

"The white path. It's the most scenic and least strenuous. I normally take the same path Mom and Dad took us on." Clara's throat tightened as the word *us* lodged itself within her. "Let's head straight toward the lake where the campsite's located so we're not out here too long. The woods get extra dark."

Jenna handed the arrangement of flowers to Clara, and the two of them walked across the street to the trail. "Great, lead the way." Her arms stretched wide, gracefully parting the path before her.

Just like Dad used to do, Clara thought. *Maybe reliving the night will remind her that she is a member of our family, and that*

Jack Drewitt is nothing more than an imposter, kidnapper, and killer.

Clara glanced behind her to find Jenna trailing behind as they made their way across the street towards the trailhead. She arranged the vibrant flowers in a cotton tote bag before tying them to her backpack. Ascending the aged, groaning stairs, she entered the calm darkness beneath the majestic trees, beckoning her to delve into her history. Desperate to persuade Jenna of her real history, Clara aspired to relive and retrace every part of the fateful night.

JENNA

Jenna's spine tingled up each vertebra as she placed her foot on the decaying stairs. The ancient wood creaked as her weight pressed against the distressed fibers. The old beams groaned under the intensity of each step, threatening to give way at any moment. The shadows danced around her, taunting her with their ominous presence. She had been so excited about this adventure, but now she couldn't shake the feeling that something was terribly wrong. The rustling leaves and eerie silence made her question the truth behind ghost stories. Any mystical force could cause trouble in these forests. The darkness closed around her, suffocating her with its icy grip. Upon entering the dense woods, she sensed a profound transformation awaiting her. A profound and unforgettable transformation seemed to be on the brink of taking place, one that would shape her whole identity. She would not leave the same person.

The trees seemed to be hiding something from her, and she

couldn't shake the feeling that something sinister was watching her from a distance. The longer she walked, the more confused and uncertain she became, unsure of what was real and what was just her imagination. It was as if the woods had absorbed all the secrets and fears of those who had passed through before her, and she was now caught in their tangled web.

The air between her and Clara was thick with tension, as if a storm were brewing just beneath the surface. Every word spoken was laced with discomfort, and every movement could shatter the fragile peace. Clara's strong determination to hold onto a history she barely remembered puzzled Jenna. She studied Clara, searching for any flicker of understanding.

Jenna observed Clara's lively strides and mirrored her pace. Her feet barely touched the ground as she leaped and bounded on the rocks, mimicking the energetic movements of a youthful child. She found Clara's outgoing personality to be quite unfamiliar. The appearance seemed coerced, as if there were hidden motives at play.

Clara's voice filled with excitement as she turned to reveal the magnificent rock formation before her. "Behold! The legendary Shipwreck Rock!"

"Any ship that dares to collide with that monstrosity shall undoubtedly meet its watery doom," Jenna said.

As Clara hiked up the rocky terrain, and she let out a small laugh as she climbed onto the low rock platform. "The last time I climbed up here, you would have thought I had just conquered Mount Everest. Now it's just a big step." Sunlight sneaking through the leafy canopy brightened her face. "You tried, but your fingertips barely grazed the edge."

FOREVER FAMILY

Jenna's heart raced as the crunch of dried leaves echoed in her ears. In her mind, she saw a young girl desperately chasing after her friend, who was steadily climbing higher and higher, out of reach. Clara never offered to help her. Jenna couldn't help but feel a pang of jealousy as she watched Clara's father sweep her up in his arms and spin her around.

Jenna often imagined herself, feeling the wind rushing through her hair and the exhilaration of defying gravity. However, life never presented her with the opportunity to take flight, leaving her dreams grounded and unfulfilled.

Jenna noticed a towering rock face and eagerly raced ahead of Clara on the trail, determined to conquer the challenge. She longed for the exhilaration she had been deprived of.

"Be careful. It's too dark," Clara said. Despite the remaining sunlight, the shadows cast a deep darkness over the forest. Her momentary confidence faded, replaced by her typical worry.

Jenna carefully selected her footholds, her body twisting and turning as she ascended the eight-foot summit with ease. She stood at the edge of the cliff, with the wind rushing past her as she outstretched her arms, her hair billowing behind her like a flowing brown silky cape. "I can fly!"

Clara cupped her hands around her mouth. "Jenna, it's not safe up there."

Perched on the edge of the world, Jenna paused to savor the sweet taste of triumph before embarking on her daring descent. Before going down the stone face, she secured each footing, knowing the shadows were deceptive. While descending, she watched Clara positioning herself closer to the base to ensure Jenna's safety. She propelled herself from the stone right before reaching the ground.

"That was exhilarating. You should try it." Jenna brushed the dirt and gravel off her hands as she grinned from ear to ear.

"Not today." Clara continued to walk along the trail.

Jenna knew Clara couldn't fathom the idea of climbing something that high. It wasn't the height that was unsettling, but the thought of falling.

"This way, Jenna." Clara pointed to the square white signs etched into the trees. She lost her peppy step and Jenna couldn't help but smile.

The girls stepped over fallen branches and ducked under low-hanging vines as they hiked along the winding trail. The forest was so dense that what little sunlight remained barely filtered through the thick canopy. Leaves rustled and birds chirped, heightening the thrill of the unknown.

Looking ahead, they could see the tree line breaking apart to reveal a spectacular sight: enormous rock formations towering into the sky, shielding the sun's rays from the earth. A haunting melody whispered through the depths of the canyon. Only one person could fit through the narrow doorway.

"Feast your eyes on Fat Man's Peril. Seriously, I didn't make it up. Some call it Fat Man's Squeeze." Clara's laughter filled the air as she spun in circles, surveying the breathtaking rock formation.

Jenna said, "It looks pretty tight" as she examined some suspicious stones resting precariously on hazardous ledges.

"Maybe for you." Clara winked.

Jenna whipped her hand at Clara's shoulder, a mischievous smile lighting up her face. The brave adventurers navigated the rocky terrain, side-shuffling through narrow gaps. Jenna's mind

FOREVER FAMILY

conjured images of fierce Native American warriors raining down arrows upon the deadly enclosure. Her breath quickened, her chest rising and falling in rapid succession, as memories of the stories Tom Wilson had shared flooded her mind.

In the end, they emerged unscathed. Jenna lowered herself onto the rough surface of a protruding rock, her fingers instinctively plucked at the tall blades of grass that grew beside her. She tugged at each strand, carefully tearing the blade down its center vein. She watched as the separated pieces descended, joining the scattered pile of dried leaves at her feet.

"That was cool, right?" Clara spun around, looking directly at Jenna. "Indian groups used to live in this area. Now and then you can find arrowheads or mortars sitting around." She walked over to the giant flat rock and sat down next to Jenna.

"Right. Didn't you find one of those things? I remember you picked up something and gave it to your dad." Jenna's fingers delicately explored the textured surface of a grass blade, discovering its distinct sharpness as it tapered into a fine point. Her hands held the power to shape its destiny. Jenna listened to the rustling of the grass blade as it tore, finding it satisfying, soothing her overcrowded thoughts.

"Yeah. Daddy found an arrowhead and I picked it up for him. He let me keep it. I hid it in an old teddy bear I used to have."

Of course, he let you keep it.

Jenna saw another broken blade fall at her feet.

Clara smiled, then patted Jenna's knee. "One of the most beautiful sights in the park is just around the corner."

Jenna took a few deep breaths, stood, and saluted Clara. "Lead the way, navigator Clara."

CHAPTER 45

CLARA

A mixture of fear and protectiveness filled Clara's gaze, imaging Jenna as a small child. Each time Clara came to the park, she was whisked back in time. Jenna's presence gave vitality to the past. *How can Jenna not see?*

Clara stood a moment, assessing Jenna as she tore grass blades apart. She let out a deep breath. Maybe if they kept going, Jenna would start to understand and remember the truth. Her fingers grazed the ground, evoking memories of the tactile sensation of gritty dirt and the contrasting smoothness of the flint arrowhead she once grasped. Her father's face lit up with joy as he watched her. The memories of her father's embrace, the shared laughter, and their unbreakable bond filled her heart with an

FOREVER FAMILY

indescribable ache.

Clara rose from the rock and studied the next rock formation ahead. A gentle smile graced her lips, exuding warmth and conjuring a wave of nostalgia that encompassed her entire face. Clara's and Jenna's footsteps harmonized with the natural symphony as they explored the winding trails on their hiking journey. Clara's parents would be overjoyed to learn of her reunion with Lucy.

"Things okay?" Jenna's voice cut through Clara's thoughts.

"Yeah, this place holds a lot of memories." She paused for a moment. "Let's go."

Jenna stumbled over a protruding root, causing her to lose her balance and crash into Clara, who stood still as a statue. Clara's hand reached out, firmly grasping Jenna's arm to prevent her from tumbling onto the sharp rocks.

"Oh, that was close. Thanks for saving me." Jenna's hands trembled as she steadied herself against the nearby tree. She carefully brushed away the dirt and debris that clung to her cargos, trying to regain a sense of composure.

"Sisters always look out for each other. Let's go, Lu-Lu." Clara's attention shifted back to the trail, where she briefly caught sight of Jenna's faint frown, delicately traced on her face. Creases formed on Clara's forehead as her expression pinched in disappointment. She snatched a small package of peanut M&M's from the pocket of her bag. Regardless of how she feels, she keeps moving forward, her steps a testament to her perseverance.

"Clara, can I ask you a question?"

"Sure," Clara mumbled through a mouthful of M&M's.

"Instead of honoring your parents where they were killed,

why don't you do it where they rest in peace?"

Clara finished chewing. "Um, well, it's where I picture our family together, laughing and smiling. Our parents had a strained relationship before that day. Every word was a weapon, sharp and cutting. They couldn't agree on anything, each conversation a battleground. We were sent to our room whenever they needed to have a discussion. The tension in the air trickled through the walls. On that camping trip, even Mom, who hated the outdoors, was happy. Dad shared the history of the area and showed us how to identify different plants. And we tasted our first s'mores." Clara's mouth watered as she reminisced about the past, unaware of Jenna's cold and distant behavior.

Clara's eyes trailed the endless expanse of wooded land, branches and leaves swaying and twitching with the gusts of the wind. She was lost in the moment. The world around her faded away, leaving only the raw beauty of nature and the overwhelming sense of awe that it inspired. The breeze brought the sweet aroma of honeysuckle and the sharp scent of pine. The contrast between the cool shade and the warm air created a sense of mystery and intrigue, as if anything could happen in that moment.

JENNA

Jenna's spine shuddered at the mere recollection of the name Lu-Lu. The name lingered in her thoughts, a constant presence that cast a shadow over her every move. It was a reminder of the secrets from her past that she had unearthed. She felt a tightness in her chest as the full weight of the name's meaning and the anguish it caused engulfed her.

FOREVER FAMILY

Clara felt a strong sense of belonging within the family, her heart warming at the thought of that name, judging by her smile. Jenna's emotions were overwhelming, as if she were caught in a never-ending cycle of misfortune. She had a name that was only meant to be temporary, a placeholder until she could finally be reunited with her father.

Jenna's heart was beating rapidly as she tried to figure out why Clara kept saying they were sisters. Why didn't she just leave it alone? A world with Nick as her father and Clara as her sister could never exist. The insinuation carried the cost of calamitous consequences. The atmosphere crackled with an electric current as she struggled to unravel the perplexing puzzle before her.

Her father warned her of the immense influence that lies hold in crafting a narrative, dictating the course of events, unexpected turns, and character growth. The flames of her wrath were not kindled merely by the tantalizing prospect of their shared bloodline. Clara firmly believed that Jenna's father was a merciless serial killer who had murdered her parents and abducted her to raise as his own.

As Jenna ventured deeper into the mystical woods, a whirlwind of unsettling emotions began to swirl within her. Each step intensified the tension crackling in the air between her and Clara.

A far-off noise caused her breath to slow and her heart to still, all in an effort to enhance her ability to hear. A subtle hum started to emerge, as if the wind were whispering a secret. Approaching closer, the noise intensified, evolving into a powerful chorus of deafening roars reverberating through the atmosphere, demanding attention.

Clara leaned her back against the chilly rock wall, and Jenna followed suit, mirroring her actions. Clara's eyes twinkled knowingly as she exchanged a secret smile with the ever-inquisitive Jenna. With a gentle touch, Clara gripped Jenna's hand, their connection sparking an electric current of excitement. With hearts pounding and curiosity as their guide, the daring damsels initiated a courageous mission beyond the protective embrace of the towering wall and were rewarded with a breathtaking spectacle that fueled their imaginations and left them in awe.

"Welcome to the Minnehaha Waterfall." Clara enthusiastically gestured with her arms, showcasing the magnificent waterfall.

Jenna's vision was deceived by the dancing shadows, causing her to hallucinate images of a man dramatically introducing the natural wonder with a similar sweeping gesture of his hands. A gentle breeze rustled through her hair, whispering words that sounded masculine in her ears.

"Careful. The rocks are slippery," Clara said, but her voice sounded older.

Blinding light engulfed Jenna's mind, overpowering her senses. Unfamiliar memories surged forward, launching a relentless assault on her very existence. The little girls giggled and chased each other, their feet hopping from one jagged rock to another. The powerful waterfall showered them with its relentless downpour. The canyon reverberated with their laughter.

More laughter filled the air as the man joined in their revelry, his humorous nature shining through. Meanwhile, the woman's face lit up with joy despite the underlying anxiety she felt. The man embraced her tightly, lifting her up and swiftly moving her away

FOREVER FAMILY

from danger. She felt safe and secure in his embrace, shielded from any harm that may have come her way.

"Lucy?" a distant voice echoed.

The trees blurred and appeared to twirl. Jenna's mind raced as she struggled to hold on to consciousness, but a suffocating darkness enveloped her, swallowing her whole.

* * *

Jenna's eyes fluttered open to find herself face-to-face with an unidentified figure. The person's visage appeared hazy and elusive, their features teasingly indistinguishable.

"Jenna, are you okay? Say something." The voice trembled with concern and doubt.

Jenna's throat emitted a low, ghostly moan as her body jerked upright. She tightly gripped her pounding head, squinting to discern the silhouette that stood out against the bright afternoon sunlight.

"Jenna?"

Her fingers stretched toward the swirling world, desperately seeking an anchor amid the chaos. Her vision blurred as a figure materialized in front of her. She stretched out her arms, offering support to help her regain her balance amid the dizziness.

"Easy. Don't sit up too fast."

"I'm fine." Jenna's annoyance built up like a volcano, and she mumbled under her breath as she reflexively rejected Clara's advances. She scanned her surroundings, trying to figure out her location. The waterfall overpowered her senses and was truly breathtaking. The rocks beneath them were covered in a light mist, hinting at their slippery surface.

Jenna's body tilted forward as she pushed herself off the ground. Clara's fingers tightened around Jenna's elbow. Jenna quickly stood up, gently brushing Clara off before confidently continuing to walk on her own. "I'm good. Really."

"Do you want to head back into town? Rest a bit?" Each word radiated concern.

"No. I said I'm fine." Jenna brushed off the leaves clinging to her cargo pants and trailed after Clara, farther away from the collecting water. As she watched the cascading water, a ghostly whisper brushed against her neck. *"I don't want you to fall. I told you to be careful."*

In the depths of Jenna's imagination, a figure materialized from the shadows of the tree line. The woman gestured at the waterfall, her silver bracelet chiming on her wrist, adding a touch of magical chords to the ghostly scene. Her heart raced, a knot forming in her stomach as her thoughts twisted and turned, distorting her perception of reality. Clara's presence seemed to have a toxic effect, confirming her dad's earlier warning.

Jenna's legs propelled her forward, swiftly narrowing the gap between her and Clara.

"If you're sure." Clara gave Jenna another look before turning and continuing on the trail. The weight of their impending conversation hung in the air, as if the silence held its breath in anticipation.

"Jenna, look over there." A shadowy figure perched atop of a cluster of jagged boulders.

"Is that ...?" Jenna squinted at the shadows.

A mischievous raccoon stood upright on its hind legs, its nimble paws, adorned with razor-sharp claws, holding a mysterious object.

"What's he eating?"

FOREVER FAMILY

With a deafening screech and a guttural croak, the creature let out a final cry of desperation as its chance for freedom slipped away. The raccoon was unfazed by its victim's piercing scream.

"I think it's a frog," Clara said. "Gross. Let's get going. We're almost there."

Jenna's lingered a moment before she resumed her journey on the path alongside Clara. The girls steadied their hands on the rough bark of a fallen tree trunk, their fingers finding purchase as they hoisted themselves up and over. They exchanged smiles, for their daring acrobatics over the tree.

As the girls walked closer, a small field came into view. Jenna's hair whipped in the wind, framing her face as she stood on the brink of the vast open field. She stood at the edge of a rolling hill, mesmerized by the sight before her. The grass, a vibrant shade of green, danced in response to the soft breeze. The ground took on a dark hue as the sun disappeared below the horizon, casting long shadows. The elm trees stood tall, their branches blocking out the sky, casting a wide shadow over the continuing wood line. As they strolled through the field, Clara untied the flowers from her pack and delicately added a few to the bouquet. As the forest drew nearer, it seemed like a fleeting moment of relief from the vastness of space had suddenly snatched away.

"Clara?" Jenna said.

Clara stared at Jenna, her face reflecting a blend of curiosity and concern.

"While you were buying flowers, I had a conversation with my dad."

Clara came to a halt before turning to face Jenna.

"Please avoid making assumptions and just listen to what he

told me." Jenna's hands came together, fingers intertwining, as she pressed them against her lips. She took a moment to gather her thoughts, carefully choosing the right words to say.

Clara stood tall, her posture rigid and her jaw tight. She held her arms tightly across her middle, her narrowed eyes revealing a steadfast determination, as if her convictions were carved into her very soul.

Jenna sensed that this was her final opportunity to sway Clara's opinion. Her hands lowered, yet her fingers stayed tightly linked. "My father's name was Jack Drewitt. He was at our campsite that night." The girls had reached an agreement on this particular matter. Jenna prepared herself with a deep breath and focused her mind on the upcoming part. She was aware that the facts would be challenging to comprehend.

"I can't think of any gentle way to say this. My father killed your parents."

Clara's body slumped onto a nearby boulder, her face drained of all color.

"He didn't flat-out say that," Jenna said abruptly, "but he said he did what he needed to do to bring me home. My real name is Jayla Drewitt, but your parents raised me as Lucy."

The towering elm trees shivered as a cold wind whispered through their branches, sending chills from Jenna's neck down through her arms. The sky transformed into a canvas of deepening hues as the sun dipped beneath the canopy of trees, surrendering to the embrace of the encroaching night. Clara's body remained completely still as she perched on the boulder. Jenna furrowed her brow, her mind racing with thoughts she couldn't quite grasp. She watched Clara's face closely, searching for any hint of what she might be thinking.

"He admitted to killing our parents and you still defend him?"

"*My* father found me the night of our camping trip. *Your* parents would never let me go, so he risked everything to bring me back to safety, to protect me from harm. Knowing the media would blame him, he took proactive measures to protect us by changing our name and keeping us hidden. Your parents probably lost Lucy and replaced her with me through illegal adoption. It didn't matter what obstacles my father faced or what sacrifices he made, as long as I was out of harm's way."

Clara leaned back, putting space between them. Her skin crawled with unease, a slithering tension having taken hold. "Jenna. Why is it hard to believe you're my real sister? He's making up these lies."

Jenna's face twisted into a snarl as her hands clenched into tight fists. She avoided any direct connection with Clara's adamant denial of the facts.

"My parents wouldn't lie to me."

Jenna's lungs filled with air as she summoned the courage to alter her voice. "Right. Like they were honest about the affair, marital problems, and creepy Roger."

Clara's face twisted with anger as she jumped up from the boulder. "Don't call him that."

"Look, fifteen long years is a long time. Neither of us know the complete truth, only secrets and half-truths. I *do* know that my dad would never allow anything to happen to me and I would never allow anything to happen to him."

CLARA

Clara came to a sudden stop, her arms hanging loosely by her sides. *No, no, no. She believes him!*

Doubt and anger stealthily invaded Clara's mind, weaving their way through the labyrinth of her thoughts. She remembered the laughter of her childhood echoing through the trees and the warmth of her family's affection. But now Jenna displayed a disturbing detachment despite her recent recollections. The days of shared secrets and whispered confessions were long gone. Clara noticed Jenna's growing estrangement from her real family, as if an invisible force was tugging her toward deception. Little did Clara anticipate that the serendipitous encounter with Lucy would thrust upon her the formidable task of convincing her of their genetic sisterhood.

Jack Drewitt was the one responsible for it all. Jenna was imprisoned within the clutches of her kidnapper, a master manipulator who had strategically twisted her mind. Clara's face turned red, and her fingernails dug into her palms. Clara's heart shattered as she witnessed the lifeless eyes of her parents, stolen by the monstrous being that now haunted her nightmares. In the blink of an eye, her sister was ripped away, snatched by this abomination who continued to roam the world, leaving a trail of devastation. Clara's determination to seek justice for her family burned fiercely, fueled by the failure of the system.

Clara's mind went blank as she stood there, entirely stunned. *How could she believe those obvious lies? How am I supposed to respond?*

"I know you've been told all these years that I went missing, but the truth is that I returned home. We can still be sisters. You

FOREVER FAMILY

can come to my house for weekends and holidays. We can go on road trips together. My dad makes an amazing turkey at Thanksgiving."

"There is no way in hell I am eating a family dinner with *my* parents' killer! He has brainwashed you and you blindly believe every word. That man didn't just kill my parents. He killed others. Were they trying to hide you, too? I should have called the police the moment I suspected." Clara's passionate emotions manifested in her fists, clenched tightly around her bouquet of flowers, and a spray of saliva that accompanied her strong outburst.

Jenna's expression shifted as she withdrew, her pupils constricting to the sudden surge of rage.

"I'm sorry, Jenna. I didn't mean ... Forget I said anything." Clara turned and headed off down the path. It was imperative that she contact the police before returning to campus so that they could investigate and arrest that man. She felt terrible about inflicting pain on Jenna, but she saw no other option.

With a guilty heart, Clara pressed on, overcoming the obstacles before her as she scaled a few boulders blocking the path. Just before the campsite, she spotted a little field she recognized. "The site's just up ahead."

She now felt the urge to place the flowers, then rush home to contact the authorities. Previously, they were not helpful, but perhaps they could be of assistance now.

As Jenna climbed over the final boulder, Clara turned to lend a hand. After a moment of hesitation, during which she examined Clara's palm as though it were laced in poison, she accepted.

Two young women stood in unison, gazing upon their intertwined past, and contemplating the mysteries of their future.

CHAPTER 46

CLARA

Nature claimed what was once the frequented campsite, as the sprawling weeds and growing saplings asserted their dominance. The sun had vanished behind the trees, leaving behind pools of darkness that concealed the details. Clara sensed that their time in the park was running out, as overnight visits were no longer permitted.

"Let me show you around." Clara led the way across the clearing. "This is where Dad set up the tent. Do you remember Dad trying to position the poles?" She forced a chuckle.

"Tom learned the hard way that asking for help can be a real pain in the butt ... literally! He asked Mary for help and fired her immediately after she tried to skewer him!"

FOREVER FAMILY

"That's right! I can't believe you remember. We laughed hysterically as she tried to apologize with the pole still in her hand! It was like watching those old comedy episodes."

"His camping skills were abysmal. Don't forget, it was Mary who single-handedly ignited the flames of the campfire," Jenna said.

"Yeah." Clara expression softened and a wide smile spread across her face. "That was just over here." She gestured over her shoulder with her thumb. "Mom built a *ginormous* fire. I remember the flames tickled the stars in the sky." Clara flung her arms high above her head and spun around, reliving the memory of the fiery embers soaring up into the heavens.

Jenna laughed. "I don't know about that, but it was effective enough to make some delicious s'mores."

"Yes. That would have perfected this hike. I should've planned better." Clara caught Jenna's eye and wondered what was really on her mind. *Is she upset that I yelled at her?*

Jenna crossed the exposed roots, which were all that remained of the campfire, and sat down on the exposed root. She ran her palm down the coarse strands, which threatened to splinter anyone who dared to get too close.

Clara hesitantly lifted her foot over the roots, finally settling down beside Jenna. Her face scrunched up in a frown as she glanced at the overhanging trees. She trembled, her heart pounding as they closed in on her, leaving her feeling vulnerable and trapped. She almost thought she could see the tree breathe.

"Remember the s'mores?" Clara said, taking her mind away from the nightmare memories.

"We begged for more, but we were forced to go to bed,"

Jenna said.

Clara welled up with tears. She suppressed her emotions and battled against the urge to cry.

"Do you remember the gift we gave your mom before we left?" Jenna continued staring off into the distance.

Clara winced involuntarily, her face contorting in discomfort, as Jenna uttered the words "your mom." A single tear fell. "Yes. Mom collected charms for her bracelet from our family adventures. The morning of our camping trip, we woke her up and gave her a s'mores charm. Mom was wearing it that night, but I never received it from the police."

Jenna's eyebrows tensed and her lips pressed together, concealing her true emotions hidden beneath a veil of mystery. Her expression was cryptic and difficult to decipher.

"Remember that day? Remember how happy our parents were?" Clara leaned in closer to Jenna with genuine curiosity. She needed her to remember.

"*Your* parents," Jenna whispered with clenched teeth. She brushed the ground with her foot. "This is where they were found."

A pyramid of stones marked the spot where Clara's parents had once camped, a solemn tribute to their memory.

"On this very root, they were sitting by the fire and attacked from behind. Benji and I built this marker for them a few years ago." Clara's fingers grazed the rough surface of the buried stones, feeling their coolness against the earth. As she looked at the stones, their surfaces formed a perfect heart shape. The once-happy area, where a family shared laughter, had been altered into a haunting sight. She glanced around, a sense of relief washing over her. Each year, without fail, the site and memorial remained untouched by morbid partiers.

Clara closed her eyes. *I miss you, Mommy and Daddy.* She gently arranged the bouquet of wildflowers, creating a beautiful display as she carefully positioned them over the stones. *But look, I found Lucy. Even if she doesn't remember now, she will. And we'll lock up the murderer who stole her.* As Clara's eyes fluttered open, she was met with Jenna's unreadable stare.

"They would be very happy you came back," Clara said.

"Clara, I don't want to ruin your moment, but did you listen to what I said earlier? I know it's hard to understand. Our pasts were fabricated by the very individuals raising us. You must see it."

"I'm sorry you believe him over me." Clara glanced over to see Jenna staring into the forest. It was only then that Clara truly comprehended the sheer density of the trees in this area. There were numerous hiding places, which made it easy to surprise her parents. The small campsite felt cramped and confined.

Clara stood up, trying to put some distance between herself and the haunting memories of finding her parents motionless and covered in blood. She raised her hands, studying the visible scars that remained. The subtle traces of her history had faded to a delicate mark, barely revealing their importance. Phantom pains still haunt her.

Jenna's footsteps rustled through the dried leaves as she trekked the western end of the campsite, where the yellow caution tape had long since disappeared.

"Be careful," Clara said. "I rescued you once from falling into that crater. Don't make me save you again." She let out a nervous laugh.

Jenna meandered near the crevice and peered down into the

darkness. "Do you remember falling asleep that night?"

"Yes. You were scared, and I tried to cheer you up with Clare Bear."

Jenna lowered her backpack gently to the ground after swinging it off her shoulders and presented Clara with a worn-out brown teddy bear missing its red bow.

Clara's heart quickened as she caught sight of her long-lost companion, her chest rising and falling with overwhelming emotion. Tears welled up, threatening to spill, as her legs trembled with uncertainty.

"I think this belongs to you," Jenna said.

With utmost care and tenderness, Clara received the teddy bear as if it were a priceless gem. She traced the outline of the neck where the crimson ribbon once rested. She clung to him with all her might, as if the very act of releasing him would shatter her heart into a million pieces. Tears escaped as she smiled into her bear. The conflict between the intense longing in her heart and the unwavering determination in her mind continued to battle without respite.

Her hand trembled as she reached again where the bear's bow tie was fastened, feeling for the open seam. Her fingers wiggled inside, searching for her father's last gift. The arrowhead was still hidden within the tangled fluff, waiting to be revealed.

As Clara placed the final puzzle piece of her past in its rightful spot, tears streamed down her face. Without hesitation, she rushed Jenna and wrapped her arms around her in a tight embrace, finally reunited with her long-lost sister.

"Lu-Lu, I knew I'd find you!"

She experienced an immense surge of happiness and comfort,

aware that her sister stood beside her, and that her days ahead were brimming with hope and possibility.

Jenna briefly returned the embrace and then slowly held Clara at arm's length, scanning her with an unfamiliar expression.

Clara nervously tapped her fingers, eagerly waiting for Jenna's reaction. But as Jenna's hold tightened, a sense of unease crept over her. What had started as relief now felt like confinement.

"We could have been happy, but you are determined to destroy my family."

Confusion twisted Clara's face.

Jenna aggressively shoved Clara, not giving her a chance to react to the unexpected attack.

With a look of sheer horror etched on her face, Clara's feet faltered, desperately seeking purchase on the ground beneath her. But the earth crumbled, into the gaping chasm of darkness below. The treacherous leaves, slick with moisture, sealed her tragic destiny. Clara's body instinctively convulsed as she tumbled into the deep crevice, her arms frantically stretching out for anything to stop her fall.

As the hands frantically searched for safety, one of them suddenly stumbled upon a protruding root. The massive network of roots vanished into the shadows, reminiscent of her haunting dreams.

"Lucy, help me!" Clara cried.

JENNA

Clare Bear descended into the depths of darkness. The shadows consumed every thread. Jenna turned to Clara's shaking body, tears streaming down her cheeks. "I explained what happened, but you were adamant about the lies. My father said you would never understand. That you would break our family apart. Now you want to call the police and destroy my reality with your delusions. It's not my fault you don't have a family. I won't let you take mine. I started to believe your stories, but my dad was right. You are toxic!"

"He's not your father!" Clara's determination was palpable as she dug her fingertips into the tangled roots, searching for a foothold with unwavering resolve. Sweat dripped down her face. She cautiously adjusted her legs, searching for a solid place to step. "He's the man that killed Mom and Dad and stole you away from me. He's tricked you to be his. Can't you see?"

"You will not destroy my family with your pseudo-illusions. It was your family that kept me from mine! I remember hiding in my room as they yelled at each other threatening divorce. I remember staying outside for hours, waiting for Mom's friend to leave so I could go back inside to use the bathroom. They hid me away, not even allowing me to play with neighboring kids. I remember them giving you praise and attention while I tagged along. I remember trying to run away but only making it into the backyard to hide because I didn't know where else to go. I remember the peace I felt when my real father found me in these woods and brought me home."

Clara's hands tightened around the roots. Her resilience surprised Jenna. The echoing sound of stones loosening and tumbling below reverberated through the twisting roots, leaving their destination shrouded in mystery. *If dad can do what it takes to protect our family, so can I.*

"Help me, Jenna. We can talk about this." Clara's face was

pelted with dirt, yet she froze in place, paralyzed by fear and terror.

"My father and I have a very special bond. We'll do *whatever* it takes to protect each other." Jenna's words hung in the air, heavy with dangerous intent.

"Wake up," Clara whimpered to herself. "I'm not here. It's not real. Wake up!"

Jenna slowly reached into her pocket, her fingers curling around the cold, hard handle of her knife, a symbol of her father's love and protection. The glimmering stars reflected off the sharp edges of her blade. The edges were still crusted with dried blood from previous encounters. She noticed Clara's struggling fingers and determined that cleaning the blade could wait.

"Please, Lucy. Please!" Clara cried.

Jenna took a deep breath. "My name is Jayla Drewitt." As she exhaled, she swung her blade with force, striking Clara's struggling fingers. Jenna's lips curled into a contented grin as Clara's hand spasmed, causing her to lose her grip. As Clara fell, her gaze met Jenna's and a mix of panic, pain, fear, and treachery flashed through her eyes. The darkness eagerly consumed her body as the ground beneath greedily swallowed her up.

Jenna maintained her calm demeanor as she gazed down into the inviting black void. She steadily removed a cell phone from her lower cargo pocket and tossed it over the side, releasing the heavy burden. Its sticker caught the sparkles in the night sky as it descended into the darkness.

At that moment, she realized the depth of her father's love for her. Family was the most important thing in the world. *Family is forever.*

"I'm coming home, Daddy."

CHAPTER 47

NICK

Amid the beeps of machinery, the incessant hustle of feet, and the never-ending overhead announcements, Nick's mandatory rest was cruel and unusual punishment. The hospital smelled like a bleach factory exploded and mixed with a bunch of random smells that were having a turf war in his nostrils. He had to get back to his house. For Jenna's sake, he had to hurry home.

Hospitals were always a place he tried to avoid. The constant stream of inquiries and curious glances disturbed him. However, his attempt to steer clear of medical facilities had ended abruptly when his neighbor discovered him collapsed on the steps leading out of his apartment. Concerned about his well-being, they immediately dialed 911.

FOREVER FAMILY

She remembers. Nick experienced conflicting thoughts about this revelation. She had no recollection of her life before, but she did remember everything that had happened since her return. His satisfaction was short-lived as he realized that her recollection of those memories could lead to perilous consequences. The world had always been against them being together, even when he was Jack Drewitt.

* * *

I know they're out there. They're always out here.

Under the half-moon's eerie glow, one could disappear into the shadows while still being able to make out the shapes lurking in the darkness. The trees loomed ominously, their branches warning the nighttime hunter to stay away. Faint wet beads of revenge and justice perspired from his forehead. The gravity of the situation seemed to overshadow the bone-chilling coldness in the air.

As Jack trailed the scent of smoldering timber, the fiery ashes cast an eerie glow that danced off the misty leaves, conjuring an otherworldly constellation in the forest. He admired the encouragement nature displayed for his forthcoming ritual. Feeling the presence of others drawing near, Jack gradually slowed his rapid strides to a silent stalk.

The darkness ahead seemed to be thinning, revealing a clearing. As he peeled away the foliage, he noticed their grinning faces, as if they knew something he didn't. They perched on a decaying log, huddled around the flickering flames of the campfire, as if trying to ward off an unseen chill that permeated the air.

How can they be so heartless? I know. I know what they did. I saw everything.

His cold, calculating fingers crept down the side of his boot, where the power to dispense justice lay waiting. With a sinister grin and a disturbing tenderness, he unsheathed the blade and ran a finger along the grooves, savoring the feeling of power it gave him. The gnarled handle clung to his rough palms, as if it had a life of its own. He was captivated by the retribution his comrade would soon obtain. They'd endured countless trials and tribulations together. Working side by side, they had corrected the wrongs against them.

As Jack's grip tightened around the blade, an energy emanated from him, transforming his once-kind demeanor into something dark and foreboding. His body tensed with anticipation, a force matching the strength of his stronghold.

The couple huddled together, their shadows dancing eerily in the flickering light of the campfire. The woman's voice was barely audible as she whispered into the man's ear, and yet he laughed with an unsettling sense of delight.

It only angered Jack more.

The location was ideal, directly behind the unsuspecting murderers. *They will pay for their sins.*

Quietly, he moved a low-hanging branch to the side as he progressed forward. The perpetrators were lost in their own world and didn't perceive the trespasser infiltrating their encampment. Jack's eyes gleamed as he held the StrongArm, its blade glinting in the dim light. He positioned it carefully, the sharp edge pointing at the man's neck, ready for a swift and precise cut. Swift intervention was imperative to reduce the unsettling sounds emanating from the vicinity.

Women usually scream or paralyze when justice is served. Which will she be? A sinister smile emerged. *She'll probably scream.*

Methodically, Jack traced an unswerving path toward his objective. They were oblivious to his proximity, despite how near he was. As Jack exhaled, he pounced on the man, slicing his throat from ear to ear. The man's fate was sealed, either to bleed out or suffocate in a slow and agonizing death. The serrated edge sliced nicely through the soft flesh, ignoring the friction created against the vertebrae. The man frantically clutched at his throat and dropped to his knees, but his struggle for life was futile.

With a sudden twist of the knife in his hand and a swift placement of his thumb on the front quillon, Jack plunged the blade into the woman, silencing her before she could even scream. The blade glided effortlessly off the ribs, through the soft cartilage, and into the woman's heart.

Petrified. I was wrong. The work of vengeance was predictable and unimaginative.

Her hand gravitated toward the blade, as if it had a will of its own. She was powerless to resist its pull and knew that any attempt to defend herself would be vain. Jack couldn't help but feel a chill run down his spine. It was as if she had resigned herself to a dark and inevitable fate, or perhaps she was simply too paralyzed with fear to alter the course of her future. Time stood still. He attempted to decipher the unsettling emotions and inquiries that the woman was conveying through her vacant stare.

Is she scared? Is she sorry? Does she wish she could have made life better for her family? Does she regret allowing Jayla to die?

Fear clouded the woman's eyes with an oblique film. The proximity to his victim fascinated Jack.

They will never hurt us again, my sweet Ju-Ju. Never again.

He felt his anxiety melt away as the woman took her last

breath.

A warm sensation trickled along his forearm, pulling him back to reality. The crimson liquid glimmered under the pale moon as the forest fell silent in awe of the ceremony. Even the crickets understood the need for a moment of quiet reflection. The physical existence of this vital fluid brought security, contentment, and satisfaction. The world wouldn't understand this desire for order—this desire for power—this desire for retribution.

The man took the bracelet from the lifeless arm of the woman and with a swift motion freed his blade by pushing her shoulder back. The gleaming crimson ribbon adorned his blade. Satisfaction washed over him, filling him with a strange sense of fulfillment. His fingers caressed the sticky surface as he absorbed its energy; then he pressed it to his lips, feeling the power course through him.

The moment after a kill sent shivers through his body, a twisted satisfaction that grew stronger with each passing moment. He stood between the two lifeless forms, shut his eyes, and felt an intense sense of pride. As he inhaled the cold, metallic aroma, he felt himself merging with his creation.

A barely audible disturbance jolted him from his blissful state. He clenched the bracelet in his palm and gripped his knife, ready to attack the trespasser.

What creature dares to interrupt The Ritual?

His head turned unnaturally, as if controlled by an unseen force, to follow the direction of the noise. Behind him, a little girl stood just outside the camping tent, silently caressing a brown teddy bear that was almost as big as she was. The tangled mess of her brown locks hinted at a night plagued by unsettling dreams.

Jack slowly shifted, his grip on the hunting knife growing

tighter, while the little girl's sight was on the lifeless figures lying motionless by the flickering flames. The campfire light distorted her face, making it difficult to understand her expression. Jack cautiously approached, stepping over the roots and crouching down to meet the girl's eyes. As he searched her face, an alarming realization crept over him.

It can't be! "Jayla?"

The girl's focus drifted away from the ritual and settled on him with an unsettling emptiness. Jack slowly approached the girl and peered deeply into her eyes, as if searching for something recognizable lurking within. His heart pounded by a sense of familiarity that left him defenseless, causing him to release his knife to the ground without a second thought.

"My sweet Ju-Ju! You've come back to me!"

Jack embraced the girl with a smile that eerily mirrored the man's mutilation. The love that was forever lost reemerged through his soul, cascading down his face and drenching the strands of her hair with his tears. Jayla had forgiven him. The culmination of his schemes and achievements bore fruit in a chilling harvest of retribution and righteousness.

Life has awarded me a second chance. Jayla has been reborn from the blood of my sacrifices. Jack was overwhelmed with an emotional epiphany. *Jayla has finally come home.*

This day sparked a new purpose for Jack's life. Instead of justice and revenge, he modeled a new intention to protect and not let the past repeat itself. He abandoned the past by creating a new future with his long-lost sister. He might have failed to protect her that day in the tub, but he would never allow danger to harm her again. Though his heart might have been filled with rage, he would now channel it into a force for good, a defense against the evils of the world.

"Let's go home, little sister. We have a lifetime to make up." With the little girl in his arms, Jack hiked back to his green work truck. Over his shoulder, the little girl clutched her teddy bear tightly and stared the motionless forms of her parents.

CHAPTER 48

BENJI

In the midst of his professor's endless ramblings, Benji stared out the window. Over the course of the weekend, he'd heard nothing from Clara, and her absence from today's class was worrisome. After the junkyard event, he couldn't believe he'd forgotten his phone. He didn't realize how much he needed his phone until it was gone. This morning Benji hoped to greet her with a coffee, but she never came downstairs. He didn't know if she was still upset or angry or considering his words.

Blame solely belonged to him. It might not have been the right time, the right moment, or indeed the right place. After the police station, he hitched a ride to his father's house. He'd thought of the what-ifs and the *I should've*s all weekend. Solitude was his processing ground.

Roger and his buddies were gambling, drinking, and getting into mischief in Vegas. Benji had forgotten he'd be gone until he arrived at the empty house. It was opportune since he needed the time alone to figure out how to approach Clara after his spew of love sentiments at the police station.

Fear of her anger and resentment was his primary concern. He'd completely missed her memorial weekend. The thought had never crossed his mind until Labor Day. He drove her to Nelson Ledges every year to place flowers on her parents' memorial marker they'd created. He sat with her as she shed a few tears and promised to find Lucy.

This year, he'd abandoned her. His words tormented him as they replayed in his mind, asking her to forget about her family and be with him. *How selfish could I be? She may never forgive me.*

He wanted to apologize and rebuild their friendship when he brought the coffee and donuts this morning. He wasn't surprised by her absence. *She must be overwhelmed with facing the memories alone and forgotten by her only true friend.*

Jenna isn't a true friend. Benji's thoughts soured his tongue. *She's a passing fad. Once she's no longer interested in Clara's story, she'll move on to the next exciting thing.* Jealousy twisted and warped his thoughts, filling him with resentment. When Jenna lured Clara away from Benji with a mirage of happiness, he had become hostile. *Jenna couldn't fathom the damage she could do to Clara's psyche. She didn't care.*

It's likely Lucy passed away in the woods that day. Due to her delicate and fragile bone structure, nature had provided her with a natural burial. He wished that the bones found in Nelson Ledges

FOREVER FAMILY

belonged to Lucy so Clara could start grieving with closure.

Benji's thoughts returned to the present when he was hit with something on the side of his face—a wadded piece of paper. He scanned the room, and everyone was staring at him.

"Mr. Lawrence. Welcome back to my class. Would you care to enlighten us with what is more important than my valuable knowledge?"

"Nothing, sir. Sorry." A few students chuckled as others rolled their eyes. He swatted the wad of paper off his desk and took some notes. Clara would need them later.

* * *

The walk back to his dorm was sluggish. He was tempted to stop by Clara's again but decided against it. The students around campus strolled with a slower gait. *Probably still recovering from the long weekend.* As he passed the café, he decided to get a sacked lunch and eat in his room.

The cafeteria sounded like a cluster of cars revving up before speeding off. Students were full of idle chitchat and superficial problems. Benji absently collected a few items, ignoring the surrounding gossip about weekend adventures and mishaps. His monotonous movements were interrupted by two boys talking about police on campus.

"... police at the dorms. Jeremy saw the flashing lights on his way to class," the taller student whispered as he handed the lunch lady his student card.

"What do you think they're investigating?" The other student leaned in for the tantalizing gossip as he moved his tray farther down the tubular tray slide.

"Probably that missing student. Maybe they found the

suspect on campus." His voice brimmed with excitement. He picked up his tray and scanned the area for an open table.

"Excuse me," Benji interrupted. "When were the police at the dorms?"

"Dude, they're still here. Something's going down. Four cruisers and several unmarkeds. They busted into a student dorm, but he wasn't there. They're tearing up that place. We thought about going to snoop, but I don't want them asking any questions." The student shook his head as if he had been in trouble with the police before.

"Which dorms?" Benji asked.

"East Hall."

"That's my dorm." Benji's face expanded in shock.

"Dude." The guy deeply chuckled. "You've got a psycho neighbor somewhere."

Ignoring the immature mannerisms oozing from this guy, Benji paid for his meal and headed toward his dorms. His steps quickened with curiosity as he noticed the police cruisers near his dorm entrance. A crowd formed around the building as students eavesdropped and gaped at the exciting campus activity. Benji assessed the group and didn't recognize anyone that lived in this building.

Pushing through the horde of nosy onlookers, Benji approached an officer clearly in charge of crowd control.

"Excuse me, Officer. What's going on?"

"Keep your distance. I have no comments," the officer stated.

"But I live in this dorm … on the second floor."

The officer turned and examined Benji with interest. "What's your name, son?"

I'm not your son. "Benjamin Lawrence."

The officer's eyes widened, as he placed his hand on his gun. He lifted the caution tape, and Benji lowered his head to pass. At once, the officer turned Benji around and twirled his hands behind his back.

"You are under arrest."

Benji let out a sigh but listened to the officer. *That junkyard guy can't press charges now, can he? This is overkill.*

"You have the right to remain silent."

He felt the cold steel encircling his wrists.

"Anything you say or do can and will be used against you in a court of law."

His other wrist was detained.

"You have the right to an attorney. If you cannot afford an attorney, one will be appointed to you." The officer held Benji by his handcuffed wrist and rotated him to face him. "Do you understand your rights?"

"I don't understand what this is all about! Why are you cuffing me?"

"Do you understand your rights?" the officer repeated.

"Yes. Yes. I understand my rights. Will you tell me what's going on?"

In his other hand, the officer pressed a button on his radio. "I have the suspect in custody just outside the dorms."

Benji stilled. *Suspect?* His heart forgot how to beat. His lungs forgot how to breathe. His legs turned rubbery as he failed to support himself. He felt guilty but didn't know why. He looked around the crowd, and the students whispered, gawked, and theorized about what he'd done. He felt humiliated.

Three other officers ran to his location and escorted Benji to the back of a patrol car. "Watch your head," one of them said as he was lowered into the back of the vehicle.

What just happened?

* * *

"This is your WBRC news update with Patricia Hudson. Police identified and apprehended the suspect in the gruesome murder of a female Penn State college student this weekend. On Monday morning, Nelson Ledges State Park groundkeepers found Clara Wilson dead at the bottom of a ravine. The medical examiner concludes that despite significant injuries consistent with a high fall, her ultimate cause of death was drowning.

"She apparently survived a forty-foot drop from the top of the rocky canyon. She sustained multiple bone injuries, including a punctured lung, only to drown in the small brook that flows from Minnehaha Falls. In a bizarre twist, this is the exact location her parents, Mary and Tom Wilson, were found stabbed to death fifteen years ago.

"Police were not forthcoming with a suspect until after the arrest of Benjamin Lawrence, a costudent at Penn State University. While motives are unclear, police are confident they will have a conviction soon. When asked what made them so sure of that statement, the officer said the victim clutched the suspect's cell phone in her hand as she died. Time will tell what will unfold with this outrageous murder. This is your local news with Patricia Hudson, signing off."

EPILOGUE

PREVIOUSLY KNOWN AS JENNA

Jenna felt the wind in her new blond pixie hair and the setting sun on her face as she cruised down the California highway in her open-top convertible. She was lost in the music as she belted out the oldies and waved her arm to the rhythm of the beat. The sounds were loud and muffled, filling the air around her. The salty kelp that saturated the air was much different than the musty pine scent of her previous home.

The sun floated above the ocean, sending waves of red and orange reflections into the sea. She checked the time on her dashboard, adjusted her sunglasses, and pressed the gas pedal in her pearl-colored car. After turning off the scenic route, Jenna caught a glimpse of her destination's marquis. An attendant reached for her door handle as she skidded to a stop.

"Good evening, Ms....?" The young man smiled in a very Cheshire fashion.

"Harper. Ms. Ivy Harper." Jenna tossed the attendant her bulky key chain.

With a swift motion, he snatched it from the air, clutching it tightly to his chest. He offered his other hand.

Jenna accepted the attendant's hand as she disembarked. Not enjoying the way his smile stretched across his face, she averted her gaze, but reminded herself that it was no worse than her barista days.

A second man drove her car into the parking garage after handing her a claim ticket, which she slipped into her sundress pocket. The young attendant scurried around her and opened the restaurant door.

Scoping the bar after she pushed her sunglasses up into her hair, she noticed her father was also late. *New life, new standards, I guess.*

"How many for dining?" the hostess asked.

"Two for the bar," Jenna said as she walked past.

The hostess gave a dismissive look and gestured toward the dimly lit bar.

Jenna searched the crowd and discovered a pair of empty seats at the center. The cushion crinkled and released pocketed air as she sat and set her pocketbook on the counter.

The bartender addressed her with a tilted smile before she got settled. "May I help you?"

"Crown and Coke." With a coy grin, she elegantly crossed her legs, exposing the supple skin beneath her flowing dress. She didn't take her eyes off the bartender as she reached for her pocketbook, storing her fake driver's license.

The man waved at her attempts to provide identification. He seemed more interested in showing off his impressive mixologist routine, twirling bottles and shakers with ease. But even his impressive display failed to elicit a smile from her.

She got what she wanted. No need to lead him on.

A man sitting farther back in the pub noticed the bartender's undivided attention and decided to check out the new patron. Jenna noticed the figure at the edge of her sight. She attempted to repel him with her mind, but he glided off his perch, adjusted his shirt, and drew near with a strut that resembled being jolted by electricity.

Straightening his collar, the man drank his courage and said, "Hi, my name is Scott. I would like to buy you drinks until my charm becomes irresistible." With a mischievous grin, he savored his quirky words and leaned against the counter next to her.

Jenna inspected his entire form with a scrutinizing intensity, as if she examined a piece of meat and dissected each detail with precision and control. "Impossible." Jenna's lips curled into a forced smirk as she turned to her cocktail.

He pleaded with a pained expression on his face. "Don't be like that, baby," he whispered, gently stroking her hand. But she pulled away, her eyes cold and distant. He looked at her with a twinkle in his eye and said, "I find you attractive!"

"The sentiment is not reciprocated," she said, her voice devoid of any emotion.

The man sat down on the stool next to her. "You have no idea what you're missing! Tonight, I could have any girl I desire, and I pick you."

"Leave until I know what I'm missing."

The man massaged her thigh with his hand.

As she eyed his hand, she plotted every possible way to inflict pain upon this man. Her mind raced with vengeful thoughts, each one more sinister than the last. She couldn't help but imagine the satisfaction she would feel as she watched him suffer.

He leaned in close to her, his warm breath tickling her earlobe. "I can give you anything you want," he whispered, his voice low and creepy. He tightened his hold on her thigh.

"Remove your hand."

"*Anything* you want." His hand tightened around her thigh once more.

A voice, rough and raspy, burst forth from behind. "Is this man bothering you, Ivy?"

The man's hand shot back as if it had been burned. As he spun around, he was met with the sight of a towering figure. The man before him was easily twice his size, with bulging muscles that strained against his shirt.

Jenna returned to her drink and said, "He was just leaving, Carson."

The man was met with a cold, menacing glare from her father, who watched him scurry away, throwing a measly twenty on the counter before slinking out of the building. Now that he knew Jenna was safe, he could sit back and relax.

"Thanks, Daddy." Jenna embraced him and planted a kiss on his cheek.

FOREVER FAMILY

He patted her back and ordered a Guinness. "Do you need me to ensure that doesn't happen again?" His tone was low and sincere.

"You can't clean the world of all the sleazy guys. That's a full-time job!"

"If it kept you safe, I would."

She knew he meant every word. It was both comforting and terrifying to know that he would do *anything* to protect her. Jenna shifted gears and changed the conversation. "Have you finished getting ready?"

"Yep. My suitcase is in the car. You?"

"Yeah. Two, in fact."

Her father gave her that expression that screamed, *We've talked about this.*

"Don't worry. Two small cases. A girl has needs." As she took a sip of her cocktail, she couldn't help but smile.

"This will be good for us, I think," her father said softly.

"I'm excited!" Jenna said. "I've never been to South America. I'm ready for a new adventure." The idea of South America had always been a distant dream for her. She had heard stories of its vibrant culture, breathtaking landscapes, and warm people, but had never experienced it for herself.

"It's time to call it a night and get to the airport. Once we've cleared customs, we'll find something to eat before boarding. I have everything in order."

"Sounds good." Jenna took the last of her drink in one gulp, and her father finished half of his before putting the bottle down.

He placed a few bills on the counter, enough to cover the cost of their drinks and leave a generous tip for the server. He then placed his hand gently on the small of Jenna's back, guiding her toward the exit of the restaurant.

Jenna and her father presented their claim tickets to the young man standing at his post.

Jenna noticed the young man ignoring her this time. *Dad is a man repellant.*

"We'll drop your car off and take mine."

"Why don't we drop your car off and take mine?" Jenna asked. They had intended for someone to steal the automobile after leaving it idling downtown with the keys still in the ignition. It was horrible treatment of her beautiful car.

"I don't like the sun beating on my head as we drive. We'll do as I say."

"Of course, Daddy. Don't worry. I'll just miss my car." Jenna's lower lip sagged dramatically, revealing her deep disappointment.

"We'll get you a new one in Brazil."

A smile spread across Jenna's face, illuminating her features with delight. "Oh, Daddy. You certainly know how to make a fantastic day marvelous!"

The attendant waited with the door open as Jenna climbed into the first arriving car.

"I have one errand before I join you at the hotel," her dad said.

Jenna followed his gaze to the corner where a man was smoking a cigarette; it was the same man who had been making advances at her earlier in the pub. When he saw her dad staring at him, the man dropped his cigarette and dashed to the next parking lot, where he quickly got into a car.

"Dad, it's not necessary."

"A father knows best. I'll see you at the hotel."

FOREVER FAMILY

"Okay, Daddy. See you there! Don't be long."

With a careful hand, her dad shut the door behind her and climbed into the vehicle that was waiting for him. His focus never left his target.

Jenna pulled out of the restaurant and drove down the road. The hum of the engine filled the car, drowning out the sounds of the city. Jenna felt a sense of freedom wash over her as she accelerated down the road, leaving the hustle and bustle of the restaurant behind. In the rearview mirror, she saw the man pull out in the opposite direction with her father close behind.

ABOUT THE AUTHOR

Tammy Bragg made her literary debut with Forever Family. With degrees in Anthropology, Criminal Justice, and Nursing, she possesses a diverse range of knowledge and interests that lend her writing a unique perspective and voice. While fulfilling her current role as a school nurse, Tammy is able to channel her inner nerd to combine her love for imagination and learning with her dedication to helping students with their health needs.

www.tjbragg.com
tj.bragg@hotmail.com

Acknowledgments

Shoutout to my amazing husband, David, who, when I shared my idea of writing a book, reassured me by saying he's heard of crazier ideas. He even promised to wait for the reviews before diving into my masterpiece. What a guy!

A special mention to my energetic son, Collin, for allowing me to concentrate on my book while also injecting some hilarious comedic moments.

My mom's bravery in tackling the initial drafts is something I find hard to fathom. She definitely deserves some recognition for her unwavering dedication. Garland McFarland is absolutely extraordinary!

All of the readers and editors who helped bring my work to fruition, especially James Abbate, Dan Larson, and Joyce Bishop, have my deepest gratitude. All credit for the stunning cover art goes to Jerry Todd. You described the genre of the book with amazing insight.

Big props to Derek Murphy from www.creativindie.com/ for providing some valuable insights on book formatting. His expertise is truly worth checking out! You saved me a ton of time in formatting my own book.

A heartfelt thank you to Foxtail Coffee Co. I immersed myself in the enchanting atmosphere, relishing each and every sip of a flawlessly crafted cup of coffee.

I want to express sincere appreciation to all those who have taken the time to read my book. Your support means the world to me.

Thanks for reading!

Please add a short review on Amazon

and let me know what you thought!

https://a.co/d/cr8RuW2